THE SEASONAIRES

JANNA KING

PEGASUS BOOKS
NEW YORK LONDON

THE SEASONAIRES

Pegasus Books, Ltd.
148 W 37th Street, 13th Floor
New York, NY 10018

First Pegasus Books edition May 2018

Interior design by Maria Fernandez

Library of Congress Cataloging-in-Publication Data is available.

ISBN: 978-1-68177-739-9

10 9 8 7 6 5 4 3 2 1

Printed in the United States of America
Distributed by W. W. Norton & Company
www.pegasusbooks.us

For Izzy and Jake—my life.

PROLOGUE

July 4th

Mia could see the shapes of revelers sitting on the dark beach. Their conversations were swallowed by the fireworks over Nantucket Harbor, the sea grass and yards of sand. She turned inland and flashed a bright smile as a red, white, and blue burst fanned out behind her. She dropped the smile, glanced at the selfie, and captioned it:

Happy 4th! #BeWyld #seasonaire
#dreamsummer #fireworks

As she pressed the "+" icon on the Instagram Story screen to post, the phone was smacked from her hand. It skipped off the concrete deck into the pool. She turned to see Presley's face, furrowed in anger.

"What the fuck, Mia?" snapped Presley. The word "fuck" sounded wrong in her lilting Georgia Peach accent.

"Lyndon'll be pissed if we don't post," Mia replied.

"And if we *do*, everyone'll know we were here. That's worse."

"It was just my face and some fireworks. No one could tell where I am." Mia fished out the phone before it sank. "Besides, you knocked it out of my hand before I posted."

She showed the phone to Presley, screen black, water bubbling beneath the cracked glass. "Now it's broken."

"Good," said Presley.

Their attention turned again to the middle of the pool. The lifeless body was floating, face down, arms and legs splayed out like a golden starfish.

"He *did* have a nice ass." Presley cocked her head. "But he was a damn dog, hounding nonstop. Didn't understand the word 'no.'"

"Fuuuuuuck," muttered Mia, crouching down, knees weak and hands shaking. She swallowed the swell of tears, knowing that if she released them, she wouldn't stop.

Another blast of fireworks made her jump, despite the thumping house music echoing from the estate empty of revelers. The bassline met the hard beat of Mia's heart as she watched the blood turn the pool's crystal surface to tie-dye, like the shirts she used to make at Y summer camp a decade ago. Tie-dye was the start of Mia's obsession with fashion. Now she represented Lyndon Wyld, one of the world's hottest clothing lines, spending a dream summer in Nantucket as a seasonaire for the brand. It was all expenses paid as long as she shared every moment with her Instagram and Snapchat followers.

But Presley was right. This wasn't a moment for sharing. Mia's mind raced. *I should've gone with Jade.* Jade's dad's annual Blue Bash at his Hamptons mansion was in full swing. It was widely known that every celebrity on earth was there, but as far Mia knew, no dead bodies.

She couldn't look away, as much as she wanted to. She had never seen a dead body before. The closest thing was her mother, who had grown so sick, pale, and gaunt, her frail bones were just a hanger for her tissue-paper skin. She was fading away. But she hadn't been . . . killed.

"Get your tiny ass in *here*," Presley demanded, breaking Mia's trance. She took long strides toward the pool house that flickered with light from the candles burning inside. Mia followed past the flagpole, where the red Wear National flag fluttered beneath Old Glory. She stepped over plastic cups, cigarette butts, and soggy potato chips. Shaking, she wrapped her cardigan around her sundress even though the night air was warm.

When Mia crossed the threshold of the open door she stopped in her tracks. Ruby was lying on the red-and-white-striped daybed, unclothed and unconscious, her right eyelid swollen to twice its normal size.

"Oh my God, Ruby!" she cried.

The septum ring in Ruby's nose was covered in blood. Blood was also smeared across her face.

"As if that bullring wasn't fug enough." Presley scowled. Save for her earlobes, Presley's flawless body was void of piercings and tattoos. Mia had one tat, a small sunflower just above her ankle. Ruby had too many to count.

Woven bracelets and a thin blue enamel bangle hung from her limp wrist. Next to her hand, with its chipped silver polish, was a Smith & Wesson revolver in matching gun-metal.

Overwhelmed, Mia's stomach roiled and forced out its contents.

Presley pulled a makeup compact from her purse, opened it, and held the mirror to Ruby's mouth. She looked and saw faint breath fog. "He messed her up, but she's alive."

Mia released a sob, then lifted a plush white towel from the ground. She moved to lay it over Ruby's naked body.

"Don't," ordered Presley.

"She's just so . . ."

"It's better if they find her like this. Doesn't take a law degree to see it was self-defense," said Presley.

"This is insane." Mia's eyes were glued to Ruby as if she could, like a magician, will her to be okay. "I can't believe anyone would do this."

Presley just shrugged.

"What the hell, Presley?" Mia motioned to Ruby.

Presley waved a hand. "I shouldn't dis the girl in her current state, but she makes my trailer park cousins look like royals."

A smartphone on the floor buzzed. Presley picked it up. The screen's wallpaper was a selfie of Ruby in a tiny bikini covered with Wear National logos, her long blond hair with violet streaks blowing in the beach breeze.

"But you were right about *this*." Presley turned the phone around to show Mia a text from Mac:

Are u ok?

"She was for sure buying drugs from him. They were probably fucking, too."

Presley grabbed the towel from Mia and wiped the phone before she let it drop to the floor. "Regardless, any scumbag who would do this to a woman deserves what he gets."

"Why were you here anyway?" asked Mia. "You'd eat dirt before going to a Wear National party."

"I thought Mac was here, bringing a keg from the bar. I came to apologize to him because I was being a first-class cunt." She nodded to Ruby's smartphone. "But now I know my cuntiness was warranted. He wasn't here, but—"

"Enough with the soap opera shit, Presley!" Mia exploded. "We need to call nine-one-one!"

"Whoa!" Presley leaned away. "I was going to do that, sugar, when *you* arrived." Presley lifted the wall phone receiver.

The fireworks finale started outside with a steady stream of pops, bangs, and booms. Presley and Mia froze, waiting for silence. After the finale ended, Presley dialed.

The operator's voice rose from the receiver. "Nine-one-one. What's the emergency?" Presley hung up, wiping the phone with the towel.

Mia glared at her. "What? Why would you hang up?"

"They'll come. Caller ID."

Presley mopped up Mia's vomit with the towel and saw a tiny diamond-tipped coke spoon in the corner. "That's pretty, but I'll leave it."

Mia's dismay turned to disgust when Presley shoved the balled-up barf towel at her. "Your hurl, girl." Presley grabbed her arm and strode toward the door.

Mia resisted. "What are you doing?"

"*We* are leaving," said Presley. "The fireworks are over. The other brand sluts will be back soon."

"We can't leave!" said Mia.

"We called nine-one-one, we did our job. But I didn't sign up for this. Did you?" Presley's arms were spread wide, as if presenting the scene to Mia.

Mia took a long last look at Ruby, then walked out the door with Presley. *No, she didn't sign up for this.*

ONE

Memorial Day Weekend

M y suitcase is way too small," grumbled Mia as she sat on a large piece of luggage.

"Move over, lil sis."

Mia slid right and her only brother, Sean, sat next to her on the suitcase. She reached underneath and pushed a couple skirts and shirts into the opening. She had watched every BuzzFeed video on packing hacks, but rolling sweaters and sticking underwear in her shoes didn't help.

"Lose either the boots or the sewing kit," said Sean.

Mia nodded to the old sewing machine on her desk. "I'd fit *that* in here if I could." Grunting, she zipped around the suitcase's perimeter. She stood and brushed her hands together, grinning triumphantly. "Didn't have to lose anything."

Sean chuckled. "You're pretty cocky for someone who's never been out of Southie."

"We visited Dad once in Paramus." Mia picked up a satin jewelry pouch from the nightstand, dropping in four thin blue enamel bangle bracelets that had been sitting next to a framed photo of a younger Mia and Sean with their mom, Kathryn, a radiant brunette with sparkling green eyes. There were no photos of her dad anywhere in this small bedroom. Ray, a handsome job-less bullshitter, had cheated on Kathryn countless times. When Mia was six, her parents split and Ray left South Boston. Mia saw him once a year around the holidays, when he visited from New Jersey, where he lived with his new wife and two kids. She didn't know what her half siblings looked like, which was fine with her. When she was ten, Ray gave her twenty bucks for Christmas, but made such a big deal out of it that she vowed she would never take another handout. She'd forge her own way and take care of her mom, who had devoted her life to Mia and Sean.

Kathryn worked at the Gillette factory during the day, coming home to make dinner and help with homework. Then, she got up at 3:00 a.m. and went to work at the neighborhood bakery, preparing treats for the morning customers. When she woke Mia and Sean for school, she smelled like a vanilla cupcake.

Four years ago, Kathryn got tired, *really* tired. She thought it was because she ran herself ragged, but after another year, when she could barely get out of bed, she finally went to the doctor. She was diagnosed with non-Hodgkin's lymphoma. Mia's part-time job at a neighborhood thrift shop helped pick up the slack. When Sean wasn't at school, he worked at McGoo's Pizza. They were hanging on in their little apartment, but barely.

One February afternoon, Mia was arranging merchandise at the thrift shop. The snowy weather wasn't ideal for shopping, so the store was empty, save for Mia's boss, Pam. Pam spent most of her time taking selfies, since Mia had proven she was good at making a sale. A pretty thirty-something entered and started browsing, one eye on Mia. Mia noticed her put-together winter outfit, which included an Hermès bag, a chic felt fedora over her long blond hair, and a sapphire solitaire necklace around her neck. She was a different type of clientele than the usual neighborhood women who visited in a chatty clump.

Mia picked a piece of lint off a magenta silk top she was straightening on a hanger. "Can I help you?"

The woman touched the silk top. "My Lyndon Wyld tweed trousers would look brilliant with this," she said in a British accent.

"I love Lyndon Wyld," Mia replied.

"I could've called that when I walked in here."

"But those clothes are a little pricey for me, and they never end up here because people hang on to them like gold."

"That's true," said the woman. "But they don't cost a penny for seasonaires."

"For who?" Mia shifted under the woman's gaze.

"Lyndon Wyld chooses six brand ambassadors to go to Nantucket for the summer."

"Nantucket? I've never been lucky enough to visit. Come to think of it, I don't know anyone who has." Mia continued to straighten the racks.

The woman smiled. "Seasonaires party, loll in the sun, wear great clothes, and get paid twenty grand to do it."

"Sounds too good to be true. Where do I sign up?" Mia said, still only half paying attention.

"The application is on the website. You have to make a video. Just be you, because your style is the dog's bollocks."

Mia offered a perplexed chuckle.

"That means 'fabulous.'" The woman motioned to Mia's ensemble. "Classic with just a hint of edge."

"Thanks." Mia glanced down at herself. "All gently loved. Mom's turtleneck, boots are from here, and these"—she smoothed her high-waisted jeans—"were my friend's. She gained the Freshman Fifteen and now they're mine."

The woman clapped her hands once. "Her gain was your gain."

Mia wanted to say that she would've gladly gained the Freshman Fifteen all her girlfriends loathed. They got to go to college. She had applied to MassArt for fashion design, but the steep tuition tanked her plans, even with financial aid. During what would have been her freshman and sophomore years, she'd taught herself everything: how to draw designs, make patterns, sew by hand and machine. She needed to get out of Southie, and fashion would be her ticket.

The woman pointed to the silver framed cutouts at the ankles of Mia's jeans. "I *lust* the grommets."

"I added those," said Mia.

"Smashing!" The woman leaned in and whispered, "I know people, so I'll nudge if you throw in that fab scarf with the top." She nodded to a paisley scarf hanging on a nearby hook.

Mia's boss was busy taking selfies in berets, so Mia slipped the scarf in a bag with the top and rang up the sale.

That weekend, Mia went on the Lyndon Wyld website. Sean helped Mia make a video. He manned her smartphone camera while she went about "Favorite Activities," as the website instructed. She sketched and stitched lace into a vintage blouse, talking about how she had been lucky enough to inherit her grandmother's sewing machine. She cooked pasta, made snow angels, and revealed her obsession with documentaries. South Boston's beaches were nearby, but Mia's fair, slightly freckled skin had never seen a day there, so she chuckled when she said she'd need "a boatload of sunscreen" for eight weeks in Nantucket.

At the end of the video, she and her mother kissed toward the camera. Kathryn's sparkling eyes were the only feature that remained from the photo on Mia's nightstand. Cancer had robbed her of her radiance.

"Way to tug at the heartstrings," Sean said sarcastically as he transferred the video to Mia's laptop.

"Why are you being a dick?" Mia shot back. "You've had fun every friggin' day playing baseball while you work toward *your* dream. I should get a chance at mine." Sean had received a full baseball scholarship at Boston College, and the majors were already recruiting him.

Mia pointed to the Lyndon Wyld site with its bold headline beneath a slideshow of catalog-perfect bodies and smiling faces doing everything the blond woman at the thrift shop described:

A seasonaire's summer is the dream of a lifetime! #BeWyld

"I get it, Mia." Sean looked at her with empathy. "I just think that showing Mom is a little . . . manipulative."

"I'm supposed to share my life," Mia replied. "Mom *is* my life."

Before uploading the video, Mia filled out the online application. Sean noticed the age requirement: *21–24.*

"Well, *that* sucks," said Sean.

Mia keyed in *21.*

"What are you doing?" Sean furrowed his brow. "You're not twenty-one for another ten months."

"We need the money, right?"

Sean couldn't argue—they *did* need the money.

They read the release form: *Participant assumes all risks, to include, without limitation, serious injury, illness or disease, death and/or property damage.*

"Because lounging on the beach in trendy clothes is dangerous," scoffed Sean.

"They're covering their asses." Mia clicked the form's *Accept* box, thinking, *What's the worst thing that could happen?*

The e-mail came in April. Mia shrieked, then danced around her room like a goofball. She ran to the liquor store down the street for a bottle of sparkling apple cider to celebrate with her family. She bought a box of crackers and placed them next to the homeless woman sleeping against the dull brick building next to hers. Most of the buildings on her block were dull and brick. Parts of South Boston were changing with an influx of upwardly-mobile hipsters, but until this e-mail, she feared life would never change for her.

Sean texted that he was taking an extra shift at work, so Mia and Kathryn toasted alone.

A check for half her seasonaire's fee arrived a month later, with the rest coming at the job's end. She stared at it for ten solid minutes because she'd never seen that many zeros in real life. She deposited it in the household account.

"Use the debit card to buy whatever you want there," Kathryn said as she swallowed her meds at the kitchen table with Sean.

"How about a yacht?" Mia put the spaghetti she'd cooked on plates. "That's what Nantucketers buy, right?"

"Don't say 'Nantucketers' or you might end up at the bottom of the Sound." Sean sprinkled Parmesan cheese on his spaghetti and dug in.

"Bite your tongue, Sean." Kathryn gave his hand a play-slap, then looked at Mia. "I know you'll be careful."

Memorial Day couldn't come soon enough. Sean pretended he didn't give a shit that Mia was leaving, but he ended up pulling her in for a bear hug.

"Bye, turd," he said. "Have a really terrible time."

Mia laughed, tears welling for a beat.

"Don't do anything I wouldn't do," said Kathryn. She had been pretty wild at Mia's age—that's how she'd ended up with Sean. She took Mia's face in her hands and kissed her forehead, her cheeks, and her nose, like she had when Mia was little.

"Mom," Mia chuckled.

Mia took the bus to the Hyannis harbor terminal. She stared out the window for the entire ninety-minute drive, because she was afraid if she spoke to anyone she would burst into tears. She felt guilty for leaving her mom and even guiltier for saddling Sean with all the responsibility.

At the harbor, she stepped onto the ferry and walked through to the bow, passing parents putting life jackets on excited children, their bored teenagers texting. Mia imagined that the couples with their arms around each other were heading for a romantic getaway. The few people near her age were already drinking beers and joking around before the boat even set off.

Mia's guilt seemed to wash away in the wake as she floated farther and farther from Southie. She took a photo of the calm waters and clear blue skies ahead, posting to her Instagram account, miamamasgrl:

Here's to the dream. #BeWyld #summer

TWO

I will end that fucking rodent for biting off me," snapped Lyndon into her smartphone, which she gripped with meticulously French-manicured fingers.

The young male flight attendant approached and placed down a tea setting—fine china, engraved with the Lyndon Wyld logo, which also adorned the green and beige seats on the private jet. Lyndon lifted the teapot lid, then lowered the phone to her side.

"It's not hot enough, I can tell," she said in her clipped British accent.

"I apologize, Ms. Wyld." The flight attendant picked up the tray.

"Thank you," added Lyndon with a smile that said, *I value you, but I own you, too.*

The flight attendant returned to the galley and Lyndon went back to her phone call. "Did you just dare say to me 'Imitation is the best form of flattery?'" Her smile had turned to a glower. "Tell

Otto Hahn that if I see one item—one fucking sock or headband or pair of knickers—that looks remotely like mine, I will sue him so fast, his tiny todger will fall off."

She clicked off the phone and swiftly exhaled.

Grace, Lyndon's younger sister and personal assistant, reached into her tote for a gold pillbox. She handed Lyndon a Valium.

Lyndon swallowed the pill with a sip of water from the logo-adorned bottle Grace held toward her. "As if it's not bad enough that he opened a Wear National store down the street from ours, he's also calling his paltry band of brand ambassadors *seasonaires*."

"What did Elaine say about that?" asked Grace.

"You mean the idiot who calls herself my attorney? She said I don't have a lock on the name."

"We'll find a new attorney." Grace shrugged. "I can't fart without hitting one waiting to be your counsel."

"Poor things." Lyndon grimaced. "I shared a room with you growing up, remember?"

"If you can't toot in front of your sister, who can you toot in front of?"

"Attorneys, apparently."

Grace broke into a laugh, which loosened up Lyndon. She chuckled.

When Lyndon and Grace were young and poor, which was the case over two decades earlier, they worked at a posh resort in the Cotswolds. They pined over the clothes that their wealthier peers wore. Grace lamented that "everyone should be able to look that toff." Lyndon, never one to play victim, took that idea and ran with it. She zipped through a fast-track undergraduate business degree at Staffordshire University, but learned the most rising through the ranks working at Selfridges department store. The result was her self-named clothing line.

Now, on the cusp of forty, Lyndon looked closer to thirty thanks to some strategic nips, tucks, and injections. With her smooth golden bob and Pilates-toned body, she was impeccably classic, yet accessible-by-design. That's why her line was impeccably classic, yet accessible-by-design. Lyndon had always been the beauty and the brains. Grace, a curvy ginger, was the humor and the help, following behind her older sister because she didn't have the drive or focus to steer her own ship.

Grace opened her laptop. "Forget about Otto's manky little tarts. Let's review our picks for this summer since we're going to meet them shortly." She clicked on the file: *Seasonaires.* "Fresh meat!"

This elicited a chuckle from Lyndon. "Don't be wretched, Grace!"

Lyndon paid homage to her salad days working at the resort by calling her brand ambassadors "seasonaires." They came and went with the vacation seasons—summers in coveted locales like Martha's Vineyard, Cape Cod, and Ibiza; winters in Aspen, Gstaad, and the French Alps. Her first crew of trendsetters converged on Nantucket eight years earlier, and after that summer, her brand's margins exploded.

Six sub-folders opened on Grace's laptop screen: Grace clicked on the one marked "Cole" to reveal a photo of a handsome twenty-something with emerald green eyes and a gentle smile.

"I still don't understand why you wanted this lad," said Grace. "He's got the look, but no social following."

"People appear out of nowhere and succeed," replied Lyndon. "Look at Otto. I was already busting my arse for years when he popped out of his hovel." She pointed to Mia's folder. "Remind me about this pretty bird."

Grace opened the folder. "Mia from Boston." She played the video without the sound. "She's the one with the sick mum."

"Right, right," said Lyndon. "We should bring the mum out for a weekend. Put her up at The Wauwinet with a butler. Take her on the yacht, get her a massage, have the girl snap and post the whole thing. We'll look like bloody heroes."

Lyndon's phone buzzed with an Instagram notification:

thenewpresley just posted a video

She clicked on the notification and a video played. Freshly made-up, long corn silk–hued hair curled to beach-sexy perfection, Presley stood in front of the Lyndon Wyld Nantucket store. "I'm baaaack, y'all!" she drawled. "This summer is going to be wild. Lyndon Wyld, that is!"

The video ended. "Our reigning queen just hit nine hundred and thirty thousand followers," said Lyndon.

"Your idea to bring her back was brilliant," remarked Grace.

"And your scrappy Southie is positively ace." Lyndon nodded to Mia in her video. "A little healthy competition never hurt anyone."

THREE

Despite the full ferry, the ride was the most peaceful two hours Mia could remember. Hundreds of sailboats were a white tufted welcome into Nantucket Harbor, skimming the water like a choreographed dance.

A man with his arms around a woman pointed to the sea of boats. "Figawi weekend is the start of Nantucket's summer season," Mia overheard him say.

"Figawi?" The woman glanced back at him.

"In 1972, when three drunk friends in a sailing race here got lost in the fog, one shouted in his thick New England accent 'Where the fuck aw we?' Figawi."

The woman laughed. Mia chuckled to herself.

The ferry was close enough that she could see the detail on the matching white, gray, and brown wood-shingled homes and buildings framing the harbor. The beautiful view was a far cry from her Southie neighborhood's dull cityscape.

She took a selfie and group texted Sean and her mom:

Miss u already.

Sean's text popped back:

Bullshit.

Her mom's text followed:

Language!

Her mom sent a kissy face emoji that Mia returned. Her heart beat faster as the ferry pulled into the harbor. A Mercedes G-Wagen convertible, wrapped in Lyndon Wyld green and beige with a chrome logo on the grill, waited on the dock. The driver leaning on the car was shirtless and in plaid board shorts that hung below his V-line. He was smooth, chiseled and bronzed, like an Abercrombie & Fitch model.

"Oh, shit," Mia muttered under her breath as she dragged her overstuffed suitcase to the car.

"Hop in the G," Mister A&F said with a devilish grin, jumping in without an offer to help. Breathless from the effort and the nerves, Mia climbed in the passenger's seat. Mister A&F leaned over, startling her. He held up his smartphone for a selfie of them. Mia thought she smiled, but it happened so quickly, she wasn't sure. Mister A&F was already posting on Snapchat. He put the car in gear. "I'm Grant."

"Mia." She stuck her hand out for a shake, but it was ignored, so she pulled it back and tucked her hair behind her ear.

Any awkwardness she felt vanished when she saw that they were driving down Easy Street. She chuckled. "That can't be the name."

"Oh, yeah, Mia. We are on Easy Street." Grant nodded, his grin growing bigger.

They drove through town, with its cobblestone streets and quaint storefronts. The Lyndon Wyld store sat among mainland fashion favorite Ralph Lauren and some local stores, all cloaked in shingles, fresh paint, and well-designed Americana authenticity. People jogged, rode bikes, and walked their designer-breed dogs. Kids scampered along, eating ice cream.

"Nantucket is a little different than South Boston," remarked Mia. "How does it compare to where you're from?"

"Mars," answered Grant.

Mia tilted her head at him. "You're *from* Mars or this is *like* Mars?"

"Both." Grant laughed.

Mia gave up trying to get more out of him and turned to the sights. "It doesn't seem real, it's so pretty."

"Yeah. Pretty . . . rad!" said Grant. "I got here this morning, so the 'hood's all new to me too, but it's fucking off the hoooooook!" He threw both arms in the air.

"Hey, hands on the wheel." Mia reached for Grant's muscular arm. His laugh was raucous and infectious as he acquiesced. Mia giggled, easing up.

Grant checked the car's navigation. "Gotta make a stop before we go to the homestead. Presley asked me to bring back strawber-ries. Fridge is stocked with blueberries and raspberries, but I can't resist a hot girl begging."

"Who's Presley?" asked Mia.

"You'll meet her soon enough." Grant let out the kind of whistle used when words didn't suffice.

The groomed trees, manicured grassy patches, and nurtured garden boxes reminded Mia of Disneyland, which she'd seen only on TV. "This is the cleanest place I've ever been. Do they even allow trash here?"

"Apparently, they do." Grant drove past the Wear National clothing store at the end of the block, with its red flag and window display of tanks and tees. The backdrop photo showed two girls in tanks and nothing else, their arms lying strategically across their laps. He parked in front of the market across the street and jumped out.

"I'll be right back. Stay here to keep an eye on your stuff. And don't fraternize with the enemy." He nodded toward the alleyway next to the Wear National store, where a whip-thin girl was talking to a guy with a scruffy-sexy beard holding a black apron. The girl, with her long, wavy blond hair and violet streaks, displayed her extensive tattoo collection in a cropped tank and denim cutoffs. She was one of the girls in the window's photo.

"Wear National is the enemy," explained Grant.

"Come on," Mia scoffed. "Is that really a rule?"

"Unspoken." Grant gave her a once-over. "But you don't look like much of a rule breaker to me. Sweet as those stray kitties." He pointed to a calico slinking between some hydrangea bushes nearby.

"They're not stray." Mia straightened and shifted in her knee-length polka-dot skirt she wished was more edgy than classic. "They're feral."

"Right." Grant shrugged and jogged inside the market.

When Scruffy-Sexy Bearded Guy walked off down the street, the girl with the violet streaks turned and locked eyes with Mia. She smiled, her silver septum ring lifting with the crinkle of her nose, and entered the store. She didn't belong here. But then again, neither did Mia.

FOUR

G rant and Mia drove back through town and into Nantucket's picturesque residential area, with its rows of saltbox homes. As they headed toward the shore, the houses grew more expansive, sitting on larger, lusher grassy lots. Grant steered them into the curving driveway of a sprawling shingled estate, surrounded by landscaping that was just the right amount of wild. Mia got a taste of the beach view.

"Boosh!" Grant shouted. "We're here."

Like most of the other homes on Nantucket, the estate's name was branded on hand-carved quarterboard: *Wylderness.* A badminton court was to the right. A meticulously manicured lawn was to the left, set up for horseshoes and croquet. White wood Adirondack chaises were dotted about, so no one was ever without a place to chill. A line of brand-new beach cruisers in Lyndon Wyld green awaited rides.

Mia and Grant disembarked. Mia picked her jaw up off the ground. "This is amazing!"

"No pool though," Grant scoffed.

"Pools are *très gauche*." The Southern belle lilt that butchered those French words came from a stunning beauty with long corn-silk locks who was stepping out of the house in a cut-out one-piece and sheer matching sarong. She held a red plastic cup and wore a pageant queen smile.

"Well, hi, there," she said to Mia. "Aren't you cute as a button?"

Mia didn't know what to say, because it sounded remotely patronizing. Pageant Queen sold it as a compliment when she pulled Mia in for an embrace. Mia caught the look of sympathy-meets-amusement from the nice-looking guy who approached with four more red cups.

Pageant Queen released Mia. "I'm a hugger," she explained, then motioned to herself as if she were a game show prize. "Presley."

"Mia."

Presley turned to Nice-Looking Cup Holder. "Well, hand Mia a drink, Cole. Have some freakin' manners!"

Cole handed a cup to Mia. "I'm Cole. Vodka cran okay?"

"Sure. Thanks." Mia took a sip and tried to stifle a cough as the drink went down with a burn. Taking care of her mom hadn't allowed for much partying.

"We make 'em strong here at the Lyndon Wyld house," said Presley with a laugh.

Grant grabbed the last cup and took a healthy gulp as Cole put his down to lift Mia's suitcase from the car. He set it next to her.

"Thank you." Mia was drawn to his emerald green eyes, which immediately made her feel comfortable, more comfortable than Presley's overfriendly hug. She noticed a scar above his right brow.

"We don't have a pool because we have the ocean right outside our back door," said Presley, who took the bag of strawberries from Grant with a "good boy" stroke of his hair. "Also, I hear the Wear National house has a pool, and we are *nothing* like those brand sluts."

"I bet Otto Hahn has boned everyone who's stepped into that pool, and summer's barely started," said Grant as he drained his drink.

"Who's Otto Hahn?" asked Cole.

"The revolting founder of Wear National." Presley shuddered. "He's older than my daddy."

"That's because your red state parents got married before they had pubes," remarked Grant.

"Dude, that's gross." Cole shook his head toward Mia.

"My parents *did* get hitched young. That's how we do it where I'm from." Presley glared at Grant. "In sickness and in health . . . for richer or poorer. Unlike my parents, I say richer." She laughed, taking a sip from her cup. "Where you from, Mia?"

"Boston."

"Pats all day!" hollered Grant. "Brady is king!"

"Julian Edelman is the real unsung hero," countered Mia.

Grant and Cole looked impressed.

Mia shrugged. "I like football. Baseball more."

"Too bad the Phillies always make the Sox their bitch," said Grant.

"Maybe not this season." Mia grinned. Grant mimed a crotch stroke.

"I hate sports." Presley admired her fuchsia nails, causing Mia to glance at her unpolished ones. "I was a cheerleader in high school, but I didn't watch a minute of the games."

"Well, you'd better learn to like them," said Cole. "I saw a game of touch on tomorrow's schedule."

"Touch? So we'll all get to know each other better." Grant raised his eyebrows and smirked.

Mia and Cole exchanged another glance.

A black Escalade crunched over the driveway's gravel. The group moved back onto the lawn as it pulled up, windows tinted, wheels sparkling chrome. The driver—a mountain of a man with a shaved wrecking ball head, wearing a dark suit and sunglasses—got out. A second mountain got out of the back, also in a dark suit, with a slicked ponytail and hands that could crush a skull like a nutcracker. The Escalade's passenger-side window slid down a crack.

"Which one of you assholes is gonna try and deflower my baby?" The deep voice was smooth as velvet.

Wrecking Ball opened the passenger door. Out stepped Maz, music and entertainment mogul, and a brand unto himself, as reflected in his first-name-only moniker. He sauntered up to the group, laser-focused on the boys.

"I will not only kill you. I will kill you once here and then kill you again in front of the parents that spawned you."

Grant virtually shit his plaid board shorts, giving Cole, next to him, a side leg tap.

Maz broke up, laughing. "I'm just fuckin' with ya." He slapped Grant on the back. "My baby can take care of herself. She's like her mama. Never trust a woman who can't take care of herself."

Presley grinned at Mia, who managed a small smile.

Grant, simultaneously terrified and awe-struck, squeaked, "Maz. I'm a huge fan."

"Damn straight, you are." Maz ignored Grant's attempt at a shake.

Skullcrusher opened the back passenger-side door. The longest legs Mia had ever seen emerged in bright white M-Kat platform kicks. M-Kat was one of Maz's several brands. When the legs finally ended, they were covered, barely, with Lyndon Wyld shorts. The rest of the statuesque figure revealed herself.

"Jade," Presley growled to Mia. "What a joke." She might as well have had claws.

Jade's skin, like her dad's, was the color of the richest café mocha. Her sensuous features and runway body were all her mom's, Tatiana Chen, one of the world's most famous supermodels. *Why did she even want this job?* Mia thought, smoothing her hair, which now seemed mousy and unremarkably wavy.

"Can I take a pic with you, Maz?" Grant looked like a five-year-old meeting Santa for the first time.

"No, my friend, you can't. This is my Jade's game."

"What's up?" Jade said to the group, paying more attention to the several trunks Skullcrusher was unloading.

"Where's the boss lady?" asked Maz.

As if on cue, because when Maz called the universe listened, Lyndon Wyld's white Tesla pulled up with Grace driving and Lyndon in the passenger's seat. Lyndon got out and with a broad smile, strode over to Maz. The seasonaires froze. Meeting Lyndon Wyld was as epic as meeting Maz. Lyndon and Maz kissed on the cheeks then embraced like family members.

Grace approached slowly, letting the two have their moment. Mia noticed her touch her sapphire solitaire necklace with one hand as she pointed Skullcrusher toward the house with the other. "Upstairs, third room on the right." Skullcrusher lumbered off with Jade's trunks.

"Gracie! My girl!" Maz hugged Grace.

Grace smiled. "How are Tatiana and the tots?"

"I'm outnumbered by femmes." He grinned, motioning to Jade.

"Jade! I haven't seen you since you were practically in nappies. You're positively gorgeous," gushed Lyndon.

Jade smiled as Maz put his arm proudly around her. "Listen, I have to jet. Take care of my baby," Maz said to Lyndon.

"I take care of all of them." Lyndon looked at the group on the lawn.

Maz gave Jade a hug, whispering something in her ear. For a moment, she stopped smiling, but when Maz parted from her, she turned on the megawatt smile again.

Maz pointed gun-fingers at Grant and Cole as Wrecking Ball escorted him back to the Escalade. The black doors shut. As the car disappeared out of the driveway, a guy in jeans, a pinstripe button-down, and bare feet ran from the house holding an iPad.

"Cocksuckermotherfucker! I wanted to show him—"

The others glared at him, Grant bursting with a single nose chortle. He then saw Lyndon, looking at him with a wry smile. "Juan Pablo?"

"J.P. Yes. Sorry," he said, pushing back the thick black bangs that had fallen over his eyes. Tall, dark and handsome, and filled with nervous energy, he straightened his shirt. "I have a hat line I think Maz would like. Haberdasheries, you know, because you're . . . British," he stammered. Jade rolled her eyes. "I'd like to show it to you, too."

"Entrepreneurial. I love that," Lyndon said with an encouraging voice that relaxed J.P. Cole offered Lyndon a small wave.

"You're Cole, right?" Lyndon nodded to him. Grace looked at the ground with a tiny head shake.

Lyndon smiled warmly at Presley. "Presley, darling, it's good to have you back!"

"Proud to be back." Presley stood taller in the spotlight, like a preening peacock.

Lyndon gestured to the estate. "Let's all go in and have a welcome chat, shall we?"

A slim man in his thirties with a trimmed beard and his hair in a low bun came out of the adjacent guest cottage. A camera was slung across his gauzy collarless shirt. Lyndon turned to him.

"Photos first. Vincent is our on-site photographer." Lyndon motioned to Vincent's camera. "Remember, always photos first."

Lyndon joined the seasonaires, crossing in front of Mia.

21

"Thank you for letting me be a part of this, Ms. Wyld," said Mia.

"Thank you for *wanting* to be a part, Mia." Lyndon gave Mia's arm a maternal touch. Presley caught this, her eyes never leaving Lyndon.

They surrounded Lyndon. Presley was on one side of Mia, Cole on the other. Grant pressed his bare chest into Presley, who restrained her irritation. J.P. inched next to Jade. Mia was painfully aware that she was a good head shorter than both Presley and Jade. She felt Cole's hand at the small of her back and glanced at him. His smile made her stand straighter.

"Ready?" said Vincent, with Grace next to him, supervising.

"Say 'Wyld!'" Grace emphasized the smile on the "D."

"Wyld!" repeated the group. Presley tilted her head, her hair falling over half of Mia's face. Mia moved in time for Vincent to snap the shot.

FIVE

Mia's eyes grew wide as she entered the estate, her mouth agape.

"You're catchin' flies, sugar," said Presley, passing her.

The airy living room looked like it could've been on the cover of *Elle Decor*, one of Mia's mom's favorite magazines. Overwhelmed by the grandeur and the floor-to-ceiling harbor view, Mia backed into a chair, almost sitting on Cole's lap.

"Sorry."

Cole chuckled. Mia instead sat on the cream linen couch next to Jade, who offered a perfunctory smile. J.P. took the ottoman closest to the couch, though Jade pretended not to notice. Presley had disappeared.

Lyndon stood in front of the fireplace. "I'm not going to stay long because this is *your* summer. But I wanted to welcome you personally." She smiled warmly. "You were all hand-picked to represent my brand because your videos proved you have the drive, the story, and the look."

"Smashing!" added Grace. That's when Mia remembered: Grace was the woman who came into the thrift shop that February, though her hair was now red.

"We go over and above the other clothing lines represented on the island," continued Lyndon.

"Over, not *under*." Grace mimed. "No booty shorts with underbum, no crop tops with underboob." Part of Grace's job was to say what Lyndon was thinking.

"But sideboob is okay?" From the loveseat, Grant eyed Jade, whose loose tank dipped low beneath her armpits.

"When done chicly." Lyndon nodded her approval.

Vincent focused his lens on Jade and Mia. Jade posed in an effortless and natural way, leaning her arm on the couch back, long legs crossed at the knee. Mia pressed her knees and ankles together and sat tall, offering a stiff smile. Realizing she was stiff made Mia even stiffer.

"Vincent's camera can wirelessly post to our social media," explained Lyndon. "But we expect you to grow your own social by cataloging everything you do."

Grace held up her smartphone. "You know the drill. Snapchat is moment-to-moment, Instagram is that big daily post. Instagram Stories should be visual snippets of your day."

"Four posts every twenty-four hours," instructed Lyndon. "Tag the brand. Tag each other."

Two "pops" from the kitchen diverted everyone's attention.

"Champers!" Presley glided into the room, holding a tray with two bottles of Dom and eight glasses.

"Presley is our returning seasonaire," said Lyndon. "The seasonaire with the most followers across all platforms will be invited back as our star influencer."

"Presley could return again if no one catches her," added Grace.

"I wasn't named 'Presley' for nothin'," said Presley. "But who needs The King when you have the queen?" She looked so full of herself she could've burst into a spray of hot pink confetti. As she walked around with the tray, everyone took a glass. Grace poured from one bottle, first for Lyndon, then herself. Presley poured for everyone else, spilling a drop on Mia's lap.

"Oops, my bad," she chirped.

Mia gave the wet spot on her skirt a quick brush.

"Let's toast." Lyndon lifted her glass. "To a perfect summer."

The group clinked glasses. Vincent took more photos.

"Look each other in the eye when you toast," said Grace. "It's good luck."

Mia and Cole locked eyes with an awkward chuckle.

"Seven years of bad sex if you don't," said Grant, trying to lock eyes with Jade, who rolled hers.

"That's a French superstition. *Parlez-vous français?*" Vincent asked Grant in his charming French accent.

"Two years of high school Spanish that I don't remember. But we had a foreign exchange student who taught me a few things." Grant winked. Vincent furrowed his brow and went back to his camera.

Lyndon put her glass on the mantel and picked up her purse. "I'm going to leave you to your adventures. You have the calendar of events. Make the most of everything!"

"But don't make too much of a mess." Grace took both her and Lyndon's glasses to the kitchen. "Our housekeeper, Nadege, comes only once a week," she called. She returned and handed Lyndon her work tote. She picked up her own, then tossed LW monogrammed T-shirts to everyone from a canvas shopping bag filled with them. She left the bag next to the front door. "Pass the rest out tonight at The Rabbit Hole."

"Sunday nights The Rabbit Hole is our hangout." Presley sat in an armchair and sipped her champagne.

"We'll be watching your social, so stay out of trouble." Lyndon's subtle smirk deliberately contradicted the warning. "And stay on the island."

J.P. rushed to hold open the door. "Pleasure to meet you, ma'am."

Lyndon cupped J.P.'s chin. "*Never* call a woman under forty ma'am."

"Apologies." J.P. glanced at his feet as Lyndon released his chin. "What should we call you?"

"Lyndon." She smiled at everyone and was gone.

After the door closed behind Vincent and the sisters, Presley turned to J.P. "How do you breathe with your nose so far up there?"

"Through my mouth."

Everyone laughed.

"No one likes a kiss-ass." Presley glanced at Mia.

"A little bro-mow before The Hole?" Grant peeked into his shorts, then at Cole and J.P.

"Those who bunk together don't manscape together," said Cole. He moved to pick up Mia's suitcase as everyone started up the stairs.

"I'm okay, thanks." Mia pulled up the rear with the heavy bag as they reached the second-floor hallway.

"I'd better have an ocean view," remarked Jade, with a sniff. She stopped at the open door that revealed her trunks at the foot of a plush king-size bed. There was an incredible view. "This is me."

"Private room? Nice," said J.P.

Mia saw Presley's eyes flash anger as Jade disappeared into her room. The three guys entered theirs. Presley turned to Mia, her pageant-winning smile glued back on.

"I guess that makes us a team."

SIX

"It's been forever since I've ridden a bike," said Mia as she approached the line of beach cruisers in front of the estate.

"They say you never forget," replied Cole, who was already on one. He pressed his heel into the kickstand, which flipped back.

"Well, I guess I'm going to test that theory right now." Mia mounted one of the bikes, teetering on it, her toes barely touching the ground.

"I'd tell you to wear a helmet, but we don't have any." Presley fluffed her hair. "Helmet head is tragic." She and Jade had managed get on their bikes with more poise than Mia, who pushed off to a wobbly start. Mia and her brother had shared the one bike their mom bought for $10 at a yard sale when Mia was seven. The chain broke after six months and it ended up in the junkyard. But thirteen years later, Mia was surprised at how quickly she got comfortable. "I guess the old saying is true," she mused to herself as she pedaled along just behind the others.

They cruised over to The Rabbit Hole while Vincent followed in the G, stopping them at spots to take snaps.

"These cobblestones are the worst," complained Jade as they jostled along. "They hurt my damn V."

J.P. laughed.

"Riding is the only way you can wear heels," said Presley, who was peddling in tall white espadrille wedges. "Two out of three female seasonaires sprained ankles last year. Guess which one ended up unscathed." She put a hand to her chest.

Grant popped a wheelie up the curb and rode on the sidewalk, arms up. "Ahhhhhhhhhh," he yelled, his voice fluttering with the bumps.

A black Crown Victoria driving down the street slowed. A man in a plain short-sleeve button-down shirt called out to them. "Bikes off the sidewalk."

Grant looked at him, but kept peddling along.

"Off. Now," demanded the man.

Mia noticed he had one brown eye and one blue eye.

"Do it, dummy," Presley said to Grant.

Grant popped off the sidewalk and joined the group riding in the street.

The man in the car nodded and continued on.

"That's the po-po," Presley explained. "They like to flex their muscles during the summer to make sure we're not having too much fun."

They parked their bikes in front of The Rabbit Hole and entered. Vincent followed. Despite its dive vibe, the place was packed with people jostling amid the worn wood panel interior, TV's bordering the ceiling, pool table, dartboards, ping-pong table, and jukebox. Ironically, the low-rent atmosphere attracted upper-crust customers: offspring of moneyed summer residents, flush young tourists, and brand ambassadors for everything from clothes to liquor. A small stage awaited Tidepull, the night's featured band, according to the scrawl on the blackboard.

"This place is lit!" yelled Grant over the din as the group waded through the crowd.

A trio of thirty-somethings abandoned a table as if invisibly bullied out of the bar by their younger, better-looking counterparts. Grant and Cole grabbed it while J.P., holding the canvas shopping bag, followed Jade. She hadn't bothered to wear her Lyndon Wyld tee like the others, who styled them in various outfits, Mia's with white cuffed jeans and a woven belt, Presley's tied at the waist and paired with a denim snap-front skirt. Jade accessorized her jersey maxi dress with a well-practiced "I don't give a fuck" expression.

Presley took Mia's hand. "We'll get drinks because I don't trust any of you jokers."

"A pitcher," hollered Grant.

"Please," added Cole with a smile at Mia.

Mia stepped up to the bar with Presley. She recognized the bartender as Scruffy-Sexy Bearded Guy who had stood with the Wear National girl in the alleyway. He was skillfully mixing drinks, pouring beers, and ignoring the shouts of "Bro! Here!" and "Where's my damn drink?"

Presley leaned over the bar. Her beauty and confidence caught the bartender's eye. "Strawberry daiquiri. And not the kind that comes out of that machine." She pointed to the machine behind him, whirring with fluorescent pink and blue slush.

"Shall I get you a chalice, too?" The bartender pulled the handle on the daiquiri machine and put the flamingo-hued drink on the bar in front of her.

"Is that how you talk to a patron?" Presley's eyes narrowed at him.

"A patron is one who *pays*. Your boss is paying." He motioned to Presley's Lyndon Wyld tee, appearing unfazed by the flat stomach she proudly showcased.

"If you think this whole 'bad boy' thing is going to get you into my drawers, you're sadly mistaken," Presley drawled, knowing full well that no one said "drawers" anymore.

"You're right," snapped a brunette waitress who put a tray of empty drinks on the bar. "You bougie bitches come in here like you own everything on the island, but honey, you do *not*."

"I don't remember *you* from last summer," Presley said to the bartender. "But I remember *you*." She sized up the waitress's curves, voluptuous enough to cause accidents. "What's your name again?"

"I never shared that with you. I'm not sharing *anything* with you, and that includes him." The waitress nodded toward the bartender. She sauntered into the kitchen.

Presley looked at the bartender, who continued to make cocktails, impervious to the drama. "Your girlfriend's got the line on spunk. In more ways than one, I'm sure." She strutted off, taking a sip of her pink drink from the straw. "This is shit, by the way," she called back.

Mia eked out an embarrassed smile to the bartender. "Can I get a pitcher? Please."

"ID."

Mia took her wallet from her purse and showed him her driver's license, holding her breath but keeping her gaze steady.

"Nice job with that." The bartender filled a pitcher and chuckled. "Kidding."

"Funny." Mia took the beer and a stack of glasses. "Thanks." Heart racing, she headed off.

The curvy waitress returned from the kitchen to grab her tray.

"You might want to try to avoid catfights with the customers," the bartender said to her as he set four tequila shots on the tray.

"That deb twat with the stick up her ass isn't a customer." The waitress nodded to the bar's entrance, where the Wear National girl with the blond hair with violet streaks entered. "Now *that* is a customer."

The paunchy, middle-aged manager, face full of weary wrinkles, approached them. "Hey, Mac, canoodling time cuts into set time." He waved off the waitress. "Eve, move it."

"Sorry, Frank," Mac said. He turned to pluck a bottle of rum from the shelf, side-eyeing Eve as she walked away with the tray.

Mia returned to the seasonaires' table, where Vincent was snapping photos. Grant relieved her of the pitcher while Cole took the glasses. Mia sat next to Presley.

Jade put her fingers under her nostrils. "It smells like a fucking frat house in here."

"Calling a fraternity a frat is like calling your country a cunt." Grant poured himself a beer. "Sigma Sig, Penn State!" He pumped his chest and chugged.

Presley pointed to herself. "Rho Pi at Georgia. Sigma Sigs were always decent hookup material." She turned to Jade. "Have you ever even been in a fraternity house, Jade?"

"At NYU, no. But I slummed it with a friend once." Jade lived in a Manhattan penthouse that her dad bought her.

"RISD doesn't have a Greek system," said J.P.

"Oooh, artsy!" remarked Presley. "What do you study there?"

"When I started, I wanted to sculpt. My mother was an artist."

Disinterested, Jade took a selfie and posted on Snapchat.

"But then I took an apparel class and realized that I wanted to design hats," J.P. continued. "So now, I'm sculpting masterpieces on heads."

Mia did a small spit take with her beer. "Ironic for a college with a scrotum for a mascot."

Everyone laughed, including J.P.

"But RISD is a great school," added Mia. Rhode Island School of Design had been one of Mia's dream colleges.

"Where do you go to school, Mia?" asked Cole.

"Nowhere." Mia didn't flinch.

"I graduated, too," said Cole.

"I didn't graduate because I didn't go to college." Mia wasn't going to hide *this* because she had done the best she could.

"Oh." Presley sniffed. "Hm."

"School of life. Best education and no debt." Cole lifted his glass to Mia.

A rocking cover of Free's "All Right Now" started to play from the stage. Mac was at the mic, singing and jamming on the guitar with his band. His bluesy voice and cocksure presence inspired the girls around the stage to cheer.

The song ended and he introduced his bandmates, rounding it out with, "I'm Mac, and we're Tidepull." To more wild cheering, they dove into another rousing rock cover.

As the seasonaires watched, Presley grinned. "Interesting. I might just let him in my drawers."

"Dude, you would *so* bone that guy." Grant nudged her.

Presley pushed him away. "Hey! I'm still a virgin!"

"What? Get out!" Grant cackled.

"The golden ticket requires four carats, princess cut." Presley wiggled the fingers on her left hand.

"But you just said you hook up," said Grant.

"Business up front. Party in the back." Presley sipped her daiquiri.

Grant leaned into Vincent with a scoff. "American girls, *oui?*"

"*Non,*" replied Vincent. His eyes were on two hot guys playing darts.

Grant paused.

By the time the band hit their third song, the house was in full groove. Presley's attention was on Mac, except when his eyes landed on her. She looked away as she waved her arms in the air, swaying her hips. Mia never went clubbing in Southie, so she let herself move to the beat. The night became a gyrating, sweaty, alcohol-fueled dance party.

When the band finished their set, Presley grabbed the Lyndon Wyld shopping bag and took to the stage. She tossed T-shirts into the crowd that went crazy, lunging and grabbing at the swag. Jade, not to be outshined, joined her, helped up by two guys whose hair looked like it took longer to style than Presley's.

"You should go up there, *chérie*," Vincent said to Mia. "I'll get some good shots for Lyndon."

"I'm not an onstage kind of girl," said Mia.

"Well, that better change."

Mia cringed and relented. She climbed up to meet Presley and Jade. With all the commotion below, she looked like a deer in the headlights. Drunk girls removed their tops to replace them with the tees. Vincent took photos of Grant, Cole, and J.P. laughing as they watched.

Mia loosened up with all the cheering. She hopped off the stage, picked up a pool cue at the pool table, and returned to bat the tees to the back of the house. Whoops and screams exploded. She saw Cole lift his phone to take photos of her, which spurred her on. As Mia picked up a tee, she noticed Mac high-five the Wear National girl at the side of the stage, her blond and violet-streaked hair now piled messily on her head. Putting extra finesse into her swing for Cole's snaps, Mia wondered if Cole captured the thin packet of white powder between their palms. At least that's what she thought she saw before she caught Mac's eyes and turned away.

SEVEN

Breakfast with the beach view could almost make Mia forget about any weirdness from the night before. No one else seemed to care about the view as she brought over her coffee and a bowl of fruit. Faces were buried in phones as everyone checked their social.

"Morning," said Mia.

"Hey." Cole was the only one to look up.

Mia sat next to Presley. She wasn't going to mention the possible drug swap. It was a party and there were drugs at parties. *No big deal, right?* She turned her attention to Instagram because she'd already Snapchatted that morning—a selfie with the dog-face filter. She'd captioned it:

Morning dog breath

She was surprised to see that her Instagram followers had tripled overnight. "Wow!" she exclaimed.

She noticed she was tagged in Cole's post of her batting the T-shirts.

What a swing! #BeWyld #tomboy

"My elbows could be higher," she remarked to Cole.

"Well, *I* was impressed." He smiled.

Presley scrolled through her phone. "I guess hashtag 'tomboy' is trending."

"Are you stalking me?" Mia laughed.

"I'm *supporting* you, sugar. See?" Presley reposted.

Mia noticed all the comments on Cole's post:

Love you @miamamasgrl! from her Freshman Fifteen friend, Liz.

Always could hit! from another high school friend. Then, dozens of comments from followers she didn't know:

Get it!
Adorbz
Baller
#likeaboss

This attention was new to her. She grinned at Cole, who offered an easy shrug.

Grant made everyone Bloody Marys to kick off touch football, which ended up being a lot of touching and not much football. He managed to get his hands on each female ass until Cole hoisted him toward the ocean, where he was dropped, laughing hysterically. The girls created what Presley called "a masterpiece sandcastle." They buried the guys from the neck down and wrote "Lyndon Wyld" in the sand with a piece of driftwood.

Vincent caught it all on video. Though they were happy hanging out at the shore below the estate, he encouraged them to take a walk down the beach for some stills. A family from a neighboring estate was picnicking. A little boy skipped over to Mia with a bucket full of sand, holding out a broken shell for her.

"You have treasures!" Mia exclaimed as Vincent snapped a shot of the sweet moment before the boy trotted back to his parents. Cole's eyes were on Mia.

Presley jumped on Grant's back, taking a video as he galloped. After a few yards, she dismounted and Snapchatted.

As they all made their way along the shore, a savory sage-meets-skunk scent wafted through the salty air. They looked to see the Wear National girl lounging under a red-and-white-striped umbrella next to two rail-thin guys with shaggy hair. That was the brand's look: nineties heroin chic mixed with seventies boho, a little hipster-nerd thrown in. The girl was smoking a joint, which she passed to the guy on the right, but not before blowing smoke in his open mouth then kissing him. As their tongues touched, his sterling bolt glinted. He passed her a bottle of Jack Daniel's. The guy on the left was lazily strumming a ukulele. While the girl snapped a pic of him, the wind blew a pack of rolling papers off their oversize beach towel toward the surf. Mia grabbed them before they hit the tide.

"Finders keepers," said Grant.

"It's cool. We have more." The girl grinned.

"I don't smoke," said Mia, walking the rolling papers to the threesome. "Well, I tried it once. Ended up in a corner thinking everyone was staring at me."

"That's what we're all here for, right? Attention," replied the girl. "I'm Ruby. This is Axel." She kissed Ukulele Boy. "And Quentin." She kissed Tongue Bolt, who ran his hand up her thigh, which had a rainbow tattoo cresting into her bikini bottom. With a wasted grin, she took the papers from Mia.

"Looks like we've wandered into the ghetto," Presley sneered, then looked at Jade. "No offense."

Jade gave her the finger.

"It's so early in the summer to be such a hater," Ruby said to Presley, her grin never faltering.

Presley's sneer remained. "I'm not a hater. I'd have to *care* to hate you."

"You don't know me. We all just got here. No one knows anyone, right?" Ruby looked at Mia.

Mia shrugged at Presley. "She's right."

"Your top's in the wrong place," called out a nasally male voice that made Vincent look up from the camera lens he was cleaning.

"Otto Hahn," whispered Presley to Mia with disgust.

Otto stepped across the sand from the sprawling estate with the Wear National flag. He wore seersucker pants, a bright orange button-down, and a white bucket hat on top of his thick, bushy brown and silver hair. His mutton chop–handlebar mustache and white-rimmed sunglasses topped off the sleaze vibe. An antique box camera hung around his neck.

"You gonna let their tits outshine yours?" He motioned to Axel and Quentin as he untied Ruby's bikini top. It dropped to the sand. Ruby didn't attempt to pick it up, but instead shifted her body toward him so he could properly appreciate it. Otto pushed his white-rimmed sunglasses up on his head.

Mia averted her eyes, feeling like she needed to take a shower.

Otto surveyed the seasonaires. "*You* aren't mine." He squinted at Presley. "You wear too much makeup," he said, then turned to Mia. "But *you* are a sweet little nymph."

"Ew," Presley muttered and strode off.

Cole touched Mia's shoulder. "Let's go."

Mia lingered, oddly fascinated as Otto moved to hug Vincent, who didn't hug back. "Where's the love, love?" Vincent refrained from response. "How long are you going to let Lady Macbeth squash your talents with her glossy, high-brow, and very dull dookey?"

"As long as the checks clear," answered Vincent, walking away.

"You're missing out on treats." Otto twisted the cap off a vial and tossed white pills to Ruby, Axel, and Quentin. Ruby washed hers down with Jack Daniel's from the nearby bottle.

Otto turned to Mia and Cole. "Treats?" He shook the vial.

"I'm good, thanks," said Mia. As she moved off with Cole, Ruby waved. Her face was open and friendly. Mia and Cole caught up with Vincent and the rest of the seasonaires down the beach.

"That chick is a hot fuckin' mess," said Grant.

"I read he doesn't pay the models in his ads." J.P. stepped around a plastic shovel left in the sand. "Sometimes he takes photos and doesn't tell them. One chick ended up on a Times Square billboard. Surprise!"

"When you work for him, he can do anything," said Vincent, staring out at the water.

Mia looked at him, then glanced back at the group under the umbrella. Otto was hunched over his box camera, aiming it at her. She quickly turned around and walked faster.

EIGHT

That night, while Presley slept soundly, pink satin sleep mask on, Mia tossed and turned. She picked up her smartphone and started scrolling through Instagram, checking out Wear National's account, which was filled with NC-17 posts cast with the 1977 filter. Morbid curiosity prompted her to open her laptop and Google search Otto Hahn. She quickly found his origin story: two decades earlier, he founded the clothing line in his Bard dorm room, where he made cotton tank tops between classes.

As a child, he immigrated with his parents from Germany to New York. His mom had been a seamstress who taught him how to sew. The tanks were a hit with the coeds, and he couldn't make them fast enough. Word spread and when he graduated, he set up shop in an abandoned Brooklyn auto garage, where he sold the goods out of a service window. Wear National went from that one window to two hundred stores worldwide. The company won Retailer of the

Year, knocking Zara off the top of the retail hierarchy. Lyndon Wyld dropped to third. Otto's credo was "Make for the asses, sell to the masses."

Otto triumphed despite his very public controversies, both personally and professionally. Besides openly admitting to relationships with several of his young employees, female and male, he often walked around his Manhattan office in a kimono and nothing else. There were a couple sexual harassment suits that were ultimately dropped. He had the same refrain as so many powerful men facing the same allegations: "All are untrue."

Mia closed her laptop, wondering how much of the legend was true and how much of it Otto spun. She went to sleep, trying not to think of Otto's box camera aimed at her.

The next morning, she and the other seasonaires dressed in the required "nautical chic" for the yacht Lyndon had chartered.

"I'll never understand why Wear National is even allowed here in Nantucket," said Presley. "There are architecture guidelines that don't allow tacky homes to ruin the aesthetic but the powers that be allow that garbage."

"It's commerce, Presley." J.P. put on a captain's hat with a logo of a finch on the band. "Otto Hahn pays the pricey rent and brings more tourists."

"Well, while his brand sluts give each other stick-and-poke tattoos and hepatitis, we're going on a gorgeous yacht."

They hopped in the G and headed for the Boat Basin, where they found *The Lady Mary*—all one hundred feet of her with her shiny green hull.

"Lyndon loved *Downton Abbey*," Presley informed the others. "She told me she was crushed when it ended. Lady Mary was her favorite character."

"My mom used to watch that show while I studied for my SATs," said Grant. "So fucking boring, except when the servants dressed those rich bitches. That was hot."

"Bet you crushed those tests," said Jade, letting a crew member help her onto the yacht.

"Does it matter? I'm here," answered Grant. "Right, Mia?"

Mia climbed onto the yacht without help. "Yep." Grant's comment stung. Mia had actually done pretty well on her SATs, yet he was the one who'd managed to go to college.

They spent the warm, cloudless day at sea just outside the Sound, lounging on *The Lady Mary*'s deck, drinking mimosas and working on their tans. Lyndon sent a care package of sunscreen especially for Mia. When Mia couldn't reach her back, Cole lent a hand. Lying on her stomach, with the sun and the breeze caressing her body, she released a long sigh.

"Magic hour," exclaimed Vincent right before sunset. "In this light, everyone looks *très magnifique*." He snapped Grant at the yacht's bow, shirtless.

"My ab game is strong." Grant ran a hand along his eight-pack.

After capturing more photos of the group, including one with the grizzled captain, who left them to their devices, Vincent made his way inside the yacht to edit and post.

The champagne ran out, so orange juice was paired with vodka for screwdrivers.

Mia sat, crossed-legged, on edge of the deck, staring out at the calm sea. Cole brought her a cocktail. "I've had more to drink in a week than I have in my entire life," Mia remarked.

"We're all going to need new livers by summer's end," Cole replied.

"Well, I know a lot of decent doctors," said Mia. Cole gave her a curious look. Mia added, "I've been taking care of my mom for a long time. She has cancer." The words came out before Mia could catch them.

"I'm sorry." Cole's kind face put Mia at ease.

"Drinking didn't fit in," she continued. "It wouldn't have been great if I was buzzed and gave her the wrong meds. Or got a DUI on the way to her treatments."

"That's gotta be rough."

Presley rolled her eyes behind her sunglasses as she lounged nearby with Jade. "How about a little Truth or Dare?"

"Yaaaaas! The dare is to strip down and hit the water!" Grant rubbed his hands together in anticipation.

"Since it was my idea, I'll start," said Presley. "Grant, truth or dare? When did you lose your virginity?"

Grant took the dare, mostly to shock khaki-and pearl-necklace-wearing country clubbers on a nearby yacht by mooning them and flipping into the water. The uptight ladies' expressions were priceless.

"Truth or dare, Mia?" Grant called, treading.

Mia was a crappy swimmer so the dare wasn't an option. "Truth."

"Have you ever cheated?"

"Yes," she answered, avoiding Cole's gaze.

Presley gasped. "Saint Mia!"

"Looks can be deceiving," said Jade.

Mia finished off another screwdriver and turned to Jade. "Truth or dare? Who do you love more, your dad or your mom?"

"That's a truly fucked-up question," snapped Jade.

"So you're taking the dare," said Presley.

"Always." Jade pulled her strapless one-piece down from under her sundress and stepped out of it, then lifted the dress over her head. She dropped it in J.P.'s lap and did a swan dive off the deck. Presley snapped a photo and posted to her Insta Story, tagging Jade:

We have the clothes. Some of us can't keep them on.
@1jaded.1 #sorrynotsorry

Jade swam to the yacht's ladder and hung on the side. "J.P., truth or dare? Before this summer, have you ever had a job?"

After a long beat with all eyes on him, J.P. removed his board shorts.

"Didn't think so," said Jade. Grant swam over and grabbed her from behind. She cackled raucously as they splashed. "Keep your shrunken pinky dick away from me!"

Everyone laughed as Jade swam away from him.

A motor cut above the laughter as a powerboat wrapped in the Wear National colors with a red logo flag sped toward the yacht. Axel was driving, with Quentin next to him. Ruby was passed out on the backseat, an open bottle of Cuervo between her legs.

"Losers starboard!" shouted Presley.

Axel, whooping, cut in toward the yacht, getting perilously close to Grant and Jade in the water.

"What are they doing?" Mia grabbed Cole's arm.

"I don't know."

The powerboat came back around and cut in again, its wake swallowing Jade. Her arms thrashed, head barely above the surface, mouth trying to find dry air. Grant was pushed farther away from her. J.P., still naked on the yacht's deck, dove in.

The powerboat did one more doughnut, then zipped away with Axel's and Quentin's war cries.

J.P. managed to drag Jade out of the wake.

The water calmed and the three climbed onto the yacht. Mia put a towel around Jade, who coughed and shivered.

Presley's phone buzzed with an Instagram notification:

lyndonwyld tagged you in a post.

She opened it to see one of Vincent's postcard perfect shots: all the seasonaires on the deck, beaming in the golden pre-sunset light:

Magical. #BeWyld

NINE

At the estate, Vincent retired to the guest cottage without saying goodbye to the group. His smartphone was to his ear.

"It was the usual summer telenovela." He sniffed, lighting up a Gitane and side-eyeing Grant, who stormed into the main house. "We have one hothead."

In the living room, Cole suggested a game of Monopoly "because nothing cheers you up like passing Go and collecting two hundred dollars." The mood brightened as houses and hotels were purchased.

Grant refused to play, pacing and swigging from a bottle of Jäger instead. "Motherfuckers!" he yelled at the top of his lungs.

Everyone turned.

"Grant, what on earth?" Presley held her chest.

He displayed his phone. Wear National's Instagram featured a selfie of Axel and Quentin on the powerboat, grinning, their hair whipping in the wind:

Water wars with @lyndonwyld. #WearNational #killinit

"Chill, dickweed. It's over," said Jade as she disappeared upstairs. J.P. followed with an annoyed glance at Grant.

"You might want to slow down there." Cole motioned to the Jäger.

"Yeah, Grant, you don't want to end up like that brand slut in the back of the boat," Presley added. "What's her name?"

"Ruby," answered Mia.

"I bet those dogs had a good time with her." Presley gave a "tsk."

Grant slammed the bottle on the mantel, then bolted outside.

"Presley!" Mia glared, then ran after Grant.

"What?" Presley lifted her hands innocently and followed with Cole.

Grant got in the G.

"Where are you going?" yelled Mia.

Presley answered for Grant. "It's Wear National Night at The Rabbit Hole."

"Shit." Cole jumped in along with Mia and Presley.

Grant floored it. He careened through town and made it to the bar, parking with one tire on the curb. Mia grabbed at his shirt as he clamored out and rushed inside.

"This'll be fun," said Presley, striding in.

As Mia and Cole entered, Mia saw something out of the corner of her eye: Mac and Ruby were against the side of the building in the shadows, sharing a smoke.

Inside, Grant drunkenly shouldered his way through the partying crowd, craning his neck, searching. He found Axel playing pool with Quentin and coldcocked him, then climbed on top and punched relentlessly. Quentin stepped back.

Presley caught the curvy brunette server, who passed by with a tray, ignoring the brawl. "Strawberry daiquiri, *Eve*. I have a memory like a steel trap. Oh, and some popcorn."

"You're all such chodes," said Eve, who moved off.

"Grant! Stop!" Mia yelled as she squeezed through the patrons. Some filmed the scrap with their phones. Cole struggled to pull Grant off.

Mac muscled in, picking up Axel, whose face was bloody. "You okay?" Axel shrugged away from him.

Grant poked his finger at Axel. "If you ever try that shit again, I'll fucking crush you!"

"We were just playing around!" Axel spat blood on the ground.

"It's true, man," said Quentin from his safe spot in the corner.

Grant stormed out of the bar. Cole followed, scowling at Axel.

A hush came over the crowd.

Presley, propped on a bar stool, applauded, breaking the silence. "Opening act was decent. Now where's the headliner?" She grinned broadly at Mac.

Mia's phone buzzed from her back pocket. After a stunned beat, she looked. Lyndon Wyld had been tagged in an Instagram video of the fight on some random account—hounddogdayz:

It's on. #teamwyld #teamnational #seasonaires

❧

In his room at the quiet estate, J.P. glanced at the Instagram post of the fight. "That's mature," he said to himself with a sniff. He was sitting on his bed in sweats and a tee, working on the business plan for his haberdashery on his laptop.

His phone buzzed. He gave a "tsk," then saw it was a text from Jade:

Enter.

J.P. stared at it. He emoji'd a thumbs-up, then winced. Leaping off the bed, he jetted out the door. He found Jade's door open a crack and knocked.

"I already said 'enter.'"

J.P. pushed the door wider. Jade was wearing an M-Kat Records tank and boys' skivvies. Her long legs took up the bed's length.

"I have that shirt," said J.P. nervously.

"I'm sure you do." Jade propped up on her elbow.

"Your dad's record label has some of my favorite artists." J.P. put his hands in his sweats pockets.

"Most of them suck." Jade patted the bed. "Sit."

J.P. sat.

"You're like a Labrador puppy, J.P."

"Labs are generic. I'm more like . . . a pitbull."

Jade laughed. "Oh, yeah, a pitbull." She reached into her night-stand and opened a *Vogue* magazine with her stunning mom on the cover. A joint was tucked in the spine. She lit it with the matches next to a Diptyque candle, and inhaled.

"We probably shouldn't smoke in here," said J.P.

"While I'm here, this is *my* room. Take a hit."

J.P. took the joint from Jade, their fingers touching, and he toked.

"You'll do anything I say, won't you?" Jade smiled.

"I like you." J.P. shrugged, exhaling.

"Bullshit. You have a boner for my dad."

"I admire your dad, but I like *you*. You're beautiful and smart. NYU."

"All you need is a sizable contribution to go to NYU, which means *you* could've gone there, too." Jade retrieved the joint. "What is it that you want from my dad? A job?"

"I want to know how he got where he is. I've studied him, but I want to hear it from *him*."

"You'll never be my dad," said Jade, her smile vanishing. "My dad started with nothing. Your *abuelo* owns everything on the other side of Trump's Invisible Wall."

J.P. looked at her, curious and offended.

"I did a little studying myself." Jade exhaled, smoke curling around J.P.'s face.

"Yeah, well, you're here because your daddy's in bed with Lyndon Wyld," replied J.P.

"Everyone's in bed with everyone. That's how it works." Jade shifted her silky legs. J.P.'s eyes lingered over them. "I saw you today, *jefe*," Jade purred. "*All* of you. I felt you when you carried me back to the boat. Impressive." She ran her hand along J.P.'s thigh. "I should thank you."

J.P. looked at Jade's hand, which moved up. "You don't have to thank me." He wished he weren't aroused, but he was. "Your dad threatened to kill me not once, but *twice*, if I deflower you."

"He knows I'm no fucking flower. He likes to wave his guns around for shits 'n' giggles." Jade gently squeezed. "But you'll do what I say because what he *wants* is for me to be happy. You'll make me happy this summer, right?"

"*Sí, claro*," replied J.P. as Jade pulled him on top of her.

—⊷—

"I think you made your point, Grant." Mia helped Cole pull Grant away from the crowd. "Let's go."

Mac took to the stage with his band, leaning into the mic. "Now that you're all fired up." He grinned at the whooping crowd and launched into Ozzy Osbourne's "Crazy Train."

Grant yanked away from Mia and Cole, heading out the door. Mia passed Presley, who hadn't moved from her stool.

"You coming?" asked Mia.

"Nope." Presley's gaze was cemented on Mac, jamming and singing.

"Do you want me to stay?"

"I don't need a caretaker, Mia."

Mia's eyes flashed hurt. Presley gave her arm a stroke. "I heard you tell Cole about your sick mama today on the yacht. Is that the story you used in your application?"

"It's not a story. It's the truth."

"The truth *is* a story. It's okay, honey, we all have one. My story is 'from country bumpkin to Insta-famous.'" Presley lifted her daiquiri, took a selfie, and posted while continuing to Mia, "You're not responsible for everyone here. Take care of yourself for once."

"Fine," said Mia with a swift exhale. "Have fun."

"I always do."

As Mia left, she caught Eve's eyes on Presley. If looks could kill. Eve's stare shifted to Mia, who looked away and hurried after Grant and Cole.

TEN

Grant, Cole, and Mia headed toward the G, still askew on the curb.

"Aw, leaving so soon?" They turned to see Ruby weaving toward them.

"Ruby, right?" said Grant, a bite to his voice.

"That's me." Ruby smiled, wasted.

"My dick's bigger than both of those pussies inside."

"When did you have time to measure? You've been pretty busy." Ruby waved her smartphone, playing the video of the fight.

"I'll show you right now." Grant started to unbutton his shorts.

"Grant, don't be a pig," said Mia.

Grant rebuttoned.

"Pigs are cute." Ruby put her finger up to her lips, dropping her phone as she pointed at the cop car passing the bar. "Shhhhhh. Don't tell *them* that."

"Great." Cole motioned Grant toward the G, then picked up Ruby's phone and handed it to her. "Grant, you'll get popped for assault." He nodded to Ruby. "And you for being drunk in public. You can share a cell."

"He's never been in prison," Ruby chuckled at Grant. "Pretty, pretty boy."

"And you have?" scoffed Grant.

"Petty theft." Ruby laughed hysterically. Mia didn't know if she was joking, but she was certain Ruby was trashed because she tripped as she headed toward the bar's entrance. Mia caught her by the arm before she hit the ground.

"You're amazing." Ruby looked into Mia's face, then turned to Cole and held up her phone. "And *you* are a gentleman." She staggered into the bar. Cole watched her enter, and Mia watched him watch her.

"That chick does *not* want a gentleman," scoffed Grant as he climbed in the back of the G. The three drove home.

When they got back to the estate, Grant grabbed the bottle of Jäger that he had left on the living room mantel and stomped upstairs. Cole tried to follow him to their room, but Grant shoved him. "Back the fuck off." He slammed the door shut.

Cole stood in the hallway with Mia.

J.P. slipped out of Jade's bedroom. "Hey," he said, quickly heading into the guys' room.

"You might not want to go in there," said Cole, but J.P. was inside before he finished his sentence.

"Hm," said Mia as she glanced at Jade's door.

"Yup," replied Cole. The two stood for an awkward beat.

"What a day, huh?" Mia broke the silence. "You want to go outside for a bit and let the kraken drink himself to sleep?"

"Nah, I can handle it, because he's already probably passed out." They laughed. Mia moved to her door and lingered.

"'Night, Mia," said Cole.

"'Night."

Mia washed off the disappointment with her makeup and got into her pajamas. She was exhausted but not sleepy. On her bed, she opened her laptop. The time read 11:30 p.m. She pulled up Skype, then closed it and shut her laptop, picking up her smartphone and moving to the window seat. She pressed "Favorites" then "Ma" with the icon of Kathryn when she was healthy, cheeks full and rosy, hair a thick brown cascade. She put the phone to her ear.

"My girlie!" Kathryn exclaimed when she answered. Her delight managed to rise above her tired rasp.

"Hi, Mom." Mia looked out to the beach, a triangle of the blue-black water lit by the moon.

"Are you okay? It's late," said Kathryn.

"I know. I'm sorry."

"Never apologize for calling me. I'm always up for you, sweet love. Are you having the best time?"

"I am." Mia put a smile in her voice.

"Tell me all the exciting news."

"Oh, there's so much." Mia wanted to say more, but all she could think about was the day's chaos, and that would worry her mom. "Wait until my memoir is out."

"You hate writing, so I'll be waiting forever."

"How are *you* feeling, Mom?"

"Like a million bucks."

Mia was relieved she'd decided to call instead of Skype, because the picture would've told a different story. "You're a terrible liar."

"Takes one to know one."

Mia changed the subject. "And Sean? How's he? I texted him, but he hasn't texted back."

"You know he's bad at that. All boys are."

There was a long pause. "I just wanted to hear your voice. I miss you," said Mia.

"I miss you, too, honey. Have fun for me."

"I will."

"Love you so much."

"Love you, too."

Mia hung up. She stared out the window and noticed a figure to the right of the moonlight. Cole was on the beach by himself, talking on his phone.

Presley, the last customer at The Rabbit Hole, sat on a barstool and watched Mac wash and dry glasses. "Where's your lovely girlfriend? What's her name? Kelly? Beth?"

"Eve."

"Eve." Presley hung on the "v."

"She went home," said Mac.

"To *your* home?"

"We don't live together."

"I'm an old-fashioned girl myself." Presley recrossed her legs. "She didn't want to wait for you tonight?"

"Nope." Mac placed glasses on shelves.

Presley put an elbow on the bar, chin in hand. "You're at the top of her shitlist?"

"No. *You* are." Mac flipped down the lid to the garnish tray in front of Presley.

"Wouldn't be the first time." Presley shrugged. "Won't be the last."

They sat in silence for a few minutes as Mac wiped down the bar. Presley looked at the small stage.

"Your band is marginal at best," Presley said. "If I'm gonna be honest."

"Don't you need your beauty rest? You seasonaires have all that twatting and Snapshitting to do." He wiped harder toward her, forcing her to lift her elbows.

"No one under thirty tweets anymore," said Presley. "And I can Snapchat in my sleep. Nothing's on my schedule until our appearance at the store at eleven."

"Your appearance," Mac snickered. "Like you're a fucking celebrity."

"I *am* a fucking celebrity." Presley showed him her Instagram, but he didn't bother to look.

"Eleven?" Mac slapped the towel over his shoulder. "My other job starts at seven a.m."

"What job is that?"

"I teach sailing to kids. Summer camp."

"Awwww. You are one hard worker." Presley knelt on the stool to reach over and point. "Though you missed a spot right there."

Mac smacked the towel down on the invisible spot and got in her grill. "Listen, what's your name? Kelly? Beth?"

"Presley."

"Why wouldn't it be?" His jaw muscles flexed tightly. "Presley. We're closed. Go home."

Presley didn't back down. Their eyes locked. "I need a ride."

"I'm not a fucking chauffeur," snapped Mac.

Presley broke the death stare, teasing him. "How about a Lyft driver? That's a good way for a starving musician to make extra cash."

"You might not believe this, with your cushy summer play-job, but no one wants to live here year-round. I want to leave, and people like you, *Presley*, are a big reason."

"I *earned* this cushy summer play-job." Presley's voice grew serious. "My life isn't so luxurious where I'm from either." This was the first time she couldn't look at him. Seeing this vulnerability slip, Mac's expression softened. Letting silence fill the room, he finished wiping down the bar, including the invisible spot.

Presley sat back down and turned on the sparkle. "Are you gonna give me a ride or what?"

Mac tossed the towel into the sink. "The Lyndon Wyld fancy flophouse is out of my way."

"Where do you live?" asked Presley.

"On a boat in Old South Wharf."

"Lemme guess." Presley put her finger to her temple. "It's called *The Eve*."

"*The Taken Aship*," Mac said, then off Presley's glare, clarified, "It's not my boat. It's my cousin's. He gets the hell outta here during tourist season and I Airbnb my apartment."

"Resourceful," said Presley.

"Yup."

"I accept your offer to go out of your way." Presley lifted a shoulder.

Mac rolled his eyes and removed his black apron. He grabbed his keys from a hook. "Lemme lock up."

Presley smiled, satisfied.

ELEVEN

I opened my eyes this morning to see my baby's bare ass right here! Right the fuck here!" Maz waved his twenty-four-karat-gold-encased smartphone at Lyndon, who sat behind the green lacquer desk of her Manhattan penthouse headquarters. Enraged, he pointed to Presley's Instagram post of a nude Jade diving off the yacht.

Lyndon sipped tea as Grace leaned in to look. "Oh, that *is* her bare bum, isn't it? Looks a tad different than when I used to diaper it babysitting during your Blue Bash."

"Why is it on this bitch's Instagram when you're mama bear, Lyndon?" Maz yelled. "You can actually see *more* than Jade's ass if you zoom in!" He zoomed in and shoved the phone closer toward Lyndon, who waved it away.

"Maz, my darling, you know that all press is good press," said Lyndon, ever calm and collected.

"Not when it comes to my family." He shoved the phone in his pocket.

Lyndon put down her cup. It clinked on its matching china plate. "You shagged two of your nannies and have a child with one. Your mother caught your wife with her personal trainer's face between her legs and had a heart attack. And your oldest son went to jail for statutory rape."

"That was thrown out. And now he's a multiplatinum DJ!"

"Exactly. After each transgression, your family's stock rose."

Grace put a file folder down on the desk. "Though it's fun to reminisce, you two should get down to business. Lyndon, you have a Skype call at ten—that's in fifteen minutes."

"Did you double book? *Me*?" Maz cocked his head at Lyndon. "I best not be your double book."

"Oh, please," chuckled Lyndon. "You always double book. We're both brilliantly efficient. It's one reason we are finally collaborating. And here's the other one." She opened the file folder and fanned out shoe designs across her desk, all with an MWyld emblem. "I wanted a quick meeting to show you how our line is shaping up!"

Maz relaxed as he reviewed the designs. "That's fire. That's fire. That's fire. All fire! Excellent."

Pleased, Lyndon made check marks with her Tiffany pen.

"But wifey hates the name," Maz said. "She's half Colombian, so we should reconsider."

"I'll persuade her. I always do," Lyndon replied.

"What . . . the . . . fuck?" Grace stared at her iPad, brow furrowed. Lyndon and Maz turned toward this interruption. Grace placed her iPad on the desk. *Fortune* magazine's cover featured Otto Hahn holding a globe wrapped in a Wear National tank top:

OTTO HAHN—ENTREPRENEUR OF THE DECADE
What will he do next?

"He's a maggot!" Lyndon threw her pen on the desk.

"An offense to maggots everywhere," remarked Grace.

"How does this happen?" Lyndon swiveled her chair away from the iPad. "Fuck!"

"I was last decade's pick. It's no big shit." Maz touched his collar.

Lyndon pointed back at the iPad, though she didn't look. "I know exactly 'what he'll do next' because he does everything I do *first*! Yet he's ahead! He's probably co-branding footwear!"

Maz massaged Lyndon's shoulders. "Deep breaths. Look at the bonsai I bought you. It's meditative." He pointed to the potted bonsai on her desk.

Lyndon refused to turn back around. "You know I can't meditate. That's why you bought it for me."

Maz bent down and stared into Lyndon's eyes. "Look. I'm playing nine holes with him on Tuesday. I'll find out what his next fail upward will be. He's not that stealthy."

"How can you golf with him?" Lyndon spoke through clenched teeth.

"Chill, baby. It's part of the bigger game," said Maz. "I'm on your team . . . as long as I don't ever see my daughter's treasures on social again." He swiveled her in the chair and pointed to the bonsai, then leaned into her ear. "I gave you that because I knew you could take care of it." His voice was now more like gravel than velvet. "I don't believe many people can."

Grace watched, holding her iPad close to her chest.

Lyndon rose and pulled gold pruning shears from her desk. "Don't doubt my ability," she said to Maz. "I don't doubt yours. Win on Tuesday. Maybe that fucker will get stuck in a sand trap."

"Or better yet, quicksand," added Grace.

"I'm a scratch golfer, ladies." Maz headed for the door. "I have a meeting in ten minutes." He winked as he exited. "Efficient."

After the door closed, Grace turned to Lyndon. "Keep your friends close and your—"

Lyndon cut her off with a glare. "I will cunt punch you if you say it."

Grace mimed a zipper mouth.

Lyndon angrily snipped a branch from the bonsai.

TWELVE

E xcuse me." Mia pulled her coffee mug in as she slipped between the kitchen door frame and Grant, who gripped his hands on the top of the frame, stretching.

"Fuck, I'm hungover." Grant winced in the morning sun that bathed the living room.

"No shit." Cole was drinking orange juice on the couch. Mia passed the space next to him and sat in the loveseat, avoiding his perplexed look.

"This almond milk is atrocious." Jade put her tea on the mantel. "We should get the maid to make it from scratch. It's easy."

"If it's easy then why don't you do it?" J.P. ribbed her as he took her mug into the kitchen. Bigger than Mia, his size forced Grant to move.

Grant chuckled at Jade. "Oh, now that he's fucking you, he's gonna pretend he's not a big pussy?"

Jade didn't respond, instead turning to the mirror over the mantel and applying lip gloss.

Grant brushed by her on his way to manspread on the ottoman. "We know what you guys were doing while we were gone."

Mia stared out at the beach.

J.P. reentered with two mugs of tea. He handed one to Jade and sat on the couch next to Cole. Grant flicked J.P.'s shin. "You put *fresh squeezed* almond milk in her tea?"

"That's so wrong," Mia said to Grant, a bite to her tone. "Why do you think that's funny?"

"Because it is." Grant smirked.

"It's really not," said Mia, aware that Cole's eyes were on her. "I know guys like you in Southie. You're good-looking but your personality makes you a total tool. We get it. You're insecure."

Grant clapped. "I knew you had a mouth piece behind the mom gear."

"I don't dress like a mom." Mia crossed her legs in her sundress.

"You do a little," retorted Grant. "You think it's some cool retro vibe, but it's fucking boring."

"How about this?" Mia uncrossed her legs and leaned forward toward Grant. "I let the real me slip out more and so do you."

Before Grant could agree to this deal, the Skype window on the flat-screen TV came to life. Presley, holding the remote, popped next to Mia on the loveseat as Lyndon's and Grace's faces appeared. She and Mia exchanged a glance.

Everyone in the living room straightened up, except for Jade, who leaned against one of the French doors behind the group.

"Good morning, lovelies!" chirped Lyndon. "You're looking tan and healthy . . . most of you."

Grant put his hands in his pockets to hide his scabbing knuckles.

"Put some frozen peas on those fists, Grant," said Grace.

Nailed, Grant winced slightly. "I will."

Grace held up her smartphone, showing the Instagram video of the fight.

"That's the last replay I want to see like that." Lyndon pointed to the video. "Do you understand?"

Grant nodded.

Grace lowered the phone.

"From the looks of social, you're all taking advantage of the island," said Lyndon.

"But don't let the island take advantage of you," added Grace.

Presley shifted on the couch next to Mia.

"Make today at the store memorable," said Lyndon. "I expect your followers to increase exponentially."

"Remember, the peasants who can't afford to holiday in Nantucket want to imagine they are," said Grace.

Lyndon put her arm around her little sister. "We were two of those peasants growing up. You're selling their dream at the store and online in the form of purchasable fashion." Her eyes went to Mia. "Mia, you need to up the social momentum."

"Okay." Mia straightened.

"After your cute little T-ball showcase at The Rabbit Hole, you got a spike. Keep it from getting flat," added Lyndon.

"You're the one with the most sales experience here, working at the thrift shop," said Grace.

Mia nodded. Grace had never acknowledged finding Mia at the thrift shop until right then.

"Mia, do you know how to work one of those old-timey registers?" Jade sneered.

Grant pulled an imaginary handle. "Cha-ching!"

Mia's face flushed with embarrassment, but she covered by scratching her head toward Grant with her middle finger. Cole caught this and silently chortled.

"Nothin' wrong with a thrift shop," Presley snapped at Jade and Grant.

"Show everyone how it's done, Mia," said Lyndon. "Show *me* how it's done, because you're not just going to the store to show your face—"

"*Grant*," emphasized Grace.

"They should want the clothes right off your backs," said Lyndon. "Jade, my darling, I'm not being literal." She held up her smartphone and the Instagram post of Jade's skinny-dip dive.

Jade shifted her gaze out the window.

"Your daddy doesn't like seeing every man's eyes on you this way," added Lyndon.

"All eyes on him," muttered Jade.

Grant yawned, making Presley yawn.

"Presley, love, go make yourself an espresso," said Lyndon. "You look tired. Don't work so hard."

"If this is work, I never want to retire." Presley put on a perky face. Mia glanced at her.

"We'll see everyone at the Summer Solstice Soiree this Saturday," said Lyndon. "It's the first real party of the season."

"Can't wait. Tah!" Grace waved. Lyndon blew a kiss. The screen went black.

"We'd better get to the store," said Cole.

Vincent entered, jangling the car keys. "*Allons-y*. Let's go." He went back out. Jade traipsed after him, J.P. right behind.

"I'll meet y'all outside in a sec," said Presley.

Mia brought her empty coffee mug to the kitchen. Presley followed.

"How was your night?" Mia put her mug in the dishwasher.

"Listen, let's not chat about that with the others," said Presley. "Keep my private life private."

Mia turned to her, eyes wide. "Are you serious? All you do is post your private life."

"Yeah. *I* post it. And I'm not posting anything about last night, though someone posted Grant's stupid fight pretty quick." She looked at the Instagram video of Grant's scrap on her phone.

"Did you just hear Lyndon?" asked Mia. "I can barely remember to post about myself, so you don't have to worry about me outing you."

"That's true." They headed back through the living room.

"So . . . how was it?" Mia slung her mini satchel across her dress.

Presley grabbed her purse. "Are you asking me if the bartender and I had sex, because I already told you, I don't—"

"I'm not." Mia stopped at the front door. "I don't know. He just doesn't seem like your type."

"He isn't. At all," said Presley. "That's what makes it perfect. I'm not going to law school so I can marry a freakin' bartender. Lawyer, doctor, stockbroker, politician, but no bartender. Especially one who lives on a boat called *The Taken Aship*."

"Ew," Mia chuckled. "Really?"

Presley leaned in. "It's his cousin's who's gone for the summer. I didn't see it. All we did was sit on the beach and chat."

"That sounds nice." Mia flashed on Cole, alone on the beach.

Presley twirled a lock of her hair. "It *was* nice."

Mia considered telling Presley what she thought she'd seen the first night at The Rabbit Hole: Mac giving Ruby drugs. But she remembered the time she told her mom her brother stole a Snickers from the liquor store. Kathryn was pissed at *Mia*. Mia wasn't sure it was the tattling that caused the anger. She'd ruined her mom's fantasy of Sean, her perfect little boy. Mac was a perfect summer fantasy for Presley. Who was Mia to spoil that over something she was unsure about?

Mia started for the door, but Presley stopped her.

"All I'm saying is let's not tell Lyndon I was hanging out with the locals. They're not really 'on brand.'"

"Why would I tell her?" asked Mia.

"Because girls are cunts." Presley's Southern lilt sweetened the word.

"Maybe the girls *you're* used to." Mia looked into Presley's eyes. "Where I'm from, we have The Girl Vault."

"The Girl Vault." Presley smiled. "I like that. I'd show you the Rho Pi handshake, but then I'd have to kill you."

Presley pushed past Mia to the car. Mia followed, shaking her head with a laugh.

THIRTEEN

The Lyndon Wyld store always had customers. The season locals shopped during the summer weekdays. They never asked for help, lightly clicking around with averted stares, as if the sales staff should know what they wanted simply by looking at them. Saturdays, the tourists created a different, steadier buzz, their excited faces revealing that they wanted to be treated the way they *thought* the locals were treated. It was the best day for the seasonaires to help out.

The store was split in half—women's clothes on the right, men's clothes on the left. Jill, a tall, slim brunette, was the store manager. In her late twenties, she had never been chosen to be a seasonaire, despite applying for multiple summers. To overcompensate, Jill took her job very seriously. She had a specific way of folding the jeans.

"Slap them on your legs like this." She whipped a pair of straight-leg selvedge denim, hem downward, against her thighs. "Fold in half, then in fourths." She folded. "Then place them on the display, pocket up, price tag in. Lyndon likes them this way."

Cole followed her instructions.

"Nice," said Jill. Mia noted the exchanged smiles.

"Wouldn't it be better to hang them?" J.P. wasn't really asking. "Then you could see the style."

"And we wouldn't have to refold them," added Grant, eyeing two cute blondes waiting outside for the store to open.

"You are one lazy *conasse*," remarked Vincent as he snapped a photo of Grant.

"Just say 'asshole,' dude." Grant laughed. "I *did* retain a couple French words from our foreign exchange student. Or 'arsehole' because 'arsehole' is acceptable if you say it with a British accent like the boss." He unsuccessfully attempted a British accent. "'You are one lazy arsehole.' I'm just going to speak like this for the rest of the time here because it sounds better. *Arsehole*."

"Nope, it really doesn't," said Mia with a chuckle.

"I agree," said Jill, her expression dour.

Vincent caught a shot of Jade, who tied a featherweight scarf around her head as she arranged others on a display table in artful swirls and loops. "This store desperately needs more pop," she remarked. Mia noticed that everything looked chicer after Jade touched it.

When Jill unlocked the doors, most of the seasonaires avoided folding the jeans and instead took photos with customers. Grant zeroed in on the vacationers' pretty daughters, who waved around their parents' credit cards like American flags in a July Fourth parade. He welcomed STDs as if they were gold medals.

Thanks to her work in the thrift shop, Mia knew how to compliment customers, always making eye contact to connect with them. "That color makes your eyes pop." "This style is *so* flattering on you."

"Your *derriere* looks amazing!" The compliments quickly turned into more sales for the store and more followers for Mia. "School of life," she mused to herself, thinking back to Cole's comment.

"That woman looked like a damn sausage," Presley said after Mia encouraged a chubby soccer mom to buy skinny jeans.

"She felt good in them and that's what counts." Mia waved at the woman, who left with her shopping bag. Mia posted a photo with her to her Insta Story.

"You don't really believe that." Presley took a selfie in some sunglasses and posted.

"I do." Mia looked up at her.

Presley put the sunglasses back in the display. "You're a good person, aren't you, sugar?"

Mia examined Presley's face, trying to figure out if this was a pageant trick. Presley slid on another pair of sunnies.

"Eyes here, people," interrupted Jill when the store was empty for a beat. She held up a pair of long red shorts with an anchor pattern. "Anything in Nantucket Red sells out every summer, though the locals wouldn't be caught dead in it. I need someone to help me grab more from the back."

"I'm a front of the house guy." Grant jogged to a tall redhead who entered.

"I'll help you," said Mia.

Jill's smartphone buzzed with a text. She scrolled and shook her head. "You're crushing it on social today, Mia." She looked at Mia. "Lyndon wants you to stay out here and keep it up."

"Go, Mia!" Presley offered an overenthusiastic cheer.

"I'll help you, Jill," said Cole.

Mia watched him follow Jill into the stockroom.

Presley leaned into her. "Wonder how many employees hook up back there. You ever hook up in the thrift shop stockroom?" Mia furrowed her brow, moving off to a mom with tween girls stepping through the door.

The flow of customers ebbed into a quiet lull. Jade swayed in the store's wicker swing, scrolling on her phone. She felt Vincent's camera on her, so she crossed her legs and gave him a smile.

"You know what's missing at this store?" J.P. knelt next to her with his phone.

"I'm sure you're going to tell me," answered Jade in a blasé tone.

"Hats." J.P. punched in his password to unlock his phone.

"What do you call your haberdashery?"

"Perch." J.P. handed his phone to Jade, website up. "*Perchero* means 'hat stand' in Spanish."

"Clever. But no one knows what a haberdashery is anymore," said Jade. "Millennials are 'stupid.'"

The tween girls gave Jade the stink eye as they made a beeline for Presley in her sunglasses.

"Relax, chicas," Jade said to them. "You're Gen Z." She turned back to the Perch site on J.P.'s phone. J.P. caught a tiny grin cross her face.

"Aw, see? You like them." J.P. nudged Jade.

"I like them, but your mission statement is so fucking pretentious." Jade read from J.P.'s phone: "'My goal is to inspire people to express the beauty that's inside their heads.'" She shoved the phone back to J.P. "My dad'll hate that." J.P. stared at his site, flummoxed.

Mia and the tweens' mom held gold hoops to their ears. "With your hairstyle, these are fantastic." Mia snapped their selfie.

The tweens nervously approached Presley. "Are you Presley?"

"Sure am." Presley beamed.

"We love your Snapchat Stories," giggled one tween.

"You have awesome style," said the other.

"Thank you." Presley beamed at them and touched the floral tops on the display next to her. "You're both prettier than roses in spring. Will you take a selfie with me?" The girls moved in close to Presley. She took the pic and posted. "Now you're part of my story." They traipsed back to the mom, but not without items that Presley chose for them.

Presley slipped behind Mia, who was standing at a T-shirt shelf, staring toward the stockroom. "I was teasing you before, honey. Cole's a good boy, I can tell. He's got that soulful eyes thing going on." Presley reconsidered. "Though he *does* have that scar. Maybe he's not such a good boy."

"I'd actually like to get to know someone instead of guessing." Mia went back to folding.

"Guessing is part of the fun, sugar." Presley smoothed a tee.

"Games suck," said Mia. "I don't get it. On the yacht, it seemed like he was interested. Then last night . . ."

Cole returned from the stockroom with Jill. Mia straightened a tee stack.

"No worries. Her hair's too neat," whispered Presley.

At closing time, each seasonaire received a bag of Lyndon Wyld merch from Jill. As they exited, the door's alarm went off. Jill approached them.

"Sorry, guys, I'm going to have to look in your bags. There were some sticky fingers last year."

"Why would we take shit when you're already giving it to us?" asked Grant.

"Some people are never satisfied." Jill looked in the bags.

Vincent shook his head and left the store. Jill riffled through Mia's bag. After a beat, she pulled out a floral top with part of the sensor still attached. "Really?"

"I didn't take that," said Mia, her body prickling with humiliated heat.

"It's in your bag," countered Jill.

Mia avoided Cole's eyes. At that moment, she felt like everyone in Nantucket knew she was from Southie, that she didn't go to college, and that she needed the $20,000 more than anyone else.

"That's mine." Presley grabbed the bag. "Our bags got switched. We work our tails off, Jill. Jill, that's your name, right?"

Jill's glare was her answer.

"I think we deserve a little more than we're getting." Presley handed the other bag to Mia.

"Then you should talk to Lyndon about that," replied Jill.

"I will." Presley fingered the floral top Jill held and sniffed with disdain. "Have your shirt. It's not one of my faves anyway."

The seasonaires left the store, Mia without a word to Jill.

Mia stopped Presley on the way to the G. "I didn't take that shirt," she said.

"It's okay if you did." Presley put a hand on her arm, leaning into Mia's ear. "But next time, you have to do a better job with the sensor. I use a rubber band."

"Someone put that shirt in my bag," said Mia.

"Who would do that?"

"I don't know."

"Maybe it was a mistake," said Presley. "Everyone gets so insane in that store."

"Why did you say you did it?" asked Mia.

"Because like *you* said, we've gotta have each other's backs." Presley released Mia's arm and walked to the G. Mia was the last to get in, squished next to Cole. As they rode back to the estate in silence, Mia scrolled through Instagram. She saw Presley's post with the tween girls, captioned:

Future seasonaires. #BeWyld #mentor

At a closer look, Mia noticed they were standing by the display of floral tops.

FOURTEEN

M ia stared across the table at the harbor.

"How do you like it cooked, Mia?" asked Nadege, the housekeeper.

"Hm?" Mia shifted her attention to Nadege, who was grilling steaks on the barbecue. "I'm sorry."

"Your meat—how do you like your *meat*?" Grant chortled as he inhaled his steak. The long table was set for the seasonaires. Vintage Edison string lights twinkled above. They were drinking an expensive Cabernet from the wine cellar.

"I was starving." Grant leaned back, his plate clean. "Man, I'm beat."

"Work is hard," chuckled Vincent, taking photos. "Especially when you've never done it before, *arsehole*." He brushed the top of Grant's head.

Grant lightly slapped Vincent's hand away. "Dude, I took this job because it's *not* work. Growing up, I went to the gym at four every fucking morning with my dad and meathead brothers, then ran five miles before bed so I would make varsity in high school. I had to score the winning touchdowns, because"—he used a deep, gruff voice—"'that's what men do.'"

"Not all men," remarked Vincent with a small compassionate smile.

Mia watched Grant drain his wine and stare into the empty red-stained glass.

Collective buzzes and dings rose from the smartphones sitting on the table. It was a group text from Lyndon:

Wicked job today! Winner: Mia. 42k total IG Likes.

"Hard work pays off." Cole patted Mia's leg. Mia smiled at him, though the platonic gesture made her tense up.

Presley applauded and everyone joined, including Jade. Their sincere kudos told Mia to let go of the floral top incident. *The world is not against you, Mia*, she reminded herself.

"Your prize . . ." Presley gestured to Mia. "The first shower."

"I'm slightly offended by that prize," joked Mia. "But okay." She headed inside, passing Nadege, who carried dirty plates.

"A package came for you today, Mia," said Nadege. "I brought it up to your room."

"Thank you, Nadege. Dinner was delicious."

"The only one who knows the words 'thank you' around here," Nadege whispered to Mia as they both entered the house. "You from Boston?"

"Is my accent that bad?" Mia put her fingers to her lips.

"No," Nadege spoke with a Creole inflection. "It's familiar. I live in Mattapan."

"Southie."

"City girls, the two of us," said Nadege as she turned toward the kitchen.

"Good night, Nadege." Mia walked upstairs and entered her room, seeing a large box on the floor. She opened it to find a sewing machine and a monogrammed Lyndon Wyld card with perfect script that read:

Create something Wyld. xo, Lyndon & Grace

Presley entered the room. "Well, look what you got!"

<hr />

Mia had been too exhausted to sew. After her shower, she flopped into her bed with her sketchpad and fell asleep before she drew one design. She woke in the morning to find Presley sleeping. Even though Mia didn't fully trust Presley, she felt comforted by her roommate's presence. Yesterday had been weird—alternately fun and stressful—like every day since she had landed on Nantucket. Mia still couldn't get her bearings and surprisingly, the sewing machine, which remained in the box, didn't make her feel more comfortable. She quietly got dressed.

She dropped her purse, contents clinking, and winced. Presley stirred, lifting off her pink satin sleep mask.

"Hey." Presley yawned and stretched. Her makeup was still perfect because she liked to be Insta-ready first thing. She snapped a pic and captioned:

Morning, lovelies. #riseandshine #BeWyld

She looked at Mia. "Did you post?"

"No. I need coffee," responded Mia, picking up her purse off the floor.

"Post. You're on a roll."

Mia sat on her bed and took an Instagram selfie. She captioned it:

Got coffee? ☕ #elixiroflife #BeWyld

She posted. "I'm going to shop for an outfit to wear to the Summer Solstice Soiree." Mia looked at Presley. "Come with?"

"Aren't you going to put your gift to good use?" Presley nodded toward the sewing machine box.

"The Solstice Soiree is in two days. I don't have time to make something."

"I'm assuming you're a design wunderkind." Presley winked.

"I don't think even a wunderkind could whip up something party and paparazzi appropriate that quickly. That's a lot of pressure." Mia rose. "I can't believe you're going to pass up shopping."

"I have a blowout appointment. You could use a little . . ." Presley motioned around her head.

Mia chuckled. "I'd rather stick pins in my eyes than have someone brush my hair for an hour. Spa days sound like torture."

"Oh, honey, I'll pretend you never said that," replied Presley.

Mia flashed on giving her mom a pedicure the week before she left for Nantucket. She'd added tiny roses to Kathryn's big toes. Her mom loved roses, especially red ones. Then her mind landed on the floral shirt in her swag bag at the store.

"Thanks again for yesterday," said Mia.

"You can thank me by coming with me." Presley pouted. "C'mon. We'll do a girls' day Snapchat story. You and me—*The Roomies*."

"Honestly, I would ruin it for you." Mia strapped on her mini satchel. "I'd just bitch about it the whole time. And then you'd put devil horns on me—hashtag: hellspawn."

"Wow, you're really sellin' it," said Presley.

Mia left the room while Presley took more selfies.

She entered the kitchen to find Cole sitting at the island, eating cereal and reading the back of the box. "Morning," he said.

"Morning." Mia poured herself coffee.

"You sleep okay?" asked Cole.

"Why wouldn't I?" answered Mia. Her tone sounded bitchier than she would've liked. J.P. and Jade walked in. J.P. moved to the espresso machine.

"We've got a free day." Cole touched the schedule on the fridge door before pulling out a bowl of berries. "After Grant wakes up—"

"Whenever that is," scoffed J.P., making an espresso.

"We're going kayaking," finished Cole.

"*You're* kayaking. I'm going to sit and watch *you* row." Jade took the demitasse cup from J.P.

"I have some stuff to do in town." Mia sipped her coffee.

"Ooh, stuff." Jade sipped her espresso.

"Yup." Mia poured the last few black drops into the sink and put her mug in the dishwasher. "I'll see you guys later." She left.

She peddled into town. The rule was you had to wear at least one Lyndon Wyld piece at all times. She had on a light blue skort, which was good for bike riding, although Grant begged the girls to wear dresses or skirts. "A beaver shot is like a surprise birthday present when it's not even your b!"

Mia knew it was okay to shop at stores other than Lyndon Wyld, but she felt like a traitor on her way to the Modern Vintage boutique on Easy Street. Presley would've made her feel worse—she went all brand, all the time. Mia didn't want *any* of the other seasonaires' opinions on her choices. When she reached the store, she caught herself glancing around like one of those sneaky cartoon burglars before stepping inside.

She was looking for a classic A-line skirt that would go with her ruched Lyndon Wyld top. It was nice to shop alone. It was nice to just *be* alone, since she wasn't used to having a roommate . . . or housemates, for that matter. She felt at home among the preloved clothing and found some good skirt options, though the prices were double what they'd be at the thrift shop in Boston. She had barely spent any money since she'd arrived and wanted to keep it that way.

The teen girl behind the counter sat next to two registers: a vintage model with the "cha-ching handle" for show and a new one for actual sales. She barely glanced up from her smartphone. "The purple raw linen knee-length would look amazeballs with your eyes." Mia found the purple skirt on the rack. She wondered if the girl had looked up long enough to notice her eyes. But Mia *did* like the skirt. She would at least try it on.

When she reached the dressing rooms, she looked below the doors for feet, finding an empty one. She entered, surprised to find Ruby.

"Sorry!" exclaimed Mia, lifting her hand.

Ruby had both feet up on the bench. She was dabbing a new white Ralph Lauren sock on the cross-hatch of cuts inside her right forearm. Vintage items were in a heap on the floor.

"I ran out of Hello Kitty Band-Aids," explained Ruby.

Mia took her makeup bag out of her purse. She put Band-Aids in it because Grant was prone to wiping out on the beach cruiser. "They're not Hello Kitty." She handed a few to Ruby.

"Thank you." Ruby took them, peeled them open, and placed them over the cuts. She shoved the trash in the nylon Wear National fanny pack open next to her.

Mia hesitated. "Can I ask you something?"

"Yes. I did this to myself," Ruby revealed. "Mindless distraction, you know?"

"That's . . . not what I was going to ask."

Ruby giggled. "Well, now we know each other better. At least *you* know *me* better."

"I used to pull out my eyebrow hairs," said Mia, feeling like there should be relative parity.

"Really?" replied Ruby. "Saved yourself waxing time and money! Did you make your way down and give yourself a Brazilian?"

"I was a little young for a Brazilian." Mia tapped nervously on the wall. "So . . . I have to ask . . . What's the deal with your boss?"

"Otto?" Ruby waved. The stack of silver bangles and beaded bracelets on her wrists jangled. "Everyone thinks he's this deviant devil. He's harmless."

"He puts you in ads and doesn't pay you?"

"It's my choice to pose for him. I'm a big girl." Ruby zipped her fanny pack.

"I saw you in that window display photo," said Mia. "Did he think of giving you *pants*?"

Ruby laughed. "The human body is beautiful. And wages aren't the most important thing. I couldn't afford rent and he's made sure I always have a place a live. And that I eat, because I forget to do that sometimes."

Ruby cocked her head, admiring Mia as if she were a museum painting. "You're so pretty."

"Thank you." Mia tucked her hair behind her ear. "You're pretty, too."

Ruby beamed. "I just realized, I don't think I've eaten since yesterday. Time flies when you're having fun."

"Want to get something?" Mia asked, abandoning her skirts in the dressing room.

"Are you buying those?" asked Ruby. "The purple raw silk one is—"

"'Amazeballs,' I know." Mia flicked the price tag. "Too rich for my blood, though."

She and Ruby left the store and walked toward Nantucket Coffee Roasters.

"We're not supposed to hang out," said Mia.

"That's a shame," replied Ruby, taking photos of flowers in a window box.

"It's ridiculous." Mia ran her hand along the wood shingle of a shop. "Ooh," she exclaimed at the splinter stuck in her forefinger. Ruby plucked it out and kissed her finger. The girls laughed. They ordered drinks and snacks at the coffee café.

"My treat," said Ruby.

"Thanks!" Mia noticed that Ruby used a credit card bearing her name—Ruby Taylor—with "Wear National, Inc." underneath.

They sat at a table in the front courtyard. Ruby sprinkled four sugars in her latte and picked at a blueberry muffin while Mia ate a lemon scone. She told Mia she'd been on her own since she was fifteen. She was originally from Stockton, California, and her mom was a junkie. Her dad, a motorcycle gang road captain, was in prison for armed robbery and attempted murder.

"He tried to kill my mom's drug dealer. Not for giving her drugs but for shorting her. She used our grocery money, of course."

Mia put down her cup. "That explains the petty theft."

"What?"

"The other night, when I saw you outside The Rabbit Hole," added Mia.

"I don't remember seeing you." Ruby squinted at Mia. "But I don't remember much about going to The Rabbit Hole." She laughed. "There are things in life I forget by accident. And things I forget on purpose." She sighed, poking at a blueberry. "Or at least try to. My job helps me do that. *Otto* helps me do that."

She caught Mia's incredulous expression.

"He's an enigma," she said. "It's easy to make him a target."

Mia thought about Otto's box camera aimed at her on the beach.

"I showed you mine, now you show me yours," said Ruby. "What are you about, Mia?"

Mia took in Ruby's welcoming face. There was something familiar about it even though they had never met before Nantucket. She didn't look anything like Mia's Southie girlfriends, who were all now away at college, but she felt like one.

A text buzzed from Ruby's phone. She looked at it. "Gotta jet. We should do this again soon." The girls rose. Ruby surprised Mia with a hug. "I owe you some Band-Aids." She walked off.

Across the street, partially hidden by a lamppost, Presley stood, her corn silk hair severely straight, post blowout. She snapped a pic of the Nantucket Coffee Roasters rendezvous, then put her smartphone in her purse and sashayed off.

Mia didn't see Presley because she was too busy watching Ruby enter the liquor store a few doors down. After a few beats, Mac stepped out, looked around, and walked in the opposite direction of Presley, who had disappeared.

FIFTEEN

"The Summer Solstice Soiree is the best party of the season because we're all getting close, but not close enough to know shit we don't want to know," said Presley as she sat at the vanity in her bra and panties, applying her makeup.

Mia, in sweats and a tie-dye T-shirt, was working at the sewing machine. She hadn't gone back to the vintage store after her snack with Ruby, but Presley surprised her by giving her a cast-off Lyndon Wyld sundress to work with. "I never wear it," remarked Presley. She shared stories about the previous summer on Nantucket as Mia sewed. One seasonaire had even gotten pregnant because "being in paradise makes people horny and stupid."

"Lyndon paid for the abortion and Grace took her," she said. "I'm the only one who knew about it because the girl was my roommate. Everyone else thought she had the stomach flu. But honestly, if she had the flu we'd all have had the flu because, well, everyone is horny and stupid." She laughed as she stared into the vanity mirror, placing single false eyelashes on the outer corners of her lids.

"I can thread the tiniest needle but I can't put on fake lashes," said Mia, sewing a fringe hem along the bottom of the emerald green sundress.

"You already have gorgeous lashes. But let me add a little sultriness," said Presley.

"You gave me this dress and now you're going to give me sultry eyes, too?"

"The dress was meant for a gamine like you, not a curvy Barbie doll like me." Presley lifted a shoulder, then watched Mia sew. "I can understand why you needed to make it shorter, since I have four inches on you, but the fringe?"

Mia finished the hem, holding up the dress. "A little passementerie never hurt anyone."

"I don't know what that is, but the dress looks hot," said Presley, surprised.

"Thank you." Mia surveyed herself in the mirror. "And passementerie is a fancy name for decorative trimming." She touched the hem.

"Call a duck a duck, Mia. It's fringe." Presley stood and examined Mia. "But that dress is on brand for you—basic with a hint of quirk," she said, half-joking.

"I still can't get used to that," said Mia. "*Things* are brands, not people."

"Leave everything you know behind," Presley said in a creepy voice, taking Mia's hand and leading her to her bed. "And join our world."

"You're freaking me out a little." Now it was Mia who was half-joking as she sat facing Presley.

"You're having fun, aren't you?" Presley leaned close, using tweezers and glue to place lashes on Mia.

"Yes." Mia examined Presley's face. It was poreless. Mia also noticed that she didn't avert her eyes when theirs caught.

Presley told her about other hookups the summer before, regular blackouts, one bad Molly trip, and a broken leg when three seasonaires went tubing on one tube and wiped out.

"Most of the shenanigans stayed off social. But one girl got so drunk at the Soiree that she did a cartwheel on the dance floor—without panties on. Someone snapped a shot and her goods were all over the Internet. She lost the job she had waiting for her after college at some high-power hedge fund."

"Sounds a lot like high school," said Mia.

"*Life* is a lot like high school, honey."

"God, I hope not." She also hoped Presley wouldn't poke her in the eye with the tweezers during this lash application. "So you stayed out of the fray?"

"I'm back, aren't I?" Presley pulled away and scrutinized Mia's face.

"If you had a super power, what would it be?" Mia asked Presley.

"I already have a super power," answered Presley.

"Oh, yeah, what?"

"Irresistible charm." Presley grinned. "It makes people forget what they want."

"How did you get so much confidence? Honestly." Mia shook her head.

"I was born with it." Presley brushed mascara on Mia. "Humility is overrated, though that's *your* super power."

"Doesn't sound like much of a super power," said Mia.

"Look at your social. That's the reason behind the follows and the likes. It's not an insult, Mia. You're workin' it just like everyone else. And tonight at the party, you need to pull that shit out, sugar."

She brought Mia to the vanity mirror. "Voilà! Sexy thang." Mia was amazed at what six little false lashes could do.

Mia thought about what Presley had said. The seasonaires' relationships skimmed the surface. They were all still trying to impress one another, presenting the image they wanted out there on social. Even she was getting the hang of that. She now understood that she was a "Basic Bitch" who, like a straight-leg pair of jeans, never goes out of style. You could wear them with anything. They looked good on everyone and you could wear them everywhere. It was all about the accessories.

She picked up her smartphone off the nightstand. "Let's post style tips."

Presley filmed her as she showed a forearm weighed down by bracelets. "Put all the jewelry you want to wear on, then take off one piece." Mia kept on only her four thin blue enamel bangles because "they were my grandma's. *Real* vintage," and a Lyndon Wyld cocktail ring. She Instagrammed, tagging the brand.

Presley tied a jersey wrap shirt on top of a satin skirt that stopped mid-thigh. Slingback heels tied the ensemble together—all from the store. "I think I'm getting too tan." She smoothed her legs. "I look better pearlescent."

"That sounds oddly shiny," said Mia.

Presley offered Mia a style tip: "Here's the best way to position your boobs." She bent over and let them fall into place in her bra, so that when she stood, she had perfect cleavage. "Symmetrical nips. Nothing's more awkward than having a conversation with a boy—or girl—who's distracted by off-kilter snake eyes."

Mia laughed. "Don't post that! That's the dumbest thing I've ever heard."

"Says you, but it's good to be tits-forward. Especially when you're talking to Grace."

Mia gave her a curious look. "Are you saying . . . ?"

"I'm not saying anything. But if you like a little pussy in your life or you *think* you might like a little pussy in your life . . . you could suck up to the boss's sister."

"Love is love," said Mia with a shrug.

"Have you ever been with a woman?" asked Presley.

"No." In sixth grade, she practiced kissing with Olive Hamilton when Olive's mom was at work. That was it. But they were definitely not women at the time.

Presley handed Mia her smartphone. "All this talk about clam gives me a beauty tip idea."

"For a Southern belle, you're downright filthy."

"I'm multilayered," said Presley. While Mia filmed, Presley skillfully worked her hair into a fishtail braid, describing the steps. She ended with "A fishtail braid is a touch of mermaid glam for any outfit."

When Mia and Presley went down to meet the others and head to the party, everyone was turned out. Jade wore cream Lyndon Wyld wide-leg sailor pants with Miu Miu studded platforms that made her look eight feet tall. The guys wore light cotton or linen suits with pastel ties. J.P. topped his with a Perch straw fedora. Mia was accustomed to seeing Cole in cargo shorts and a T-shirt, so the sight of him dressed up was jarring, in a good way.

"You look great," he said to her.

"Thanks. So do you."

"Who's ready to slay it on the runway during our Summer Solstice Soiree fashion show?" Presley sashayed across the living room and back. Jade watched her, hand on hip.

"I've never been in a fashion show," said Mia, nervously turning the bangles on her wrist.

"Me neither," replied Cole. "I'm sweatin' a tad just thinking about it." He yanked at his collar.

"We need some pre-party lube," said Grant as he poured tequila into the shot glasses that lined the mantel.

Presley handed Mia a shot. "Don't worry, sugar. I'll show you how it's done."

SIXTEEN

The Summer Solstice Soiree took place at the Seascape Restaurant, an open-air shoreline restaurant. Families flocked there during summer days for sliders and lobster rolls between dips in the ocean. This evening, it was filling with millennials playing dress-up.

A long banquet table inside held a clambake. Grant walked by and picked up a crab from the colorful pot and pushed it in front of Mia like a puppet. "Save me!"

"Too late," said Presley, who put her arm through Mia's, walking them off. Vincent snapped Grant holding the crab.

The seasonaires each took an Aperol Spritz from the beverage table. The cocktail's orange sunset color bounced off the rest of the party's decor. Mia noticed that everything was white, from the folding wood chairs to the tablecloths to the clusters of tiny tea lights that gave the room a magical sparkle, like anything could happen. And boy, did it, when Lyndon and Grace arrived. Lyndon wore a Stella McCartney garnet-hued sequin skirt with pink tulle at the hem and a simple silk tee from her own line that made the sequins elegant instead of gaudy.

Grace was wearing a white Lyndon Wyld sleeveless jumpsuit. Her thick red hair fell over her shoulders, ablaze against her outfit. She rounded up the group as Lyndon waved at the other guests she knew, like Jill, who was sitting at one of several booths hugging the walls. Though this was her brand, her "baby," Lyndon didn't belong here among the twenty-somethings who still had so far to go in life. She strode to the circle of seasonaires, her arms gesturing to them like they were prized livestock.

"What a gorgeous lot! It's so good to see you all in person again!"

"It's good to see you, too, Lyndon," said Presley, beaming.

Lyndon's eyes stopped on Mia's dress. "Is that from last season?"

"Oh, um, yes." Mia clasped her hands, obscuring the dress.

"Let me see!" Lyndon scrutinized it.

Mia dropped her arms, shifting uncomfortably.

"It was mine," said Presley before Mia could answer.

Mia's face grew hot.

"And Mia made it hers! I love that new length," said Lyndon, examining the hem. "And the passementerie!"

Presley muttered under her breath, "Fringe."

"Did you do that, Mia?" asked Lyndon.

The heat radiating through Mia turned from embarrassment to excitement with Lyndon's interest. "I did. I'm used to working with hand-me-downs. Sad, huh?" She caught herself: *There was the self-deprecation Presley was talking about.*

"It's not sad, is it, Grace?" Lyndon turned to her sister.

"It's resourceful." Grace turned to Jade, motioning to her hand-shredded M-Kat tank paired with the Lyndon Wyld pants. "Like cross-promotion, yet different." Her tone was disapproving.

Jade shrugged. "It matches."

Lyndon's tight smile said that this annoyed her, but her voice was bright and encouraging. "Fashion show time, lovelies!"

In the back office, the group got in and out of outfits from items on a rack separated by plastic dividers with their names. A bedsheet was tacked to the ceiling for privacy. Mia was the only one to change behind it.

They took to the plank runway constructed above the sand, with the guests sitting in folding chairs on either side. The sun lowering into the harbor served as the backdrop. Jade was first. Mia and Presley watched her effortlessly work it.

"This must feel like small potatoes to her," Mia whispered to Presley.

"She's totally phoning it in." Presley exhaled sharply.

Vincent and some other photographers from local to national media snapped photos. Grant ate up the female attention as the girls in the audience started "the Grant Chant." At the last minute, J.P. took off the Lyndon Wyld hat he was given, handing it to Jade. When the time came for Mia to head down the runway, she was ready to bolt. Cole jumped up with her and the two walked side by side. His laughter at the whole affair relaxed her.

"Watch a pro," said Presley as she stepped up on the runway. She brought the house down with a beauty pageant sashay and wave that inspired cheers.

Lyndon was pleased, air-kissing and hugging the seasonaires inside after the show. "Brilliant job!"

"Cole, I know you're new to social media, but this was a chance to feature each of you individually," said Grace.

"Sorry." Cole and Mia's laughter subsided.

Lyndon patted Cole on the arm. "I thought it was sweet and entertaining."

Grace's brow knit for a beat. She handed each of them a stack of business cards that touted a discount at the store. "Make sure everyone here knows that the party doesn't end tonight. Summer celebrations on Nantucket aren't complete without some frivolous shopping."

"But don't be obnoxious." Lyndon wagged a finger at the group. "Save that for The Rabbit Hole." Her finger stopped at Grant, his knuckles still bearing a few scabs from his fight. Her gaze was chiding. "Have fun tonight."

J.P. excused himself to the bathroom. "Drink went right through me."

Jade touched the Lyndon Wyld straw fedora on her head—the one J.P. had handed her. "See? I've got you, Lyndon." She air-kissed Lyndon and Grace, then followed J.P.

Grace motioned to Presley, Grant, and Cole. "I'm parched! You?"

Presley got the hint. "Dry as a tumbleweed!" She put herself between Grant and Cole, linking their inside arms, then grinned at Lyndon. "Amazing party, as usual!" With Grace, the trio walked toward the bar. Cole glanced back at Mia, who was left alone with Lyndon.

Damn them, she thought as she shifted under Lyndon's steady gaze.

"What happened at the store, my talented lovely?" Lyndon sounded more curious than angry.

"I didn't take anything. It was a misunderstanding." Mia glanced out at the restaurant's deck where guests drank, ate, and chatted in the moonlight. She wished she could get some air.

"That's unfortunate," said Lyndon. "It's not right for the staff to humiliate my seasonaires in front of one another. That creates a lack of trust, a crack in the fabric of my brand."

Mia put on a smile. "It's fine. Honestly. No harm, no foul."

"Well, you let me know if you ever feel that you aren't being treated fairly." Lyndon caressed Mia's arm. "You're not like the others, Mia."

"No disrespect, Ms. Wyld, but I don't know whether to take that as a compliment."

"It's Lyndon. And you should. I understand why you'd be drawn to a diverse group of friends."

Mia tried to keep her brow from furrowing in confusion.

"I know I'm not your mother," continued Lyndon.

A lump lodged in Mia's throat.

"But it's part of my job to take care of you while you're here." Lyndon pulled her smartphone from her garnet clutch, revealing an Instagram post of Mia at Nantucket Coffee Roasters, sitting with Ruby:

Make new friends. #teamwyld #teamnational

Mia swallowed hard, her neck and face growing hot. She didn't recognize the account: hounddogdayz.

"Like in any family, loyalty is rewarded." Lyndon touched Mia's chin. "Be the smart girl I pegged you for." She turned on her kitten heel and walked off toward Grace, who was perusing the buffet.

Heat filled Mia's whole body. She was pissed at the shame she felt for hanging out with Ruby. *No one should pick my friends.* This was *not* high school, but she might as well have been fourteen, caught cheating.

The bar was crowded. Presley stopped Grace, Grant, and Cole at one of the tall tables guests used for their drinks and food. "You all wait here. I'll grab us some bubbly."

"You're the best, Presley," said Grace.

"I know." Presley gave her skirt a swing as she turned and strutted off. She swiped a half empty flute off an abandoned tray and put it down in front of the bartender, who was shaking a cocktail. She craned her neck to look behind the bar.

"Can you pour four of those from a fresh bottle?"

"Sure," replied the bartender. "We're out up here, so if you'd wait a couple minutes . . ."

"Of course, sugar. Patience is a virtue." Presley tapped the bar with her newly manicured Ballet Slipper nails.

"Right." As the bartender started for the back, Mac appeared with an unopened bottle.

"Nice of you to show up," the bartender grumbled to Mac and moved down the bar to take orders.

"You whined, princess?" Mac tossed Presley's flat beverage into the sink.

The candles along the bar seemed to flame with the energy between them. Presley, feeling Grace's eyes on them, doused any spark with a sharp response. "I didn't know you worked here, too."

"It's a side gig." Mac grinned. "I told y—" He stopped, seeing Presley's eyes shift toward the tall table where Grace, Grant, and Cole talked.

"I get it. Your bosses are here." Mac opened the bottle with a tense smile. "Don't want them to think you'd hang with the likes of me. My girlfriend doesn't want me hanging with likes of you either, but—"

"Does she pay you?" Presley turned the bitchiness up louder. "What I'd *like* is bubbly that's actually bubbly. That's not too much to ask, is it?"

Mac's grin became forced. "You should always get what you ask for. You're a *seasonaire*." He poured champagne into another flute.

"I want four of those," demanded Presley.

Mac poured three more and put them in front of her. Presley lifted one by the stem and tilted it toward her, pouting. "Sad pours."

Mac stared into her. She held tight to her bitchiness. He poured more champagne into each flute. "Better?"

"Much." Presley sashayed off with the four glasses.

Cole stepped up to Presley and took two of the champagne glasses. He caught eyes with Mac, then moved to Grace's table.

"I'm going to mingle." Grace walked off with her champagne, aiming toward Jill.

Presley's eyes were focused across the room. "Mia looks like she's in the corner with a dunce cap on." Cole and Grant turned to look at Mia. Her eyes were toward the floor.

SEVENTEEN

Lyndon finished doing an efficient lap around the party, graciously greeting guests. She returned to Grace, who was talking to Jill in a corner. Grant and Cole drank at the tall table while Presley handed discount cards to a pair of douches in aviator sunglasses despite the fact that they were indoor and it was night.

"I have some work to do, so I'm going to go," said Lyndon. "I'll meet you back at the hotel."

"Want me to join?" asked Grace.

"No. I'll see you in the morning at the hotel. Breakfast in my suite?"

"Only if I can have flapjacks." Grace shifted to Jill. "You Americans call them 'flapjacks,' right, Jill?"

"I call them evil carbs," Jill chuckled, sipping a sparkling water.

Lyndon and Grace laughed. Lyndon air-kissed both women. "Have fun." She slipped out the front door.

Mia was still frozen in the same place Lyndon had left her. Watching Lyndon exit the restaurant, she let out a sigh of relief that seemed to unglue her feet from the floor. She did a slow 360 and scanned the party. J.P. and Jade emerged from the hallway leading to the restrooms. Jade strutted ahead, smoothing the front of her pants. Grant had a giggling strawberry blonde against a wall near the deck, his face close to hers. Presley was on the deck, posing for Vincent with the harbor behind her.

Hot breath grazed Mia's neck, sending a buzz down her spine.

"I never pegged you for a wallflower."

She turned her head to see Cole behind her. He sipped from a beer bottle. "You have all this Summer Solstice Soireeing around you and you're standing here by yourself?"

"I'm taking it all in," said Mia.

The jazz ensemble on the small stage started playing Katy Perry's "Firework." The bassist, drummer, and keyboardist at the Moog synthesizer could've been any seasonaire's grandparents. The singer, two decades younger with the same nose as the keyboardist, belted out the lyrics. Her crimson-slicked mouth opened wide at the mic.

"This is a very weird cover," Mia chuckled. "I'm sure the band was Grace's idea."

"Dance?" Cole held his hand out to her.

Mia balked at the empty dance area in front of the band. "No one's dancing."

"Let's start a trend." Cole took Mia's hand. "That's our job, right?"

"Hashtag trendsetters!" exclaimed Mia in a faux enthusiastic voice as she posted a selfie of them to her Insta Story.

Cole led her onto the parquet floor placed over the hardwood. He was a decent dancer.

"Wow. Who knew?" Mia motioned to him.

"I do have mad dance skills." Cole moonwalked.

"Very impressive." Mia laughed until she saw his eyes move past her. She did a rhythmic spin so she could look in that direction. Jill was talking to Mac at the bar. With the distance and the music, Mia couldn't hear their conversation. Cole moonwalked the other way and brought Mia's attention back to him.

At the bar, Jill frowned at the wine Mac was pouring. "Rosé? Whose hack soiree is this?"

"Do you work for Lyndon Wyld?" asked Mac.

Jill gestured to her flowing palazzo pants and silk blouse. "How'd you guess?"

"Then I'd have to say it's *your* party," answered Mac. "But you look too sophisticated to be a seasonaire."

"Is that your charming way of saying I look old?" Jill squinted at him. "I just started managing the store. You should come in."

"Is that a charming way to say I'm poorly dressed? Because this is a uniform." Mac gestured to his vest and white shirt underneath. With the suspenders and the scruff, he looked like a saloon keeper in an old Western, the kind with a dead wife and a vendetta who made all the lasses loosen their corsets. "What can I get you?"

"I'm not thirsty." Jill tilted toward him. "I'm looking for something stronger."

Mac recorked the wine bottle. "I'm sorry, but I can't help you."

Jill plucked a drink umbrella from the container in front of Mac. "Rumor has it, you're here because you can."

Mia tore her focus from the conversation she could only see but not hear across the room. She found the rhythm with Cole.

"She takes her job way too seriously," said Mia. "Jill."

"I admire that." Cole gave Jill one more glance. "I mean, don't you think you should do your best whether you're the president, a proctologist, or a plumber?"

"I don't want any of those jobs," replied Mia, amused.

"What job *do* you want?" asked Cole. J.P. and Jade sashayed onto the dance floor with J.P. singing. Jade put her hand over his mouth. Mia chuckled and took some rhythmic steps back away from them. Cole followed.

She danced closer to Cole. "Lyndon's. I want Lyndon's job."

"Seriously?"

"Yes. I want to be a fashion designer." Mia corrected herself. "According to a self-help app I downloaded, then deleted, I'm supposed to say, 'I *am* a fashion designer. I'm just not getting paid for it.'"

"You're getting twenty grand this summer. Sounds like pay to me," said Cole.

"I barely have time to sleep, let alone design." Mia shrugged her arms like a ragdoll. "Although the sewing machine Lyndon and Grace gave me is a start."

The song ended and the singer slowed it down with "Feeling Good." Cole took Mia's hand, but instead of pulling her in for a slow dance, he steered her to two tall stools at a high table. Mia's disappointment was palpable since everyone else seemed to be swaying against each other to the music.

"If I wanted to be a fashion designer and all I was doing all summer was chilling and going to parties, I'd hate that," Cole teased Mia. "I mean, what could be worse?"

Mia lightened up, flicking him on the arm. Cole nudged her affectionately with his shoulder.

"Okay, so it's fun," conceded Mia.

"Can I quote you on Instagram?" Cole took out his smartphone.

"Sure, why not?" replied Mia. "At least you're *asking* to take my photo."

"What do you mean?"

"Nothing." If Cole didn't know about the post with her and Ruby, she wasn't going to tell him. It was only a matter of time before he saw it.

He took a selfie with her and typed:

"OK, so it's fun"— @miamamasgrl
#BeWyld #summersolsticesoiree

"I feel like a tool doing this. I didn't *have* an Instagram or a Snapchat account before I landed this job." He posted and showed Mia. She thought she saw Jill and Mac talking in the background, but Cole put his phone back in his pocket too quickly.

"What are *your* career plans?" asked Mia.

"I'm not sure yet. Are you asking me to decide?"

Mia put her hands up. "As someone said to me tonight, 'I'm not your mother.'"

"Thank god, because that would be awkward." Cole leaned close. Mia blushed. He went on, "Because I don't know my mother. She ran off when I was seven. My dad and my grandparents brought me up."

"Oh. That must've been hard." Mia thought about her mom. She'd rather have a mother who was sick than no mother at all. She took another Aperol Spritz from the tray of a passing server and tried to push the thought of losing her mom out of her mind. She sipped. "These are so refreshing. It's muggy in here."

Cole looked toward the open back doors. "Let's go outside."

They stepped onto the deck, standing off to the side, partially hidden by a heater. Since it was a warm night, nobody gathered around it, so the two had the small block of space to themselves. The singer's voice wafted out to them.

Cole polished off his beer and placed the bottle on a nearby table. When Mia finished her drink, he pulled her in to slow dance. Cole's cheek grazed Mia's. She could feel his smile.

"Does this feel a little like the prom?" he asked.

"I didn't go to my prom," replied Mia. "Can I ask *you* something? Who were you talking to on the beach?"

THE SEASONAIRES

"Mia." Cole pulled back. His smile disappeared.

"I'm sorry." Mia's response was genuine. She wished she could delete her question like a lame hashtag. "I don't really care who you were talking to." Their hands remained intertwined. "I just want to know if you have any interest in me at all, because I'm trying pretty hard and I'm getting mixed signals."

Cole let go of her hand. "Listen, Mia. Summer's just started. I'm trying to concentrate on the job because I got it as kind of a fluke. I mean, look at me." He pointed to his face. "I'm not Grant."

"Okay, no," Mia shook her head with a scoff. "I'm the queen of the humblebrag and that shit doesn't fly with me."

"I'm serious. I'm just a guy from Detroit, lucky enough to earn some cash screwing around on Nantucket. No obligations except to sell some nice clothes. I mean, what were the chances?"

Mia looked out toward the beach. Off to the side, through a mound of thick green sea grass, she could see Ruby's face glowing in the orange light of a vape pen.

"I get it." Mia turned back to Cole. "I'm going for a walk. And this time, I'm not asking you to come."

Cole started to follow her. She put her hand on his chest and left him on the deck. Cole stood for a beat, then disappeared inside the restaurant.

Mia slipped off her sandals and held them in her hand as she stepped off the deck into the sand. Her feet slid down into the cool, grainy mounds. She made her way toward Ruby, who skipped toward the shoreline in her loose, barely-there dress.

"What up, Miiiiahhhh?" Grant's voice startled her as he emerged from the darkness to the left of her. He zipped up his pastel plaid trousers. "Had to pee like a racehorse." Mia looked past him and saw vacant Adirondack lounges dotting the sand. Mia caught a whiff of weed as he grabbed her by the hips.

"Come dance with me," he begged.

97

"I'll be up in a minute," said Mia. "I'm gonna go for a swim."

"I thought you didn't know how to swim."

"Then it's about time, right?" Mia lifted his hands off her. "Especially when it's totally dark and everyone around you is wasted."

"You're a funny girl." Grant gave her ass a pat before he jogged to the restaurant. He never looked back at Ruby, who was twirling languidly, her arms in the air.

"What a beautiful night!" As she twirled, she saw Mia. "Hey, I know you!"

Mia stepped closer to her. "If you're trying to crash the party, you're a little far away." They were out of the guests' direct line of sight.

"Nope. I don't crash parties. No one should ever be where they're not wanted." Ruby beamed at Mia. "But I'm happy you're here."

"Are you okay?" asked Mia.

"Amazing!"

"Grant's such an idiot sometimes." Mia waited for a response. Ruby kept twirling, rolling her wrists, her fingers swiping the air like a belly dancer.

A motor echoed off the Sound. Ruby stopped twirling. She teetered, looking toward the noise. A single headlight cut through the black night, coming toward them.

"Mermaids!" Otto rode up to Mia and Ruby on a red-and-white custom ATV. He made a half circle and skidded to a stop, spraying wet sand. "How did I get so lucky to find you magical sylph-like creatures here?" He dismounted and plucked his box camera from the net storage pouch under the handlebars.

Mia eyed the festivities at the restaurant. She wanted to go back up, but couldn't abandon Ruby in her wasted state.

"Who are you, enchantress?" Otto asked Mia.

"Oh, I'm so rude," said Ruby, grabbing Mia's hand. "This is Mia. She's a Lyndon Wyld seasonaire."

"We met," Mia said to Otto. "At the beach a couple weeks ago."
Ruby held her hand tight.

"A seasonaire. I could've called that by your dress." Otto swiped
his fingers along the waist of Mia's dress. Now it was Mia who
gave Ruby's hand a squeeze.

"Cotton-poly blend." Otto seemed more interested in the fabric
than Mia. He snorted. "When will Lyndon up the ante to one
hundred percent cotton?" He squinted at Mia. "I'm asking you,
Magical Mia."

"I don't know," replied Mia.

Ruby took another pull off the vape pen. She passed it to Otto,
who smoked.

"Don't you have a joint, Ruby? Or that hash pipe? The lighter, the
fire, the smoke are what makes the process so fun." Otto shook the
vape pen. "This is bullshit." He offered it to Mia, who lifted her hand.

"No, thanks."

Ruby stuck out a hip. "Where are you headed, Otto?"

"I'm going to that boring as fuck party of yours, *Mia*." He
squinted at Mia, then took another hit. "But before I go up, you
should let me shoot you." He touched the box camera hanging
over his chest. You're like yin-and-yang naiads, so different but
so the same." He framed the girls with his hands. "Fuck photographers. *I'm* behind the lens now. All my ads are *me*."

"I've seen your ads," said Mia flatly.

"You don't like them. I can tell by the tone of your voice. Unless
you're always so uptight." Otto snickered.

Mia straightened. "My opinion on your ads shouldn't matter."

"No, it shouldn't. But I'm entertained by opinions. Opinions
are the most intimate way to get to know someone." Otto looked
into Mia's face.

Ruby giggled. "I thought you were going to say, 'Opinions are
like assholes. Everybody has one.'"

Otto kissed Ruby on the lips. "I love you. You're so silly."

"You say that to all the girls," Ruby giggled again.

"I do, but there's a lot of love to go 'round." He smoothed his handlebar mustache.

Mia's stomach turned, though she stood as still as the owl decoys on top of the restaurant's roof to keep the seagulls from crapping on it.

"I'm gonna go pass these out." Otto pulled condoms from his clam-digger pants' pocket. The shiny red wrappers were emblazoned with the WN crest. "What's your opinion on that, *Mia?*"

"I don't think you should go at all."

"That settles it. I'm going. Never do what people tell you." He shook his finger, then turned to Ruby. "Coming, sweetness?"

"I'm looking for a bracelet I lost today." Ruby shook her armful of them. "I came here for lunch with Axel and Quentin and when we got back, it was gone." She pouted. "From this season's collection."

Mia glanced around on the sand. "I'm like a pirate when it comes to treasure hunting." Mia held up her hand and the Lyndon Wyld cocktail ring. "Found this. I'll help you."

"You're not sharing trade secrets, are you, baby girl?" Otto brushed a lock of Ruby's hair from her face. Her eyes shifted down toward a broken shell. Barefoot, she pressed the bottom of her big toe on its jagged edge.

"No."

"Good." Otto trudged up the beach. Mia lifted her phone from her mini-crossbody bag and clicked on the flashlight, shining it on the sand. She and Ruby sifted with their feet, searching for a few minutes. With the light, Mia caught three red marks on the top of Ruby's feet, between her toes.

"I didn't lose a bracelet," said Ruby.

"I know." Mia stopped sifting.

Ruby hoisted on her woven rainbow backpack and pranced to the ATV. She got on.

"What are you doing?" asked Mia.

"Going for a ride." Ruby grabbed the handlebars.

"You shouldn't do that."

"As Otto said, that's all the more reason I *should*. Come with." Ruby grinned.

"I can't." Mia glanced up at the restaurant. The deck was empty. Through the open doors, she caught Cole dancing with Jill.

"No one's going to see you," said Ruby.

Mia got on behind Ruby and slipped on her sandals. "Do you know how to ride this thing?"

"My dad's in a motorcycle gang, remember?"

"Oh, right."

Ruby pressed the Start button and turned the throttle toward her. The tires spun in the wet sand as the ATV carried both girls off.

EIGHTEEN

I nside the restaurant, the dance floor was crowded. The band
ended a rousing version of the "Macarena," which made the
partiers laugh. Despite the chuckles, when the singer announced
they were taking a break, a disappointed "Awwwwww" filled the
room. As the band left the stage, Otto entered from the deck. He
commandeered one of the empty tables.

Presley took selfies with the two female guests she was dancing
with. "Come see me at the store." She handed them discount
cards. "I'm usually there Saturdays. I'll give you first dibs on the
new merch." Her eyes moved to Otto across the room.

Jade and J.P. threw back tequilas at the bar. Jade put her shot
glass down and noticed Otto. She looked back at Mac. "Two
Patróns. Silver. Neat."

Mac poured two tequilas. He garnished them with limes, his
eyes on Otto. Jade reached over and grabbed a salt shaker. She
started toward Otto's table. J.P. followed.

"Stay here," said Jade. "And get your camera ready. Video."

"What?" J.P. looked perplexed.

She leaned in to his ear. "Do it for me." She bit his lobe.

J.P. let her move off. He pulled his smartphone from his pocket.

Grant and Vincent stood by the restroom hallway. At the sight of Otto, Vincent pulled a box of Gitanes from his breast pocket and headed for the front door. "I'm going for a smoke."

Otto leered at Jade, who took long, leggy strides to his booth. "My daddy sends his regards." She leaned over to put the tequila shot in front of him, her frayed tank top draped to reveal her breasts. "And a drink."

"Arsenic?" Otto snickered.

"You're hilarious. My dad loves you."

"He knows I don't like to drink alone." Otto patted the seat next to him.

Jade slid close, her leg touching Otto's.

Otto looked into her eyes. "I always said your parents made beautiful babies."

At the bar, J.P.'s brow furrowed as he held his smartphone low and filmed. The band started to play again, so he couldn't hear Otto and Jade's conversation. But he didn't need to. Jade leaned back. Otto poured a small mound of salt on the top curve of her cleavage. Jade laughed. He licked it off, then shot the tequila and sucked on the lime.

Presley approached Mac at the bar. "We have an infiltrator." With a disgusted expression, she looked toward Otto, who cuddled closer to Jade. Mac had been watching "The Jade and Otto Show" while making two Manhattans. He placed the Manhattans in front of two millennials who were making out at the bar, like many of the other intoxicated guests. Some had gone back to dancing, including Cole and Jill. Mac walked around from the bar and across the floor to the Otto's booth.

Grant sidled up next to J.P. "Some entertainment up in this bitch!" He nodded toward Mac. J.P. stopped filming, slipping his phone back in his pocket.

Mac reached the booth. "Mr. Hahn, this is a private party. Invitation only."

Otto looked up and tilted his head to touch Jade's. "This gorgeous creature invited me."

"You're gonna get me in trouble, Otto." Jade offered a full-throated laugh.

Mac was laser-focused on Otto. "I'm gonna have to ask you to leave."

Otto smiled. "I have another engagement anyway." He kissed Jade's neck and held her hand for a beat, then slithered out of the booth. He looked Mac in the eye. "But I'm glad I could drop by."

All eyes were now on the scene. Jill and Cole watched from the dance floor, so engrossed they were barely keeping beat. Cole snapped a photo with his phone. As Otto left through the front of the restaurant, he winked at Jill. Cole's brow knit.

In the booth, Jade opened her closed hand and looked: a vial of cocaine with a tiny gold diamond-tipped spoon. She tucked it into her pants' pocket.

Presley, standing at the bar, couldn't take her eyes off Mac.

―――

Ruby drove Mia down the shore to Brant Point. Exhilarated, Mia smiled the whole way there. They parked near the lighthouse that stood at the water's edge, surrounded by rocks, and got off the ATV. Mia didn't bother to smooth her windblown hair. She smiled forcefully. "Do I have bugs in my teeth?" Ruby giggled. Mia pulled her smartphone from her purse and clicked on her camera to examine. When she looked up, Ruby had disappeared.

"Ruby?" Mia glanced around.

"Over here!" Ruby's voice came from the opposite side of the lighthouse. Mia crossed through the ramp and climbed the rocks to Ruby, whose backpack was sitting in a crevice.

"I love this spot!" Ruby's voice soared over the harbor. "No one comes out here at night. It's so peaceful." The rippling water glowed rhythmically with each flash of the lighthouse's red lamp. Ruby lifted her right foot and crooked her knee so she could survey the bottom. It was dark gray with dirt and sand. Blood seeped from cuts in her big toe and her heel. She shrugged and put it back down.

"You don't seem to mind getting hurt." Mia's eyes fell on a long horizontal scar on Ruby's right wrist. When they met for coffee, Ruby's many bracelets had covered it, but tonight, it peeked out.

"After a while, you don't feel it anymore. Which is *why* you do it." Ruby looked hypnotized by the triangle of moonlight reflecting off the water.

"There are other ways to feel," said Mia.

"I don't care about the pain. It's the other stuff I care about. Joy, happiness. Those are harder to come by." Ruby glanced at Mia.

"Would you wear all the bracelets if you didn't care about the pain?" asked Mia.

"Well, the bracelets are part of my vibe." Ruby gave a short giggle. Her eyes welled with tears. "People see these scars, and they automatically think I have so little respect for myself, it doesn't matter what they do to me. But these scars don't make me weak. They make me strong." She sniffed and smiled. "So that's my only regret—that I can't make people see them that way."

"People only understand what they can see right in front of them," replied Mia. "They don't look for the whole picture."

Tears spilled over Ruby's cheeks.

"I happen to love your vibe, by the way." Mia's tone lightened. "But I think you need one more bracelet." Mia removed one of her thin blue enamel bangles and lifted Ruby's right hand. It was bony and cold. She slipped the bangle on.

"You said your grandma gave this to you." Ruby examined the bangle, then looked up at Mia. "I saw your Instagram style tip video."

"She did." Mia took a deep breath. "She killed herself." She touched Ruby's wrist scar. "Not *that* way. She didn't want to watch my mom die. She would say 'No parent should outlive their child.' I think she felt guilty."

"Mamas need to take care of their cubs," said Ruby. "That's how my mom ended up like she did. She tried to handle everything. It was so much pressure. The drugs relieved that, but, you know, it's a slippery slope."

Mia nodded.

Ruby threw herself onto Mia in a hug, holding tightly. "Thank you." Mia relaxed into Ruby, embracing her. After a long moment, Ruby pulled back, then looked out to the water. She wiped her tears.

"Let's go swimming." She clamored down the rocks.

Mia followed. "What? Swimming?"

On the sand, out of the tide's reach, Ruby pulled her dress off her shoulders and let it fall. She yanked down her lace thong and tossed it aside. Naked, she ran into the water before Mia could catch her.

"Ruby! What are you doing?" Mia's heart pounded. She glanced around—no one anywhere. She looked out at the dark water. She couldn't see Ruby. She scanned the areas lit by the moon and the red lighthouse lamp. The water's natural ripples were uninterrupted by any swimmers.

At the Y pool during summer day camp, Mia had never gone past the shallow end. She'd walk until she reached the buoys that were slung across. They differentiated the swimmers from the non-swimmers. She was fine staying with the non-swimmers. But now, all she could think about was Ruby, her bloody foot, the self-inflicted wounds along her arms, and what Mia assumed were needle marks between her toes. She threw off her sandals, put her purse on the sand, and waded into the ocean. When water hit her thighs, the freezing shock stole her breath and stung her body.

"Ruby!" she yelled. Her teeth chattered. Her arms were out in front of her, searching while simultaneously helping her balance in the current. She pushed at the sandy bottom with her feet, glancing around. She wiped the burning saltwater from her eyes because she didn't want to miss any sight of Ruby. "Ruby!"

As she moved farther out, the current became stronger. Her feet slipped from the bottom and she dropped under the water. Instinctively, she waved her arms and ran in place with her legs, getting enough momentum to lift her head above the surface. She coughed and spat. As the current yanked control from her, she grasped at the water. It flowed through her fingers. Her head went under. All her frantic movement seemed fruitless and ineffective against the power of the undertow.

Suddenly, hands grabbed the back of her dress and lifted her enough for her to catch her breath without choking. Through the blurry film covering her eyes, she could see Ruby's face. Ruby's expression was determined as she swam with Mia back to the shore.

"Kick!" she yelled.

Mia flapped her legs, wishing her feet would touch the ground. They finally did as she and Ruby made it to shallower waters. She tried to leap to shore, but her legs felt heavy. Her dress clung to her. Ruby never let go.

They both fell onto their hands and knees and crawled onto the shore, then turned over and flopped on their backs out of the reach of the water. Both were breathless. Mia's dress was caked in sand.

"You can't swim, can you?" asked Ruby.

"No." Mia's chest heaved as she sucked air.

"And you went out there to save me?" Ruby looked at her with disbelief.

"I didn't know what you were doing," answered Mia. "But *you* saved *me*."

"We saved each other."

Mia turned onto her side facing Ruby. "Fuck. That was cold."

"Doesn't it feel good?" Ruby opened her palms toward the night sky. "Brings you back to life!"

"No. It doesn't."

They both started laughing.

When the lighthouse lamp pulsed on, Mia saw paw-size bruises on the insides of Ruby's thighs.

—∞—

Presley smoothed her skirt over her legs as she stepped out of the restaurant. She took a deep breath, scanned the area, and, confirming that no one was around, sashayed to the side of the building where the kitchen door was located.

Mac smoked a cigarette by the closed door. He saw Presley. Her face was flush, her eyes burning, as she strode toward him. He tossed his smoke to the ground and grabbed her. They kissed with passion and urgency. After long hungry moments, they parted. Presley turned on her heel and strode back off. He dropped his head, shaking it.

NINETEEN

M ia couldn't bring herself to say anything to Ruby about the bruises. They drove back on the ATV. Mia, still soaking wet, fringe hem dripping water, shivered in the wind. When they were a few yards away from the restaurant, Mia tapped Ruby's shoulder and leaned in to her ear.

"Stop here."

Ruby took her hands off the throttle and the ATV slowed to a smooth stop.

"I think it's best if I get off here," said Mia.

"Not door to door?" Ruby glanced back, smiling.

Mia dismounted. "No. If for no other reason than you're not my servant." Mia tilted her head toward Ruby's. "You're not *anyone's* servant." They hugged. They both jumped at the buzz of a text from the phone inside Mia's purse pressed between them. Mia lifted it out and looked. She had a text from Presley:

Where r u?

"I'd better go up before someone sends a search party," said Mia.

"I'll see you soon," said Ruby. "Next time we'll swim with dolphins."

"You are *really* overconfident," Mia chuckled. With a wave, Mia scurried up the beach, still shivering. Through the open deck doors, she could see that the party was breaking up. She ducked around the side of the building and walked to the G. She texted Presley:

At the car.

She leaned against the car, which blocked some of the breeze. Presley and Grant exited the restaurant. Other guests left and split off, most good-and-inebriated.

"Some crazy shit at that party!" exclaimed Grant.

Presley's attention was on her phone. She looked up to see Mia's wet state.

"What on God's green earth?"

Grant laughed, touching Mia's damp dress. "You weren't kidding about swimming, were you?"

"Serious as a heart attack." Mia brushed his hand away. "Because the water is so cold, I almost had one."

Vincent emerged from the restaurant. "I want to get the *bella* roommates of Lyndon Wyld together in front of the restaurant." He looked curiously at Mia, then pulled a towel out of the car and handed it to her. "But only one of you is dry."

Mia wrapped the towel around her shoulders.

"I'm always camera-ready." Presley furrowed her brow at Mia, then moved off with Vincent for some photos.

Grant leaned in to Mia. "That Ruby chick is a total tease," he said in a low voice.

"Maybe she's not interested in you like that." Mia wrapped the towel tighter.

"She gave me her number." Grant waved his smartphone. "Because all the ladies are interested in me like that."

"That day you picked me up from the dock, you told me to stay away from her. That doesn't apply to you, Grant?"

"I said them's the rules and *you're* not a rule breaker." Grant shoved his phone in his pocket.

Cole, J.P., and Jade exited the restaurant. Cole mouthed "What happened?" to Mia, who shrugged.

Presley finished posing.

Vincent motioned to the three guys. "Gentlemen, one more shot."

"I never pegged you for sexist, Vincent," said Jade, who joined the guys for a photo. She planted herself in the middle of Grant, Cole, and J.P. Presley scowled as she watched. The group parted, giving each other high fives.

"Aw, Presley," said Jade. "You can't always be the center of attention."

As Mia stood alone, wet in her fringed Lyndon Wyld dress with the monogrammed towel around her shoulders, Vincent snapped a candid.

Presley stepped up to Mia. "I thought you couldn't swim."

"I can now," said Mia "We're in Nantucket. Had to do it sometime, right?"

"At least you had your own personal lifeguard." Presley held up her phone and showed Mia Wear National's Instagram. It was Otto's selfie on the beach, walking toward the restaurant, captioned:

The life of every party. #WearNational
#smokinsummer #killinnantucket

Mia and Ruby were in the background.

Presley put her phone back in her purse.

Mia gripped the towel and looked down. "Why?" she said softly.

"That's my question," retorted Presley, equally as soft.

"I'm hungry." Jade looked at J.P. "I want a burger at Stubbys."

"That sounds good," said J.P. "Later." He waved at the others and walked off down the street with Jade.

"Let's hit the Spark," shouted Grant. "I heard when the bubble machine comes out, the tops come off."

"I think I'll pass," said Mia.

"Mia's not coming. She's moist already." Grant gave a drunken cackle.

"Ech. I hate that word." Presley grimaced. "As a matter of fact, I hate it so much I'm not going to go."

"I'll go," said Vincent.

"Vinnie! I knew you had it in you!" Grant threw an arm around Vincent, who was pushed off balance by the enthusiasm.

Vincent tossed keys to Presley. "You can take the car back." They fell through her palms and clattered on the ground.

"Nice catch," teased Grant. "Presley's got nothing on you, Mia."

"I just had a manicure." Presley daintily picked up the keys.

Grant grabbed Cole in a headlock. "Cole, you're my wingman!" They wrestled each other to the ground, laughing.

A black Crown Victoria drove by and stopped. The man with the two different colored eyes got out. "Let's tone it down, fellas." He tapped Grant, who was laughing on top of Cole. Grant rolled off and caught his breath, looking up at him.

Cole stood and glared at the man. "You might want to think before physically accosting anyone."

"Cole, dude, chill," said Grant. "We don't want trouble."

The man pointed at Grant and Cole, then got back in the car and drove off. "Behave."

Cole took a deep breath and composed himself. He looked at Vincent. "You still coming?"

"You boys need a babysitter," replied Vincent, rolling his eyes toward Mia and Presley. He got between Grant and Cole and walked off.

Mia and Presley climbed into G. Presley took the wheel and drove them off. "That Cole—kinda hot, huh?"

"Kinda dumb." Mia huddled down to avoid the wind.

"Speaking of . . . why'd you leave the party to go off with that urchin?" asked Presley.

"I don't know," answered Mia.

"And having coffee with her in town?" Presley's eyes shifted to Mia. "Everyone saw *that* Instagram post. Why, Mia? I don't get it."

"For the same reason you went off with Mac." Mia's response was surly.

"Oh, you like her?" smirked Presley.

"Oh, you like Mac?" mimicked Mia.

"Mia!" Presley's eyes went wide. "I thought you didn't do women."

"I'm not *doing* her, Presley. But she's a friend. I like her. Mac's *your* friend."

"He's not my *friend*." Presley tossed her hair. "I'm just toying with him. Summer here requires toys."

Mia shook her head in disbelief.

"That girl is bad news, Mia." Presley motioned to Mia with one hand, steering with the other. "I mean look at you."

"What?" Mia crossed her arms. "I'm *moist*."

Presley shuddered.

"She taught me how to swim." Mia chucked the wet towel in the back seat. "You know what? Summer might be about toys for you, but I'm not a damn puppet. I am *not* going to have anyone tell me who I can and can hang out with!"

"So you're hanging out with her to spite me?" snapped Presley.

"Has anyone ever told you you're a narcissist?" Mia snapped back.

"Never!" Presley burst out laughing.

Mia lightened up. She looked up at the moon, which was a sliver-shaped crescent, like the scar on the inside of a Ruby's wrist. She grew serious. "She needs a friend, Presley."

"She's got plenty of them, in that Wear National house. They can all rot there, for all I care. You should have seen Otto prance into our party like it was his."

"Otto isn't her friend," said Mia.

"That's not your problem, sugar. Like I said, you're a fixer. My sister is a fixer. She's been married three times because some people can't be fixed. And then they break *you*."

They drove in silence, out of downtown and into the residential neighborhood, toward the shore.

Mia thought about her high school boyfriend, Trevor. Trevor was broken. He grew up with parents who fought constantly, like hers did when she was little. He was in Sean's year. Mia and Sean had given him a ride home from high school one day after baseball practice. His dad was standing on the sidewalk in front of their apartment building while his mom chucked clothes and shoes out the window. An alarm clock followed, hitting Trevor's dad in the head.

"Time to get the fuck out, Henry!" screamed Trevor's mom.

Neighbors had been peering out their windows. Mortified, Trevor had shrunk down in the back seat.

Mia glanced at him. "Let's go get ice cream."

The three had driven off without Trevor's parents noticing, they were so self-involved. That year, Trevor started drinking and smoking pot. He never stopped, even when it cost him his college baseball scholarship and he was kicked out of school. That's when Mia began dating him. He was her first. She'd liked how he'd buried himself in her as if he could hide there. He couldn't get enough of her, of anything that felt good. Though he was trying to get sober, he craved pleasure, so Mia assumed that when he started getting regular texts from "Sharon" that he was cheating on her. The betrayal led Mia to a one-time hookup with a guy who worked at the fabric store she frequented. She then discovered from friends that Sharon was Trevor's AA sponsor.

Trevor had confronted Mia while she was at a busy Starbucks with Sean. He'd told her that AA rules frowned on hookups in the program. "I wouldn't do that!" Then he called her a "cheating slut" and Sean punched him in the face. A week later, she saw Trevor and Sharon outside the Y where the AA meetings took place. They were all over each other.

Mia let that memory flow through her brain file. Her mind fast-forwarded to Ruby tonguing Quentin and Axel on the beach at the summer's start.

"Broken people can't help themselves," Mia said to Presley.

"Bullshit!" Presley slammed on the brakes. Mia gasped and grabbed the dash handle. "Damn cats!" hissed Presley. A black cat scurried past the headlights into the shrubs around the estate's driveway.

"I think Ruby was abused," Mia continued. "More than once. And it might be happening now."

"You *think* she was?" scoffed Presley. "Well, I *know* I was. By my uncle."

Mia searched Presley's face for a tell, then felt terrible she thought Presley would make this up in some sort of sick competition.

Presley's blue eyes grew teary, though her jaw was tight. "As my daddy used to say, 'Gotta nut up,' though Lord knows I didn't tell him about his demented fuck of a brother. He would've chopped his balls off and fed 'em to the neighbor's pitbull. And then he would've fed *me* to the pitbull."

Mia stared at her, still searching.

"I took care of it myself." Presley sniffed back the tears before they fell. "The second time he tried, I fought back." She caught

Mia's stare and chuckled bitterly. "You don't think I can fight, do you? It's amazing what adrenaline'll do. I was a quarter of his size, but I punched and scratched and kicked with everything I had. Knocked two of his teeth out. He told everyone it happened in a bar fight. 'You shoulda seen the other guy,' he said. Yeah, shoulda seen her." Presley spat the last three words.

"Presley, I'm sorry that happened to you," said Mia.

"Can't throw your life away because you were handed some crappy cards." Presley tilted her head at Mia. "No amount of your pity—sorry, I mean, *friendship*—is going to stop that sinking ship. That girl, she's out to self-destruct."

Mia looked away. "That's a little dramatic."

They pulled up in front of house, its windows dark.

"She's a junkie whore, plain and simple." Presley shrugged.

"Presley!"

"Not a figure of speech. Not hyperbole, but truth. Mac told me."

Mia whipped toward Presley. "Mac enables her!" she blurted. "He sells her the drugs."

"What are you talking about?"

"I saw Mac give her a packet of white powder."

Presley's mouth was agape. She shook her head. "When did this happen?"

"A few weeks ago. That first night at The Rabbit Hole." Mia's words tumbled out in a ramble. "I didn't want to tell you what I saw because I wasn't sure. Everything was new and coming at me. Then, you liked him and, you know, The Girl Vault." Mia exhaled. "But I saw them meet again at the liquor store in town."

"So you're telling me he's a drug dealer?" Presley balked.

"I'm saying that he might not be just some fun-time bad-boy fantasy. Believe me I've had those."

"Get out!" Presley pointed. "Get. Out."

Mia got out of the G and closed the passenger door.

"What are you doing?" asked Mia. "Aren't you coming in?"

Presley didn't turn the motor off. "No. I'm going to find out if what you're telling me is bullshit."

"Don't do that."

"Why? Because it's *bullshit*?" Presley tucked her hair behind her ear as if she was ready to hear a different truth.

"No. I just think you should leave it," answered Mia. "What good is it going to do to find out this information?"

"No one drags me into the mud without a fight," said Presley. "And if what you're saying is true, by being with him, I'm muddy. He knew that."

Mia kept her hand on the passenger door handle.

"Move." Presley revved the motor, prompting Mia to pull her hand away. "If anyone asks where I am, tell them I went back to the party to help clean up."

"How is *that* believable?"

Presley's eyes turned skyward as she concocted. "I wanted to do a fun after-party Snapchat story . . . that's going to *coincidentally* fail to post." She started to drive away, then stopped. "Better yet, *I* won't say anything, if *you* won't say anything."

Presley drove off. Mia walked up the porch steps to the front door. She stopped and looked at the closest beach cruiser.

TWENTY

"T his is a little out of the way," J.P. said to Jade. They leaned into each other in the back of an older Lyft Subaru as it wound around the long, curving roads of Nantucket's largely uninhabited northeast shore.

"It's part of what makes The Wauwinet special," said Andy, the Lyft driver, according to the app on Jade's phone. Andy's dark tan implied that he drove drunk tourists around Nantucket all night so he could spend all day kiteboarding.

"We've been driving for twenty minutes," replied J.P. as he looked out the window at the landscape. There wasn't a home in sight.

"Mia and Presley went back to the house," Jade whispered to him. "We would've had zero privacy."

They pulled around the circular brick driveway of The Wauwinet, which was called an "inn." But there was nothing quaint or inn-like about the opulent East Coast resort compound, with its sprawling main building and surrounding cottages. Conforming to the Nantucket Historic District Commission's strict code, the cedar shingles remained unpainted, weathered to a soft gray.

"You meeting your folks here?" asked Andy, who opened the back door for Jade.

"Do we look like we can't pay for this joint ourselves?" Jade gave a quick nod at the hotel.

"I didn't mean that. It's just a nice place."

J.P. handed Andy a discount card. "Thanks for the ride. Come in to the store."

"You work for Lyndon Wyld?"

J.P. nodded. "But check out Perch hats—www-dot-perchha berdashery-dot-com."

"What's a haberdashery?"

Jade snickered. Andy gestured to her M-Kat tank. "And you work for Maz? I spent a week's pay on a pair of M-Kat kicks."

"Why would you do that?" Jade cocked her head at him, seeming genuinely curious.

Andy was speechless for a minute, then he guffawed, pointing at her. "I get it. Reverse psychology." He got back in the Subaru. "Well, whatever sales method you're using, it's working because you're staying here." He nodded toward the palatial hotel and drove off. "Nantucket's finest."

Jade and J.P. walked up the pathway in the center of the lush, green grounds that were fragrant with garden roses. The fireflies seemed to flicker in time to the crickets' chirps.

"It feels like we're marooned on an island on an island," said J.P.

"Very meta, Scrotie," chuckled Jade.

"Hey, I didn't come up with my school's mascot."

Jade sashayed inside and up to the concierge at the long oak front desk.

"Can I help you?" said the concierge with a smile as tight as her ponytail.

"You have a room available." Jade never asked. She told.

J.P. glanced around the elegant foyer. Candles cast a warm light over the antique couches, chairs, and traditional oil paintings. The grandfather clock showed 11:05, late enough that this luxurious public space was empty. He joined Jade at the concierge desk.

"We only have a cottage," said the concierge, as if she expected the young visitors to turn around and leave with that information.

"We'll take it," said Jade. She and J.P. simultaneously pulled out their wallets and slapped credit cards on the desk. Jade's was a Platinum American Express. J.P.'s was Black. The concierge choked slightly.

"You win." Jade tapped J.P.'s Black Card as she put away hers.

The concierge slid the credit card over and typed into the computer. She looked at J.P., her tone more reverent. "How many keys will you need, Mr. Alvarez?" She handed the card back to J.P.

Jade answered, "One is fine."

The concierge motioned to the French doors. "You'll go out that way, to the beach and around the garden to the right."

Jade and J.P. exited the foyer with Jade throwing a last look-to-kill at the concierge.

The lawn that spanned the side of the property facing Nantucket Bay was filled with vacant wicker lounge chairs. The hotel was bright inside but the path around to the cottage was sparsely lit by small hurricane lanterns.

Glass broke. "Bollocks!" They turned and looked up toward the noise. On a third-floor balcony, Grace was holding the top of a wineglass. Rising next to her was Jill, holding the stem. They laughed, tipsy.

In the dark corner of the path, Jade grinned. "That's—" J.P. clapped his hand over her mouth.

They watched Grace grab Jill by the back of her head and kiss her hard.

Before Jade could say another word, J.P. pulled her along the path. He looked at the room key and found the cottage.

"Don't ever shut me up," snapped Jade.

J.P. unlocked the door and motioned her in. "I'm sorry. But I don't really think we're supposed to be here."

"We're not their slaves, J.P." Jade lay back on the chintz comforter, her Miu Miu platforms still on.

"I thought you wanted privacy." J.P. walked around the room, touching the hand-painted floral stencils on the pine wood walls. "If Grace sees us, that's far from private."

"She's not going to see us."

"Wow, this is so . . ." J.P. searched for the words.

"Sweet?"

"I think that concierge was surprised we youngsters had the funds," laughed J.P.

"She was definitely surprised when you whipped yours out." Jade crossed her legs.

J.P. tossed his hat on the wicker rocker in the corner, kicked off his Top-Siders, and leapt on the bed. He bounced around Jade, touching the ceiling between each bounce. "Jump on this bed with me."

"Never." Jade tried not to laugh.

J.P. dropped on his butt, flopping back on the plush pillows next to Jade. "You're no fun." He pulled a peach from the basket of fresh fruit on the nightstand and took a juicy bite.

Jade shimmied her shoulder close to his. "I'm sure that video you took at the party says different. Let me see it."

"Really?" J.P. threw his head back with a groan.

"Really."

J.P. put the peach back in the basket and wiped his hands on a napkin with The Wauwinet seashell logo. He pulled his smartphone from his pocket and tapped in his password. The footage of Otto and Jade in the booth at the restaurant played: Otto leaning into Jade, licking the salt off her.

Jade put her hand on the inside of J.P.'s thigh. "Did that turn you on? Watching."

"It was simultaneously repulsive and a turn-on."

"That's how I feel about your haberdashery mission statement." Jade chuckled. She pointed to the video. "Post it on Instagram."

"No way. That will *not* go over well with your dad."

"On the contrary." Jade ran her finger up J.P.'s torso and unbuttoned his shirt. "If you post that video, my dad will assume you're not fucking me. It will absolve you."

"That's a stretch," replied J.P. "I'm not posting it." He pressed the side of his phone and the screen went dark. He placed it on the stenciled nightstand.

"Fine, but I'm disappointed." Jade yanked her hand off his bare chest. "You'll have to make it up to me."

"I think I can do that." J.P. leaned over her and kissed her. She responded, pulling off his shirt. He made his way down her body. She closed her eyes and let her head sink back into the pillows. Her lips parted in a moan.

TWENTY-ONE

Inside *The Taken Aship*, an old thirty-six-foot power cruiser, Mac and Eve sat on the floor at the glass coffee table, their backs leaning against the base of the faded and cracked leather couch. A brick of heroin wrapped in plastic was in the center of the table next to a pack of Marlboro Reds, a Zippo lighter, and two open beers. Ruby stood in front of them, holding her woven backpack, its top flap open. She looked sick, her skin pale and waxy. Her hair was still drying, tangled from the harbor plunge earlier.

Eve grinned at the heroin and winked at Ruby. "Good girl."

"I'd like to buy an eight ball." Ruby's voice was weak. She found her Hello Kitty wallet in her backpack, fumbled for cash, and held the bills out, her hand trembling.

Mac shook his head. "I can't believe Otto doesn't give you a taste for your troubles."

"He wants me to do it the right way," replied Ruby. Sweat beaded around her hairline.

"I get it. We all have to be accountable." Eve unwrapped the off-white brick. She slid an orange marine first-aid case from the side of the couch and flipped open the top, sifting around the contents and lifting out a small scale. She nodded to Mac, then Ruby's money. "Count it."

Mac reached for the cash. Ruby tripped as she passed it to him across the table, catching herself with her hand.

"You okay?" asked Mac.

Ruby nodded. She twitched as she watched Eve scrape the brick with a scalpel, weigh out the powder, and drop it into a tiny zip-lock baggie. Eve clutched the baggie until Mac was done counting.

"All here," confirmed Mac.

"*Such* a good girl." Eve handed the baggie to Ruby.

Ruby took it with a wan smile. She lifted her nylon Wear National makeup bag from her backpack and unzipped it, pulling out a rubber tourniquet. "Do you mind?"

"Yes, we mind," snapped Eve. "You're not doing that here."

"Okay, sorry." Ruby put the makeup bag and the heroin in her backpack. She hoisted the straps over her bony shoulders and headed out.

Eve shooed her. "Enjoy."

"Ruby . . ." Mac wore a concerned expression.

Ruby turned to him.

"Be careful," he said.

"Yeah, be careful no one sees you leave here." Eve followed Ruby to the door, making sure it was locked behind her. She walked back to Mac and straddled his lap, draping her arms around his neck.

"If I were the jealous type . . ." she purred.

Mac's hands remained by his sides. "You're not. You like to pretend you are."

"If I *were*, I'd say you've got a hard-on for little miss junkie mule."

Mac glanced down at his crotch. "Nope."

Eve tilted her head. "Then what's gotten into you, baby?" Her tone was condescending.

"I'm not down with the arrangement." Mac stared at the door.

Eve reached into the first-aid case, brushing her breast against Mac's shoulder. She pulled out a box of gauze, opening it to reveal cash. Mac tucked Ruby's money inside.

"That cocksucker Otto built the store here so he could keep closer tabs on us," he continued.

"Stop blowing yourself," said Eve with a scoff. "He could've kept tabs on us without building the store. Who cares? It's a means to an end."

"I'm not sure if this is the way," replied Mac as he put the gauze box back in the case. "Don't you ever think about what we're doing to people?"

"People like her?" Eve nodded to the door. "No. We don't do anything to them. They do it to themselves. It's not my business. *This* is." She reached around for the brick and held it between them.

Mac's eyes narrowed at her. "When did everything become a transaction for you?"

"When *you* stopped paying off." Eve's eyes, sad for a beat, locked with Mac's before she placed the brick in the first-aid case with the scale. She dropped in the scalpel and covered it all with a folded thermal blanket, boxes of Band-Aids, bottles of peroxide and ipecac, and sundry ointments. She leaned into Mac's ear. "We're together now for one reason, to stop serving drinks to assholes in the summer and losers in the winter." Eve shut the case's lid and sat back, hands on Mac's thighs. "Or do you want to end up like Frank—fat, bald, and sad?"

"I might want to find another way." Mac's hands remained by his side.

"Yeah, right. Like your music." Eve climbed off. "Keep blowing yourself, because I'm sure as shit not going to."

"That's a shame," muttered Mac as Eve disappeared into the bedroom at the hull.

She returned with a duffel. "If you find your balls while you're at it, let me know." She yanked on her UGG boots by the door. "Until then, I'll be at my sister's." She exited with a slam.

Mac rose and put the orange first-aid case in the boat's upholstered storage bench, arranging life jackets on top of it. He sat back down on the floor against the couch, grabbed a cigarette, and lit it, tossing the Zippo on the table. He leaned his head back and exhaled.

The moon was high and the waters bordering Old South Wharf were calm. Presley parked the G among the line of cars. She applied lip gloss in the rearview mirror, giving her lips a smack. She put the gloss in her purse and started to get out when she saw Eve striding angrily down the dock. She shut the door and ducked down.

"Zero balls," Eve grumbled to herself. She didn't look in Presley's direction because she was singularly focused on a beat-up, blue VW Beetle a few yards away. She chucked her duffel in, took the driver's seat, and peeled out.

Presley exhaled. "Jesus." After the coast was clear, she got out of the G. Taking long strides down the dock, she scanned the names of the boats. "Where is this stupid dinghy?" she muttered to herself, then saw *The Taken Aship* and scoffed. She smoothed her hair and rapped on the door.

"Eve, why do we do this every fucking time? I mean, you have a damn key." Mac opened the door. "Hey," he said, surprised to find Presley.

"Howdy." Presley smiled, her lips shining with gloss.

"If I knew we were having a party, I would've dressed up," said Mac, deadpan.

"Come again?" Presley looked confused, glancing around the empty boat.

"Never mind. What can I do for you, princess?"

"Party supplies, like you just said." Presley peered past him. "Where's your lovely girlfriend?"

"Shitlist," said Mac. "Permanently on there."

"That doesn't sound fun."

"You might be shocked at this, but life's not all about fun." Mac held the doorknob.

Presley stepped inside.

"Sure, come on in." Mac scratched his head and chuckled dryly.

Presley scanned around the small living-kitchen area. "So, this is *The Taken Aship*? It's quaint."

"I'd give you the five-cent tour, but this is pretty much it." Mac motioned wide with both arms.

"I don't want the tour. What else you got?"

Mac didn't flinch. "I have some very addictive cherry pie from the Island Pie Shop."

Presley paused. She didn't press. Maybe she didn't want another answer. "Cherry. My fave."

"I knew it." Mac pulled the pie from the refrigerator. He plucked two forks out of a drawer, yanked some paper towel off the roll on the counter, and brought it all to the coffee table. He and Presley sat next to each other on the floor with their backs against couch.

"You're forgetting something," said Presley.

Mac looked at her inquisitively.

"Ice cream," she answered.

"That's a crime." Mac mock-furrowed his brow. "Ice cream on *this* cherry pie." He gestured for Presley to do the honors. "This is the pure stuff."

"Okay," said Presley, incredulous as she dug her fork into the pie's golden lattice crust. She lifted a biteful of red sweetness, sliding it into her mouth. "I hate to admit it . . ." She chewed. "*Ever.* But you're right."

She took another bite. Satisfied, Mac dug in as well.

"You mentioned that your life might not have been the Georgia peach debutante picture you paint it to be."

"Did I mention that?" Presley took another bite, quickly wiping the cherry juice that dripped on her chin with the paper towel. "You can take the girl out of the trailer park but you can't take the trailer park out of the girl."

With amusement, Mac watched her enjoy the pie.

"I grew up in Baxley," said Presley. "I was the poster child for the ongoing war on welfare. You know that hundreds of thousands of Georgia families are on welfare?"

"I didn't. But I'm familiar with the welfare situation." Mac took a bite.

"We were one of those families. I lived in a double-wide with my parents, my sister and brother, and my uncle and his two a-hole sons." Presley placed her fork on the paper towel. "From the time I was ten, I worked my ass off so I could go to college—odd jobs, while studying every minute. That's why this summer job is easy, as, well—" she took another bite, "—pie."

"Hm. I'll bet." Mac looked impressed.

"See, I'm not who you think I am," said Presley.

"I'm not who you think I am either," Mac replied.

Presley looked in Mac's eyes. "Who are you?"

"Do you think that because you told me your story, I should tell you mine?"

"Alrightee." Presley rose. "Thanks for the pie." She started for the door.

Mac got up, wincing at his harsh words. "I'm a guy who's trying to put one foot in front of the other."

"If you do that on this island, you'll fall off." Presley touched the wall.

"That's the whole point," said Mac. "I do *not* want to live here forever."

"Then what are we doing here?" Presley dropped her hand. "You could've asked me to leave."

"We're eating pie and getting to know each other better." Mac stepped in close to her.

"What if all we discover is that we're both addicted to cherry pie?"

"Then we go our separate ways."

Mac kissed her. Presley responded, putting her hand on the back of his neck and pulling him in. He picked her up in his arms and carried her to the bedroom.

Eve stepped up to the boat. At the door, she could hear the sounds of sex. She looked into the hull's small round window, then slid to the side, her eyes burning with rage. She pulled her smartphone from her purse, turned back to the window, and started to film. After a few moments, the wood planks on the dock rumbled. She looked around and the rumbling stopped. Eve put her phone away, ran down the dock to the VW, and drove off.

She didn't see that she had passed Mia on her cruiser, hidden between the shadow of a yacht and its large anchor moor. Mia glanced at the G down the street, then at the boat's window, where Eve had stood. Torn for a long moment, she rode off on her bike, back down the dock and away from the wharf.

TWENTY-TWO

Lyndon sat on a tall stool at the bar in Topper's. The restaurant's warm but elegant decor matched the rest of The Wauwinet, with its gorgeous wood floors and exposed wood beam ceilings. Lyndon was the only customer because it was close to midnight and the hotel's older highbrow crowd were ensconced in their rooms and asleep.

The bartender put a scotch on the rocks in front of her. "How's your summer going, Ms. Wyld?"

"Brilliantly," replied Lyndon. "How's yours, Jeremy?"

"Great. Thank you."

"I'm famished." Lyndon took a sip of her drink. "Do you happen to have any oysters left?"

"Saved some just for you—Fanny Bay."

"The bee's knees!" Lyndon clapped.

The bartender disappeared into the kitchen.

"Did I hear the word 'fanny'?" said a male voice with a nasal pinch that came from doing too much cocaine. "I would recognize *that* fanny anywhere."

Lyndon took a healthier sip of her drink without turning around. Otto mounted the bar stool next to her.

"That seat is taken." Lyndon didn't look at him.

Otto rubbed his shoulder to hers. "It is, by *me*."

"Isn't it enough to get booted once a night?" said Lyndon. "I heard about your little show at my Solstice Soiree."

"I wasn't booted. I left to come find you." Otto put his elbows on the bar, chin in his palms. "What can I say? I like your parties."

"Anything is better than your crack house orgies," remarked Lyndon. "You know that went out with the grunge era."

Otto reached over the bar to grab a highball glass and the bottle of Macallan scotch that the bartender had left when pouring Lyndon's drink. He poured his own.

"Tell me you're not staying here," said Lyndon.

"Oh, no. It's too stuffy for me. I stay at the White Elephant in town. I like to be near my babies when I come in. I know you prefer to be more . . ." Otto looked up for the word. "Removed."

He held his glass out to Lyndon for a toast. "But I wanted to buy you a drink as thanks."

Lyndon side-eyed him. "Thanks for what?"

Otto sipped. "First, for sending Maz to chat me up about my business. You know I love to talk about myself. His golf swing needs work, but he brings stellar kush."

The ice cube in Lyndon's glass clinked as she put down the empty drink.

"And second, for introducing me to Ines Paxton, your old mate." Otto struck the "t" hard.

Lyndon side-eyed him. "That was two years ago and I didn't introduce you. She was doing a story on me and she thought you'd be a good source instead of the lying sack of shit you are."

"I said you were a skillful puppeteer." Otto drained his drink. "All good business people are. It was a compliment not a lie."

Lyndon rolled her eyes.

"I know you two have lost touch, but she's gone from working at BBC to MTV," said Otto. "Did you know that?"

"No, but that sounds about right," Lyndon sneered. "Hack."

Otto continued, "She wants to do a reality series about Wear National and cross promote online and over social. We all know that brick-and-mortar stores are becoming as obsolete as, well, those flats you're wearing." He crinkled his nose at Lyndon's gold flats with an LW medallion flourish.

Lyndon circled an ankle in the shoe. "My stores are doing fine. So are my online sales."

"Now who's the liar?" Otto tilted his glass toward her. "You're still too stuck in your high castle to join the twenty-first century. The TV show is going to follow my seasonaires here in Nantucket next summer."

"Your seasonaires?" Lyndon gritted her teeth at the words. "Who's going to watch your meager band of skeezy strung-out strumpets?"

"They're already watching." Otto showed Lyndon a Wear National Instagram post with two hundred thousand likes: Ruby on her knees frolicking in shallow water wearing a bikini bottom. Her breasts were strategically covered with wet sand. "I took that one," he said proudly. "She's like a magical sprite, isn't she?"

"I'd never put my charges in that position. It's revolting." Lyndon turned away.

"Not according to my line's 4.5 million followers." Otto grinned. "I'm Entrepreneur of the Decade. Everyone everywhere wants to see what I'll do next. Haven't you read?"

"No one anywhere gives two shiny shits about a wrinkled limp-cock tosser like you," replied Lyndon.

"I'll admit I might personally be out of the MTV demo." Otto poured more scotch in his glass. "But viewers *will* tune in to watch my young, hot, and hung seasonaires get into naughty mischief with nary of yours in sight. Is that still a word? 'Nary.' Is that how to use it?"

Lyndon didn't respond.

The bartender brought over a plate of oysters with a cloth napkin and some silverware, including an oyster fork. "Here you go, Ms. Wyld."

"Those look yummy," said Otto, eyeing the platter. "I met up with *your* delicious morsels at the party. They're not as delicious as mine, but mmm—"

Lyndon picked up her oyster fork and stabbed it into Otto's right hand.

"Motherfu—!" Otto laughed raucously. He pulled the fork from his skin. "You know they script everything on those reality shows, right? So maybe you can do this again." He pointed to the blood seeping from the holes in his hand. "Everyone loves a good villain." He knocked back his second drink. "I have a helicopter to catch back to the city. I have a meeting with Ines in the morning."

Otto left. Lyndon stared at the oyster fork on the bar.

In the hotel cottage, J.P. slept naked, on his stomach. He snored lightly. The other side of the bed was empty. From behind the closed bathroom door, a toilet flushed, then water ran and turned off. Jade padded in, barefoot, in her panties. Without making a sound, she picked up J.P.'s phone and typed in the password: perch. She posted the video of her and Otto at the Summer Solstice Soiree on Instagram.

Mia squirmed awake at the feeling of a warm body getting into bed with her.

"I just broke every one of my rules," said Presley, still wearing her clothes from the Solstice Soiree.

Mia opened her eyes to see Presley's soft smile. She touched her arm. They both closed their eyes and fell asleep.

TWENTY-THREE

"Morning!" chimed Presley as she and Mia entered the kitchen. Grant was making Bloody Marys.

"Hair of the dog." He handed one to Cole, whose head was resting on his elbows at the kitchen table.

"Not so loud," moaned Cole. He wouldn't look at the drink.

Grant patted Cole on the back. "This man gave up the chance at a sister, so I got them both."

Mia and Cole exchanged a glance.

Vincent snapped a photo of Grant tucking a piece of bacon from the nearby pan into the top of the bright red cocktail. "Bloody with bacon, Vinnie?"

"I don't eat meat. I also don't get hangovers."

"I forgot that the French drink wine from the teat." Grant sipped the drink and crunched a bite of bacon. "Mm." He held a Bloody Mary toward Mia, but she waved it off, instead taking two bottled waters from the fridge. She placed one next to Cole.

"Hydrate."

"Thanks." Cole didn't pick his head up.

Mia reached past Cole to the Advil sitting next to a bowl of cherries. She winced because her body was sore from treading water in the harbor.

"Where are Jade and J.P.?" asked Presley. She took a selfie holding the cherry bowl and Snapchatted:

Life's a bowl. 🍒

"We can't wait all day for them." Presley applied peach lip gloss in the camera frame of her phone. "The country club brunch and trunk show starts in twenty."

"Pre-Bloody Bloodies," said Grant, finishing his cocktail.

Presley tapped his glass with the lip gloss tube. "Jade thinks she's in a glass by herself, but she'll find out she has no control over the consequences." She lifted her phone and showed Mia, Cole, and Grant the video on J.P.'s Instagram of Jade in the booth with Otto.

"J.P. didn't come home last night," said Cole. "I wonder if he ended up shark chum. There's an entire subreddit, Maz Beatdowns, dedicated to Maz's goons kicking the crap out of people at clubs, the mall, even Six Flags."

"Who knows if those stories are true?" said Mia. "How do you know what to believe?" Her words were pointed at Cole. She exited the house and walked toward the G. Vincent was in the driver's seat.

"Mia."

Mia turned to see Cole and stopped. Presley walked past them, smiling at Mia before being scooped up by Grant and carried to the car. She giggled.

Cole stood with Mia. "I want to make sure we're cool," he said. "I got home last night and knocked on your door, but you didn't answer."

"I'm glad I didn't because it sounds like you were pretty toasted," replied Mia.

"I was." Cole kicked a pebble. "When you left to go out to the beach, you didn't seem very happy with me. I was having a good time hanging out with you."

"I wasn't really sure about that," said Mia.

Cole looked at her. "You should be."

Mia let this sink in. "Okay."

Cole motioned his hand between them. "So, are we—?"

"Cool? Yes." With Mia's smile, Cole relaxed.

Driving into town with Cole sitting next to her, Mia thought about the party, his breath on her neck when he came up behind her, his cheek against hers when they danced. But she moved an inch away because there was a push-pull to him that kept her off-balance.

They arrived at The Highview Club, a bright yellow clapboard "amusement park" for the pearls-and-khakis set, with yachting, tennis, squash, croquet, and poolside drinking.

The North Lawn was set up like an outdoor pop-up store with Lyndon Wyld clothes and a champagne brunch buffet. When the group arrived with Vincent, Jill was arranging racks. She and Cole exchanged a smile.

"Do you need help?" Mia asked her.

"Nope." Jill arranged pastel socks on a table. "I'm good."

Presley's eyes moved past Mia. "Look what the cat dragged in."

Jade and J.P. approached. J.P. strode ahead of Jade, looking around. "Is Lyndon here?"

"Not yet," said Cole.

Jade grabbed a men's polo shirt and shorts off a table, and handed them to J.P., since they were both wearing their clothes from the night before. She checked the size of a dress on a rack, then pulled it off the hanger.

"What are you doing?" Jill motioned to the items. "Those aren't free swag."

"I'm buying them. Relax, lover girl." Jade handed cash to Jill, whose expression went from annoyed to perplexed.

Jade and J.P. put on the purchases in the green-and-beige-striped changing cabanas erected for the event.

Grant played croquet, snapping selfies until he got stung by a bee. By the time Grace arrived ten minutes later, his cheek had started to swell. Grace surveyed the scene. She rearranged some merchandise on a table where Jill was standing. "Nice job." Their eyes locked for a beat. She crossed to Mia and Presley, who were greeting guests. "Mia, can I talk to you a moment?" She motioned for Mia to follow.

Mia whispered to Presley. "Another wrist slap if she saw me and Ruby in Otto's Instagram post."

"Hang in there, sugar." Presley squeezed Mia's arm as she moved off.

Mia stepped up to Grace near the changing cabanas. Grace put finger to cheek. "On second thought, I think everyone should hear this." Mia's breath quickened as Grace motioned for Presley to gather the others. Presley came to Mia's side, holding her hand.

"Lyndon apologizes for not being here," Grace said to them. "She needed to get back to New York, where the hustle happens while you loll around on Nantucket." She chuckled. The seasonaires gave an expected laugh. "But she wanted me to make an announcement, first to you and then to our guests."

Mia shoved her hands in the pockets of her white jeans as if hoping to find magic dust she could toss in the air to make herself disappear.

Grace turned to Mia. "Lyndon and I loved what you did to the dress you wore last night."

Mia motioned to Presley. "It was Presley's dress, but—"

Grace interrupted. "She gave it to you, so now, it's yours. You made it one hundred percent yours."

Presley let go of Mia's hand.

Grace continued, "Out of all the clothes worn on the runway during the fashion show, that dress won the most attention on our social. So we decided we are going to design one exactly like it called the Mia."

Mia's mouth dropped open.

"Woot! Woot! The Miiiiahhh!" cheered Grant. His swollen cheek from the bee sting didn't dampen his enthusiasm. Mia grinned at him. She saw Cole's smile. Everyone clapped, though Jade's and Presley's applause was weak.

"It's already trending on Instagram." Grace held up her smartphone.

The seasonaires checked their phones. The Lyndon Wyld account featured Vincent's candid shot of Mia standing, wet and serious, against the G outside the Summer Solstice Soiree.

Stay tuned for the Mia. #modern #mermaid #BeWyld

"*C'est fantastique!*" Vincent beamed at Mia, who was still speechless.

"You may as well have been wearing my fishtail braid," muttered Presley.

Grace scanned the others. "Let this be a lesson to you slackers. You might think that this is the Summer of Fun, but if you want to get something out of it, you're going to have to put more in."

Jill brought over a mounted blown-up screenshot and set it on the easel she unfolded. Mia couldn't believe her eyes.

Grace waved off the seasonaires. "Now get to work. Sell some merch and, more importantly, sell yourselves."

Presley was the first to walk away. Cole was the last, leaning into Mia and whispering, "See, you're doing some designing after all."

Mia smiled.

"This dress is so freaking cute!" One country club daughter pointed to the Mia display.

"We're taking pre-orders," said Jill, overhearing.

Grace noticed Mia's wide-eyed gaze. "If you want us to wait to move forward until you talk to an attorney, we will. Lyndon just feels that we should strike while the iron is hot."

"This is just so, um—" Mia stammered. "Surprising."

"Why? You're talented. *Own it*." Grace put her face close to Mia's. "You know, I didn't go to college either."

Mia shook her head.

Grace caressed Mia's arm. "I had a feeling we were soul sisters when I saw you at the thrift shop."

From the buffet table, Presley eyed them. She took a swallow of champagne.

"I have to admit," Mia said to Grace. "I was surprised to see you welcome us that first day. I didn't put two and two together." She chuckled. "See? College probably would've helped."

"Bullshit. You're whipsmart, Mia. Both Lyndon and I are very aware of that." On her smartphone, Grace showed Mia the popular Wear National Instagram post of Ruby in the water, kneeling in the bikini bottom. "There's *her*." She held it next to the blowup of Mia. "And there's *you*. You are *us*." She dropped her phone in her purse and walked with Mia to the buffet table.

Jade and J.P. were eating grapes off the same plate. Grace tapped the plate. "You're going to have to stop with the sideshow, Jade. You're not so famous that we won't send you home." Grace left the event.

"She won't send me home." Jade popped a grape in her mouth. "She has zero say. That's why she grabs the low-hanging fruit." Her eyes were on Jill, who helped two women with handbags.

"What does she mean by sideshow?" asked J.P. "She wasn't at the party when Otto crashed it."

"She didn't need to be, thanks to you." Presley displayed her phone: the video of Otto and Jade on J.P.'s Instagram.

"How did that . . . ?" Heated, he turned to Jade.

"Why would you post that?" said Jade, glaring at him with her hip cocked.

"Are you shitting me right now?" snapped J.P. He pulled his phone out of his pocket, deleted the post and stormed off.

Jade shrugged. "He'll get over it."

"Guess it's dog-eat-dog." Presley eyed Mia.

A young girl approached. "Mia, will you take a picture with me?"

"Of course." Mia looked back at Jade and Presley as she walked with the girl to the easel topped with her likeness. Vincent snapped a few photos, then took some with the girl's phone. The girl grinned at Mia.

"Thank you."

"Anytime," replied Mia.

When the girl walked off, Presley stepped up to Mia.

"You know exactly what you're doing, don't you?" she said to Mia.

"Working." Mia looked puzzled at Presley's tone.

"You had this all planned."

"The only thing I had planned was to do a good job."

"Right," Presley sneered, leaving Mia standing by her own wet and alone image.

TWENTY-FOUR

Presley had barely said two words to Mia in over a week. She ignored her through whale-watching, tubing, a game of poker, and two trips to the Lyndon Wyld store.

Before a beach barbecue, Mia asked her to help with false eyelashes. "I still can't get the hang of it."

"You're talented enough to do them on your own," said Presley, applying her own makeup at the vanity. Mia went without the eyelashes. She couldn't tell if the silence was due to jealousy or lack of trust. Maybe Presley was distracted by Mac. She had gone off on her own a couple times and returned no more or less interested in talking to her.

It was Sunday, a free day, and Mia had been roped into cooking dinner the next night. She and Grant had bet on the Red Sox–Phillies game. Grant would make everyone tacos if the Sox won.

Mia would cook spaghetti with homemade sauce if the Phillies were victorious. Mia lost.

After a night of drinking and dancing at the Chicken Box, everyone was still asleep at eleven, so Mia grabbed a couple recyclable totes and headed out the door to bike to the Farmers & Artisans Market.

"Bitch, wait up."

Mia turned, surprised to see Jade putting on her aviator sunglasses, her hair in an impressively high topknot, spiral curls springing out of the top. They got on cruisers and peddled to town.

"Where's your BFF?" asked Jade. "Pres-ley."

"She's pissed at me," replied Mia.

"You mean jealous."

"Pissed, jealous—both look the same." The breeze felt good on Mia's face.

"Haters gonna hate. Have you read comments on my social?" Jade snickered.

"I don't think Presley's a hater." Mia stopped at a bike rack near the entrance of the buzzing Farmers & Artisans market.

"Don't fool yourself, but don't give a shit either." Jade lifted her long leg off her bike. "You're here to succeed, right?"

Mia locked up the bikes. "I want to move forward in my career, yes."

"You want it? Then get it. Be a fuckin' boss."

Mia stopped at the bakery stand and pointed to a vanilla and maple morning bun. "I want that."

"There you go!" Jade laughed.

They bought two pastries, strong cups of coffee, and ciabatta for dinner.

Nantucket's resident three-piece acoustic band, Dolphin Shine, performed its quirky brand of folk music while the two girls walked around the stands. The bursts of summer color were bright against the whitewash of the surrounding buildings. Mia picked out ripe tomatoes, fresh basil, and garlic, along with salad ingredients. Jade put together two huge bouquets from the flower stand.

The patchouli, lavender, and mint of handmade soaps wafted through the air as Mia perused long sea glass necklaces crafted by a local jeweler. She rubbed the smooth translucent blue and green pendants between her thumb and forefinger.

"Mermaid tears," said the jeweler. "Legend has it that every time a sailor drowned at sea, the mermaids would cry and the sea glass was their tears washing up on the shore." The jeweler moved off to ring up a customer.

"Cheesy," Jade said under her breath.

"Maybe. But I happen to like tales." Mia left the necklace. "You don't have to believe them to like them."

The singer of Dolphin Shine, who wore a kooky hat topped with a fin, was giving out free hugs. Mia tried and failed to duck out of one. Jade laughed.

They walked by a T-shirt stand with red, white, and blue Nantucket tees and sweatshirts.

"I can't believe it's almost the Fourth of July," said Mia. "This summer is going by so fast."

"Time flies." Jade waved a mini American flag, then put it back in the display.

"I heard the fireworks are amazing here," said Mia. "Fireworks on my side of Boston consist of sparklers and the occasional obnoxious Red Devil before the cops confiscate everything."

"My dad puts on his own fireworks." Jade ate a strawberry from a stand. "I'm going to his annual Blue Bash in the Hamptons."

"It looks like a killer party. I've seen photos online," said Mia.

"It'll beat The Rabbit Hole, that's for sure." Jade made duck lips for an Instagram selfie. "Come with. I'm going to drag J.P. He's still pouting over the Otto video I posted on his Instagram, but he'll do anything to get in with my dad."

"Why did you do that?"

"To mess with my family. It might've been a lapse in judgment, which is why I deleted it." Jade blew on a patriotic pinwheel. "Come with us."

"We're not supposed to leave the island," said Mia.

"Lyndon didn't implant microchips, Mia. Although I know she wants to."

Mia pointed to Jade's phone. "Our social media is basically a microchip."

"That's true. But if we didn't want it that way, we wouldn't be here."

"Can I ask you something?" asked Mia.

"Yup." Jade shrugged and leaned over to smell a candle.

"Why *are* you here?"

"I want to make my own life," said Jade. "I've always been the daughter of the royal couple. This job was my way to be me."

"'Remember, we're not microchipped,'" replied Mia, tossing Jade's words back at her. "Your dad doesn't control you."

"He controls the purse strings."

"Buy your own damn purse." Mia touched woven bags hanging on a rack.

"Those are fug." Jade scrunched her nose with distaste.

"I'm just saying, 'Be a fuckin' boss,'" said Mia with a grin.

"I get it." Jade hooked her arm through Mia's as they continued walking. "I'm still going to my dad's party because the thought of spending our country's birthday in that stinky fucking Rabbit Hole dive makes me want to hurl my morning bun."

"Well, don't do that."

"I won't. In fact, I want another one." Jade settled for a blueberry turnover at the Island Pie Shop stand, where they bought a cherry pie for dessert.

Jade gobbled down the turnover. "I have my period and there aren't enough carbs to make me happy right now."

They stopped at the pharmacy for "lady products," as Jade faux-delicately put it. Entering, the air-conditioning hit them with a cold blast after walking in the sun. They walked to the feminine care aisle and Jade picked out tampons. As they continued down the aisle, she perused the condoms.

"Magnummmms, where are you?" She found them. "There you are!"

"TMI," Mia chuckled.

"Really? TMI?" Jade raised an eyebrow. "You saw J.P. on the boat during Truth or Dare. Don't pretend you didn't look." She hip-bumped Mia.

"I'm sorry, but Mr. Hahn needs a paper prescription and he'll have to come in himself with his ID."

The name "Mr. Hahn" made Mia and Jade look toward the pharmacy window. Ruby was talking to the pharmacist. An empty vial sat on the counter between them. Mia and Jade hung back in the aisle, unseen.

"He's a super busy man." Ruby offered a friendly smile to the pharmacist, who didn't return the pleasantry.

"Oxycodone is a Schedule 2 drug so we can't fill it any other way," said the pharmacist.

Jade nudged Mia and whispered, "Don't you want to say 'hi'? According to Presley, you two are tight."

They watched Ruby dial her phone. "Hey, Otto, it's me, Ruby. The pharmacist needs to talk to you."

"I don't want to interrupt," Mia whispered back to Jade. "She's making a phone call."

Ruby clicked off her phone and spoke to the pharmacist in her sweetest voice. "See? He's *so* busy, he's not answering his phone. But you'd be doing me such a solid if—"

A siren's blare outside drowned out Ruby's words. Through the window, Mia and Jade could see firetrucks pass.

Ruby's phone pinged with a text. She looked. "Our store is on fire." She raced out the door with other customers, missing Mia and Jade. Mia followed, but Jade grabbed her.

"Hey, my items!"

"Jade!" Mia glared at her, making Jade abandon the tampons and condoms, though not happily.

On the street, Mia called for Ruby, but her voice was no match for the sirens.

When they arrived at the Wear National store, firefighters were dousing the flames devouring the right side. The front window was shattered from the heat pressure, and the display bearing Ruby's image was melted and singed.

"Holy shit," muttered Jade.

Paramedics were loading Quentin into an ambulance. The left side of his face was burned and covered in gauze. He moaned in pain.

"He's that Wear National seasonaire," Mia said to Jade. They stayed behind the invisible line that a cop indicated with wide arms because lookie-loos had started to gather.

Ruby hugged Axel, who stood with another cop and a weeping salesgirl. She was too preoccupied to notice Mia and Jade.

The black Crown Victoria drove up to the curb. The man with the two different colored eyes got out and stepped up to the crowd control cop. "Detective Miller," said the cop with a nod. Miller nodded back.

The ambulance screamed off. Jade pulled Mia away. "Enough disaster porn."

TWENTY-FIVE

Presley's eyes were closed, her head tilted back. She felt Mac's gaze, so she moved even more slowly and sensuously, holding him back. When she opened her eyes, she saw him staring at her face, not her body. This made her heart beat faster.

"Why are you looking at me like that?"

"You're fucking beautiful," said Mac.

Presley brushed her hand over her face.

"Don't stop." Mac pulled her into him.

She put both hands on his chest and let him look into her eyes. They both finished and she fell into his arms. She curled up next to him and together they breathed. Their bodies glistened. The boat's tiny bedroom was hot.

"I've been the other woman before," said Presley. "Usually I don't care."

"I could've figured that about you."

"But with you, I don't like it." Presley scratched her fingernails lightly down Mac's stomach.

"You mean you care," replied Mac.

"Maybe." Presley scratched harder.

Mac winced and smiled, grabbing her hand. "That's okay. I care, too." He released.

"Have you cheated on Eve before?" She caressed him gently.

"Neither of us are saints, that's for sure."

"Then how can she claim you?"

"Ha. No one claims me."

"I could claim you."

"Oh, you could, could you?" Mac kissed her forehead. "Eve and I make better coworkers than a couple. I'm not even sure about that anymore."

"What do you mean?"

"It's not anything I want to talk about with you."

"Oh." Presley removed her hand from his chest.

"Because this is really nice," said Mac as he pulled her in tightly. "I'd like to keep it that way. I want to make changes in my life."

"What kind of changes?" asked Presley.

"Just . . . changes." Mac kissed her deeply. His facial scruff was rough against her skin.

"Your beard is scratchy." Presley giggled.

"Do you want me to shave it?"

"No." She touched his chin. It was square with a dimple hidden inside his beard. She kissed him. They made love again, then dozed in and out of sleep for the next half hour. Mac started awake and looked at his smartphone on the windowsill.

"I have to get to my shift."

They dressed. Mac zipped Presley's sundress, nuzzling into the nape of her neck.

"Tell Eve I say 'hi,'" said Presley, slipping on her sandals.

"I won't," replied Mac.

Presley stepped out of the boat and headed up the dock with an extra swing in her strut. She put on her oversize tortoiseshell sunglasses, but didn't bother to smooth her hair. She glanced back at the boat, then turned to see Ruby heading toward her. Her face flushed with anger. Ruby's expression was peacefully buzzed.

"Fancy meeting you here." Presley blocked Ruby's path. "The last time I saw you on a boat you were unconscious."

Ruby smiled. "The sea is relaxing."

"Especially with an empty bottle in your lap," replied Presley.

Ruby looked around, smiling at all the blue around them—the water and the sky. "It's a beautiful day. What are *you* doing here?"

"Enjoying the harbor." Presley put a hand on her hip.

"Maybe you're here for the same reason I am," said Ruby.

Presley let two fishermen pass before responding. "I doubt it."

"You and I aren't so different," said Ruby, tilting her head and staring into Presley.

"Oh, honey, please." Presley rolled her eyes.

"You put on the face, the hair, the clothes, but I can still see it." Ruby smiled. "I know what you've been through. Anybody who looks in your eyes knows it."

Presley's expression hardened. "You don't know shit about me and don't you *ever* assume that you do."

"It's okay." Ruby touched Presley's arm. Presley noticed all Ruby's bracelets, including the thin blue enamel bangle. With a caress, Ruby walked around her. Presley stood and watched as Ruby continued down the dock, her woven backpack heavy on her thin frame. Ruby knocked on *The Taken Aship*. The door opened and she stepped inside.

Presley turned and walked away from the dock.

TWENTY-SIX

Night fell over Manhattan. The last of the Lyndon Wyld employees walked past Lyndon's glass-enclosed office and out the door. Lyndon and Grace sat on the couch with Lyndon's iPad on the coffee table in front of them.

Grace was reading a new story: "Here's a quote from Otto Hahn: 'The most important thing is that no one was killed.'"

"You have to use a voice like a parrot in a torturously tight waist trainer," said Lyndon, sipping her tea.

Grace did her best imitation of Otto as she continued reading. "'Stuff can be replaced. People can't.'"

"What a fucking tosser," replied Lyndon. "I think the meth lab in the store's basement exploded." She crossed her arms.

Grace read silently for a beat. "The poor lad suffered third-degree burns. Otto had him airlifted to his hometown's hospital and he's not returning."

"He's not photogenic for Otto anymore," scoffed Lyndon.

"Or fuckable," added Grace. She pointed to the trending Twitter hashtag:

#WearNationalFire

"Rumors are that it was arson. Otto probably torched it for the insurance money."

"Do you think the kids know?" asked Lyndon.

"Vincent checked in this morning before the fire." Grace showed her a text from Vincent. "The boys went wind-surfing. Mia and Jade went to the farmers market."

"Hopefully Mia kept Presley and Jade from ripping each other's hair out," remarked Lyndon.

"He said Presley didn't go. She appeared to be miffed about the Mia dress."

"She stayed home to pout-n-primp?" asked Lyndon.

Grace scrolled through Presley's Instagram, showing Lyndon. "There's nothing for most of the day until this." She showed Lyndon a selfie of Presley holding a lobster roll with Old South Wharf in the background:

East Coast cravings. #BeWyld #nomnom

"That's Jeffrey's Deli, Old South Wharf—best on the island," said Grace.

"Good God, Grace, how can you eat so much mayonnaise?"

Grace peered at her phone, scrutinizing Presley's selfie. "She looks a little more tousled than usual," remarked Grace.

"Let's call them." Lyndon nodded to the iPad.

Grace group texted on her phone:

Skype now.

Vincent pinged back:

I'll round everyone up.

"MTV will eat this up, I'm sure." Lyndon shuddered. "It creates sympathy for Wear National. Goddammit!"

"I think you're giving Otto too much credit," said Grace.

"He didn't get where he is by talent," replied Lyndon. "You know that."

Grace got another text from Vincent:

Ready.

She opened Skype and pressed the icon with the group photo of the seasonaires from the first day at the estate. Vincent was in the middle of the screen. He moved back to reveal everyone in the living room.

Lyndon's smile was warm and concerned. "Hello, my darlings. I'm sure you've heard the news about the Wear National store fire."

Mia nodded and glanced at Jade, who was sitting next to her on the couch. J.P. watched Jade from the ottoman. His arms were crossed.

"I wanted to make sure you're all okay," Lyndon said. "I needed to see you all with my own two eyes."

"We're peachy here," exclaimed Presley. "Not to worry, Lyndon!" She was sitting next to Grant on the loveseat, even though there was plenty of room next to Mia.

"It's just a reminder to make the most of life," said Lyndon. "I feel very protec—" Her voice caught with emotion.

"We both feel protective," added Grace.

"Will we be seeing you next week for Fourth of July festivities?" asked Mia.

Lyndon sniffed back her tears. "No, my darling. We go to London to see our mum."

"God save the queen and all that." Grace offered a regal wave.

"The Summer Solstice Soiree was our big event," said Lyndon.

"We let you handle Independence Day *independently* at The Rabbit Hole," added Grace.

"My baby sister is so punny." Lyndon put her hand on Grace's shoulder.

"We will light it up!" Grant pumped his arms in the air.

All the seasonaires glared at him.

He brought his arms down. "I didn't mean it like that."

"Watch yourselves," said Lyndon. "Watch one another."

"We'll check back soon," said Grace as she and Lyndon waved. Grace clicked off and the screen went black.

Lyndon stood. Her smartphone buzzed on the desk. She picked it up. "Son of a bitch!" she shrieked and threw the phone against the wall, missing Grace's head by a millimeter.

"What the hell?" chuckled Grace. "Remember the Play-Doh container you threw at me, when they used to have metal bottoms?" She pointed to a tiny scar on her chin. "Ten stitches."

"I wasn't throwing my phone at *you*."

"Why were you throwing your phone at all?"

"He just broke up with me!" Lyndon yelled. "Over text!"

"Why you little tart." Grace raised her eyebrows. "I didn't know you were dating anyone."

"I'm not!" Lyndon paced, breathing heavily.

Seeing that Lyndon was sincerely upset, Grace grew serious. "Who broke up with you?"

"Maz! He killed our footwear line deal!"

"Shit," whispered Grace.

"This is Otto!" yelled Lyndon. "He fucked with Jade at *my* party to turn Maz against me! He knew Maz would find out!" Lyndon paced.

Grace followed Lyndon around the room. "We'll fix this. It's going to be fine."

Lyndon pointed to the desk phone. "Call him."

Grace picked up the receiver and dialed. "Maz, please. I have Lyndon Wyld on the line." She listened for a beat, then hung up and looked at Lyndon. "He's gone home for the day."

"It's six o'clock. He never goes home this early!"

Grace speed-dialed Maz on her smartphone. "He's blocked my calls."

Lyndon stopped and stared at Grace. "Or maybe Maz thinks we had something to do with the fire."

"The arson is a *rumor*, Lyndon," replied Grace.

"Otto could've put that bug in his ear! *He's* the maggot that needs to be squashed!"

Lyndon lifted the bonsai off her desk and whipped it at the wall with all her might. The clay pot shattered, dirt spraying across the floor. The mini tree lay there, roots naked and exposed.

TWENTY-SEVEN

Mia placed one of Jade's farmers market flower arrangements on the dresser in the bedroom.

Presley entered. "I put away some of the groceries."

"Do you deserve a prize?" Mia's tone was snarky.

"I do!" Presley exclaimed. "The first shower. I gave *you* the first shower for doing something you'd never done before here when you racked up the most likes. I've never put away the groceries, so I'm giving myself a prize."

"Why have you been such a bitch to me?"

"I'm not being a bitch. I'm giving you space to grow." Presley's sarcasm was thick. "Grow your social media, grow your relationship with Lyndon. The only reason you're getting anywhere is because I'm letting you."

"You're letting me?" exclaimed Mia.

"Yes," replied Presley. "I *gave* you the dress."

"And I thanked you. But I did the work." Mia put her hand on the sewing machine.

"You cut-and-pasted."

"What's your problem, Presley?"

"My problem is . . ." Presley took a deep breath. "I need a shower." She removed her clothes, dropped them on her bed, and disappeared into the bathroom. Mia shook her head, her mouth agape. While the water ran in the bathroom, she sat on her bed and opened Skype. She clicked on the photo of her mom, who answered after two rings. Kathryn lay in bed, wearing a Boston College Eagles hoodie with a wool comforter pulled up under her arms.

"Are you okay?" Kathryn's question was immediate. "I saw the news."

"Mom, yes. Everyone here is fine."

"Nantucket is only fourteen miles long! A fire could spread."

"It could, but it didn't."

"Thank God."

Mia perked up. She wasn't going to let Presley make this day any worse. "Want to hear some good news?"

"Always."

Mia beamed. "Lyndon Wyld is going to sell a dress that I designed."

"That's incredible, baby!" Kathryn's eyes lit up against her pale skin.

"You would love the fringe, Mom. I'll make sure to get not just one, but two in your size."

"I'm a zero now." Kathryn made an "0" with her fingers. "I have to shop in the kids' department. Those fashionistas you're hanging out with would be jealous."

"I'm not jealous," said Mia. "I'm worried."

Sean came into frame, handing his mom a glass of water and a rainbow collection of pills.

"You'd better be eating Sean's food, Mom," chided Mia. "I know he's cooking for you."

"I made spaghetti tonight," said Sean. "Grandma's magic sauce."

"We're on the same wavelength." Mia exchanged a bittersweet look with her brother. "I'm making it tomorrow night. I lost a bet."

The water turned off in the bathroom.

"It wasn't a big a hit here." Sean side-eyed their mom.

"Mom, you have to eat." Mia pushed in closer to her laptop camera to make her point.

"I'm trying," said Kathryn.

"Try harder, please."

Kathryn changed the subject. "I'm so proud of you, honey. You're incredibly talented and now the world gets to see it." Kathryn turned to Sean. "Aren't you proud of your sister?"

Presley exited the bathroom, hair wet, wrapped in a towel. "Oh, hi!" she said, ensuring that she was in the Skype screen for Sean to see. "Don't mind me."

"This is Presley." Mia nodded back to Presley.

"Good to meet you, Presley." Kathryn smiled.

"I can see where Mia gets her beautiful eyes," chimed Presley.

"You're sweet," said Kathryn.

"There's a whole family resemblance, that's for darn sure." Presley gestured to the screen. Sean glanced down and shook his head with a dry chuckle, then looked back up. Presley pulled a sheer nightie out of the dresser and held it up, stepping into the screen's frame. "Well, I'm gonna get ready for bed."

"Somewhere else, of course," said Mia, prompting.

"I hope I get to meet y'all soon in person." Presley offered up a "toodles" wave, then traipsed back into the bathroom.

"And by get ready, she means *selfie-ready*." Mia mimed applying cosmetics to her face.

"She seems nice," Sean said flatly.

"From *your* selfies, it looks like you're having an amazing time." Kathryn beamed. She took a deep breath and closed her eyes for a beat, then smiled. "I should let you go. You probably have tons to do tomorrow. You must be getting ready for the Fourth of July there. I'm sure it's huge on Nantucket."

"It is." Mia's stomach twisted with guilt. "What are you both doing?"

"Ordering in barbecue from AK's, watching *Stand by Me*." said Sean.

"No Red Devils out front this year?" asked Mia.

"Nope," said Sean wearily. Mia noticed the dark circles under his eyes.

"Those are dangerous anyway." Kathryn furrowed her brow at Sean. "Remember when you almost lost a finger?"

"Not the important finger." He flipped off Mia. She returned the gesture. This was usually done in jest, but as Sean kept his middle finger up, his jaw was hard.

"Okay. Well, I miss you both," Mia said. "Let's talk soon."

Mia and Kathryn blew each other kisses. Sean clicked off.

Mia could see the Lyndon Wyld icon still active on Skype. She looked back at the bathroom door. The water was still running. She held her breath and pressed the button. The Skype bell rang five times. Mia reached out to click off when Lyndon answered.

"Lyndon, hi!"

"Mia, my darling." Lyndon's brow knit. "Are you all right? Grace just went home. Do you need to speak with her, too?"

"No, I'm fine," replied Mia. She pulled one of the decorative pillows onto her lap. "I didn't get the chance to tell you how grateful I am for the opportunity with the dress."

"You deserve it! It's a brilliant piece," said Lyndon. "I'm sure Grace told you how much I adore it."

"I'm so glad. That's a huge compliment." Mia twisted the etched silver ring on her forefinger. "I was thinking . . . what if I did a photo shoot?"

"With the group?"

"Maybe with one other person . . ." Mia paused. "Like Cole."

"I loved what you did together on the Solstice Soiree runway." Lyndon clapped her hands together. "A photo shoot would be smashing!"

Mia smiled.

"While I have you on the phone . . ." Lyndon's mood sobered again. "Did you see what happened with Otto at last week's party? Grace and I had already left, so we're trying to get a handle on it."

Mia pulled the pillow in tighter. "I didn't."

"Has he been harassing you?"

"No."

"If anybody ever makes you uncomfortable or you see something that you think isn't right, you know you can tell me." Lyndon leaned into the screen.

Mia heard the blow dryer go on in the bathroom. "You'll probably say that it's not my business," continued Mia.

"If you feel like it's your business, it is," said Lyndon. "And if it's your business, it's *my* business."

Mia blurted the words. "I saw bruises on Ruby."

"Ruby?" Lyndon looked confused.

"Ruby Taylor, the Wear National brand ambassador I know."

"I would ask you how you saw these bruises except I know how that girl dresses," remarked Lyndon. "She doesn't leave much to the imagination."

"It worries me," said Mia. "She's gone through rough stuff in her past. I think some abuse. I hope it isn't happening here."

"Has Grant gotten his paws on her?"

Mia paused. "No."

"Although Ruby is not really my problem, I'll hurt Grant if he's an insufferable wanker to any woman or man on this island. He's already been in one scrap that's all over the Internet." Lyndon huffed. "Or I'll send Grace to hurt him, which is worse." Lyndon gave a dry chuckle.

"I honestly think he's more bark than bite," said Mia.

"I hope you're right," said Lyndon. Mia felt her smartphone buzz once in her lap. She glanced down. It was a text from Sean:

They can't just make a dress u designed. Using u.

"Grace e-mailed you the contract for your dress," said Lyndon. "It's very exciting."

"It is." Mia smiled at Lyndon, putting her phone screen-side down on the bed.

"Read it. Take your time," replied Lyndon. "But not too much time. And thank you for the information about the Wear National girl. Everyone should feel safe there." Lyndon leaned close. "Between you and me, the only way that will really happen is if Otto is voted off the island."

Mia forced out a laugh, but the conversation made her squirm.

"Let us know what you think of the terms for your dress." Lyndon waved and clicked off. The Skype session ended. Mia checked her e-mail and found one from Grace:

Mia—
    This is the start of something huge! We'll need all the appropriate documentation, including your driver's license and social security number, but don't fret about that now.
    Cheers,
    Grace

Mia's brow knit as her eyes fell on the words "don't fret." She opened the PDF attachment—the contract. She skimmed it and got the gist. This deal was exposure versus pay. At least the dress would bear her name. She thought about what Lyndon said: *"your dress."* But it wouldn't be her dress anymore. Lyndon Wyld would own it. She closed the document, put her laptop to the side, and looked out the window.

Presley exited the bathroom in her nightie. Her hair was coiffed and her makeup done. Her eyes went to the closed laptop and she sighed. She pulled down the comforter on her bed and slid inside the sheets, then picked up her pink satin sleep mask from the nightstand.

"Is your brother as smart as he is handsome? Because when you have looks and no brain, you've got . . . well . . ." She raised a shoulder. "Grant."

Mia considered Sean's text. "Yes, he's smart. Why does it matter? He's in Boston." Mia lowered her voice. "I thought you were seeing Mac."

"You thought wrong." Presley's eyes welled for a beat, but she quickly covered them with her sleep mask, slid down in bed, and turned away. Mia stared at her, then pulled her laptop back on her lap and opened the contract.

TWENTY-EIGHT

Mia walked on the beach all morning, thinking about the paperwork for her dress. Stepping back onto the estate's deck, she washed her sandy feet off with the hose in the white ceramic pot and stomped them on the LW welcome mat. She looked through the glass French doors and saw Jill and Cole talking next to a large box from the store.

"Great," she muttered to herself, then entered.

"Lyndon wants you to post a virtual July Fourth greeting card on the brand's Instagram," explained Jill. "There's swimwear inside." She patted the top of the box, then looked at Mia.

"You can keep your pick."

Vincent entered, surveying his camera bag for lenses. "I have plans!" He looked at the group and rubbed his hands together excitedly. "First, I'm going to shoot a seasonaires' pyramid on the beach."

"Have fun." Jill looked at Cole. "See ya." She left.

Cole looked at Mia. "We need scissors or a knife, something sharp."

"Yup," replied Mia. "We do."

Grant bounded in, seeing the box. "Swag! I want to open it!" He ripped the box open with his bare hands to find bikinis and board shorts in red, white, and blue. "Sweet!"

Presley, Jade, and J.P. entered. Presley went directly to the box. "Ooh, treats." She sifted through it and pulled out a string bikini top.

J.P. was reading his iPad. "Did you read the news about the MTV series?"

"I don't need to read the news. I *am* the news." Jade sat on the couch and threw her long legs over the arm.

"Oh, wow," scoffed Mia.

"I didn't mean it that way," explained Jade. "My dad is doing an MTV series with Otto Hahn."

"What?" Presley held the bikini top up to her chest in the mirror over the mantel.

"It starts filming next summer," said Vincent, snapping close-ups of all the hands sifting through the styles.

"Lyndon can't be very happy about that," said Mia.

"No one is going to watch that garbage if it includes Wear National," said Presley. "That name brings down everyone in association with it."

"It's a one-billion-dollar company," said J.P. "Your personal opinion is not the collective opinion."

"But mine is the only one that counts." Presley pulled out a one-piece with red, white and blue crochet in the center.

Jade grabbed a two-piece. "My dad can't be brought down." She changed from her T-shirt into the bikini top right there. "He's untouchable."

"We have more appeal in one Instagram post than they'll have in an entire TV series. Let's show Lyndon we can sell it."

Presley turned to Mia, who was standing at the French doors, staring out at the beach. "Mia's gonna sell it because she's got the most skin in the game. She got her contract for *the* dress last night."

Mia glared at Presley, who wore that pageant grin. There was only one way Presley could've known about the contract.

"That's awesome, Mia." Cole offered up a genuine smile. "Congratulations!"

Mia shifted her feet under all their gazes as she stood across the room, separate from them.

After they changed into the suits and made their way to the beach, they formed their pyramid. The three guys were on all fours at the bottom, with Presley and Jade on the second level, and Mia, being the smallest, on the top. They put on their brightest smiles as Vincent snapped photos. They were a picture of the American dream on America's biggest day.

"*Fini!*" shouted Vincent with the last shot.

They collapsed the pyramid into the sand, laughing.

Mia and Cole started to roughhouse in the sand. Cole tickled her. His smartphone slipped from his pocket. Mia noticed he had received a text from "Unknown" and no preview showed. Cole picked up the phone, his thumb hitting the Home button. The screen opened to the text:

We r close.

Mia saw it. She stopped laughing.

Cole pushed the phone back into his shorts' pocket as if nothing had happened. "What's wrong?"

"I don't like being tickled." Mia wasn't lying. Being tickled made her feel like she couldn't breathe, but for some reason, until she'd seen the text, it wasn't so bad with Cole. Brushing the sand off, she got to her feet and walked toward the estate.

Cole threw his hands in the air and flopped back in the sand. "Where are you going?"

"I have dinner to cook."

"My Phillies-win din!" Grant threw his arms in the air.

"It's not attractive to gloat," said Presley, kicking water at him.

Jade laughed. "That's funny coming from you."

"Guys, let's get some shots diving off the dock," said Vincent.

"Dock out with our cock out!" yelled Grant. He took off toward the estate's private dock.

"I don't need a dock to see that," Jade said to J.P.

In the kitchen, Mia looked through Cole's Instagram, which, oddly enough, didn't go back much past the start of the season. She smiled when she saw she had been tagged in several posts. Her smile disappeared when she found an Instagram post from the Summer Solstice Soiree with @stilljilll, arm-in-arm on the dance floor. But there were no others with Jill. As much as she hated herself for doing it, she found Jill's Instagram. There were four posts with Cole and a few with people Mia didn't know at the store and in town. The one-to-four ratio made Mia believe that Cole and Jill had a "thing," but that the thing meant more to Jill.

Or that's what Mia wanted to believe.

"I can boil water," said a spun-sugar voice.

Mia turned to see Presley. Jade was by her side. Mia clicked off her phone as Presley pulled a large pot off a hook.

"I'll chop," said Jade, grabbing a knife from the knife block.

"Let's get cooking." Mia pulled vegetables out of the refrigerator.

At the dock, Vincent took advantage of the late afternoon sun, letting the rays streak across his photos of the three guys, who drank beers and jumped. As the bottles drained, the water play got fancy. Cole did a cannonball. J.P. jackknifed. With his back turned toward the harbor, Grant hollered and threw himself backward, tucking in his knees and doing a flip.

Cole took a selfie with J.P., and Grant photobombed from the water. Cole posted on Instagram:

Divebomb. #BeWyld #bromance

Grant climbed out.

"I give that backflip a six," remarked Vincent, chuckling.

"Oh, really? You can do better?" Grant raised his eyebrows in a challenge.

"I can, but I'm doing my job here." Vincent wiped a splash of water from his camera lens.

"How about if we get a photo of *you* showing *us* how diving is done," said Grant.

"Lyndon *did* say we should live life to the fullest," added J.P. with a grin.

"Ooh. Peer pressure?" Cole gave a good-natured shrug at Vincent.

"I'm a decade older than all of you, so you're not my peers," said Vincent, handing Cole his camera. "But being the elder statesman here, I'm compelled to prove myself."

Vincent slipped off his loafers and removed his shirt. He was lean, his body hairless. Wearing just his calf-length linen shorts, he stepped to the edge of the dock. He motioned to Cole. "*You* can take the shot," he said.

"You think I'll drop your precious baby?" said Grant, mock offended.

"*Absolument.*"

Mia walked down the dock to them, holding a chilled six-pack. "Thirsty?"

Cole turned to see her and snapped a photo.

"Hey, I'm pretty good at this," he said.

Mia looked at the photo. "My eyes are closed. Don't quit your day job."

Cole furrowed his brow.

"Mia's got an eye. Let her take the photo," said Vincent, shaking out his legs like an Olympic diver.

Cole handed Mia the camera.

Vincent took a deep breath and dove off the dock, slicing the water with barely a splash. Mia got three action shots. After a beat, Vincent resurfaced, wearing a triumphant grin.

Grant kneeled on the dock. "An eight, if I'm gonna be generous."

Vincent climbed his way back up. Lifting his leg onto the dock, he froze in pain. "*Merde!*"

Mia rushed over. "You okay, Vincent?"

"My back," croaked Vincent. Grant and Cole helped him the rest of the way.

"But you nailed the dive!" exclaimed Grant.

"Fucking right I did." Vincent put his hand to his lower back.

They returned to the estate with J.P. and Cole supporting Vincent on either side.

"I've got something that'll help," said Grant, bolting into the main house.

Mia, Cole, and J.P. escorted Vincent to the guest cottage.

"I'm okay." Vincent waved them off at his door.

"You sure?" asked Mia.

Vincent nodded. "Thank you. I just need to rest." He disappeared inside. Mia, Cole, and J.P. walked off.

"It was actually an amazing dive," said J.P.

Grant ran back out, passing them. He flashed the two pills in his hand. "Doctor Feelgood on call."

"I didn't know you had a medical degree," said Cole.

"You don't need one around here." Grant continued jogging to the guest cottage.

"Supper's almost ready," Mia called after him. When she, Cole, and J.P. disappeared into the main house, Grant knocked on the guest cottage door. Vincent opened it.

"Hey," Grant said, breathless.

"Hey," Vincent replied with an eye roll and a smile. He motioned Grant inside. "Take your sandals off."

TWENTY-NINE

The sunset cast an orange-pink glow to the deck. Mia, Jade, and Presley had set the table, Jade sprinkling blooms along it from the farmers market. J.P. brought up three bottles of rosé from the wine cellar. Still missing Grant and Vincent, the others sat, staring at the meal, which included a giant, delicious-looking platter of pasta with marinara sauce.

Mia avoided Cole's gaze.

"You're so fucking lucky, Mia," said J.P. "There never seems to be a good time to talk business with Lyndon or Grace."

"Not everyone wants to hear about your caps." Jade took a sip of wine.

"Hats," corrected J.P.

"Potato, potahto." Jade shrugged.

Presley looked at the time on her smartphone. "Well, this is rude."

"Maybe Grant's taking a shower," said J.P.

"He does take really long showers." Cole nodded.

Mia stood and topped a plate with spaghetti and salad. "Vincent should rest. I'm going to bring him some food." She grabbed utensils and a monogrammed napkin and walked with it all to the guest cottage. She knocked on the door.

"Vincent, I have food for you."

There was no answer. After a beat, Mia placed the tray on the wicker table between two matching chairs on the small porch. Beneath the table were Grant's flip-flops. She looked at them curiously and made her way back to the main house, joining everyone else on the deck.

Presley put food on her plate. "According to Miss Manners, you can start eating before everyone arrives if the food is hot."

"It's probably not hot anymore." Jade tilted her empty wineglass.

"I think it's fine." Mia looked distracted while she uncorked the wine and poured a glass for Jade. Cole put spaghetti on his plate and tucked into it.

"Compliments to the chef," he said, wiping his mouth with his napkin.

"Thank you," said Mia, sitting between Presley and Cole.

Grant leapt out onto the deck from the house, painkiller buzz going. He poured himself a generous glass of rosé and drank thirstily. Pulling over the platter of pasta, he scooped a mound onto his plate, then dug in before sitting down. He took a chair next to Cole, who eyed him.

"Mia, this almost Lenny Dykstra–worthy," he said, mouth full.

"'Almost?' How long are you going to rub it in?" Mia threw a hunk of ciabatta at him. He ducked and it flew off the deck. A seagull swooped in and pecked at it.

"I'll rub it in as long as the Sox lose, which will be often." Grant took another bite.

Vincent hobbled in to take photos, still clearly in pain.

"What are you doing, Vincent?" asked Mia, concerned. "You should be in bed, resting and eating the supper I left you." She pointed to the marinara sauce. "According to my grandmother, this sauce has magic healing powers." What she didn't say was that the sauce didn't heal her mom.

"I've got a job to do here," said Vincent.

He gingerly knelt down to take a photo of J.P. and Cole toasting. Mia noticed two red marks on the side of his neck, barely covered by a linen scarf. She flashed on Ruby's bruises.

"Nice hickey," said Presley, noticing as well.

"It's not a hickey." Vincent adjusted the scarf. "I grazed the dock pylon I shimmied up after my celebrated dive." He continued to snap photos. "Who gives hickeys anyway? They are not sexy."

Mia tried not to stare. She turned her focus to Grant, who was devouring his spaghetti like it was his last meal, and she remembered him walking up the beach that night of the Summer Solstice Soiree.

"We're finally starting to feel like a little family, aren't we?" Presley grinned at the others. "Families fight but we always make up." She gave Mia's hair a stroke. "My mama and daddy would practically kill each other, but next thing you knew they were kissing and carrying on. Neither would ever abandon ship, though sometimes we wished they would."

"Do you believe in unconditional love?" Mia posed the question to the table.

"Fuck, no." Presley took Mia's finished plate, elbowing Grant in the shoulder as she passed. "Help me clear. I'm being helpful this week, and it's the least you could do."

"What? That's not part of the deal," whined Grant as he looked at Mia.

"Your bet was with Mia, not me. I always win," said Presley.

Grant dragged himself up and dutifully gathered plates.

"I shopped, I cooked, I conquered." Jade rose. "Now, I'm taking a bath." She sashayed inside.

"I've got work to do." J.P. followed her, passing Grant and Presley.

"Is that code for 'sex'?" Presley asked him. "Because Lord knows, she makes you work for it."

"No, I really have work-work," replied J.P.

Vincent took a photo of the three at the French doors. "This is an image booster. Hashtag 'Work.' Hashtag 'Not Spoiled.' Hashtag 'We Do Windows.'"

"Hashtag 'Bite Me.'" J.P. retorted. He and Vincent chuckled as Grant went inside with Presley.

She turned to him. "Now I know why you haven't tried to hook up with me."

"Because you're not my type?" said Grant.

"Exactly." Presley strutted into the kitchen.

Mia caught Grant's glance at Vincent, who stepped off the deck.

"I'm going to capture this sunset." Vincent left Mia and Cole alone.

Mia swirled the wine around in her glass, staring into the pink whirlpool. Cole leaned toward her.

"Are you going to give me the silent treatment all night?" asked Cole.

"You don't have to sit with me, Cole," said Mia.

"Where else would I go?"

Mia looked around. "To meet Jill."

"She lives in Barnstable," answered Cole. "Takes the ferry out here to work."

"That's inconvenient, since you're getting close." Mia heard Presley's bitchiness in her own voice. She shut her eyes.

Cole leaned into her. "Jill and I aren't hooking up, Mia."

"You don't need to explain anything to me." Mia meant it. She felt bad enough that she'd stalked Jill's Instagram.

"I don't need to but I want to." Cole put his palms on the table. "Jill has become a good friend, but you've seen us. There's no chemistry."

"Cole, honestly, I haven't given much thought to your chemistry."

"Jill isn't interested in my type," said Cole.

"That's hard to believe," scoffed Mia. "What type interests her?"

"*Your* type," answered Cole.

Mia's face flushed as this information registered. "Oh." She felt like an ass.

"I promised myself that I wouldn't get involved with anyone this summer." Cole looked into Mia's eyes. "But I like you, Mia."

Mia finished off her wine. "Do you want to do a photo shoot with me tomorrow?"

Cole nodded. "I do."

"I do, too." Mia and Cole turned to Presley, walking out on the deck with dessert.

THIRTY

I don't understand why you get to do this photo shoot alone." Presley rushed from the house after Mia, who was striding to the G wearing the Mia dress that Nadege, the housekeeper, had handwashed and pressed after its soak in the sea. She had it paired with ribbed black tights and black riding boots that Lyndon had sent overnight, which gave the ensemble an avant-garde edge.

"I'm not alone. I'm doing it with Cole." Mia had done her makeup by herself in the bathroom. She looked fresh and pretty.

Vincent was in the car's driver's seat while Cole was in the back, wearing a Lyndon Wyld chambray button-down, jeans, and laced boots.

"You're a city girl," scoffed Presley. "I'll bet you don't even like horses."

"Every girl loves horses," replied Mia. "I've never seen one in person, but now is my chance."

"Who came up with this idea?"

Mia stopped and looked at Presley. "I did. Vincent thought of a location that would make my dress pop. And the powers that be were on board."

"Oh." Presley stood there stunned as Mia climbed into the car next to Cole.

"Off to greener pastures," said Cole.

Vincent motored them out of the driveway. Mia didn't look back. They ventured to the opposite side of the island, where the estates were spread out so far, each was like its own fiefdom. The car continued onto a private peninsula.

"This isn't even on the map anymore," noted Vincent. "It used to be called Brock's Lookout. A friend of Lyndon's owns it as a retreat, some manufacturing tycoon. It's seventy acres."

"What?" Mia gasped.

"There's nothing else like it on Nantucket," remarked Vincent.

The sprawling compound sat on a hilltop, with crystal waterfront on three sides. The G crossed a wooden bridge over a salt marsh and reached an electronic gate, where an old barn had been artfully turned into a gatehouse. The guard walked up to Vincent.

"We're here for the Lyndon Wyld shoot," said Vincent.

The guard motioned them on. Along the driveway were two lush green pastures where several horses wandered. In the distance sat the expansive main house, with three separate guest houses. Vincent parked by the stables, which bustled with several groomers, handlers, and stall cleaners. He, Mia, and Cole got out of the car.

"Somehow I thought it would smell worse here." Mia inhaled the scent of fresh hay mingled with sea.

While Vincent prepared his cameras for the shoot, a trainer brought around a majestic horse with a coat that looked like silver crushed velvet.

"Beautiful!" exclaimed Mia.

"This is Granite," said the trainer. "He's a gelding."

"What's a gelding?" Mia inched closer to the horse.

"He's neutered." The trainer stroked Granite's neck. "Geldings are easier to train than stallions."

Cole covered his crotch with his hands, which made Mia laugh.

Mia gently caressed the horse's nose. "Hi, Granite."

Cole pet Granite's neck. The horse lifted his snout as if to demand they continue pampering him.

"I went to summer camp, but I think those horses were actually mules, because they looked nothing like this," said Cole.

"I'll help you up." The trainer motioned to Mia.

"Where's the saddle?" Mia looked at Granite.

"You'll have a bridle but no saddle."

"It'll look better in the photos," added Vincent. "Bareback, like Lady Godiva."

"Except I'll be wearing clothes," Mia chuckled. "And I've never been on a horse, with or without a saddle."

The trainer placed a mahogany mounting block next to Granite and motioned Cole to climb on first.

"Wait." Vincent unbuttoned Cole's shirt. Cole gave a good-natured head shake at Mia and mounted the horse. With the trainer's help, Mia climbed on next, sitting in front of Cole. Cole put his hands on her hips to make sure she felt secure before they moved.

"You good?"

Mia nodded, though inside she was scared to death on this giant creature that could buck or run off any second. Petting him was one thing. Riding him was another.

The trainer got on a black-and-white-speckled Appaloosa that Granite knew to follow. Once they reached the pasture, he offered simple instructions. "Release your lower body and move with Granite. When you think 'walk' he'll walk. When you think 'stop' he'll stop. If you relax, he'll relax. He can feel your heartbeat."

Mia could feel Cole's in his chest against her back. It was steady, but he always seemed confident, even when he claimed he wasn't. His humility wasn't disingenuous. It was the difference between insecure and cocky, and that place in the middle attracted Mia.

They walked the horses easily around the wide-open space overlooking the water. The Mia dress was a vibrant contrast to the horse's silver coat, picking up the grass's woodsy hues. Mia's hair was loose, her expression relaxing as she let her body ease into Granite's languid stride.

Vincent jogged around them, his feet light on the ground, snapping photos. He called out directions: "Put your arms around her," "Lean your head back against him," "Put your hand on her thigh," interspersed with *"Ah, oui!," "Incroyable!," "C'est magique!"*

With Cole behind her, holding her, Mia felt safe and free at the same time. Seeing their growing comfort level, the trainer moved them into a graceful run. Mia let out an exhilarated whoop, beaming. She and Cole laughed. Vincent caught it all on film.

Hours passed like lightning and the shoot came to an end. Mia and Cole said goodbye to Granite and thanked the trainer. While Mia reviewed Vincent's photos by the stable, Cole sat on the wood fence yards away, watching the horses in the pasture. The caramel, coffee, ink black, and white colors of the herd knit seamlessly with the wild nature that extended for acres around them. Mia pulled her smartphone from her black faux suede purse and snapped Cole with the horses in the distance. She posted to her Insta Story, tagging him.

Nature boy @motorcityfitz #BeWyld #ride

Vincent looked at the photo. "See, you *do* have a good eye," he said. "Is your hearing as sharp?"

"What do you mean?" asked Mia.

"I know you came by the other night with dinner for me after my little dock incident." Vincent touched his lower back. "I had familiar company."

"I wanted to see if you were okay," replied Mia, fingering one of her pearl earrings. "I wasn't trying to intrude."

"I know that privacy isn't de rigueur in our line of business, but I appreciate that you respected mine," said Vincent.

"No worries." Mia smiled.

"Lyndon doesn't have to know about *everything*." Vincent noted Cole glancing Mia's way.

"Like you said, isn't the whole point of this job for everyone to know everything?" asked Mia.

"It shouldn't be," answered Vincent as Cole approached. "You two should wander for a bit." He motioned around. "It's spectacular." He walked in the opposite direction. "I'm going to. I'll be back in an hour to drive us back."

Mia and Cole walked the grounds, meandering to the wide cliffs overlooking the beach.

"Since the fire, you've seemed a little distracted," said Cole.

"Jade and I saw it." Mia's eyes were on the clear blue horizon.

"You did?" replied Cole.

"I watched the paramedics put Quentin in the ambulance. His burns were—" Mia shook her head, trying to expel the memory.

"It's sad." Cole picked up a stone and chucked it off the cliff. "No one comes here and thinks they'll end up going home like that. I wonder how the others are holding up. You're friends with Ruby."

"I haven't talked to her." Mia picked bark off the tree. "She's . . . sweet, sincere."

"My friends were stoners like her—good guys. I smoked a lot of weed in high school, but that got boring afterward. They fell into other shit and went a direction I didn't want to go in." Cole chuckled, kicking some leaves. "I don't know what direction I'm going, except that I know it's not theirs."

Mia spun around. "I know what direction I want to go."

"Fashion." Cole motioned to Mia's dress. "And you're doing it!"

"I mean right now." Mia twirled. "I want to go to the stable and visit Granite." She skipped off. Cole caught up with her and took her hand. They ran toward the stable, laughing.

The twelve-stall stable was an architectural masterpiece of curved wood ceilings with stainless steel pendant lamps hanging from the beams across. Wrought iron gates with picture-frame windows let the horses peer out into the center aisle, where Mia and Cole strolled. The workers and trainers had left the barn immaculate for its equine occupants, who were calmly munching hay and resting.

"This is way nicer than most apartments in Southie," said Mia. "I feel more comfortable here than at the estate."

"Horses don't judge."

"Or at least we can't hear them judging." Mia caressed the nose of a snow-white stallion. She whispered, "Are you judging us?"

"I know I said you've seemed distracted." Cole watched Mia. "But today, you looked really happy. It was nice to see."

"I was. I am." Mia turned to him. *Those damn green eyes*, Mia thought as Cole peered right into her soul.

Cole continued, "Because sometimes you have this look, Mia, like you're ready for the rug to be pulled out from under you. How come?"

"I don't know." But Mia *did* know. Her dad had read her bedtime stories and checked for monsters in the closet. He kissed her bad dreams away. Then he left her. Trevor had constantly told her he wanted to protect her when they were together. Then he cheated on her and lied about it. And her mom showered her with as much love as any mom could, but she was going to die. Mia understood that the rug got pulled.

"You didn't get *lucky*, like J.P. said at dinner." Cole brushed a lock of hair from Mia's face. "You earned your place here. Try and enjoy it."

"Okay, I will." Mia kissed him. His lips melted into hers, their tongues finding each other. With their arms wrapped, they felt and fumbled their way into the open empty stall at the end of the barn. It was filled with fresh hay waiting for a new gelding or stallion. Mia pulled Cole's shirt off and unbuttoned his jeans. She let him undress her. Her hands made their way down his body. His hands felt strong on her. They made love.

Afterward, they rested in the bed of hay, their breath slowing. They could hear a horse's neigh and another one's snort.

"They're judging us," said Mia.

"Do you care?" Cole pulled her close.

"Nope." Mia kissed him.

THIRTY-ONE

The July 4 *Wall Street Journal*'s website headline read:

LYNDON WYLD WILDLY MISSES ANALYSTS ESTIMATE FOR

YEAR-END RESULTS.

PROFITS DOWN 30%

Lyndon punched the "x" on the window tab to close the page. She picked up her smartphone next to the tea cup on her tray and looked at her brand's Instagram. Her seasonaires, in playful pyramid formation, were filtered and Photoshopped to look more like the ideal American melting pot dream than ever before. The caption read:

Have a Wyld Fourth! #BeWyld #WyldFourth
#dreamlife

She turned to stare out her private plane's window, her expression tense. All she could see were clouds.

———

Mia and Jade stood on the deck, polishing off the strawberry-blueberry mojitos Grant had concocted. Jade looked at the Instagram post as Mia gazed out at the three layers: dark blue water topped with a ribbon of burnt sienna, then the clear azure sky. A sea plane waited at the end of the dock. Its propellers churned up the water.

"Last chance," said Jade, singsong, giving Mia's shoulder a light bump. "Our fireworks are better."

"Thank you for the invitation, but I'm good here," replied Mia.

The other seasonaires were inside the estate, getting dressed for the night's Rabbit Hole festivities. J.P. stepped out, holding his iPad. He repositioned his straw fedora with its indigo grosgrain band and the Perch bird logo.

Jade tilted the hat slightly. "Better."

"Have a blast tonight, Mia." J.P. kissed Mia on the cheek.

"You, too," said Mia.

Jade pulled a small box wrapped with a red, white, and blue bow out of her sapphire sequin clutch and handed it to Mia. "Happy Independence Day."

Mia was surprised. "What is this?"

Jade shrugged as she and J.P. walked to the dock. Mia waved, then opened the box. It was the long necklace with the green sea glass pendant she had seen when she went to the farmers market with Jade. She softly gasped. Jade smiled at her from the dock as she and J.P. got in the seaplane, which took off.

"Lyndon is gonna flip a shit," said Presley, who was putting in a diamond stud earring as she stepped out. They watched the plane ascend.

"I don't think Jade cares," said Mia.

"And J.P. will do anything to meet Maz." Presley looked over Mia's shoulder at the necklace in its box. "That's cute." Mia put it on and took an Instagram selfie, tagging Jade:

Happy mermaid tears. Thank u @1jaded.1 #BeWyld
#surprise #notcheesy

Presley touched the smooth gem that hung above the second button of Mia's white Lyndon Wyld cardigan, fastened over a red gingham strapless dress. Mia had replaced the original buttons with ones bearing hand-painted American flags.

Presley fingered her own pearl choker. "I don't wear long necklaces because they always get caught when I lean over."

Grant met them with three pink-and-blue mojitos. "Lean over who?" he snickered.

"Wouldn't you like to know," responded Presley. She tapped one of the artful buttons on Mia's cardigan. "I saw you painting those. Maybe Lyndon will dub this 'the Mia sweater.'"

Mia brushed her hand down her cardigan to brush Presley away. "I get it. You're mad about the photo shoot."

"Do I look mad?" Presley's face was a mask of practiced cheer.

"You're so passive-aggressive." Mia sipped the final drops of her cocktail from the straw.

"Ladies, let's not fight," said Grant. "Unless there's going to be hair pulling, then go for it."

"I'm not starting petty tussles tonight." Presley hugged Mia.

"Good." Mia softened, lightly embracing Presley.

Presley threw her arms in the air. "It's a night for celebration and fireworks!"

"And getting lit!" Grant handed the girls fresh mojitos.

Mia took one, but Presley put her hand up. "I'm not drinking that—strawberries and blueberries! Do you see what I'm wearing?" She twirled in a white Swiss dot dress that flared at the tops of her thighs.

"More for me," said Grant, drinking two-fisted.

"*God bless America! Land that I love. Stand beside her. And guide her . . .*" Vincent sang as he stepped out and motioned for Grant to contlnue.

"I do *not* know the lyrics, dude," said Grant.

"You're a disgrace to your country." Vincent gave Grant's hair a quick ruffle.

"No shit. Are you hanging with us tonight?" Grant slurped from his straw.

"I'm going to come for a bit, take some photos, then meet friends for a late dinner at the Club Car," replied Vincent.

"What about fireworks?" asked Grant.

"You've seen one finale, you've seen 'em all." Vincent shrugged.

"Adulting is a snoozefest," said Presley. "Who gets sick of fireworks? That's just plain sad."

"It's *your* job to post festivities and fireworks," said Vincent. "Remember, Lyndon wants at least four for your Insta Stories."

"Mia, where's Cole?" asked Grant.

"How would I know?" Mia snapped back.

"You guys are a thing, don't deny it," teased Presley.

"Not a thing." Mia sipped, shifting her eyes away.

Grant yelled at the top of his lungs, up to the second-floor window above them.

"Cole, get the fuck down here and tandem-ride with your thing." He nodded to Mia.

"I'm in the john!" Cole yelled back through the bathroom window.

"He complains that I'm in there for a long time," scoffed Grant to the others. "He takes his phone. I think he's sending dick picks." Grant grabbed Mia's phone from her hand. "To Miiiahhh!"

Mia went to punch low, then grabbed high, getting her phone back. Grant laughed. "Scrappy."

"Maybe he manscapes more meticulously than you." Vincent smirked at Grant.

"Mia? Could that be true?" Grant raised his eyebrows to Mia.

"I wouldn't know," replied Mia. "I haven't seen your mans-caping either, so I can't judge."

Nadege brought out a basket of powdered sugar-coated pastries, placing them on the deck table. "Homemade beignets."

"Nadege, it's a crime that you're working another Fourth of July," said Mia.

"Miss Lyndon always invites us to stay," said Nadege. "The holiday is much nicer here than where we live in Mattapan. People get crazy. The firearms come out in celebration and you never know where the bullets that go up will come down."

"That's kinda what Southie's like tonight, too," said Mia.

Presley put her arm around Nadege. "Nadege's husband brings her three kids." She smiled at Nadege. "They are so darn cute, Nadege."

"I'm leaving most of the beignets up here instead of bringing them down to the beach," said Nadege. "Fireworks and sugar get my babies riled up."

"Oh, you know I will go *HAM* on these later," said Grant, chowing down on one while miming a joint.

"There's no ham in a beignet," said Vincent.

"HAM. Hard as a motherfucker," clarified Grant. "Because these are insaaaaane!" He ate another one.

"They get him riled up, too," Mia chuckled to Nadege. "Enjoy the night with your family."

Cole joined the group. "Let's roll, people!"

"To The Hole!" yelled Grant.

Mia started her Insta Story with a selfie, sitting on the cruiser bike with Presley behind her in the G's passenger seat. She drew a crown on Presley and captioned:

Princess @thenewpresley #WyldFourth

"Get your ass out of that car and bike with us." Grant yelled at Presley.

"I'm not getting overheated," replied Presley. "I'll carry the swag." She held up Lyndon Wyld canvas totes filled with mono-grammed bucket hats and white woven rope bracelets adorned with the words *Free To Be Wyld*.

They passed the beach estates, where revelers were ensconced behind their high hedges at private catered parties, like the one Maz was having in the Hamptons. As they rode closer to town, the saltbox houses were quaintly decorated for barbecues and picnics on the front lawns. Kids giggled and shrieked with glee as they threw their bodies onto Slip 'N Slides, whooshing across. A couple dads gave it a run, too, making guests laugh.

Grant stopped to watch. "I was the king of Slip 'N Slide!" he said to one of the dads.

The dad handed him a beer. "Slurp 'N Slide."

"You're going to look like an idiot going into The Hole com-pletely wet," Mia said to Grant.

"You earned your very own dress contract by being wet," replied Grant.

That shut Mia up. Vincent captured the action shot with Grant in a midair dive while the kids and adults cheered. The look on his face was pure joy. Mia grinned, simultaneously tickled by his all-encompassing lust for life and jealous of it. Some people were made that way and their lives seemed to follow accordingly. After, Grant high-fived the families around him, giving the kids fist bumps. The smile never left his face.

As Mia watched these families celebrate, she thought about her Fourth of Julys when she was a kid, playing around the street's fire hydrant. She had never been purely joyful, like Grant on the Slip 'N Slide, but she had been happy. Her dad had detonated that happiness like a bottle rocket. She looked at Cole and thought about being with him at the photo shoot, in the horse stable. It seemed like a dream. He smiled at her as he laughed at Grant, who climbed back on his bike, his Lyndon Wyld polo shirt soaked. They peddled into town, where people were out in the street, drinking and waving American flags. There seemed to be music coming out of every bar and restaurant, each with its own crowd of party people.

The Rabbit Hole event was already packed when they arrived.

"The party has arrived!" exclaimed Presley, who sashayed inside first, with Grant and Vincent following.

Cole held the door open for Mia. "After you, pretty lady." Mia grinned, absently holding the sea glass pendant.

A DJ was spinning under a Lyndon Wyld branded banner. Many of the millennials had come straight from beach barbecues, volleyball tournaments, and water sports, still in bikinis and board shorts, accessorized with a solid alcohol buzz. The NO SHIRT, NO SHOES, NO SERVICE sign meant nothing tonight. Grant whipped off his wet shirt and fit right in, grabbing two girls and taking a selfie. The other seasonaires were the best dressed there. The merch they passed out was gone in two seconds flat, giving Vincent a snap-worthy sea of partiers dancing and drinking in brand gear.

Presley took a seat at their table. Grant made a beeline for the bar. "We need some drinks!"

Cole looked at Mia, who sat next to Presley. "What can I get you?"

"Will you get me a piña colada?" asked Presley.

"Will you give *me* a blow job?" Grant laughed.

Cole shoved Grant, looking back at Presley and Mia. "We've got it."

Presley refused to look at the bar, where Mac hustled, making drinks with Frank. That hustle didn't stop him from looking at her.

Mia leaned into Presley. "Are you okay?"

"I'm amazing!" Presley pulled her smartphone from her purse. "Let's take a selfie."

Two girls approached in Lyndon Wyld swag bucket hats. Their long matching fishtail braids hung down in the back, like the one Presley demonstrated in her Instagram beauty tutorial before the Summer Solstice Soiree.

"Hi," said the girl with the darker fishtail braid.

"Hi!" exclaimed Presley.

Presley's smile stiffened when she realized the girl was talking to Mia. "Mia, can we take a pic with you?"

As Mia was pulled away, toward a Lyndon Wyld sign with the girls, she shrugged at Presley and mouthed, "Sorry."

Eve stepped up to Presley, holding an empty tray. "What can I get you?"

"I'm good," replied Presley, putting her phone back in her purse.

"Mmmm," Eve squinted at her. "You're really not." She walked off.

Presley squeezed the clasp of her purse shut, her knuckles growing white.

THIRTY-TWO

Maz's house was a seaside Hamptons Modernism masterpiece—all glass, concrete, and wood—designed by an East Coast "starchitect." Its style veered from the historical shaker shingle beach architecture just enough to make Maz a happy anarchist but not enough to cause the neighbors to veto it. The money for their cooperation was well spent. His annual Blue Bash was organized by the world's most sought-after caterers and party planners, with his wife Tatiana's discerning eye on all of it.

Jade and J.P.'s seaplane landed at the dock, fifteen yards from where Maz's thirty-million-dollar yacht sat with its ten decks and reclaimed wood dining table under a ceiling-length Swarovski crystal chandelier. J.P.'s grandfather had a private jet and one of the fastest speedboats in the world, but this yacht trumped those riches.

"That is fucking incredible," said J.P. With his eyes glued to the yacht, he tripped on a rope anchor, but caught himself.

"It's whatever," replied Jade. "We're barely ever on it. My dad has no idea how to drive a boat."

"It's not a boat. It's a yacht," said J.P. "And no one who owns something like that would ever drive it themselves."

Jade shrugged. "Bougie."

Instead of a Red Carpet, a blue one greeted guests from the list that was as star-studded as any awards show. No one dared to attend without matching that carpet.

"Unbelievable!" Everywhere J.P. looked there was another famous celebrity: actors, rappers, pop singers, sports legends, and technology tycoons.

"Your head's going to fall off if you keep whipping it around like that," said Jade, walking ahead of him. She made her way toward the house, kissing supermodels on both cheeks and having her ass grabbed by not just one but two musicians. J.P. was too distracted by the Hollywood wattage to even notice. Jade led him to the M-Kat logo backdrop for some paparazzi photos.

J.P. tried to pull away. "Coming here was risky enough without photos blasted everywhere."

"My dad will be very disappointed if we don't represent," Jade said, nodding to the logo.

"We're supposed to be representing," J.P. whispered to her. "Lyndon Wyld on Nantucket. That's why I don't want to do it."

"So you're going to fuck up this opportunity?" Jade crossed her arms.

J.P. had no choice, so they stepped up and put on media-worthy smiles.

Tatiana saw Jade from the koi pond–bordered doorway, where she stood with two nannies, each holding toddler girls adorned in cornflower blue. Tatiana showcased her forty-four-year-old model-thin body in a tube top and skintight velvet leggings the same color as the cupcake-size sapphire ring on her right hand, which competed with her conflict-free diamond wedding ring set. When Maz and Tatiana met twenty-five years earlier, Tatiana had imparted her social consciousness on her famous beau, whose clothes were rumored to be made by poor São Paulo single mothers and their children. Tatiana ensured the mothers earned fair trade wages and received health care while a school was built for the children. Yet she was the one who liked the yacht.

Tatiana waved to Jade, who came in for a hug and the required air kisses. She held Jade out and surveyed. "You look so thin, baby! I was worried that Lyndon would overfeed you."

J.P. stifled a chuckle, since *his* mother had the opposite worry.

Tatiana continued, "With the exception of Kate Moss, those Brits love their bangers and mash. You'll look incredible at the Victoria's Secret runway show."

"We're going to crush the mother-daughter theme," said Jade.

Jade handed J.P. her phone. "Take a photo, J.P." J.P. took one, the women with their hands on one hip, chests out, inside legs pointed forward. He gave the phone back to Jade, who AirDropped Tatiana the photo. They both posted to Instagram.

Jade:

Like daughter, like mother. @tatianamkat #twinning

Tatiana:

Like mother, like daughter. @1jaded.1 #fuckthehaters

Tatiana finally looked at J.P., who shook her hand. She held his for a moment too long. Jade's face tensed.

"You are much more handsome in person," Tatiana cooed to J.P. She looked at Jade. "Lyndon needs to have Vincent better filter you all."

"We're real life, Mom," said Jade.

"Oh, honey, you are *so* not real life." Tatiana shooed them inside. "Go have fun."

The estate was a blue-hued fantasy down to the menu: blue crab cakes, blue fin tacos, blueberry tarts. The Dom flowed into blue crystal glasses flown in from Murano, Italy, for the occasion. The staff wore navy M-Kat uniforms with sailor hats. A DJ played from the second-story landing—not just any DJ, like The Rabbit Hole local, but one in multimillion-dollar rotation at Las Vegas's hottest nightclubs.

"Perch hats need be part of this next year." J.P. adjusted his straw hat.

"Slow down, tiger," Jade chuckled. "You have the whole night to sell your soul to the devil."

Jade stopped at Skullcrusher and Wrecking Ball, who had dropped her off at the Lyndon Wyld estate. She got lost in their bear hugs.

"Hi, honey. You're looking gorgeous after your time in Lyndonland," said Skullcrusher. His eyes burned into J.P., who immediately started to sweat.

"Welcome!" Wrecking Ball slapped J.P. on the arm. "Be good, you two." The two giant men lumbered off through the crowd.

"You know we won't." Jade grinned.

"That's gonna leave a mark." J.P. rubbed his biceps. "Can we go outside to get some air?" He nodded to the open deck that faced the beach.

"Too much for you already?" teased Jade.

"No, I just want to see who's out there."

But before they could take two steps, they heard the booming velvet voice.

"My princess!" shouted Maz, who approached with his arms wide. He was turned out in a sapphire three-piece suit and blue suede M-Kat kicks.

"One of three," said Jade, giving her dad a kiss on the cheek. No air kisses for Maz. "Hi, Daddy."

Maz spoke low in her ear. "You've been naughty."

"Learned from the best," replied Jade.

Maz shifted his gaze to J.P. "I know you!"

"You do?" J.P.'s eyes went wide in shock.

"How could I not? J.P., you've made quite an impression on my girl. She's told me all about you."

"Really?" J.P. tried not to hyperventilate.

"I hear you have a compelling business opportunity to discuss," said Maz.

"I think you'll like what I have to show you," said J.P., absently touching the brim of his hat.

Maz pointed the way to the foyer. "I have to go make sure that the head of Microsoft is behaving himself. But I'll be back for you."

"All right!" J.P. grinned.

"In the meantime, make yourself at home. Eat, drink, there's lots of networking to be done."

As Maz walked off, Skullcrusher and Wrecking Ball flanked him.

A server stopped with a tray of blue cheese and pear on endive. The cheese's strong smell mixed with J.P.'s nerves. "I feel nauseous."

Jade waved off the server. "No, thank you." She turned to J.P. "Don't worry, baby, you got this." She kissed him deeply, and saw Tatiana watching them from the arch between the foyer and the living room.

"This is the most insane party I've ever been to," J.P. said, scanning the room. "It makes The Rabbit Hole look like Abu Ghraib."

"Yep," replied Jade.

Skullcrusher and Wrecking Ball returned. "Maz wants you up in his office," ordered Skullcrusher to J.P.

J.P. looked at Jade with the excitement of a little boy. "It's happening."

"Kill it," said Jade, touching his arm as he walked off with the men.

Jade watched J.P. wind his way up the floating staircase. The two giant men following him looked like they would sink each step that seemed to be suspended in midair. Jade's smile disappeared as she turned and walked into the nearby bathroom. She shut the door and pulled the vial of coke Otto had given her from her purse and unscrewed the cap. With the diamond-tipped spoon, she lifted a pinch of powder to her nose and sniffed, then pressed her nostril closed. She took a hit in the other nostril, replaced the cap, and put the vial back in her purse. She looked at herself in the mirror with a deadness that said she loathed what she saw.

When she stepped out of the bathroom, Tatiana was waiting for her.

"I bought a new comforter for your bedroom. Red satin, ugly as sin, but you'll like it, since you'll be staying here for the rest of the summer."

Jade didn't argue.

J.P. stepped into Maz's office, which overlooked the property's second pool, surrounded by a private courtyard that was off-limits at the event. When Skullcrusher closed the thick steel door, the party noise ceased as if the room were hermetically sealed. Maz stood at his large oak desk, pruning a bonsai with gold pruning shears.

"Mister . . . Maz . . ." J.P. stuttered. "I don't know what to call you?"

"Have you ever had a bonsai, J.P.?" Maz trimmed.

"I haven't. Come to think of it, I've never had a plant of my own."

"Bonsai is more than a plant." Maz glanced up at him.

J.P. shifted his feet.

"It's an ancient Chinese art form," continued Maz. "My wife introduced me to it. People think it's Japanese, but the Japanese redeveloped it under the influence of Zen Buddhism."

"I didn't know that," said J.P., pushing his thick dark bangs out of his eyes and into the brim of his hat.

"I already have hats in my collection," said Maz.

J.P. straightened. "I know, but you also partner with designers who bring new assets to the table."

"Like Lyndon Wyld?" scoffed Maz. "Everyone knows how that turned out."

"I'm not Lyndon Wyld." J.P. held up his iPad. On the screen was the Perch website. "Perch." He pointed to the logo. "For 'Perchero,' which means—"

"'Hat stand' in Spanish." Maz smiled. "That's clever."

J.P. looked like a little boy being given a "Best Effort" trophy, along with the rest of the team.

Maz continued to shape the bonsai, dropping the tiny trimmings into Wrecking Ball's Godzilla paws. "Bonsai is a particular representation of something much more than itself, letting each person interpret it and build upon it based on their own experiences and memories."

"Like how we wear clothes or accessories," J.P. chimed in. "They're extensions of our own personal style."

Maz tilted his head, appreciating the bonsai's new form. "They're held in such high regard that they're brought into the house, even though they contain dirt from the garden." Maz's smile seemed calculated, teeth bared wide. He looked at J.P.

"I want you to explain yourself to my colleagues here." Maz pointed the shears toward his two hulking lackeys. Then he put them down and left the office.

J.P. looked flummoxed. He stammered to Skullcrusher and Wrecking Ball. "I'm supposed to show you my pitch? Is that like a pre-pitch to him?"

"No. He wants you to show us the video," said Skullcrusher.

"What video?" J.P.'s heart raced.

"You know what video," replied Wrecking Ball. "The one you took of his daughter with that scumbag, Otto Hahn, slobbering all over her. The one you posted on Instagram."

J.P.'s face went white. "I didn't post that."

"It was on your Instagram," said Skullcrusher.

"I know." J.P.'s stammering worsened. "Someone got a hold of my phone and posted it."

The men snickered. "Yeah, right," scoffed Wrecking Ball.

"Even if that were true, why was it on your phone in the first place?" added Skullcrusher.

"I was told to film . . ." J.P. paused. "The party. But I deleted it as soon as I saw it."

"News travels fast," said Wrecking Ball, lifting his smartphone. On it was a screenshot of the Instagram post. "Two hundred thousand views with just as many likes, then shared on Twitter and Facebook."

"But it disappeared once I deleted it," J.P. said breathlessly.

"The toothpaste is out of the tube. People saw it, lots and *lots* of people." Skullcrusher jabbed his smartphone screen.

"Nothing is ever really deleted. You know that," said Wrecking Ball.

"Jade has been popular since the day she was born." Skullcrusher slid his phone in his back pocket. "Everyone wanted to be her. Now everyone wants to be *with* her."

"Maz isn't stoked about that," said Wrecking Ball.

"Jade and I are friends." J.P. lifted his hands. "I wouldn't do anything to hurt her."

"Take off that hat," demanded Skullcrusher.

Shaking, J.P. removed the hat.

"Please. I'm sorry," cried J.P.

"Relax." Skullcrusher took the straw fedora. "I just want to try it on." The hat sat on top of Skullcrusher's bowling ball pate like a

kids' party hat. "You're sorry all right. It's too small for my head."
He shoved it back on J.P. "You should have the hat on anyway.
You know why?"

"Why?" said J.P., the word coming out like a squeak.

"Because your feet are going to be cold."

"Why would they be cold? They are toasty warm in here." J.P.
offered a twitchy smile.

"If you keep your head warm, your feet will stay warm," said
Wrecking Ball. "Take off your shoes."

"I'd prefer to keep them on." J.P. let out a nervous chuckle.
"Hammertoes."

Wrecking Ball lifted J.P. and Skullcrusher snatched off the
M-Kat slip-on sneakers.

"Your toes look nice." Skullcrusher glanced down. "You
wouldn't want anyone to step on them, but you've been stepping
on plenty of toes yourself. Maz don't play that."

Wrecking Ball picked up the gold pruning shears from the desk.

"No. Nonononono, please," J.P. begged, sweat beading on his
upper lip.

"We should remind you that there is an implied nondisclosure
agreement," growled Skullcrusher.

J.P. started to hyperventilate, his eyes darting around in the
hopes that someone would save him. But the room was silent and
the pool courtyard below was empty.

THIRTY-THREE

I can't get her to move," said Mia, standing at the pool table with Cole. She nodded toward Presley across the room, still sitting in the same place, poking her straw in and out of her full piña colada.

Mia and Cole put their empties on the windowsill.

"Every party has a pooper," said Cole, racking up balls. "Are you going to let her ruin your night?"

Mia plucked two pool cues from their clips on the wall. "Nope." She handed a cue to Cole and pulled her smartphone from her pocket. They took a selfie. Mia posted to her Insta Story:

Who will win? #WyldFourth #stripes #solids

Cole looked at Mia's smartphone screen. "Nice photobomb." Ruby was in the background between them, making rock-and-roll devil horns with both her hands, tongue out. Mia turned as Ruby came in for a hug.

"Mia! Where have you been?" exclaimed Ruby. She pulled back to admire Mia's sea glass necklace. "I love that. You have the best taste in jewelry." She jangled her bracelets—one was the thin blue enamel bangle that matched the other three Mia wore. "I haven't seen you since our lighthouse adventure!"

"What lighthouse adventure?" Cole asked Mia, expression curious.

Ruby continued in her drunken slur. "The night of your Summer Soiree, Mia and I went for a swim at Brant Point. Have you been to the lighthouse?"

"Can't say that I have." Cole chalked his pool cue.

"Ooh, you're missing out!" said Ruby. "Mia saved my life there." She grinned broadly at Mia.

"She did?" Cole looked at Mia, both impressed and confused.

"Yes!" Ruby gave Mia another huge hug. She smelled like a distillery. "And because you're such a beautiful person, I brought this for you." She pulled a white capsule from her wood beaded satchel, holding it out for Mia.

Mia squinted at it. "I know some people think it's, you know, YOLO, to take something at a party without asking what it is, but . . . what is it?"

"A treat!" answered Ruby with glee.

"It's Molly," Cole whispered in Mia's ear.

Mia put her hand up. "Thank you for offering, Ruby. I want to be able to kick Cole's ass at pool. We were just going to play." She touched Cole's arm.

"I am the *worst* pool player," said Ruby with a giggle. "Which is why I wasn't here when your charming pal there beat the crap out of Axel."

She nodded to Grant, who was approaching with Presley. Axel was throwing darts nearby, side-eyeing Grant with a scowl.

"That wasn't Grant's finest hour," said Mia. "But to be fair, Axel could have been a little less, um, *showy* as boat captain."

"All in the name of fun. That's what this summer's about, right?" Ruby's spaghetti strap slipped off her shoulder. "I'm going to mingle." She turned and walked straight into Presley.

"Why are you and that other brand skank here?" Presley glared at her. "You have your own party."

"Nice to see you again, too," Ruby grinned. "We have a DJ at ours and I was craving a little live music."

Mac and the band took to the stage and started to tune their instruments.

Ruby passed Grant, who stared at her ass cheeks, peeking out from under her ultra-short WN halter dress hanging over her bikini top.

Presley stared as well, face sneering with disgust. "Remember what Lyndon and Grace said? Underbutt doesn't belong here."

"We're celebrating freedom!" Grant pulled Presley toward the dance floor. "Let's dance."

Cole raised an eyebrow at Mia. "You're a lifesaver, huh?"

"Don't ask," she said.

"It is a little weird that Ruby and Axel are here when Wear National has their own event," said Cole.

Mia watched Ruby wave to Mac, who nodded at her as he turned the tuning keys on his guitar.

"Live music," replied Mia.

"Well, if I can't ask about your lifesaving skills, let me ask you this," said Cole. "You can bat T-shirts with a pool cue but can you actually play pool with one?"

"Hell, yeah," answered Mia with bravado, then a chuckle. "Well, sort of."

"Sort of works." Cole tugged her sweater sleeve. "Let's go."

Mia put the white ball on the dot, leaned over, and broke with fair proficiency.

"Stripes," she called.

Cole smiled, turned on, as Mia landed a couple balls in their intended pockets. He played with skill and focus, though his attraction to Mia was a distraction. Mia took another turn.

"Blue stripe in the corner pocket." She aimed, but stood up, frustrated. "This angle is for math majors with a minor in pool."

"Ever hear of the Ghost Ball Method?" Cole asked her.

Mia shook her head no. Her lips curled in a seductive smile. "Show me."

Cole put his arms around her from behind. In the corner, Vincent snapped a photo of them.

"Align your body up on the line from the object ball to the pocket," Cole directed, his body against Mia's. "Use your imagination to drop that ghost ball into position. Keep your eyes on it, so it doesn't disappear on you. Then shoot straight at it."

Cole backed away slightly so Mia could follow his instructions. The 10 ball dropped in the right corner pocket.

"Bam! Ghost ball!" Mia exclaimed and whipped around, her face in Cole's. She was beaming.

"God, you have an amazing smile." Cole held Mia's waist.

Vincent took another photo. Mia and Cole were aware he was there. They turned to him.

"Want to join?" asked Mia.

"*Non, merci*," said Vincent. "I will leave you all to your excesses in a bit."

Mia slipped to the side of Cole, reached for her piña colada on the nearby wood shelf, and finished it.

"I can't believe we're not enough fun for you, Vincent," joked Cole.

"That's just it," replied Vincent. "You're all *too* much fun for me. I'd like to be cuddled up asleep in my little cottage by midnight." He grinned and walked off. His smile disappeared as he passed Grant, who was dancing with Presley as Mac and the band launched into a rock cover of the Ginuwine's raunchy track, "Pony."

Every move Presley made was for Mac. She would make him want her, though she never looked at him once. Grant didn't give a shit because he was too busy watching Ruby dirty dance with Axel. Both spaghetti straps of her dress had now fallen, so her Wear National string bikini top underneath was in full view.

Eve strode by with drinks on a tray, calling out loudly, "If you go into heat, package your meat!"

Mia was that perfect point of buzzed—relaxed but in control. She let Cole lead her onto the dance floor. He pulled her close and they moved to the beat, their bodies heating up with the pulsing rhythm and the bodies around them. Mia remembered her first slow dance in sixth grade at the Winter Ball. She couldn't recall her partner, only that they barely moved. It was a way to *almost* make out without getting in trouble. But there were no rules here.

After the song ended to massive cheers, they slipped out of the steamy crush, found a pocket of air between a wood pillar and the wall, and kissed. Mia could taste the sweet pineapple and coconut from their piña coladas on Cole's tongue.

"It's time to slow it down and cool it off a little, heathens," said Mac into the mic. Sitting on a stool with his acoustic guitar, he sang Train's "Calling All Angels." The lyrics came out deep, warm, and emotional.

Presley, at the foot of the stage, couldn't help but watch him. She turned to see Ruby swaying nearby, her hands waving in the air. Presley's face was a mass of confusion: longing, sadness, and anger as she turned back to Mac.

Mia and Cole, holding hands, moved closer to the stage. Mia caught Ruby popping the Molly.

Grant passed Ruby his beer. "No need to dry-time it."

Ruby took a swig, swallowed, and passed the bottle back.

"You gonna share with *me* now?" Grant held out his palm. "Got another one?"

"That's not an equal trade." Ruby laughed. "But you know where you can buy some. Everybody does."

"It's only worth it if it's free," said Grant.

"Nothing's free on Nantucket." Ruby's smile was bittersweet.

When Mac finished the song, Ruby whooped and pounded her hands on the stage. Presley weaved her way to the bathroom.

"We'll be back." Mac stood and returned his guitar to its stand. The band left the stage and the DJ resumed. Ruby grabbed Mac's arm as he stepped off. "Post-set smoke?"

"I'm working." Mac pulled away from her and headed to the bar. Ruby's eyes were wide, perplexed.

"I think you need to up your game," Grant said to Ruby, while nodding toward Mac. "You're not going to do that with some local rocker asshat."

"And I'm going to do it with you?"

Suddenly, Ruby's legs buckled underneath her like a ragdoll's. Mia and Cole rushed over, pushing through the crowd. With Grant, they helped her up.

"Ruby, are you okay?" asked Mia.

"I'm so good." Ruby's eyes were slits, her smile slack. "It's just hot in here. I'm gonna go back to the homestead for a skinny dip."

Mia didn't want to let Ruby go, but she didn't want to leave Cole either. She remembered what Presley had said, sitting on the exact same stool where she sat now, also watching them: *"You're not responsible for everyone here. Take care of yourself for once."*

Grant took a step to follow Ruby out. "I'll go with her."

Axel, with his arms around the two now-wasted fishtail-braid girls, blocked Grant. "Fuck off," he said, shoving Grant's shoulder.

Grant lunged at him, but Cole grabbed his arm.

Dark Hair Fishtail-Braid Girl shrugged to Mia. "Your party was fun, but we've heard theirs has better swag." The girls left with Ruby and Axel.

Grant took one more step toward the door. "That Ruby chick is into me. Fuck that guy!"

Mia touched his arm. "Leave her be, Grant. You've got your pick of the litter here."

"I've been through most of 'em." Grant gestured like a circus ringmaster.

"Come on, dude." Cole motioned to Grant. "Let's get a drink."

Cole, Mia, and Grant stepped up to the bar. Mac was behind it, tying on his apron.

"Nice set," Cole said to him.

"Thanks." Mac looked up. "What can I get you?"

Presley pushed through, interrupting before the others could order. "I'll have a strawberry daiquiri."

Mac grinned at her. "Hand-crafted, coming right up."

"The machine is fine." Presley's expression was flat, her hands on the bar as Mac pulled the handle on the drink machine.

"What did you think of the song?" He brought the slushy cocktail to Presley.

"What did I think?" Presley threw the daiquiri in Mac's face.

"Fuck!" yelled Mac, flamingo pink liquid dripping down his face.

This stopped all the partying around them as eyes went wide. Mac stormed around the bar and pulled Presley back into the kitchen, faster than anyone could snap photos and post.

"Holy shit!" exclaimed Grant.

Mia and Cole could only stare.

THIRTY-FOUR

"Don't touch me!" Presley yanked herself from Mac's grasp. The tiny kitchen at The Rabbit Hole was hot as hell.

"What the fuck, Presley?" Mac grabbed a kitchen towel and wiped his face.

"You were singing that song for her!"

"I was singing that for *you*!" He chucked the towel on the counter.

Presley slapped him hard across the face.

"Bullshit," snapped Presley. "I know what you meant by those lyrics. *And* you're a drug dealer!"

"What are you talking about?" Mac put his hands to his head. "The song is about angels!" He gestured to her. "You're an angel!"

Presley turned. "That's another reason you're full of shit, because you know I'm far from an angel!"

Mac reached for her. "Come on."

Presley stepped away and motioned to her white Swiss dot dress, which was splattered with pink. "Look what you made me do!" She had tears in her eyes that went deeper than a stained outfit.

"I didn't *make* you do anything," said Mac. "You're a fuckin' force, Presley. That's one of the reasons I can't stop thinking about you!"

"Stop!" yelled Presley. "I'm leaving. I need to go home and change."

"Let me drive you. I'm taking a keg to the Wear National party. We can talk about this."

"There's nothing to talk about, *ever.*" Presley stared into him. "When you see me here or around town, I don't want you to say a word to me. We don't know each other. We never met."

"Presley, you can't just erase what happened between us." He touched her arm.

"Oh, yeah?" Presley retorted. "Watch me." She turned and strode back out of the kitchen. Mac stormed out the back door.

Presley reunited with Mia, Cole, and Grant at the bar.

Grant laughed. "Dude, that was crazy!"

Vincent stepped up and yawned. "Listen, children, I think I got all I need here." He tapped his camera. "I'm off to meet my very civil friends."

"Give me the car key." Presley held her hand out to Vincent. "Now I have a chance to wear the fierce jumpsuit that was in the running tonight. A big event always demands a wardrobe change."

"Everyone here is drunk," said Mia. "No one will notice your dress."

"Mia's right," added Cole. "Clothes will be covered with way worse."

"*I'm* not drunk." Presley grabbed Vincent's sleeve. "Give me the damn key, Vincent! Remember that essentially, you work for *us.*"

"That's harsh," mumbled Grant.

Vincent eyed Grant and handed Presley the key.

"*Salope,*" he growled as he left. Grant watched him, looking torn.

"Do you want me to go with you?" Mia asked Presley.

"No, you stay. From the looks of Cole's tongue down your throat, you're having a good time." Presley stormed out of the bar.

"I'll go see if she's okay." Cole followed Presley out.

Eve found Mac leaning on the back wall of the building, smoking a cigarette.

"Clever exit," she said.

"I wasn't trying to be clever. I'm . . ." Mac touched his face, annoyed. "Sticky."

"So you got a little daiquiri facial. Strawberries are good for your skin. And I want to get as many facials as possible for the rest of my fucking life. Tonight's huge for us. Fireworks start in an hour and no one wants to see those straight. The rush is gonna start."

"I'm not doing this anymore, Eve."

"Don't give me that snowflake shit, Mac. You are not pussying out during the busiest night of the year."

"Yes. Yes, I am." Mac tossed his smoke down and ground his heel into it. "I'm balling up and going to tell Otto I'm out."

Eve took her smartphone out of her back pocket. "No, you're not . . . unless you want me to show this video to that stuck-up slut wearing the Lyndon Wyld label." She played the video of Mac having sex with Presley. "I'll show it to her and then I'll make sure that her boss gets it. You know we dirty locals are off-limits."

Mac shoved Eve against the wall. "Don't you fucking threaten me!"

Eve punched him in the chest. "It's not a threat."

"Hi." Cole stepped from a shadow. Mac moved away from Eve.

"What's up?" Eve squinted at Cole.

Cole's response was tentative and halting, "Um, Ruby said I could find you out here."

"She did, did she?" Eve side-eyed Mac with satisfaction. "What are you looking for?"

"Anything that will make tonight's fireworks even more, you know, memorable," answered Cole, failing to hide his nerves.

"How about advice?" said Mac. "You'll get the best view at Steps Beach. Everyone'll tell you Jetties, but Steps is a little more out of the way. It's to the side of Jetties, down a long set of stairs off Lincoln Avenue that lead down to the beach."

"That sounds nice," said Cole.

Mac continued, "There are some cozy nooks in the dunes down there. I noticed you and that little Lyndon Wyld pistol are getting pretty close."

Eve chuckled and pointed at Cole. "I don't think this gentleman is looking for free travel tips."

"Though I appreciate them," said Cole.

"Take a little toot of this." Eve pulled a packet of white powder from her bra. "Unless you like to enjoy it a different way. Believe me, with this, it won't matter where you watch the fireworks."

"I don't need a taste. I believe you," said Cole. "How much?"

"No reason to be shy." Eve smiled. "We don't judge."

"I don't judge what I don't see. This is all you." Mac pointed his forefingers at Eve and Cole. He walked off to his truck, got in, and drove off.

As Cole turned to Eve, Frank opened the back door and leaned out.

"Hey, we're drowning in here!" he yelled.

Cole shoved his hands in his pockets.

"Can't a girl have a smoke?" Eve pulled cigarettes from her black pleather work fanny pack around her waist.

"Inhale quick. The drinks don't serve themselves." Frank disappeared back inside.

Eve raised an eyebrow at Cole.

Mia sat at the bar, chin in her hand, tapping her fingers. The celebrations around her had reached a pinnacle. The DJ worked the partiers, who pumped their fists and nodded their heads until he dropped the beat and more ear-piercing insanity ensued. The pool table, darts, and ping-pong tables were all busy. She waited, glancing at her smartphone. Ten minutes passed, then twenty. She looked around, feeling like she couldn't have been more alone in a room with more people.

Grant joined her. "Hey, why the long face?" He looked around. "Where's Cole?"

"I don't know," said Mia. "I thought I did, but I don't."

He put his arm around her. "You don't need Cole, Mia. You got me."

"I appreciate the offer, Grant." Mia smiled at him. "But no thanks."

"Hey, why haven't we hooked up?"

"Because that would be like hooking up with my brother," answered Mia.

"You just made it weird." Grant pulled his arm from around Mia. His smartphone buzzed on the bar. On the home screen, he saw a text from Ruby:

Evry1's at the beach. Pool 2 myself. 😊

Grant poked himself in the chest. "Yohhhhh! I called it!" He checked Ruby's Instagram. Her latest post was a photo of a sparkling pool and her Wear National bikini top floating in it. "She's such a tease!" He groaned. The geotag *Wear National July 4th Party* revealed the estate's address. "You're right. I shouldn't go."

"Is that the only reason you're not going?" asked Mia.

"That and if I bang her, and Lyndon finds out, I'll probably get fired."

"Classy. And why would she find out?"

Grant widened his eyes at her. Mia shook her head. "I might be a worrier, but I'm no snitch."

"You, Lyndon, and Grace are *tight*." He wound his first two fingers together.

Mia took his hand and held it. "I wouldn't tell them."

"What about Cole? Are you going to tell him?" asked Grant.

"No," answered Mia. "But he's no snitch either. If he ghosts me completely, he's a dick. But he's no snitch."

"Sold! I'm gonna go." Grant jumped off the bar stool. He jogged out the door, giving a few girls a pat on the booty before he left.

"Have fun," Mia said to no one. She was alone in a bar filled to the rafters with people. They had gone from six seasonaires to four to one in what seemed to Mia like minutes. She put her elbows back on the bar, her chin in her hands. She waited twenty more minutes but Cole never returned.

The three girls huddled next to her talked and drank wine. One was the shop girl who worked at Modern Vintage. She was wearing the purple A-line skirt she'd encouraged Mia to buy. She leaned in toward the others. "My roommate was so wasted, she couldn't remember what happened." She shook her head. "She woke up on the floor of the fraternity bathroom, missing her underwear."

"That's so fucked up," said a girl with a pixie haircut. "So she was—?"

Modern Vintage Girl nodded. "She went to the administration. They wouldn't do shit—said she needed to practice 'more responsible drinking.' My roommate was doing a lot more than drinking, but that doesn't give some asshole the right to take advantage." She noticed Mia staring at them and waved. "Hey, weren't you at—?"

Mia didn't wait for her to finish, but charged for the front exit. She wove her way through the sweaty, drunk throng of partiers.

"Fireworks in ten minutes!" she heard Eve yell as she left. Some partiers stumbled out the door behind her. Mia found her cruiser next to another Lyndon Wyld bike. The third, Grant's, was gone. She rode off, not really knowing which way to go. People in town started to get settled in to watch the show, climbing on roofs and heading in groups toward the beach. Her ears were still ringing from The Rabbit Hole house music and loud insanity. She peddled along to the din of the loving families and mellow groups of friends. Some were taking selfies, but most had their faces turned forward instead of down at their phones.

She realized that she had only two Insta Story posts and Lyndon wanted four. She stopped in front of the Island Pie Shop and took a selfie. The store was dimly lit behind her, enough to reveal July Fourth decorations. She could only manage a closed-mouth smile, and captioned:

American as apple pie. #WyldFourth #sweet 🍎

She went to Ruby's Instagram and checked the geotag. The Google Maps directions revealed it was seven minutes away by bike. She followed the navigation. The cobblestones under her felt bumpier than they had on her ride to The Rabbit Hole. She stood on the pedals and pushed down with more force, angry at Cole for leaving. She exhaled with a groan, pissed that the night had gone downhill so quickly. She wanted to trust Cole and that aching desire made her feel humiliated. Her Southie posse of high school Girl Vault friends used to say, "Chicks before dicks." They would never abandon one another for a guy. Yet she'd chosen to wait for Cole instead of making sure Ruby got home okay.

Furious with herself most of all, she peddled harder.

THIRTY-FIVE

A s Mia reached the Wear National estate, the fireworks burst overhead. She couldn't see them fully because the home was sprawling and the best view was from the beach side. The property looked similar to the Lyndon Wyld estate, save for the Wear National red accents, instead of green and beige.

She leaned her bike against one of the palm trees jutting around the facade as a nod to the brand's Cali beach inspiration, though Otto hailed from Brooklyn. These trees didn't jibe with Nantucket, but neither did Wear National.

She walked to the front door and turned the knob, but it was locked. House music thumped from inside. She could see through the window. The interior was void of partiers, which surprised Mia given the rumors about Otto's underground raves and bacchanalian orgies. She remembered Ruby's text to Grant:

Evry1's at the beach. Pool 2 myself.

And that kissy-face emoji.

"What am I doing?" she muttered to herself.

She glanced back at the driveway. The G was there, which was curious, but no other Lyndon Wyld cruisers besides hers. Maybe Grant had brought his around back. She walked to the side of the house into the yard, cringing at her potential faux pas if Ruby and Grant were simply having a good ol' time skinny-dipping.

Mia's brow furrowed when the first person she saw was Presley, alone, standing at the edge of the pool, staring into it. That explained the G outside. Having changed out of the daiquiri-stained dress, Presley now wore a white Lyndon Wyld sleeveless jumpsuit, similar to Grace's at the Summer Solstice Soiree. Her arms were crossed.

"Presley?" said Mia.

Presley's attention remained on the pool. She looked as if she was deciding on whether or not to buy a new pair of pumps. Mia followed Presley's gaze. What she saw sent a shockwave down her spine.

At the opposite end of the pool, Grant floated, facedown in the water. Blood feathered out from his lifeless body.

Presley's eyes locked with Mia's. "You're here." Her voice was calm, almost flippant.

Mia spun away from the pool. "What is happening? What should I do? What is happening? What should I do?" she repeated in a whispered mantra to herself. As fireworks exploded over the harbor, her mind landed on an answer—it was like she'd been programmed: *Snap and post.* The fact that at this moment, Mia was thinking of her followers and likes, and of Lyndon's approval, made her hate herself. Still, she smiled brightly into the tiny camera hole at the top of her smartphone.

When Presley slapped the phone from her hand as she pressed the "+" icon to post, Mia was smacked back to reality. "Fuuuuuuck," she muttered, crouching down, knees weak, hands shaking, understanding that the first friend she'd made on this "dream summer adventure" was now dead. She swallowed the swell of tears, knowing that if she released them, she wouldn't stop.

Another blast of fireworks made her jump. But nothing hit harder than what she saw when she followed Presley into the pool house: Ruby, naked, brutally beaten, and unconscious. Mia threw up, unable to contain the sickening mix of horror, fear, and guilt from her desperate desire to run. The gun in Ruby's limp hand meant that the party was over, literally and figuratively, for all of them. Grant, forever.

Mia watched Presley, grace under pressure. Presley didn't post, puke, or cry. She handled it, which made Mia feel relieved and freaked out at the same time, especially because Presley was *there*. *Why was she there?*

"You'd eat dirt before going to a Wear National party," said Mia.

"I thought Mac was here, bringing a keg from the bar." Presley launched into her drama with Mac, setting Mia off.

"Enough with the soap opera shit, Presley!" she exploded. "We need to call nine-one-one!"

"Whoa!" Presley leaned back. "I was going to do that, sugar, when *you* arrived." She lifted the wall phone receiver.

The fireworks finale started outside with a steady stream of pops, bangs, and booms. Presley and Mia froze, waiting for silence. After the finale ended, Presley dialed.

The operator's voice rose from the receiver. "Nine-one-one. What's the emergency?" Presley hung up, wiping the phone with a towel.

Mia glared at her. "What? Why would you hang up?"

"They'll come. Caller ID."

Presley mopped up Mia's vomit with the towel, leaving a tiny diamond-tipped coke spoon on the floor in the corner. It could've been anyone's. So many drugs must've been consumed at this party. Mia flashed on the Molly in Ruby's palm and Ruby's legs buckling at The Rabbit Hole.

Presley shoved the towel at Mia. "Your hurl, girl." She grabbed Mia's arm and strode toward door.

Mia resisted. "What are you doing?"

"*We* are leaving." said Presley.

THIRTY-SIX

Mia felt like barfing again as she followed Presley around the side of the Wear National estate to the front. The smell of her own vomit in the towel she clutched kept her stomach turned inside out. It was hard to keep up with Presley, whose strides toward the G were purposeful, but not panicky.

Mia glanced around. The estate's grounds were still deserted, though the palm trees cast shadows that made Mia feel watched. Presley noticed the beach cruiser leaning against one of their thin trunks.

"Did you ride that?" Presley asked, her voice low.

"Yes," answered Mia.

Presley pointed to the vomit towel. "Throw that in the G because we can't toss it around here." She pointed to the bike. "Throw that in, too, and let's go." She strode to the car. Mia tossed her phone in the passenger's seat and dumped the towel in the back before rushing to the bike. She tried to lift it into the back of the G, but struggled with its weight.

"Fuck," muttered Presley. "If I chip my polish, how am I going to explain *that*?"

Together, they picked up each end of the bike. Mia's whole body felt weak. Her arms shook as the they got it in the back of the car. In the process, her long sea glass pendant necklace got stuck on the handlebars and broke. Mia didn't notice as she clamored into the car. She picked up her phone from the seat and buckled in.

"You're stronger than you look," said Mia, breathing heavily. She realized she had never seen Presley break a sweat. And she wasn't breaking a sweat now.

"Real strength has nothing to do with looks," replied Presley as she drove them off.

They peeled down the driveway to the street.

"This isn't happening." Mia stared forward, shaking her head.

"It happened," said Presley. "But not on our watch."

"What are we doing?" Mia shook her head, the wrongness of this whole situation hijacking her brain.

"We sent for help, Mia," said Presley. "You can't save Grant *or* Ruby now. You have to save yourself. We have to save each other."

Sirens blared in the distance but quickly grew closer. Presley turned down a thin alleyway behind the saltbox homes. She parked in the darkness as two police cars and an ambulance sped by, going the opposite direction, toward the Wear National estate. Mia held her breath and when she exhaled, uncontrollable sobs came out. The blood rushed from her head and her hands at the same time, making her dizzier than she'd ever felt. Her fingers tingled like a million tiny pin pricks.

"I killed him!" blurted Mia, crying hysterically.

Presley whipped her head toward Mia. "What are you saying?!"

"Grant . . . he got a text from Ruby at The Rabbit Hole," cried Mia. "I knew he shouldn't go over there. She and Axel were so wasted. Something bad was bound to happen."

"You didn't kill him!" Presley pounded the steering wheel. "He was an adult. He didn't act like one, but he made the choice to go. We have no idea what happened when he got there."

"It doesn't matter. Now, he's dead! Grant is dead! And it's my fault," wailed Mia.

"Stop saying that!" Presley grabbed Mia's shoulder. "Look at me! Don't ever say that again!"

Mia started to hyperventilate. "I . . . can't . . . breathe . . ." she gasped. Heat radiated through her entire body. More sweat beaded on her forehead and her chest. "*I'm* going to die."

Presley released Mia's shoulder and collected herself. "You're not going to die. You're having a panic attack. We call them the vapors where I'm from. Breathe in through your nose for a count of five and out through your mouth for a count of seven, like this." Presley breathed in through her nose slowly and evenly, then out through her mouth, which was shaped like she was going to whistle.

Mia tried, but she couldn't control her breaths, her body, her thoughts, or her tears. She squeezed her phone tightly in her hand, her middle finger slicing on the broken glass. Blood oozed from the tip. She was unhinged.

Presley grabbed Mia's cracked phone and cut her finger on the glass as well. She took Mia's hand and pressed their bloody fingers together. Surprised, Mia calmed.

"You didn't just do that." She stopped crying.

"Damn right, I did." Presley opened the glove compartment and pulled out a box of tissue. She wiped her finger on one, holding it in her hand.

"Who does a blood promise?" asked Mia in disbelief. With the back of her other hand she wiped the snot that dripped from her nose. "We're not vampires."

Presley held the tissue box out for Mia, who plucked one out and blew her nose, then wiped the blood off her finger. The cut was tiny, but she had the urge to slice it more. Ruby would've sliced hers more.

"I did that because I want you to know that I'm now your sister," said Presley.

"Is this some sorority shit? Because you know that's not me."

"No, there was no blood involved at the sorority, except that after living together for a semester, we all got our periods at the same time."

Mia's breath was still labored. "What are we going to tell everyone?"

Presley's tone was measured and precise. "We are not going to tell anyone anything, Mia." She reminded Mia of Miss Skinner, her fourth grade teacher, whose word was the gospel. Miss Skinner told her students that if they didn't stop chattering, she would nail their feet to the floor and their butts to their chairs. Her students believed her.

Presley continued, "We are going to go back to our house and we are going to hear the news like we're hearing it for the first time. If you were ever in a school play, then put on your invisible costume and act the fuck out of this shit. Or we could end up in jail."

"Why? Why would that happen?" Mia's crying resumed.

"Promise me, Mia, that you will follow the plan. Say you promise," ordered Presley.

Mia couldn't get the words out.

"Listen, we're not lying," implored Presley. "We *don't* know what happened. We were in the wrong place at the wrong time. We weren't supposed to be at the Wear National estate at all."

Mia tried to control her breath and her thoughts.

Presley turned off the motor. "We're going to sit here until you calm down and promise me. I'll wait, however long it takes." She pulled out another tissue, handing it to Mia. "You got some"—she mimed vomiting—"in your hair there." She pointed to a lock of Mia's hair. "Which reminds me . . ."

Presley got out of the car, pushed her seat forward, and reached into the back for the wadded vomit-filled towel. She lifted it out and held it away from her body. Mia wiped her hair with the tissue and put it on top of the towel.

Presley tossed the heap in a nearby garbage can, then got back in the driver's seat.

"Don't say I never did anything for you."

Mia sniffed.

"Here's what's what." Presley stared into Mia. "You don't know how long I was at that house when you arrived. I don't know if you were already there before I arrived. You could've been hiding."

Mia shook her head.

Presley continued, "I'm not threatening you, sugar. I'm leveling with you. We don't know shit about each other, so a promise is mutually beneficial. We're presenting a united front."

Time stood still as they sat in the darkness of the alley.

The trees rustled as if they were shushing Mia, telling her to keep quiet. She prayed that nature would protect her. That false solace was obliterated by the siren that returned as the ambulance raced by in the opposite direction.

"Do you think Ruby's okay?" Mia asked Presley.

"Even if she is, she isn't," answered Presley.

After a half hour, Mia still didn't know if she could face the other seasonaires back at the estate. Presley received a group text from Lyndon. She showed it to Mia:

Everyone meet back at the house. Now.

Mia looked at Presley and said, "I promise."

THIRTY-SEVEN

M ia tried to keep her breathing steady as Presley drove them closer to their estate, which was about twelve blocks from the Wear National house. To Mia, they were worlds apart but far too close.

There weren't many cars on the residential streets. The families who had been at barbecues and picnics had all gone in for the night. Presley turned the G at the corner with the saltbox house with the Slip 'N Slide in the front yard. The porch lights reflected off the water that slicked the yellow plastic. A tabby cat sat perched on the picnic table cleared of food and the beers that Grant had shared with the dad of the house.

"I say this with love after chatting so closely with you in that alley, but, honey, you need gum," said Presley.

"I'm sure lots of people vomit on the Fourth of July here," Mia whispered, barely having enough energy to speak.

"We're not 'lots of people.'" Presley pointed to her white patent leather handbag on the floor by the passenger's seat. "I have some in there."

The last thing on Mia's mind was her breath, although now that Presley brought it up, she realized that her mouth tasted like spoiled cottage cheese. In the handbag, she found a pack of sugar-free gum next to two condoms. One wrapper was open and empty. A white lace thong was shoved in the bottom corner. Mia put a piece of gum in her mouth and chewed. The sweet mint cooled her off.

They pulled around to the front of the estate and stopped. Cole was sitting in an Adirondack. He walked to Mia.

"Where did you go?" he asked.

"Where did *you* go?" Mia shot back. The anger that rose up in her over his ghosting her at The Rabbit Hole helped burn away her fear.

"Lyndon wants to Skype with us. Who screwed up?" said Presley. "Where's Grant?" She chuckled. Mia noticed that Presley's smile wasn't twitchy or nervous, though she avoided Mia's eyes.

"How do you know anyone screwed up?" asked Mia. "Maybe she just wants to wish us a Happy Fourth of July, since she didn't do it earlier."

Cole checked his watch, his expression curious. "It's the middle of the night in London."

A Subaru pulled up and Vincent got out. "Thank you, Andy." Mia noticed the Lyft sticker on the back.

Vincent handed Andy a woven *Free To Be Wyld* swag bracelet from several in his camera bag. "Will you put this on and let me take a photo for our social? You've got a great look." Vincent held up his phone with the Lyft app on the screen. "There's five stars in it for you."

"For sure," said Andy.

Vincent snapped a photo of Andy making hang ten fingers.

Andy looked at the bracelet. "I met a dude who shills for this company about a week ago. I think the girl he was with worked for M-Kat." He nodded to the estate. "You get dope digs—this and The Wauwinet."

"That's Jade and J.P.," said Cole.

"I guess they rendezvoused at Nantucket's finest resort, because this house isn't good enough for them," remarked Presley with a swift exhale.

Andy offered a peace sign and drove off.

Vincent joined the others. He motioned to Presley in her white jumpsuit. "You cleaned up nicely."

"Thanks." Presley put a hand on her hip, batting her eyelashes at him. "Don't be mad, Vincent. I had a moment."

Vincent headed into the house, waving his phone. "So why am I getting called back for a Skype call with Lyndon? I was in the middle of dinner."

Cole leaned into Mia. "I would've liked to watch the fireworks with you."

Mia walked away from him and entered the house.

In the living room, Presley took the loveseat and patted the space next to her for Mia, who sat. Cole settled on the nearby ottoman, trying to connect with Mia. Vincent clicked on the TV with the remote and brought up the Skype screen. Lyndon appeared. She looked like she'd been crying, her eyes red and swollen.

"This summer is going to give me gray hair." Lyndon touched her blond bob, her voice a tired rasp. "Where are Jade and J.P.?"

Everyone was silent.

Presley scrolled through Instagram on her phone. "Check Jade's Insta." She showed the post that featured Jade and Tatiana to Mia, Cole, and Vincent.

Lyndon scrolled through her smartphone. "They were at Maz's Blue Bash. I should've known." She clucked her tongue with disappointment. "She'll never learn. And J.P. is throwing his life away like . . ." She trailed off.

"Are *you* okay, Lyndon?" asked Vincent.

Lyndon looked at them, her eyes welling. She took a deep breath.

"I don't know how to tell you all this, but . . ." She held back her tears. "Grant is dead."

"What?" gasped Presley, grabbing Mia's hand.

Mia started to cry. She didn't have to fake it. The flood returned easily. Cole's jaw locked. Presley put her arms around Mia, her expression pure shock.

Vincent took some wobbly steps, then sat on the couch.

"How?" asked Presley with deep concern.

"No one is sure yet," replied Lyndon. "From what the police told me, he was shot."

Mia cried harder. Cole squeezed his eyes shut.

"He was found in the Wear National pool," added Lyndon.

"Why was he at the Wear National party?" Presley looked at the others. "When did he go? He was with us at The Rabbit Hole."

"The police are on the scene right now," continued Lyndon. "I don't know much else. Grace has been under the weather, and now she's way too upset to be on this call, but we're coming in tomorrow."

Presley nodded, holding Mia tighter.

"Lock up tight," said Lyndon.

"We will," said Cole.

"I love you all." Tears fell down Lyndon's cheeks before the screen went black.

Vincent looked comatose, muttering, "It smells like vomit in here."

"She got sick," Presley mouthed to Cole, pointing at Mia in her arms. "I found her on my way back to The Hole after I changed. We decided to go to the beach for some fresh air and fireworks."

Mia disengaged from Presley's arms and sat back in the love-seat. She stared at the ceiling, sniffing.

Cole looked at Mia, puzzled. "You didn't drink that much."

Manic, Vincent leaped back up and clicked around the TV channels. "I don't know about you, but I want to know what happened. Maybe there's something on the news."

"It's almost midnight. TV news is done," said Cole.

"This is one hundred percent fucking crazy." Presley headed upstairs. "I'm going to get my iPad. Maybe there's something online."

Cole moved next to Mia. "Are you okay?"

"No. Grant's dead." Mia pressed her thumb against the tiny cut on her middle finger. It stung.

Presley brought down her iPad and placed it on the coffee table. She sat on the floor. Mia and Cole sat to the right of her as she scrolled through Twitter. Vincent paced. She searched the word "Nantucket" and found a host of Nantucket travel blog feeds, then one local news feed: *@Nantucket411.*

"There!" said Presley. The most recent tweet, twenty minutes earlier:

Lyndon Wyld seasonaire killed at Wear National party.

Hearing Presley read the words out loud, Vincent sat on the ottoman to look. The tweet had a video link to a Nantucket Channel 14 news story. Presley clicked it. In the grainy footage, the police were putting up crime scene tape at the Wear National estate. Otto drove up in a red '63 Corvette convertible with Axel and the fishtail braid girls. He got out and jogged to the cops at the door. Although the conversation couldn't be heard, the cops were clearly telling him about what happened.

"Noooooo!" Otto shrieked, his voice rising to an even squeakier pitch than usual. He fell to his knees and sobbed in his hands.

Mia thought his reaction was too quick to even register. It had taken *her* the last hour to even begin to understand what had happened.

"Who killed Grant?" Cole stared at Presley's iPad screen.

"The story doesn't say." Presley played the video again.

Vincent pointed to Otto on the screen. "This is a huge crock of horseshit!"

"Why do you say that?" asked Cole.

"Convenient timing to be *caught* on film," answered Vincent.

Presley turned to Vincent. "You think Otto had something to do with this?"

"Can I say he's definitely involved? No." Vincent rose, disgusted. "But I *will* say he's capable of anything. He could've paid these nightcrawlers to be there for his theatrics."

"What's a nightcrawler?" asked Mia.

"A camera crew that films crime scenes to sell the footage." Vincent paced. "They're everywhere, even on Nantucket."

Presley replayed the video. "He's a horrendous actor."

"*Ça suffit!*" Vincent stormed out of the house, slamming the front door.

"It was no secret that they were close," said Presley. Her eyes were soft and sympathetic. "Oh, this is awful. That doesn't even begin to describe it." Presley's acting skills were far more convincing than Otto's.

"I can't believe it," whispered Mia. "Should we text Jade and J.P.?" She pulled her phone from her purse.

Cole noticed the cracked black screen filled with water. "What happened to your phone?"

Mia felt Presley's eyes on her. "When I puked, I dropped it in the gutter." She slid the phone back in her purse.

"This isn't something you text anyway," said Presley. "We should wait up until they come home."

Cole stood. "Now *I* could use some fresh air." He slid open a French door to the deck. Mia and Presley followed. They sat in separate deck loungers, staring out into the dark night. No one spoke. Mia tried desperately to picture Grant's smiling face in the blackness—one of his shit-eating-grin selfies. But the image of Grant facedown in a blood tie-dyed pool of water was seared into her brain.

Presley fell asleep first. Cole moved to Mia's chair, perching on the edge.

"I assumed you left, so I left," said Mia softly.

"I didn't," replied Cole.

"I don't care, Cole." Mia shrugged, her arms listless. "We hooked up. Whatever."

"I went to check on Presley." Cole tugged on his right shirt cuff. "After she left, I had to take care of some unfinished business."

"Cole—"

"I don't want you to think I left because of you," continued Cole. "It was because of you, but—"

Mia shook her head.

"I'm engaged," blurted Cole. "I *was* engaged."

Mia closed her eyes, her heart sinking.

"We broke it off last night." Cole let the weight of his secret fall from his mouth. "I didn't tell her what happened with us, but it wouldn't have mattered. We were basically over."

Mia opened her eyes, putting on a stoic front. "I wish you'd been honest with me before, Cole. But I told you that you aren't obligated to tell me anything."

"Stop doing that, Mia."

"Doing what?" Mia stared out at the beach.

"Making yourself unimportant. It's fucking stupid." Cole put his hand on Mia's arm. "You're important to *me*. I *want* to tell you."

"Fine." Mia pulled her arm away. "Tell me."

Cole rubbed his forehead, his forefinger swiping his scar. "We had already put our wedding on hold after I took this job."

"That's too bad." Mia sounded sarcastic, but she didn't mean it that way. She winced.

"She hates social media. She doesn't even have a Facebook page."

"Is she Amish?" Mia sniffed. "My brother doesn't have a Facebook page either, and I tease him that he's Amish."

"I had to respect that she didn't want her world on display, but this was a good money gig and we're young, so—"

Mia put her hand up. "Tonight has been . . . *a lot.*"

"I know."

Mia scooted over and Cole nestled close. She was pissed at him, but now she was hiding secrets, too. She let herself nod off on his chest. The last thing she felt was him kiss the top of her head.

THIRTY-EIGHT

When the morning sun woke Mia on the deck, the stunning orange-pink haze made her wonder if last night had been a nightmare. A heavy rock sank in the pit of her stomach. What had happened was real. Cole was still sleeping by her side. The arm that had been around her dangled over the lounger. Presley was gone. Mia gingerly lifted herself and tip-toed inside.

Upstairs, she knocked on Jade's door—no answer. She opened it slightly to find the room empty. The guys' room was empty as well. Mia's throat tightened at the sight of Grant's Penn State backpack on the floor. She took a breath and padded to her room, craving a shower—like a hazmat type of scrubbing. Presley was sound asleep, wearing her pink satin sleep mask. She never left the door open, but maybe she was more afraid than she'd let on.

Mia snuck into the bathroom and started to unbutton her cardigan, then noticed—the long sea glass pendant necklace Jade gave her was gone. She ran out and down the stairs, scanning the living room floor. She rushed to the deck and surveyed. Cole stirred, mumbling incoherently before settling back into a quiet snore. Mia raced to the front, kicking the driveway's gravel around the G, glancing inside.

"Shitshitshitshit!" She shot inside and took the stairs two at a time, scurrying along the hallway to her room. She shook Presley's arm. "Hey," she whispered.

Presley whined, "Noooooo," and rolled away from Mia.

"Presley!"

"You're not really waking me up are you?" growled Presley.

"My necklace, it's gone!" Mia felt around the void where the pendant had hung on her chest.

"It wasn't your best look anyway."

"I searched everywhere—inside, outside, in the car. What if it's at the Wear National house? I don't remember feeling it fall off."

"It could be anywhere, Mia." Presley huffed as she sat up and lifted her sleep mask. "You can't start doing this, worrying about every little thing."

"It's not 'every little thing.'" Mia sat on the bed. "It's my necklace. It's bad enough that Ruby was wearing the bracelet I gave her."

"That's your bad, for sure," remarked Presley. "Why you gave that to her is beyond me."

"It's a long story," said Mia.

"Don't tell me." Presley yawned.

"She needed it."

"Well, she doesn't need it now." Presley smoothed the covers over her. "Some prison guard is going to wear it or try to put it on her boyfriend as a cock ring." She considered this for a moment. "Is that what a cock ring looks like?"

"Presley!"

"You have to have a sense of humor, Mia, especially in dark times." Presley stretched her arms up.

"Are you kidding me?" Mia squeezed the back of her neck. Every muscle in her body was tense. "What should I do?"

"Whatever you were going to do before you realized the necklace was gone," answered Presley.

"I was going to take a shower."

"Good. Now please let me sleep." Presley reached to the nightstand and pressed her smartphone's Home button. The screen read 8:35 a.m. "It's too fucking early."

Mia saw a text from Jade before Presley clicked her screen to black:

#sorrynotsorry

"Have you heard from Jade or J.P.?" asked Mia, not wanting to seem like she was reading Presley's texts.

"No." Presley snuggled back into her pillow.

"Lyndon and Grace will be here in an hour," said Mia.

"I need ten more minutes or I won't to be able to focus." Presley pointed at Mia. "You need to focus, too."

"Right, focus," replied Mia, deadpan, as she trudged into the bathroom.

She took a long, hot shower. Washing her hair twice, she inhaled the steam and the shampoo's lavender scent. She scoured her body so hard with a loofah that her skin was red and raw when she got out. Blow-drying was too much effort, so she pulled her hair into a wet ponytail. She put on a Lyndon Wyld sundress with flat sandals and walked down to the kitchen, leaving Presley to sleep. Cole was there, pouring coffee into a mug. Mia grabbed an empty mug from the cupboard.

"Did you sleep?" asked Cole, pouring her coffee.

"Not really." Mia sipped. "You?"

"A little."

Cole put the coffeepot back on the maker's warmer. He showed her his iPad. The news was now covering the murder, so he clicked on one of the many links. A video of a newscast played. To the right of the anchor were separate photos of Grant and Ruby, both smiling.

"Fourth of July fireworks turned into gunfire when a young man was killed at a party in Nantucket," reported the anchor. "Grant Byrd, who worked as a brand ambassador for the popular Lyndon Wyld clothing line, was allegedly shot by a brand ambassador from competitor Wear National. The suspect, Ruby Taylor, was found beaten at the scene. She was taken to a local hospital and is expected to recover."

"Ruby," said Mia softly. She flashed on her friend, unconscious, beaten, and bloody.

"Jesus," said Cole. "What happened with them?"

Mia took another sip. The coffee burned her tongue and her throat as it slid down. They sat in silence at the kitchen counter until a text buzzed on Cole's phone. He looked. "They're here."

Presley joined Mia and Cole in the foyer, where they stood like a greeting line for the queen.

"Where are Jade and J.P.?" Cole whispered.

Presley shrugged. "Rude and wrong." She centered the thin belt around the waist of her dress, her hair and makeup flawlessly applied as it had been every day since Mia met her. Mia felt like a jittery mess, smoothing flyaway strands back toward her ponytail. Caffeine wasn't the brightest idea.

Through the thin horizontal window to the right of the door, Mia saw Lyndon and Grace pull up in the Tesla. Her heart beat hard and fast, ringing in her ears. Presley squeezed her hand once and let go. It did nothing to bring Mia's heart rate down.

As soon as the sisters entered the house, Lyndon walked straight to Mia and hugged her. Presley scowled, then put on a practiced "sad smile" when Lyndon embraced her. Lyndon rubbed Cole's arm.

Grace pulled a bottle of Belvedere from a silver lamé wine bag. "It's early, but we need alcohol. Bloody Marys in the living room." Off Lyndon's glare, Grace's eyes went wide. "Oh, that doesn't seem right at all! I'll make sunrises."

She disappeared into the kitchen while Lyndon led the others to the living room, holding Mia's and Presley's hands on either side of her. She sat in an armchair. Mia and Presley took the couch, Cole the ottoman.

"I don't even know where to begin," said Lyndon, lifting a monogrammed handkerchief from her purse, which she had set on the side table next to her.

Grace brought in a tray of vodka sunrises. "We should start with these and a toast to Grant." The cranberry red blended into the orange juice, giving Mia a flash of the pool's crimson. Everyone took a glass. Mia was the last.

"To Grant," said Lyndon, lifting hers.

"Should we pour one out?" asked Cole. "That's how we do it in my family."

"This rug is hand-hooked and costs more than your salary," replied Grace, pushing at the tufts with the tip of her tan suede loafer. "So that's not happening."

"Eyes, my loves." Lyndon locked eyes with each person in the room.

Mia swallowed a gulp, praying the vodka would kick in quickly.

"I wish Vincent were here, but he's very upset," said Lyndon.

"Naturally." Presley wore a look of concern. "We all are."

"Where are Jade and J.P.?" asked Mia.

"They aren't returning," sniffed Lyndon, putting down her drink. "This tragedy made me see that neither of them feels a responsibility to the brand or, frankly, to you as mates."

"I don't believe that." Mia looked into her drink.

Grace sat on the loveseat. "We need to be here for one another."

Mia felt Presley's leg against hers and when she moved, their skin stuck for a beat.

"We're here for you." Lyndon leaned forward. "It's important for you to mourn this loss, so I've made an excellent grief counselor available to you. Her office is a bike ride away."

"You should share your feelings openly," added Grace. "Your fans will expect it."

Mia put her hands over her face. "What are you saying?"

"Spread the Grant love on social media," answered Presley, looking at Lyndon for affirmation.

Lyndon nodded. "We're also creating a beautiful tribute for him at the store. We'll put up Vincent's fabulous photos. And yours, so send Grace your favorites."

"I can't," said Mia, a bite to her tone. "My phone broke."

"I drop mine every other week." Grace waved her hand. "I'll have a new one messengered to you."

Mia stood, looking at Lyndon and Grace. "Can I talk to you both in private?"

"Of course, my darling," replied Lyndon. She took Mia's hand and led her toward the deck, with Grace following. Presley's eyes caught Mia's, either warning or pleading.

The wind had picked up since dawn. Mia wrapped her bare arms around her body. She tried not to shiver.

"What is it, Mia?" Lyndon peered into Mia's face.

"I don't feel right here." Mia focused on the swaying sea grass bordering the estate.

"Do you mean that you don't feel safe? Because you should feel safe." Lyndon gently turned Mia's face to her. "This is a very unusual situation."

"And obviously an unfortunate relationship dispute," added Grace, putting a hand on Mia's arm. "That has nothing to do with anyone else but Grant and Ruby."

"I warned against hobnobbing with the Wear National camp." Lyndon clicked her tongue. "They're not our people."

"If Jade and J.P. get to go home, why can't I?" asked Mia

"Because unexpected circumstances are part of life," answered Lyndon. "If I've learned anything that I can impart to you, it's that you *must* forge ahead."

"I *will* forge ahead, at home with my mom and brother." Mia held herself tighter.

"That's not moving forward." Lyndon shook her head. "That's backward."

"Mia, I hate to bring this up." Grace gave Mia's arm a light squeeze. "But per the seasonaires contract, you'll give up the balance of your pay if you leave. And you can forget about the new phone."

"Grace." Lyndon maintained her cool. "Let's not be crass."

Grace dropped her hand from Mia's arm. "I'm sorry."

"I'd like to chat with Mia for a minute alone," said Lyndon.

"Of course." Grace glanced down, then walked inside, closing the French doors and joining Presley and Cole, who watched through the glass.

Tears welled in Mia's eyes. Lyndon hugged her, then held her away, looking into her face. "Oh, I don't know what's come over me. If you want to leave, Mia, I completely understand. But you will be missed. You've been doing so well here."

"I'm not sure what I want." Mia wept. "Except for this whole situation to disappear."

"Believe me, so do I." Lyndon closed her eyes, then opened them. "I have an idea." She touched Mia's arm. "Would you feel better if you had your family here?"

"Seriously?" Mia sniffed.

"One hundred percent," replied Lyndon.

Mia's shoulders relaxed. "Yes, I'd feel much better."

"What about a visit?" Lyndon brightened. "I'll put your mother and brother up at The Wauwinet. It's a secluded slice of heaven in chaotic times. You can stay there, too, if you like. You and your mum can have a spa day."

"We've never done that."

"I never had a chance to do that with my mum either." Lyndon offered a small smile, then leaned in. "Can I share something with you?"

"Of course," Mia replied, understanding the implied privacy.

Lyndon put her hands on the deck railing, motioning Mia to join her. They stared out at the choppy water curling with white, frothy caps. "My mother and father were inseparable," she said. "I've never seen two people so in love. It's the kind of love I've dreamed of my whole life, which I'm sure has fucked up every relationship I've ever had, pardon my French." She chuckled dryly. "That kind of connection comes with its drawbacks. We didn't have any money, so my father worked himself to the bone. When I was eighteen, he died of a heart attack."

"I'm sorry," said Mia.

Lyndon brushed back hair that had blown across her face. "My mother had a nervous breakdown. She couldn't live without him."

Mia shifted on her feet. She didn't know if she felt complimented or burdened by this intimate information.

"She was diagnosed with acute schizophrenia," Lyndon continued. "It can come on rather suddenly in a healthy person, often in response to a stressful event. She had to be institutionalized."

"That must've been hard for you and Grace," said Mia.

"Grace was thirteen at the time and was going to be put in a foster home. Even though I had no idea how to take care of a child—I was practically a child myself—I couldn't let that happen, so I became Grace's legal guardian. It was my job to make sure we survived, and I very quickly saw how fierce my protective instincts were." Lyndon looked at Mia. "I'm willing to bet you learned that about yourself at a young age, too."

Mia stared at the whitecaps, thinking about how much the money this summer meant at home.

"At the same time, you need to take care of yourself. I want to help you do that," said Lyndon. "But the only way I can do that is if you stay here." She put her hand on Mia's.

THIRTY-NINE

Mia pulled the fabric scissors from her sewing kit and sliced through the Lyndon Wyld messenger label, splitting open the box. Inside was her new smartphone. She brought the smaller box to her bed and opened it, lifting out the shiny device.

"I'm going to break *my* phone so Lyndon will buy me a new one," said Presley, spritzing on perfume as she sat at the vanity.

"*You* broke mine when you slapped it out of my hand," remarked Mia as she turned on the phone.

"You are an ungrateful little bitch, aren't you?" said Presley, half-joking. "That was for your benefit, remember?"

The perfume's strong jasmine–orange blossom scent bothered Mia as she clicked around the phone's screen, signing in and downloading her apps. "I don't want to go today. A merch stand at the farmers market right now seems inappropriate. We've never had one before, why start now?"

"Putting on a brave public face translates to sales." Presley slicked on a neutral lip gloss. "I want to look good, but not too good." Presley turned to Mia and smoothed her hair instead of tossing it. "What do you think?"

"You look fine," replied Mia.

"Fine as in 'hot'? Or fine as in 'mediocre'? because I like the first but want the second." Presley tilted her head.

"The second."

"Good." Presley grabbed her purse and left the room.

Mia clicked on Instagram to ensure that her Insta Story was empty. She knew it would have disappeared within twenty-four hours, and that even if she had accidentally pressed the "+" icon to post the selfie in front of the fireworks, it would be gone. But she needed to be positive. She exhaled and clicked off the phone, then glanced in the vanity mirror. She didn't look fine in any way.

Vincent drove Mia, Cole, and Presley to the farmers market. The ride over was quiet, though Presley took a selfie, looking pensive, her hair blowing in the wind. Mia side-eyed Cole, who rolled his.

The farmers market was teeming with locals and tourists, noisy with shoppers talking over one another and music playing. The colors, noise, and smells felt assaulting to Mia. She could barely look when she passed the stand that featured the sea glass pendant necklaces, with their mermaid tears.

"I miss Jade already," she said, touching flowers that begged to be arranged.

"Really?" remarked Presley, her eyes narrowing. "She sucked all the air out of the room."

"I liked J.P. He was a good guy," said Cole, touching a Nantucket cap hanging on a stand. "And Grant . . . we weren't best bros or anything, but after you bunk with someone for a few weeks, you get used to having them around."

Mia eyed Presley, who snapped a selfie with a bouquet of daisies. The three continued walking. The Dolphin Shine singer with his kooky fin hat took a break from playing the guitar to hug Mia. She held on longer than she should have. Vincent used it as a photo opportunity, which he posted on Instagram:

It takes a village. #ForeverWyld #healing

They arrived at the Lyndon Wyld merch stand, where Jill sat among the arranged clothing and accessories. She embraced each of them, including Mia.

"Horrendous," Jill said. "Grant was a piece of work, but entertaining."

"He sure was," replied Presley.

Vincent took some shots of the group at the stand. As passersby watched, Mia couldn't tell if their expressions were of pity, scorn, or morbid curiosity. "This is weird."

"News travels fast," remarked Presley. "But we have a job to do."

Mia leaned into Cole as Vincent snapped a shot. "Are we supposed to smile?"

"When you think of Grant, do you feel like smiling?" asked Cole. "Because I do."

"Yes," answered Mia, offering up a melancholic smile.

The sight of them became an increasing public distraction and after the fifth gawking person bumped into Vincent, he put the cap on his lens. "I am in hell. *Je suis fatigué.*" He trudged off to the car.

"Poor Vincent." Presley pouted. "He's taking Grant's loss hard."

"Anyone want food?" Cole motioned to the Island Pie Shop stand nearby. "We can take a pie-eating selfie and call it business."

"I'm not hungry, but I'll watch you eat," replied Mia. She had zero appetite.

"Anything but cherry." Presley sniffed.

They headed to the stand. Mia stopped at a Snapchat Spectacles pop-up kiosk. "I guess I should catch up on my social since I've been without a phone for all of a day." She gave a dry snort.

"Out of sight, out of mind," warned Presley.

Cole examined the booth and the futuristic-looking glasses. "These things are cool."

Presley waved a hand at Mia. "I'll let Mia be the guinea pig, and see how goofy they look on her first."

"Thanks." Mia put on the glasses and tapped the top left-hand corner.

Presley read the instructions on the kiosk. "Count to ten."

Mia slowly turned, scanning the street as she counted in her head. The pristine town that had been so awe-inspiring when she arrived now looked manufactured to her. She finished counting and Cole helped her link to her smartphone. She replayed the video in her Snapchat Memories and noticed Detective Miller staring at them from far down the street by the liquor store as he got in his Crown Victoria. She shivered and deleted the video before Cole or Presley looked. "Blurry."

"Pilot error, I'm sure." Presley took the glasses. "Let me try, because they looked spy-chic." She put them on and posed for a beat with her hand on her hip. Then she scanned the street and counted to ten out loud. Her smile turned into a scowl and she ripped them off. "Fuck."

"What is it?" asked Cole.

"More trash than usual," replied Presley, walking off toward the exit where they had parked the G.

Mia and Cole looked in the direction of Presley's scorn. The Crown Victoria was gone, but Mac and Eve stood outside the liquor store, talking.

"How much do you have to piss off a woman to get a daiquiri thrown in your face?" Cole asked Mia.

"Don't try and find out," Mia answered, lifting a brow. She followed after Presley.

FORTY

"M ia, you have to eat something," said Cole, tapping Mia's plate with his fork.

Mia pushed around her scrambled eggs. She, Cole, and Presley were ensconced under a patio umbrella at 45 Surfside Bakery and Café.

Presley poured syrup on a stack of waffles. "Comfort food, sugar."

"I haven't slept for three days," said Mia, rubbing her eyes. "Maybe that's why I'm nauseous."

"You're making me sleep-deprived, too," Presley huffed. "It's like having a fish out of water in the bed next to me, all the flippin' and floppin'."

"Are you going to see the grief counselor?" asked Cole.

"Head-shrinker, you mean?" Presley shook her head. "Absolutely not."

Cole sipped his coffee. "I went to a therapist a couple times after I lost my grandpa." He glanced at Mia. "I'm thinking maybe it'll help now. Plus, I'm going to start running—endorphins, right?"

"You know what'll help now?" said Presley, cutting her waffles.

"What?" asked Mia.

"Not dwelling." Presley took a voracious bite. "And waffles." She chewed and swallowed, then looked at Mia. "Did talking to Lyndon and Grace make you feel better? You never told me about your conversation."

"Nothing to tell," replied Mia, putting down her fork. "All I know is that I can't wait till my mom and brother come in."

"I can't wait either." Presley took another bite.

Three millennials drinking lattes and eating eggs Benedict huddled together at a nearby table. They stared at Mia, Cole, and Presley. One snapped a smartphone pic.

Mia lifted a menu to block her face. "Great, we're gossip."

"I hope I didn't have syrup on my chin," said Presley, dabbing around her mouth with her napkin.

After another lookie-loo snap, Mia got up.

"What are you doing?" asked Cole.

Mia tossed her napkin on her chair. She restrained giving the Eggs Benedict Millennials the finger as she passed them and jogged down the patio steps.

"Mia . . ." Presley called out to her.

Mia got on her cruiser and peddled off. She rode a few blocks and stopped next to a tree to pull her smartphone from her purse. She found a group text from Lyndon and Grace with the contact card for the grief counselor, Dr. Adrienne Lambert, who was at Nantucket Cottage Hospital. Mia found the location on Google Maps and peddled there to find a cluster of clapboard structures. Nantucket's gray shingled buildings were all starting to look the same to her. She locked her bike to a rack and walked inside the hospital's main building.

She checked the text message and searched the numbers on the doors, finding Suite 32, marked with the placard:

ADRIENNE LAMBERT, M.D.
PSYCHIATRY

She entered. The reception area was decorated with beachy touches—a couch covered in anchor fabric, framed nautical photographs, and health and travel magazines neatly fanned out on the coffee table next to a white ceramic bowl filled with seashells. Mia stepped up to the reception window.

"Can I help you?" asked the receptionist, a portly man in his forties wearing wire-rimmed glasses and a kind smile.

"I'm here to see Dr. Lambert," replied Mia.

The receptionist checked the schedule book in front of him. "Do you have an appointment?"

"No. I'm Mia Daniels. I work for Lyndon Wyld." Mia drummed her fingers on the reception windowsill.

"Oh, yes." The receptionist's eyes filled with sympathy. He glanced at the schedule book and back up at Mia. "Dr. Lambert is with a patient, but she'll have some time free in about forty minutes. Can you wait?"

"Sure." Mia sat on the couch. She thumbed through a *Prevention* magazine, finding recipes with "anti-bacterial" turmeric. She didn't know what turmeric was and didn't care. She flipped to an article on adult acne and one titled "Five Ways to Make Stress Work for You." The photo featured a fresh-faced woman who didn't look remotely stressed. Mia put the magazine down and headed out the door.

"I'll be back."

"Okay," replied the receptionist.

Mia roamed the halls. The hospital was much smaller than Boston Medical Center, where she regularly brought her mom.

She found the patient care wing and stepped up to the nurse's station. Two female nurses typed information on separate desktop computers. Mia stood for a long moment. Neither nurse looked up at her. The air smelled stale and musty, reminding her of her mom's room in their apartment.

"Excuse me," said Mia. "Do you know what room Ruby Taylor is in?"

The nurse with curly red hair glanced at Mia. "Did you check in with security?"

Mia patted her shirt. "My sticker must've fallen off."

"You'll have to get another one," replied the nurse.

Mia noticed a police officer standing guard in front of a room down the hall.

An announcement came over the speakers. "Code Blue, Room Ten-twenty. Code Blue." The two nurses hustled in the same direction, away from Mia. Mia slipped down the corridor toward the police officer, who watched her pass. The door was open. A nurse was cleaning Ruby's facial wounds. Ruby's eyes caught Mia's and filled with tears. There was so much Mia wanted to know and say, but all she could do was look sorry and confused.

"Hey," snapped the police officer. "Move along."

Mia hurried back down the corridor and wound around the hospital. She found Dr. Lambert's office and sat on the anchor-covered couch.

"I'm back," she said, trying to calm her breath as quickly as possible. She returned to the *Prevention* piece on adult acne and read the same sentence over five times because she couldn't concentrate.

"Mia?"

Mia looked up to see a woman around Lyndon's age. "I'm Dr. Lambert." The doctor's hair was gray, but the look was chic, pulled off of her serene face, which revealed she knew how to make stress work for her without reading any magazine article. "Come on in," she said with a wave.

Mia followed her into the office.

"Please"—Dr. Lambert motioned to a couch—"make yourself comfortable."

Mia's experience with psychologists extended to TV shows and movies, in which characters lay down on black leather chaises. The only place for Mia to sit was a white linen couch, and no one dressed as crisply as Dr. Lambert would want some sorry patient's dirty shoes on there. She sat, noticing a board game–size box filled with sand topped with a tiny rack on the coffee table.

"Did you buy that with the sand?" asked Mia.

"I did," replied Dr. Lambert with an amused smile.

"That's ironic in a beach town."

"You think so?" Dr. Lambert picked up a brown leather notebook from her desk, along with a robin's egg blue Tiffany pen. She sat in a tufted armchair across the table from Mia.

Mia shifted uncomfortably and put her hands in her lap. "I've never been to therapy."

"I'm glad you're here." Dr. Lambert crossed her legs. "I'm sorry about what happened to your colleague. How are you feeling?"

"Tired. I haven't been sleeping."

"I can give you something for that." Dr. Lambert pulled a small prescription pad from the notebook's pocket.

"I don't like drugs," said Mia. "My mom has cancer. She's had to take so many and I've seen their side effects."

"I understand." Dr. Lambert wrote out a prescription. "This is in no way a permanent solution, but insomnia can wreak havoc on you emotionally and physically, so you need to take care of it."

Mia reached over and took the scrip from the doctor, putting it in her purse. "I'll think about it."

Dr. Lambert nodded. "Tell me how else you're feeling."

"I'm sad, of course." Mia played with her blue enamel bangles. "I'm freaked-out, because someone was shot."

"Scared, yes." Dr. Lambert nodded again.

"And angry."

"Mm-hm." Dr. Lambert tapped her pen once on the larger notepad.

"This wasn't supposed to happen," said Mia, squeezing her hands together. "I came here to get away from the feelings I'm having now, so this is really, really fucked up. It's fucked up for everyone involved."

"What else are you angry about?"

"I don't like that everything I do needs to be for public consumption. Maybe I'm pissed at myself because I knew that going into this job. Social media has never been a huge pastime of mine."

"What are your pastimes?" asked Dr. Lambert.

"I sew, draw, cook . . ." Mia shrugged.

"Are you doing those things?"

"I was, before—" Mia shook her head.

"What have you been doing?"

Mia didn't answer. Dr. Lambert leaned forward. "When tragedy and change occur, there's comfort in the normalcy of day-to-day life."

"But life isn't normal here," remarked Mia.

"What do you mean?" Dr. Lambert leaned back.

Mia motioned out the window. "It's Nantucket, the dream life."

"The only dream life is the one you have when you sleep," said Dr. Lambert. "Do you remember yours?"

Mia shook her head. She stared past Dr. Lambert at the bowl of apples on the desk.

Dr. Lambert looked at the apples. "Would you like one?"

"No, thank you." Mia focused on an apple, a shiny red one without a stem. "I do remember a piece of a dream I had. But this was before Grant died, like a week after I got here."

Dr. Lambert watched Mia.

"I was walking home from the bodega near my apartment with apples for my mom." Mia smiled. "She loves apples." Her smile faded. "But I couldn't remember how to get back, even though I live a couple blocks away. And my phone wouldn't dial. I tried and tried to reach everyone I knew . . . and then I woke up."

Dr. Lambert wrote on her pad. Mia peered over, but she couldn't read the doctor's curlicue writing.

"You're going to say that the apple is like a symbol of temptation, right?" Mia picked up the sand tray's tiny rake. She scraped straight and circular lines.

"What do *you* think it's a symbol of?" asked Dr. Lambert.

"The answering a question with a question thing doesn't work for me." Mia scrubbed the sand with the rake.

"Apples can symbolize temptation, yes," said Dr. Lambert. "They can also mean wisdom or spiritual growth."

Mia sat back on the couch, still holding the rake. She started to cry. Dr. Lambert handed her a box of tissues from the coffee table. Mia wiped her eyes, weeping for a few cathartic minutes.

"'Embrace your grief. For there, your soul will grow,'" said Dr. Lambert. "That's a quote from Carl Jung, a psychiatrist who believed that dream images are not just our own, but part of a bigger picture."

Mia placed the tiny rake back in the sand tray. "Let me ask *you* a question, Dr. Lambert."

"Okay." Dr. Lambert leaned forward.

Mia sighed wearily. "What's a soul?" She could see that a question to her question was coming, so she got up and left.

FORTY-ONE

After another sleepless night, Mia broke down and took an Ambien. She slept like she'd been hit in the head by a ball-peen hammer. Dragging herself out of bed the next day, she picked up her smartphone and checked the time. She focused her blurry eyes enough to see it was past noon and she had a text from Presley:

> Hi, Sleeping Beauty. Went to do a little retail therapy.
> Tried to wake you, but #fail.

Mia clicked off her phone. "Coffee," she said to herself. She made her way downstairs to find Nadege weeping as she dusted the foyer shutters.

Mia went to her. "Nadege, what happened?"

"I feel terrible," whimpered Nadege. "I think they took Vincent because of me."

"What do you mean?" Mia saw the front door open. Cole entered, sweaty from a run. She gave him a concerned look with a nod to Nadege, who covered her face with one hand.

"A Detective Miller was here," said Nadege. "He asked me some questions about July Fourth."

"You didn't have to answer any questions, Nadege," said Cole as Mia led her to the bottom stairs, where they sat. Cole stood in front of them.

"My mother is here from Haiti." Nadege shook her head. "I'm not making any trouble for her. All I told him was that I didn't see any of you after you left on July Fourth. And then he asked to speak with Vincent. I pointed him to the guest cottage, then I saw Vincent follow him out in the car. Vincent's back now, but when he saw me, he turned away."

"I'm going to go see if he's okay," said Mia.

She walked along the driveway and knocked on the guest cottage door. Vincent answered. He had a bottle of Pinot Grigio in one hand and an empty wineglass in the other.

"Hi," said Mia.

"Care for some wine before I drink this whole bottle?" Vincent stepped back for Mia to enter, pouring himself a full glass.

Mia waved him off. "I already have an Ambien hangover."

Vincent shut the door behind her. "I took that shit until I woke up on my doorstep, naked, with a half-eaten Big Mac on my chest."

"I thought you were a vegetarian."

"*Exactement.*" Vincent took a healthy sip of wine.

"I came to see if you were okay." Mia looked around the mini version of the main house.

"No. I'm not okay." Vincent sat on one of the kitchen counter stools. "I was just questioned about the murder of someone I happened to like. Grant was an idiot, but I liked him."

"I liked him, too," said Mia, sitting on the stool next to him. "That's why I'm here."

"I had nothing to do with what happened," said Vincent. "I was with my friends. They told that to the police and so did everyone working at the restaurant that night."

"Why did they question you if Ruby Taylor killed Grant?"

"You know why, Mia." Vincent offered a sideways smile. "Somehow the police knew, too. Like we talked about at the stable, nothing is private and it's our own fucking fault." He finished off his wine.

"I wanted to ask you something that day . . ." Mia touched one of the magenta roses in the vase on the counter.

"I'm an open book. Catch me before I shut and lock with one of those little keys, like a . . . ?" He mimed turning a tiny key. "What's the word?"

"A diary," replied Mia.

"Yes." Vincent lifted his index finger. "Read me. I'm a diary."

"Did Grant ever hurt you? You said the marks on your neck were from climbing up the dock."

"No. *Jamais*." Vincent looked into Mia's eyes. "I don't have abusive relationships anymore."

"Was Otto Hahn an abusive relationship?"

"Ah, you are going back in my diary," Vincent chuckled dryly. "He wasn't a relationship."

"What was he?"

"A mistake." Vincent poured more wine in his glass.

A rose petal dropped in front Mia. "I read about him, and he's done some really vile things."

"A lot of people do vile things, especially in this business." Vincent shrugged.

Mia went on, "I saw an anonymous quote from a photographer who worked for him years ago. He said Otto berated him in public. He threw caviar in his face at a party! Fish eggs!" Mia searched for a reaction from Vincent, who polished off half his glass in one swallow.

"I was seventeen."

Mia let this confirmation sink in. "Why didn't you leave or report it?"

Vincent placed his empty glass on the counter with a clink. "*Dix-sept.*" Vincent put up ten fingers, then seven. "I moved here from Pont-de-Flandre, which sounds pretty but it's not. And I fell into a job with the hottest clothing line in the world."

"So many women have spoken out about his atrocious behavior."

"You know what people say? 'Sour grapes,'" replied Vincent, with a sad head shake. "That some girls were pissed because he stopped paying attention to them. He wouldn't fire them. He'd just be a shit till they left."

"I know guys like that." Mia took a sip of Vincent's wine. "They're not as slimy as Otto, but—"

"Cole is not like that." Vincent winked. He took the glass from Mia and drank.

Mia returned to the main house, still hazy from the Ambien and the conversation. She walked up to the bedroom for a nap and found Presley on the bed, reading her iPad. Shopping bags dotted the floor, including two from Lyndon Wyld.

"The police talked to Nadege and Vincent," said Mia, plunking down on her bed.

"Cole told me," replied Presley.

"I don't understand why." Mia played with her bangles.

"I do." Presley pointed to her iPad. "Toxicology reports came back. Your pity project Ruby Taylor was so wasted, she couldn't have lifted a gun, let alone pull the trigger. They released her. It may have been a drug deal gone wrong."

Mia looked at Presley. "Should we—?"

"No." Presley scrolled through Twitter. "But look what's trending."

Mia's eyes fell on the slew of tweets about the murder, marked with one hashtag:

#whodunnwyld

FORTY-TWO

At the police station, in the investigation room, Detective Miller put a baggie with a gold diamond-tipped coke spoon on the metal table in front of Otto, who sat in a chair with his hands folded.

"This was found at the scene. It had your prints on it," said Miller, leaning on the table.

"That's because it's mine," Otto replied with his customary arrogance. "I use it to put sugar in my coffee." He held his thumb and forefinger millimeters apart. "Keeps me thin."

"Was the gun yours, too?" asked Miller.

"Make love, not war." Otto made a peace sign. "That's what my folks taught me."

"Would you call what you did to Ruby Taylor making love?"

"You're getting really personal here, detective." Otto clucked his tongue.

Miller sat down in the chair across the table. "You've had a history of personal relationships with your employees."

Otto frowned at the detective. "This is my private life, you know?"

"Not according to the videos we found online," said Miller, tilting his chair back on two legs. "We didn't have to dig deep. They were right out there for all to see."

"What videos?" Otto's eyes widened, innocently.

"I'll be happy to show them to you and refresh your memory."

Otto leaned in. "There's one video that counts. It's the Nantucket Channel 14 news footage. I arrived at the house in a *car* long after the unfortunate event. Now, I don't want to do your job for you, but I wasn't close enough to walk there, like on the beach, for instance."

Miller scowled.

"Ruby texted me to come over," added Otto, showing Miller a text from "Unknown Number":

> It's Ruby. My phone broke, so I borrowed 1.
> Meet me at the house 😊

"Sweet thing," Otto smiled. "But I never went. I was otherwise occupied at my hotel with Axel, one of my seasonaires, and two girls he met. You can talk to them."

After letting Miller get a good look at the text, he put his phone back in his pocket.

"Now I'm done here. If you have more questions, talk to my attorney." Otto pinched his own nipple. "He's kind of a freak. I mean, we're all freaks, right?"

"Not all of us," said Miller.

Otto leaned forward again, grinning. "All of us, especially those of us who say, 'not all of us.'"

Mia hurried down the hallway as she read the text from her mom:

See you in a bit! 😊

"I want to come with," whined Presley on Mia's heels. "I'm the best welcome wagon. Remember when we met?"

"Yes. You're 'a hugger,'" replied Mia. "That's exactly why you can't come. I don't need you hooking up with my brother right now."

"Well *that's* presumptuous, sugar."

"You basically said as much when I was Skyping with him." Mia stopped and turned to Presley, speaking in a low tone. "Shit is complicated enough, don't you think?"

Presley's and Mia's faces were close. "Only if you make it that way," replied Presley. "You're not going to talk to them about anything, right?"

"Why would I do that?"

"Because you're you," said Presley.

"Well, you're you. You're not coming." Mia continued along the hall and down the stairs.

"I'm going to meet him later anyway," called Presley.

"Later is better than sooner." Mia blew out the front door, holding an aluminum Lyndon Wyld monogrammed water bottle so her mom had hydration on the long ride back.

Vincent waited for her at the G as Cole loped up the driveway, finishing up another run. He stopped, putting his hands on his thighs to catch his breath. "I promise not to be sweaty and stinky when your mom and brother get here."

"That would be nice," Mia chuckled.

Cole waved and jogged toward the house.

"Excited?" asked Vincent, noticing Mia's gaze linger on Cole, whose muscles glistened in a loose tank.

"Very," Mia replied, turning back to climb in the car.

Vincent raised an eyebrow and laughed.

"About my mom and my brother visiting." Mia gave him a deadpan look as he took the driver's seat and started off. She put the water bottle on the floor next to her feet and noticed something sparkle against the aluminum: it was her broken mermaid teardrop pendant necklace just underneath the seat. She slipped it into her purse, sat up, and exhaled.

Motoring through town, they passed a mint-condition gold 1960s Camaro. Otto Hahn was driving, wearing white-rimmed sunglasses and a Wear National knit cap, even though it was the dead of summer. He grinned, pointing at Vincent. "Vinnie!"

"*Fils de pute*," grumbled Vincent, driving on. He glanced at Mia. "You heard Ruby Taylor was released?"

"Yes," replied Mia, even more relieved she had found the necklace. They were silent for a few minutes, but when they hit the winding stretch of road, Mia launched into a conversation about movies to make sure the subjects stayed light. Vincent enjoyed documentaries like she did, but surprisingly, he was a fan of animated films.

"*Monsters, Inc.* is a masterpiece!" he said with a wave of his hand.

They arrived at The Wauwinet. Mia took in the lush grounds. "My mom is going to love this."

"What about your brother?" asked Vincent.

"He's going to pretend he hates it, but he'll love it, too."

They walked to the hotel's private dock and watched a shimmering white forty-five-foot boat glide in.

"There's your precious cargo." Vincent nudged Mia, who smiled.

When Mia saw Sean helping Kathryn down the boat's ramp, her body swelled with emotion. She raced to her mother, wanting to spill everything, but stopped in her tracks. Seeing her mom outside in the sunshine instead of in bed under their apartment's dim lights filled her with joy. Kathryn beamed at the sight of Mia. They continued toward each other.

Sean caught Mia in the first hug, lifting her up. "Hey, turd."

"Hey, turd." Mia wouldn't let herself cry. That would upset her mom. Mia gently put her arms around Kathryn's tiny waist. Kathryn planted kisses over Mia's face, like she used to do when Mia was a little girl.

"Are you okay, baby?" she whispered.

"I'm okay," Mia lied.

Vincent snapped heartfelt shots. He landed on one with mother, daughter, and son, and asked Sean for his social handles.

"I'm not on any of that stuff," said Sean.

Vincent sniffed, eyebrows raised. "All righty." He readied a post on Lyndon Wyld's Instagram.

"Wait—" Sean started to protest, but Mia touched his arm.

"Sean, please," pleaded Mia.

"Fine," said Sean. Vincent posted.

Mia and Vincent got Kathryn and Sean situated at the hotel.

"Who would want to ever leave here?" said Kathryn, seeing her room. Mia smiled.

"Do you like it, Sean?" asked Mia.

"It's all right," replied Sean with a chuckle. Mia exchanged a glance with Vincent.

Kathryn's awestruck gasps punctuated the ride back. She didn't care that the roads were filled with curves and turns. "It's like a Disneyland ride." She giggled, sipping the water Mia brought. "At least it's what I think a Disneyland ride is like." Mia squeezed her hand, appreciating her exhilarated expression.

They drove up to the estate to find Presley sashaying out the front door toward them.

"Well, hey there!" She wore a flowing maxi dress with a thigh high slit to show off her legs. Her blond hair was in beach-goddess waves. Mia was sorry she'd given her the time to primp.

"This is Presley," she said, looking at the driveway's gravel.

Presley hugged Mia's mom. "It's a pleasure to meet you in person, Mrs. Daniels. I love your daughter!"

Mia held her breath as Presley hugged Sean. "And you must be Sean!"

Sean furrowed his brow at Mia over Presley's shoulder.

"She's a hugger," remarked Mia.

Cole stepped out of the house and walked over to shake Sean's and Kathryn's hands. He didn't look "sweaty or stinky," but handsome in a loose striped button-down and light khakis.

Presley clapped her hands, getting the others' attention. "Lyndon and Grace are here." She tilted toward Kathryn and Sean. "They have a surprise for you."

Mia and Sean linked Kathryn's arms and followed Presley and Cole through the house. Kathryn was awe-struck. "This looks like a page from *Elle Decor*."

Mia chuckled. "It was."

They exited the French doors to the deck and walked down to the shore, where Lyndon and Grace stood, beaming.

"Welcome!" Lyndon put her arms out wide.

The beach was set up like a plush outdoor living room with a fabric cabana, upholstered loungers, plush pillows, and Lyndon Wyld monogrammed towels. Vincent snapped photos.

Kathryn noticed Nadege smiling next to a steaming hole in the sand. "Is that—?" Kathryn gasped.

"A real clambake," replied Grace.

Lyndon and Kathryn embraced. Grace stepped up to Mia. "The mama bears meet," she said.

"I've never been anywhere so beautiful," exclaimed Kathryn as Mia and Sean helped her into a lounger.

Lyndon handed Kathryn the softest new cashmere sweater. "We brought this for you, in case you get cold."

"Thank you," cooed Kathryn. "This is my first Lyndon Wyld piece."

"There's more where that came from," said Grace. "We have a shopping trip to the store planned."

Lyndon took another lounger while Grace and Mia sat on pillows. There was no room for Presley in this intimate powwow, so she moved to the beach towels where Cole and Sean sat. She was close enough to hear the conversation between the other women.

Lyndon reached for Kathryn's arm. "Can I start by telling you how wildly talented your daughter is?"

"You can, but I could have told *you* that." Kathryn beamed at Mia.

"Mom." Mia blushed.

"She's too modest," remarked Grace.

Nadege held out a tray of fruit-filled drinks, some in green blown-glass goblets, some in clear. "Sangria, virgin or regular?"

"Virgin, thank you," said Kathryn. Nadege handed her the beverage in the clear goblet.

"Mia?" asked Nadege.

Mia caught a side-eye from Sean and took a clear goblet. "Same."

The others took their drinks as well.

"I'm so glad you both could come for a visit," Lyndon said to Kathryn and Sean.

Kathryn put her drink on the rattan side table. "I'm glad, too. I felt I should talk to you in person, first to express my gratitude at giving my daughter this opportunity."

"She's definitely made the most out of it." Grace sipped her sangria.

Kathryn continued, her face growing somber. "But naturally given what's happened, I've been extremely concerned about her here."

"Mom." Now Mia's blush was of embarrassment not modesty.

"I don't have kids of my own," said Lyndon, looking at Kathryn with empathy. She motioned to Mia, Presley, and Cole. "These *are* my kids, so I've been beside myself with worry, as well. But my goal is to keep this season afloat and create the best experience possible for them."

"There may be more seasons, because Mia's earned quite a following," Grace grinned at Mia. "We bring our reigning influencer back."

"What's an influencer?" asked Kathryn.

Presley stepped over. "An influencer is a person whose social media messages impact other peoples' lives." She held up her smartphone and scrolled through her Instagram.

"That sounds important," remarked Kathryn.

"It is." Lyndon smiled at Presley. "Presley, my darling, will you make sure our other guests have what they need?"

Presley returned Lyndon's smile. "I'm the hostess with the mostess." Her smile dropped as she turned away to walk back to Sean and Cole on the towels.

Lyndon leaned in to Kathryn. "Kathryn, Mia is special. She can't let anything hold her back, even tragic events like the one that happened. She's on her way up, and life is going to try and knock her down. The strong survive. You're proof!"

Kathryn gave a weak chuckle. "I feel like crap."

Grace lifted her sangria goblet. "Well, I'll toast to your honesty. I'm all for that."

"Good, because I want Mia to come back home with me," added Kathryn.

Mia glared at her. "Mom, you can't—"

Kathryn turned to her. "I have every right to say what I want. I don't care how old you are, you're my daughter."

Cole looked over.

"Mia and I have chatted," said Lyndon. "It would be a shame if she left. She's an increasingly important part of my company."

"If you're talking about the Mia dress, I think that's fantastic," said Kathryn.

"It's not just a dress, but an *entire* Mia Collection for next summer." Lyndon motioned down her body.

"What?" Mia's eyes went wide.

Grace exchanged a glance with Lyndon as if this were a surprise.

"The deal of course will be much more lucrative than for just one piece," added Lyndon.

Grace climbed on board. "But she needs to remain a Lyndon Wyld face."

"I . . . don't know what to say," stammered Mia.

"You don't need to say anything right now," replied Lyndon. "Have a think. Chat about it with your mother, because she seems like a very smart and straightforward woman."

Grace lifted her glass to toast. "To smart, straightforward women."

Vincent snapped a photo of the four women as Presley watched. She scooted next to Sean, who stared out at the water. "Is this your first time on Nantucket, Sean?"

"Yup." Sean sipped his drink.

Cole nodded to the football on the towel. "I hear you've got a good arm."

"I'm all right," replied Sean. "Better with a bat."

"Your sister's pretty good, too." Cole eyed Mia, who approached. "I say we put that ball to the test with some touch." Cole grabbed the football and stood. Presley and Sean rose.

"I'll be on your team." Presley touched Sean's arm. "You were homecoming king, weren't you?" She squeezed his biceps. "A homecoming queen can feel it."

Mia's brow furrowed.

"I was, but all that crap was a joke at our high school," answered Sean.

"Sean, you've got the look," called Grace from her place near the loungers. "Why don't you stay? Make up for our losses."

Mid-photo, Vincent lowered his camera and gave a "tsk" of disgust.

"Too soon?" Grace grimaced.

"The words, not the notion," said Lyndon to Kathryn and Sean. "I wish you'd both had a chance to meet the others. With three gone, there's a huge void."

Presley adjusted her bikini straps. "Jade never wanted to be here in the first place. On a major holiday like July Fourth, when it's our job to stay here on Nantucket together, she traipsed off to her dad's party."

"Who's Jade?" asked Sean.

"Maz's daughter," answered Cole.

"*The* Maz?" scoffed Sean.

"One and the same." Cole twirled the football on his finger.

"Jade wasn't the brand," remarked Lyndon. She squinted at Sean. "Grace is right. *You're* the brand."

Grace nodded, crossing her arms.

"The fact that you called me a 'brand' means I'm not your guy," replied Sean, backing up on the beach and motioning for Cole to toss him the ball.

Mia turned to Presley. "*You're* going to play?"

"Of course, sugar!" chimed Presley. "Remember when you told me that I'm stronger than I look?" Mia flashed on the two of them lifting her cruiser bike into the back of the G at the Wear National estate.

Cole flicked Mia's arm, bringing her back. "That leaves you and me."

"I have to use the ladies' room." Mia grabbed Presley's hand. "Come with me." She pulled Presley up the beach.

"Your brother is a stone-cold fox." Presley leaned in to Mia. "He looks better in person. Hashtag: no filter."

"Stop," snapped Mia.

"Does he have a girlfriend? Boyfriend? Both?"

"Not that I know of."

"Even if he did, the rules don't apply when you're out of town," said Presley with a giggle.

They entered the main house's French doors and went into the guest bathroom off the living room. Mia shut the door. "Presley, I know that you and Mac are over, and that you need a new toy. But find someone else."

"Sean is not a toy!" Presley pulled down her bikini bottom and peed. "I only have a couple days to get to know the brother of someone I hold near and dear to me. I want *him* to know what you mean to me."

Mia put her hands on her hips. "Write him a letter."

"No one writes letters anymore, silly." Presley flushed and washed her hands.

"I found my necklace, by the way," remarked Mia.

"I told you you had nothin' to worry about." Presley squirted lotion on her hands from a porcelain bottle, rubbing them together.

"Right." Mia left.

———

Mia ended up sleeping at The Wauwinet with Kathryn that first night. She said that she wanted to make sure Kathryn had all her meds and that everything was set up comfortably, but she needed to be there for herself. They faced each other under the plush chintz comforter, knees touching.

"Do you want to talk?" whispered Kathryn.

"I'm okay." Mia closed her eyes as her mom stroked her hair until she dozed off.

———

Presley stared at her reflection in the bathroom medicine cabinet mirror. The pomegranate clay mask on her face was cracking. She touched it—it was dry. Her fingertips left white clay powder on her smartphone screen as she scrolled through Instagram, stopping on the post of Lyndon, Grace, Mia, and Kathryn.

A text popped up from Mac:

What the fuck is going on?

She deleted it, put her phone on the basin, and washed her face.

FORTY-THREE

Detective Miller sat at the desk in his office, talking on his phone. "Eve Wier said her boyfriend, Mac Doyle, went to talk to Otto Hahn the night of the Fourth. He told her he'd been selling drugs for Otto and wanted to get out of the game. She claimed she had no idea, which we both know is complete crap, especially after the anonymous tip."

He listened through the receiver, putting his feet up on the desk.

"Yeah, we're almost ready to go in."

He touched a file folder on his desk labeled "Grant Byrd."

"But I'm thinking that Otto might not be responsible for Grant Byrd's death after all. He's got a pretty strong alibi."

He opened the file and sifted through documents, finding a security camera photo of Otto in the lobby of a hotel that looked similar to The Wauwinet, but smaller.

"He was seen by the staff at the White Elephant that night around the time of the murder."

Miller listened, then put his feet on the floor and clicked on his computer to the video of Otto wailing at the crime scene.

"And on that video those nightcrawlers took, he arrived at the estate in a car. If he'd been on the beach, why didn't he just walk up to the house and make that ridiculous scene?"

He clicked off the video.

"You want to know what I think?" Miller waited for the person on the other end of the phone to respond. "I think someone was after Otto. Grant was in the wrong place at the wrong time."

At the store, Presley watched Mia snap a selfie with Kathryn in front of the mounted life-size poster of Mia in the Mia dress.

"Isn't that precious?" cooed Presley to a few customers who were ogling Mia. She could barely fake that pageant smile anymore.

Kathryn held Mia's face. "I'm so proud of you, baby."

"Can you see why this is pretty exciting?" replied Mia.

Kathryn nodded. Mia captioned her Instagram:

Inspiration. 😊 🙏 #mymom #myangel

She turned to Kathryn. "Let's go pick out some outfits for you." Mia looked across the room at Sean, who was folding clothes with Cole. She gestured to Presley. "Want to help us?"

Presley struck a pose. "Does a one-legged duck swim in circles?"

The three perused the store, pulling pieces off racks and shelves.

"Thank goodness we make a size zero," Presley said to Kathryn. "You're tinier than Mia! You know the Mia dress was originally mine, but it fit her better. I like to think I inspired her."

"I'm sure you've been a great support to each other after what you've all been through," said Kathryn.

Mia grabbed a floral dress from a hanger and stuck it in front of Kathryn. "How about this?" As she pulled Kathryn to the dressing room area, Mia locked eyes with Presley.

Kathryn became the center of attention, trying on the curated pieces selected just for her. As she came out of the dressing room wearing each item, Mia and Presley fastened, buttoned, and zipped clothes on her as she gazed at her reflection in the full-length mirror.

Vincent took photos. *"Bella!"*

"I'm going to get you a belt for this," said Mia, surveying Kathryn in a blue cotton dress. She walked off as Lyndon approached.

"Thank you so much for the clothes, Lyndon," said Kathryn. "They're amazing."

"Not as amazing as your daughter." Lyndon nodded to Mia, who stopped to help a woman find the right cardigan from a stack. "She knows exactly what people want." With a smile, Lyndon walked off.

Presley hung Kathryn's rejects on a nearby rack. "No offense, Mrs. Daniels, but the same can't be said for your son," she chuckled. "I'm going to give him a hand." She walked off before Mia could catch her.

Sean tried six different ways to fold. "This is my idea of hell," he said to Cole.

Cole laughed. "Yeah, it's not my favorite part of the summer."

"What's your favorite part?"

Cole's eyes went to Mia, who returned to Kathryn in the dressing room area.

"You know I'll come after you if you hurt her, right?" warned Sean.

"Absolutely," replied Cole.

Sean play-punched him as Presley approached.

"Boys, no fighting over me," she said, brushing back her hair. "Cole, let me show Sean how it's done." She relieved Cole of his tee before her eyes shifted to the store's entrance.

Jade and J.P. entered.

Mia looked up from buckling the belt around her mom's waist. She rushed over, embracing Jade. J.P. kissed her on the cheek.

"How are you?" asked Jade, holding Mia's hands.

"Better since my family got here, though Presley is attempting to commandeer my brother." She nodded toward Sean, who looked perplexed as Presley refolded one of his sorry attempts. Cole stepped up to J.P. and the two fist-bumped.

Mia waved at Kathryn, who waved back from the dressing room area. "And there's my mom."

"She's fucking adorable," remarked Jade with a smile.

"I haven't seen her this happy in a long time." Mia grinned. "Lyndon got rooms for them at The Wauwinet, which is *very* cush. I stayed there last night." She whispered to Jade and J.P., "Rumor has it you two spent a night there a while back."

"Haven't you learned anything from this job yet? Rumors are true," said Jade. She nodded to Grace, who was talking to Jill. "They were there, too."

"Really?" Mia's eyes went wide.

"Uh-huh." J.P. winked.

"Sapphic rendezvous." Jade made a V with her fingers and stuck her tongue through it. "I think Grace likes it rough."

Cole looked at his feet, eyebrows raised, while Mia chuckled, "I miss you, Jade. Are you staying for a while? Please say you are."

"No." Jade shook her head. "We're only here for the tribute unveiling."

"And for some field study." J.P. walked off, Cole following. He stopped at the scarf display and lifted a white bucket hat from the stack in the center, like those given out at The Rabbit Hole on the Fourth. "One hat style, that's it," he scoffed.

"Did you throw the game because Lyndon wouldn't make your hats?" asked Cole with a dry snort. "Thanks for leaving me alone in the house."

"I didn't plan it that way," replied J.P.

"What was your plan?" Cole plucked a peppermint candy from one of the dishes placed around the store.

"To spend some quality time with Maz," replied J.P. "But he wasn't very happy with me, to put it mildly. I didn't delete that video of Jade and Otto fast enough."

"Oh, shit," said Cole, who stopped in the middle of unwrapping the candy.

"Yeah, it was the scariest night of my life, man." J.P. put back the bucket hat. "But Jade saved my ass."

"After almost *costing* you your ass."

"She stood up to her dad." J.P. knocked once on the display. "She told me it was the first time in her life. She's always tried to get at him by doing stupid shit, but she'd never actually confronted him straight up."

They looked at Jade and Mia, faces close, laughing.

J.P. continued, "Otto tried to give her drugs and had been pulling some really nasty shit on her at Christmas parties and whatnot."

Cole put the candy in his pants' pocket. "That guy is such a scum."

"Maz never believed her." J.P.'s eyes softened as he watched Jade. "She broke down."

Cole squinted. "I can't quite picture that."

"It was intense and pretty heartwarming, except for the part where I almost lost some toes. But I guess I accidentally brought them together, and now I'm fam." J.P. nodded toward Lyndon, who walked to the center of the store. "Unlike with her." He shook his head and focused on the white hat.

Lyndon stood and grandly motioned to the entrance. "Everyone, let's convene out front." She ignored Jade as she headed out.

"I'm persona non grata," Jade whispered to Mia. Grace held the door open as the store emptied. She and Jade exchanged a look.

Outside, Lyndon held court in front of the store window, which was obscured by a green-and-beige curtain. Grace took her place off to the side as the crowd grew. Mia held hands with her mom. Presley slid next to Sean, who stood by Cole, while Jade leaned against J.P.

"You both have some balls," remarked Presley.

Vincent moved around, snapping photos along with a few news media photographers.

"Loss is never easy," Lyndon said to the group. "But in the words of Helen Keller, 'So long as the memory of certain beloved friends lives in my heart, I shall say that life is good.' Today, we honor the memory of our friend, Grant Byrd."

Inside the front window, Jill pulled back the curtain. The display was a visual barrage of images of Grant from throughout the summer with the seasonaires. In the center, in bright, bold green letters, were the words:

WEAR A MEMORY

The crowd cheered. Presley clapped with enthusiasm. "Beautiful!" Sean dropped his head. "That's so wrong."

Mia placed a hand on her stomach for a beat. She felt nauseous.

FORTY-FOUR

Remove your robes and lie facedown." The massage therapist tapped the two padded tables with round holes at the top. "I'll be back with the other therapist in a few minutes." She left the room, which smelled like lavender, as guitar muzak played softly over the speakers.

"I've never had a spa treatment, unless you consider chemo one," Kathryn chuckled.

"That's not even close to funny, Mom," replied Mia as she and Kathryn slipped off the white terrycloth robes.

At the store, Kathryn had changed alone in the dressing room. Here, Mia tried not to look at her naked body. It was so skeletal that it made Mia's heart hurt. Kathryn hung her robe on one of the door hooks and climbed on a table, pulling the white sheet over her.

She nodded to Mia. "You look like you could use this more than me."

"What did you think of the tribute for Grant?" Mia hung her robe on a hook.

"I don't know anything about marketing, so I can't really answer that, but what I *do* know is that Lyndon has very high hopes for you."

"She does," replied Mia as she climbed on her table.

"I think she's afraid I'm going to get in the way of that." Kathryn positioned herself on her stomach. "She's trying to butter me up with all this pampering." There was a light knock on the door.

"Come in," said Mia.

The two massage therapists entered and started to work. Mia's and Kathryn's initial nervous giggles gave way to long breaths and sighs as firm hands kneaded their bodies. The massage therapist rolled her forearms horizontally up Mia's back, pushing the stress out of her body.

Kathryn's massage therapist put more oil on her hands. "I'm going to use some tea tree essential oil. It has healing properties."

"Sounds perfect," said Kathryn.

Mia thought the "healing" comment was strange. Neither she nor her mom had mentioned anything about Kathryn's lymphoma. *Why would Lyndon or Grace reveal something so private?* But her mom's relaxed sighs calmed Mia. And perhaps the massage therapist simply deduced that something was wrong by her mother's wasted frame.

"I can see why you don't want to come home," said Kathryn, turning her head so she and Mia faced each other.

"You've said that twice," remarked Mia. "It's starting to sound passive-aggressive."

"Crazy things happened here," whispered Kathryn. "I can't help it if I want to take care of you."

"You can't take care of me," said Mia without whispering.

Kathryn's eyes showed hurt. She closed them.

Mia sighed. "I didn't mean it like that. I meant that I'm an adult."

Kathryn didn't respond.

"Great." Mia groaned. "You're not going to look at me now?"

After a few moments, Kathryn started wheezing, her eyes remaining shut.

"Mom?" Mia sat up and flipped over, pulling the sheet around her. "Are you okay?"

Kathryn's wheezes intensified. Her massage therapist opened the door and yelled, "We have an emergency! Help!"

Now the sirens were for Mia's mom. Mia rode in the back of the ambulance, holding Kathryn's hand, which felt plump with the swelling. Kathryn had on an oxygen mask, but her eyes were open. She looked terrified.

"You're going to be okay, Mom," Mia smiled at Kathryn.

She breathed in through her mouth, counting to five and releasing for seven through her nose. She willed another panic attack away because she had to be strong for her mother. *That* was her job. She grimaced and composed a text to Sean.

Grace drove Sean to Nantucket Cottage Hospital. Lyndon had gone back to Manhattan after the store event. Her last words to Mia, her mother, and brother had been "Enjoy, all!"

Sean sat with Grace in the emergency waiting room. He kept turning his phone over on the table to check for a text update from Mia. He'd flip it back over and tap on the Patriots cover.

"This is a top-notch hospital." Grace put her hand on his arm.

"I don't care if it's top-notch," replied Sean. "We're at a *hospital*."

They jumped up when they saw Mia enter from the hallway.

"She's okay," said Mia. "The doctor explained that it was an allergic interaction with the bleomycin Mom takes. It could've been the herbs in the massage oil."

Grace gasped. "Oh, I feel terrible!"

"Don't," said Mia. "The massages were a lovely gesture." She looked at Sean. "After a shot of cortisone, she's much better."

"He needs something for the pain!" a woman cried. Mia, Sean, and Grace turned to see a strung-out couple at the admitting desk. The guy, who looked like he hadn't bathed in weeks, was holding his arm, wincing.

The nurse stared at them without sympathy. "I told you before, he'll have to see a doctor for that. Wait like everyone else." She waved them off. The guy turned, bumping into Sean. His expression was more pissed than pained as he slogged to a seat.

"They don't look like everyone else on this island," Sean whispered to Mia and Grace.

"They're more common than you think," replied Grace. "The opioid and heroin epidemic is as big here as it is anywhere else."

"It's hidden pretty well." Sean eyed the junkies.

Grace embraced Mia. "I'm glad your mom's okay." She released her. "I'm so sorry, but I have to fly back out. I'll check in with you later. Send any medical bills to me." She pointed to Sean, smiling, as she left. "You're a seasonaire, Sean."

"Nope," Sean shook his head. He and Mia headed down the hallway. "What a crock of horseshit."

"It's a compliment, Sean," said Mia with a scoff.

They entered Kathryn's room as a nurse walked out. Kathryn grinned when she saw them. "They're releasing me!"

Sean didn't look nearly as happy as she did. "They don't want to keep you for observation?"

"No, thank goodness." Kathryn brushed lint off the blanket. "I'd hate to see a night at that gorgeous hotel go to waste."

"I'll call Presley to come get us," said Mia.

"No." Sean put his hand up. "That girl is *a lot*. Let's get a Lyft." He reached into his pocket, then remembered. "I left my phone in the waiting room." He exited.

Mia sat in the chair next to the bed. "I'm sorry, Mom."

"My allergic reaction is your fault?" Kathryn chuckled.

Mia took Kathryn's hand. "I'm sorry for what I said, about taking care of me."

"You're not wrong." Kathryn gazed into Mia's eyes. "Sweetheart, you've had the world on your shoulders at home for a long, long time."

Sean shoved the door open. "My phone's gone. What complete asshole would steal someone's phone at a hospital?"

Mia stood. "Ugh, Sean, that sucks."

Sean's eyes narrowed. "Those two junkies were gone, too."

"Honey, you should report it to the police," said Kathryn.

"Don't you have Find My Phone? asked Mia.

"I haven't enabled it yet." Sean rubbed the back of his neck. "I just bought the damn thing, with my hard-earned wages." His words were aimed at Mia.

"Don't be pissed at me because you left your phone in the waiting room," retorted Mia.

"I'm not pissed at you. I'm just pissed."

Mia threw her arms out to the side. "What are you pissed at? That you were invited to enjoy a couple beautiful days on Nantucket?"

"Does it look like Mom's enjoying it?" Sean pointed at Kathryn in the hospital bed.

Mia threw her head back. "Lyndon and Grace were trying to do something nice for us!"

"Was it really for *us*, Mia?" Sean glared at her. "I think it's for *you*. Or for *them*. They got plenty of pretty, heartwarming photos to spackle over their shitshow of a summer now."

"Sean, go to the police station and report your phone," demanded Kathryn in a terse voice. Sean left. Mia looked at her mom and shook her head.

FORTY-FIVE

They're siblings. They don't text?" asked Lyndon, turning to Grace, who held Sean's smartphone.

"They do, but we're sisters. Sisters are different. Men are—" Grace clicked around the phone's screen—"*pithier*."

Lyndon looked out over Manhattan. Below her office, the streets bustled during evening rush hour.

Grace punched the few application icons on Sean's phone: Lyft, Spotify, Candy Crush. "There's nothing on here that's meaningful."

"Any photos?" asked Lyndon.

"He has a photo of a bat in a Boston sporting goods store." Grace shrugged. "That's it."

"What about his social media?" asked Lyndon. "Snapchat, Instagram?"

"Nope." Grace put the phone on Lyndon's desk. "Not even Facebook."

Lyndon touched the new bonsai on her desk. A handwritten card hung from a gold string on the tiny trunk:

It's not personal. It's business.—Maz

"I lost Maz. We can't lose Mia." Lyndon opened a file folder and ran her fingers over sketches of the Mia dress.

"Dr. Lambert said she agreed to try Ambien for sleep, but nothing else," said Grace.

"Dr. Lambert shouldn't be sharing that information." Lyndon closed the folder.

Grace motioned to her. "You wanted to know what's happening since—"

Lyndon put her hand up.

Grace pulled her smartphone from her workbag and scrolled. "Vincent's been turned inward, or upside-down, so he's not giving us much."

"He fucked up by getting involved with Grant and he knows it," remarked Lyndon, walking to her desk. "Anything from Presley?"

"Just the usual narcissistic showboating," replied Grace, holding her smartphone up to reveal an Instagram post of Presley looking wisftul on the beach at sunset with the caption:

Girl missing boy. #Grant #ForeverWyld

"I can't have this explode anymore, Grace," said Lyndon. "It will be the death of us."

Kathryn was finally asleep in her hotel room. Mia stroked her head, then rose softly from the bed. She moved toward the door, then stopped for a beat, looking back. She left.

Mia passed the room service tray on the floor with the remnants of their dinner: three plates covered with sterling domes. She walked across the hall and knocked on the door. Sean opened it, wearing a Boston College Eagles T-shirt and sweats. He held a tiny bottle of vodka. "I'm going to drink everything in the mini bar."

"That's what it's there for," said Mia. She walked to the fridge and took out a mini bottle of rum. Unscrewing the top, she drank the entirety, then tossed it in the trash.

"I can see you *are* learning a lot here," Sean said, dryly. "Like how to underage drink."

"Give me a break, Sean," snickered Mia. "You've been drinking since you were ten. And I *have* learned a lot."

"If you're talking about the Mia dress, you haven't learned anything. You already knew how to do that. Please tell me you didn't sign any contract."

"I haven't yet."

"Good. Because it seems like you're going along with whatever Lyndon Wyld tells you."

"That's not true." Mia brushed her hair back.

"Why isn't she letting you come home?" asked Sean.

"'*Letting me?*' It's not like I'm a prisoner here," replied Mia.

"You're not?"

"No." Mia knelt and clinked around the inside of the fridge door for another mini bottle of rum. She picked it up, then put it back, shutting the door.

Sean stared at her. "You were 'required' to stay here on July Fourth, that's what Presley said."

"We had a job to do." Mia glared back. "It was the biggest night of the season and we had to promote our brand at The Rabbit Hole."

"Our brand, our brand, our brand," scoffed Sean. "What *is* that?"

"It's money, Sean! For us!"

"Bullshit, Mia. You're lying to yourself if you think that's the whole truth. You like it here—all the parties, the attention. You've become . . . what's it called? Insta-famous."

"You have no right to judge me!"

"You're so much better than this, Mia." Sean motioned around.

"What does that even mean?" Mia spun around, throwing her hands in the air.

"These people you're living with, they're walking ads. They're pictures, not people."

"No, they're *people* who have become my friends, my family, while I'm here!" Mia heard herself say the words, which rung in her ears like they were hollow.

"Those two uppity British chicks"—Sean leaned in to Mia—"you're their Cinderella story. You remember that story, don't you? I mean, you watched the movie on a damn loop when we were little."

"I don't need a refresher course, no."

"At midnight, everything turned to shit and then she had to depend on some prince to save her. Is that what you want? Who's going to save you? That Cole guy? Because he's not real either."

"What do you mean?" asked Mia.

"I thought he was. He seemed like a nice guy, but when I left the police station today, I saw him there. He didn't see me. Why was he there?"

"I don't know." Mia paced. "His roommate was murdered!"

Sean put his hand on Mia's shoulder to stop her pacing. "Let me ask you another thing."

"Please don't."

Sean pressed, "Why aren't they shutting down this whole fucking charade, huh?"

"The grief counselor said we have to get back to a sense of normalcy."

"Do you know anything about this grief counselor?" asked Sean.

"No," said Mia. "Do *you*?"

"I know that she's on the Lyndon Wyld payroll."

Mia looked into Sean's face. "When did you lose all sense of trust, Sean?"

"The exact same time you did."

Some memories never faded. Mia was six. It was a hot July Fourth and their parents had been fighting like they did every day. Seeing her mom cry always made Mia cry, so Sean brought her outside, where the neighbor kids were playing in the fire hydrant spray. The water came down in giant drops, like the rain Mia loved because she and Sean would search the sky for rainbows. They weren't fans of summer because there weren't rainbows. Their dad called them inside, handed them towels, and motioned them into the living room. Their parents' bedroom door was closed. Mia could hear their mom weeping as their dad told them he was leaving. "Some people just can't be together," he said in a pragmatic tone that wasn't meant for children. "If your mom and I stay together, one of us won't get out alive." He'd never tried to win Kathryn back. And though he was the one who left, Mia's mom was the one who wouldn't get out alive.

Now, Mia looked around the luxurious hotel room. "You're ungrateful, Sean."

Sean turned away from her.

"When you took extra shifts at work because you quote 'wanted' to—" Mia continued.

"*Wanted* to?" Sean huffed in disbelief.

"You wanted to so you didn't have to take care of Mom. You would do anything to leave it all to me. Now I'm here for one freakin' summer, and you won't even give me that!" Mia headed for the door, then stopped. "You know what? This *is* for me." She slammed the door behind her.

Sean couldn't sleep. He stared at one of the beams that stretched across the high ceiling, at a knot that was more interesting than any of the hand-painted flourishes in this flowery room. There was a knock on his door. He waited a long beat. At another knock, he winced and pushed himself off the bed. He didn't bother to put on his T-shirt, which was flung over the white wicker rocker.

"Go back to Mom's, Mia." He opened the door to see Presley.

"I am definitely not your sister," said Presley, her eyes landing on his bare chest.

Sean wasn't moved by her attire: tiny sleep shorts, a Rho Pi sweatshirt unzipped to the perfect amount of cleavage, and fur-covered slides on her pedicured feet. She tapped her nails on the door frame. "Well, aren't you going to invite me in?"

"It's late, Presley."

She slid past him into the room. "I feel like you got the shaft."

"I'm fine," replied Sean with an exasperated chuckle.

"Well then, *I* got the shaft," said Presley. "You're leaving in the morning and we barely had time to learn about each other." She ran a finger along Sean's shoulder.

"Shit happens." Sean plucked Presley's hand off him. "And shit is tiring." He ushered her back to the door.

Presley turned, serious. "Wait, Sean, I want to talk to you. It's about Mia." Sean stopped ushering. "I know you're a good brother," continued Presley. "You know how I know? Because my brother is an asshole."

"I'm sorry to hear that," replied Sean.

"I believe you," said Presley softly. "I care about Mia. You probably know that she was friends with Ruby Taylor."

Sean didn't respond.

"She's the girl who was involved with Grant the night he was killed," said Presley. "She was released."

"Then she's innocent." Sean moved to the mini fridge and pulled out a bottled water.

"She may not have committed that crime, but she's trouble." Presley stepped away from the door. "I tried to warn Mia."

"Mia is going to do what she wants to do." Sean opened the bottle and drank.

Presley tugged on the cuff on her hoodie. "I'm worried."

Sean motioned with the bottle. "About her or *you*, because she does what she wants?"

Presley started to cry. She slumped down on the bed. "I've completely lost my mind with everything that's happened." She wept as if the floodgates had opened. "Thank God for waterproof mascara."

Sean squeezed his eyes closed and exhaled, then sat next to her. "I get it." He offered her the water, but she put her hand up. He placed the bottle on the nightstand.

"I've been brought up to put on my game face, so that's what I've been doing," said Presley between sobs. "But it's exhausting." She flopped back on the bed.

"I'm sure," said Sean.

"Mia is lucky to have you and your mama." Presley looked up into Sean's face, her mouth trembling. "She wanted to go home, and I would want to go home, too, if my family gave a shit about me." She turned and curled up, her shoulders shaking with more sobs.

Sean watched her, his eyes a conflicted mix of exasperation and empathy. He lowered himself down and spooned her. Her weeping subsided and she closed her eyes. As her breathing steadied against him, it lulled Sean to sleep.

When he woke in the morning, Presley was gone.

FORTY-SIX

G race and I are so sorry you've decided to cut your trip short," said Lyndon. She and Grace filled Mia's FaceTime screen. Mia held her smartphone for Kathryn, who sipped coffee next to Sean on the deck at Topper's. Her breakfast of brioche French toast and eggs Florentine sat half-eaten.

"My doctors feel it's best I go home," said Kathryn into the phone.

"What a shame." Grace shook her head. "You didn't get a chance to enjoy sunset on the yacht."

"We have our private boat ride back," replied Kathryn. "That's plenty."

"Mia, I'm sure you want to go back with your mom," said Lyndon.

"I—" Mia started.

Kathryn put her hand on Mia's arm. "She needs to stay here."
Mia looked at her mom.

"I can see what this job means to her." Kathryn smiled softly at Mia.

"I hope you can see what Mia means to us," said Lyndon.

"I do," replied Kathryn.

Sean put down a piece of honeydew melon, his fork clinking on the china plate. Mia glanced at him.

"Well, Mia, Grace and I completely understand whatever decision you make," said Lyndon.

"Sean—" said Grace.

Mia turned the phone's screen to Sean.

"Hm?" said Sean with a stoic expression.

"Though you and your sister don't seem to do well with phones, we're going to send you a new one," said Grace.

"Thanks."

"On one condition," added Grace.

"What's that?" Sean smirked.

"You jump on social and represent."

"I'll think about it." Sean side-eyed Mia, who gave him a pleading look.

"We hope to see you both soon," said Lyndon.

"Safe travels." Grace waved. The sisters clicked off.

Mia placed her phone facedown on the table and put her hand on Kathryn's. "I'm going back with you."

"No." Kathryn shook her head. "You're not. You're finishing what you started. I didn't raise either of you to be quitters."

"Are you sure?" Mia searched her mom's face.

"Yes," said Kathryn. "I'm changing the subject now." She pointed to the lawn. "Look." Mia and Sean turned in the direction of her finger. A white-tailed bunny munched on the manicured grass.

"Lawnmower," said Mia with a chuckle.

"Cheap labor," retorted Sean.

Mia threw her hands up. Kathryn put down her coffee cup.

"I'm kidding!" Sean chuckled. "It's all good. Come on." He ate the melon on his plate. "You both like seafood, right?"

Mia and Kathryn nodded. Sean opened his mouth to expose the light green chewed mass inside. Kathryn broke up laughing, covering her face with a napkin.

"You're so gross," laughed Mia.

After they finished brunch, Mia walked them to the private boat at end of the hotel's dock. She and Kathryn held each other for a long time. "I'll be home before you know it."

"I'm *am* proud of you," Kathryn whispered in Mia's ear. "And—"

"'Don't do anything I wouldn't do,'" finished Mia, her voice catching.

Kathryn kissed Mia all over her face. Sean flipped Mia off, but she saw the love in his eyes. She returned the gesture with the same affection, then turned to walk down the dock.

Vincent waited for her, snapping a photo. "Your mother is a warrior-goddess," he said.

"She is." Mia watched the boat glide away from the dock. She wasn't sure she'd made the right decision, but she felt relief when her mom gave her the blessing to stay because she knew she would have stayed regardless. As Vincent drove them back to the estate, Mia's mind wound like the road's curves. She exhaled when the text from Cole buzzed in:

Day drinking at The Hole. Meet us.

Mia looked at Vincent. "Can we stop for a drink? I could use one."

"*Absolument*," replied Vincent.

Mia texted back:

See u there.

Vincent steered the car into town and parked in front of the bar. They entered. It was still early, just past noon, so the place was almost empty. Cole and Presley sat at the usual table. A couple of local guys were playing pool.

"We gotta get our drink on before the rest of the chudnuts show up," Mia overheard the guy in a South Wharf Plumbing shirt say as he knocked two balls in the right corner pocket.

Behind the bar, Mac and Frank prepped for the impending rush. Mac cut up limes, glancing periodically at Presley, who scrolled on her smartphone as if he were invisible.

Music played from the jukebox, Pearl Jam's "Alive."

Cole rose as Mia approached with Vincent. "How's your mom?"

"She'll be fine."

Presley put her phone on the table. "Did the fam get off okay?" She straightened, chest up. Mia saw that she was wearing Sean's Boston College Eagles T-shirt knotted at the waist.

Mia glared at her. "I'm ready for some darts."

"I'll meet you there with a beer," said Cole, exchanging a glance with Vincent.

"I'll come with you," replied Vincent. They left Mia and Presley alone.

Mia's jaw tensed. "I asked you not to, but you couldn't help yourself."

"You asked me not to what?" Presley fixed the star charm necklace that touched the neck of the tee.

"I asked you *not* to hook up with my brother."

"I didn't hook up with him."

"You're wearing his shirt," snapped Mia. "You eye-fucked him the entire time he was here, so forgive me if I don't believe you."

"You're the last person who should be slut-shaming." Presley pulled up Mia's Instagram on her phone, displaying a post of Mia standing with her mom in front of the Mia dress poster at the store. "Check out the comments."

Mia took Presley's phone and scrolled down to three comments in a row:

trevorsouthie99 Devil-slut
trevorsouthie99 Cheater & liar
trevorsouthie99 Bitch

She shoved the phone back at Presley, her body burning with anger. "That's my ex-boyfriend."

"I'll bet you still have a T-shirt of his," remarked Presley.

Mia found the post on her own phone and deleted the comments, then blocked Trevor.

"I need something stronger than a beer." Mia walked away from Presley, heading toward Mac at the bar.

"Tequila, please."

Mac nodded toward Presley, who stepped up to the jukebox across the room. "If she hates me so much, why does she even come here?"

"That's *why* she comes in here," replied Mia.

Mac poured her shot. She tossed it back and headed for the dart boards, where Cole had just landed a bull's-eye. Elvis Presley's "Hound Dog" started to play.

Before Mia could reach Cole and Vincent, two cops, one male, one female, entered and marched toward her. Her heart started pounding, but they moved past her to the bar. Cole and Vincent stopped playing.

"Mac Doyle?" demanded the male cop.

"That's me," said Mac.

"You're under arrest for the possession and distribution of a controlled substance."

As Mac was cuffed by the cop, he chuckled bitterly and exhaled in defeat.

Frank rushed over. "What the hell's going on?"

"Frank, unless you want us to shut you down for serving alcohol to minors, you'll step away," said the cop.

Watching, panicked, Mia backed into the pillar where she and Cole had kissed on July Fourth. Eve exited the kitchen, putting on her server's apron. She looked up to see the female cop ambush her.

"Eve Wier?"

"Fuck me," muttered Eve as she was cuffed.

Mac and Eve were read their Miranda rights as the cops led them to the front door. Mac caught eyes with Mia, who turned away and saw Cole staring into his beer mug. She turned back. Presley was leaning on the jukebox, tapping on the glass to the beat, entertained by the show.

"Take a picture, it'll last longer," Eve shot at her, as she was pushed through the door by the cop.

After the chaos ended, Presley turned her gaze to Mia, then opened her arms to everyone. "Drinks all around on Lyndon Wyld."

Mia watched Frank set shot glasses on the bar. "Let's go." *Business as usual*, Mia thought.

FORTY-SEVEN

As Vincent drove Presley, Mia and Cole back to the estate, Mia couldn't stop thinking about Mac's face as he was led out of The Rabbit Hole. The betrayal in his eyes—it seemed directed at her.

"I told you they were cracking down here," said Presley.

Mia touched Cole's sleeve. "Were you at the police station yesterday? My brother thought he saw you."

Cole shook his head. "Why would I go to the police station?"

Mia stared out the window. Maybe Sean had been messing with her because he was pissed. She glanced at Presley in Sean's T-shirt.

As they drove up the estate's driveway, Mia could see a small figure curled up to the side of the porch steps.

Cole squinted. "Who is that?"

At closer look, Mia recognized Ruby, knees bent to her chest, arms around her shins. Vincent stopped the car and they all got out. Mia strode to the steps. Ruby looked like she had been dragged down the pebble driveway. Her wounds were barely healed. Her face was less swollen, leaving eyes as big as those in the Keane prints that hung on Mia's grandma's walls.

"Ruby!" cried Mia. "Are you okay?"

Ruby rose, weak and wasted. She wore a Rabbit Hole sweatshirt and Levi's that were too big on her, cinched with a man's belt.

"Otto came to pick me up when I was released," she said. "I went back with him to the estate, but I left. I couldn't stay there."

"Is Otto still there?" asked Cole.

Ruby nodded. "I moved to a friend's, but now that's not a good place for me either."

Presley eyed Ruby's outfit. "I'll bet," she muttered.

"Come inside." Mia started to lead Ruby into the house.

Presley stood in front of the door. "This is my house, too, and I don't want her here."

Vincent stood, watching.

"I'll bring you some water," Cole said to Ruby. Glaring at Presley, he disappeared inside.

Mia gently touched Ruby's arm. "What happened that night?"

"I don't remember." Ruby put her hand to her head. "I've tried and tried . . ."

"That's 'cause you were more wasted than my cousins after robbing a Rite Aid," Presley sneered.

"If you're not going to let her inside, then *you* go!" snapped Mia.

"Fine, I will." Presley started, but first got in Ruby's face. "I'm onto you, girl." Ruby cowered, her eyes filled with fear.

Mia pushed Presley away. "Go!"

"Grant's still dead, Mia," said Presley. "Remember that."

As Presley headed inside, an engine roared. She stopped. They all turned to see a red vintage Corvette convertible pull into the driveway.

"I'm out," said Vincent, walking back to the guest house.

Otto was behind the wheel. He stopped in front of the porch. "Ruby, sweetie, let's go."

Mia held Ruby's hand. Ruby didn't move.

"Ru-by," Otto repeated in creepy singsong. He shoved the car into Park and got out. He strode up to her. "Let's go."

"I don't want—" said Ruby in the smallest voice.

"These fucking poseurs are not your friends," hissed Otto. He took her skinny arm in his hand. "I'm the one who takes care of you, baby."

Presley stared from the doorway, as frozen as Ruby, like Otto's words were kryptonite.

"Let go of her," said Mia, locking eyes with Otto.

"Mermaid Mia, I remember you." Otto leered at her. "You are a saucy wench!"

"Get your hand off her," demanded Mia.

Otto took his hand off Ruby and put it on Mia's arm. "There. Better?"

They heard a crash on the porch. Cole, who had dropped the water glass, launched off the steps from the front door, shoving Otto away from Mia. He grabbed him by his collar. "If you touch anyone here again, I will fucking kill you where you stand."

"I would like to see that," said Vincent, who had stopped midway to the cottage.

Cole pulled Otto closer with an even tighter grip. "I don't think a single person would care what happens to your body after I dump it in the harbor. Am I right?" He glanced at the others. Their silence said everything. He released Otto, tossing him off. Otto stumbled back to his car and snickered at the group.

"Poseurs." He roared off in the Corvette.

Mia nodded gratefully to Cole as she walked Ruby inside. Presley held the door open for them. Mia guided Ruby to their bedroom.

"You can have my bed, Ruby," said Presley, patting one of her pillows. "I've never had a bad dream snuggled in it." She spoke with unusual softness.

"Thank you," whispered Ruby.

With a small smile at Mia, Presley left. Mia felt guilty for doubting Presley's story about her uncle because today, she saw the connection with Ruby.

Mia turned to Ruby, who scanned the room. "Do you want to take a bath?"

Ruby nodded. Mia ran the water in the tub, dropping in a vanilla-scented bath bomb that she bought at the farmers market. It fizzed into strands of bubbles.

"That smells good," said Ruby with a child's smile. "Like a cookie."

Mia helped her out of her clothes, putting her Wear National nylon fanny pack on the basin counter. Ruby's body was badly bruised. There were fresh cuts on her arms. "Oh, Ruby."

Ruby started to cry.

"It's okay. It's okay." Mia brushed a strand of Ruby's hair off her face.

"It's not okay," replied Ruby, weeping. "I can't remember, and I feel horrible about that . . . for Grant. I can see your face at The Rabbit Hole, Mac singing . . ." Ruby closed her eyes. "And a girl with blond hair." She opened them. "That's the last thing I remember." She looked at herself in the mirror. "But maybe that was just me."

"You don't need to think about it right now." Mia helped Ruby down into the suds. When Ruby put her wet feet on the tub's ledge, Mia saw the fresh needle marks between her toes. "But you need to get help."

Ruby nodded.

"Relax for a little bit, okay?" Mia headed out the door.

"Mia?"

Mia stopped.

"Thank you for everything." Ruby's beatific smile returned.

Mia left the bathroom door open a crack. She moved to her sewing machine to adorn a Lyndon Wyld dolman-sleeve top with silver star appliques. Watching the needle's rapid pokes in and out of the fabric was meditative for her. After a few minutes, she stopped the machine.

The water was still running in the bathroom. She opened the door to find Ruby in the tub, unconscious. An empty bottle of OxyContin was tipped sideways on the counter. The label read "Otto Hahn."

Another ambulance siren blared. Ruby was saved within an inch of her life.

FORTY-EIGHT

I t's supposed to be one of the most peaceful places on the island," said Cole, sitting with Mia on the living room couch. He showed her a Nantucket travel brochure for the island's cranberry bogs.

"Is anywhere really peaceful on the island?" Mia sighed, looking at the cover photo of garnet red berries blanketing a pond.

"Come on. Ruby is going to be okay." Cole put a hand on Mia's leg. "You saved her. Thank God she was here."

Mia looked at Cole. His eyes always made her feel better.

Cole slapped the brochure. "We'll bike there, get a little exercise. It'll be good. Let's go!"

"Go where?" Presley entered from the kitchen with a bowl of strawberries.

"It's a free day so we were going to take a ride to the cranberry bogs," said Mia.

"Can I come?" Presley pleaded with her eyes. "I hate being a third wheel, but after what happened with Ruby, I don't want to be here by myself."

Cole glanced at Mia.

"Of course you can come." Mia folded the brochure.

"I didn't get to go to the bogs last year." Presley stood on her tiptoes and clapped. "How about if we bring a picnic?"

"Sounds good," replied Cole.

The three mounted the cruisers and peddled through town, stopping at the market across from the burned-out Wear National store with its yellow "Fire Caution Do Not Cross" tape in front. Mia glanced at the building. A few workers wearing hard hats were surveying inside.

Mia, Cole, and Presley bought provisions, which Mia put in her bike's basket. As they rode off, they failed to see Axel in a hard hat, standing in the Wear National store's charred doorway.

Mia started to breathe easier when they were out of town on Milestone Road. The sun was out, with a few fluffy clouds in the sky. This was the Nantucket Mia wanted to remember.

Cole glanced at Google Maps on his smartphone. "We're supposed to turn left when we reach the third Nantucket Conservation Foundation marker at the scenic overlook."

Presley counted every time they passed a marker. Reaching the third, she examined the stone. "Says two hundred twenty."

"That's the one," confirmed Cole.

They veered left on Larsen Road, which welcomed them with a notice on a wood post that read CAUTION: BEES AT WORK.

Mia teared up at the thought of Grant during the trunk show. His cheek had swelled after the bee sting during croquet, but he'd still cheered for her over the kudos on her dress. His Abercrombie & Fitch model features had been distorted. But the sight was nothing compared to seeing him floating facedown, bleeding out in that pool.

"This is far!" Presley huffed as she rode.

"You wanted to come," reminded Mia.

"It sure is pretty." Cole scanned the nature around them.

They peddled past the rolling hills, grasslands, and freshwater ponds of the Middle Moors. They rode along the coastline and sea-sprayed bluffs. Sheep lolled behind a barbed-wire fence.

"Um, I think this is it," said Cole, who stopped and pointed to a sign that read MILESTONE CRANBERRY BOG. They gazed out at the field-size carpet of green groundcover and white blossoms.

"Where are the cranberries?" wondered Mia.

Cole lifted the brochure from his inner windbreaker pocket and read. "I guess I missed the part where it says the berries are ripe in the fall."

"Selfie-worthy anyway," remarked Presley, pulling her phone from her backpack. She snapped, tagged Mia and Cole, and captioned for Instagram:

Life is good. #BeWyld #friends #berrygood

"This'll do for a picnic spot," said Mia, pulling the grocery bag out of her bike's basket while Presley spread a blanket.

Cole looked up. "Crap."

Darker clouds were rolling in.

"That's Nantucket for ya," said Presley. "It can change in a flash."

"I don't want to get stuck out here in the rain," replied Mia, her disappointment palpable.

"My hair's gonna frizz like a poodle," added Presley. "Let's go."

They packed up and ventured back. The clouds cast shadows on the surrounding vines. The birds launched into a constant chorus that trumpeted in their ears.

"I am not a huge fan of birds," said Mia.

"I didn't know that about you," replied Cole.

Mia thought of the finches on the logo of J.P.'s hats. Some other nameless animal made a sound that Mia was sure was a ghost or a spirit. With the impending showers, the roads were empty. Mia and Presley peddled side by side.

"I'm not seeing the chemistry." Presley nodded toward Cole, who was a few yards ahead.

"There's a third element in the mix." Mia's brow lifted at Presley.

"Are you calling me a cockblocker?" Presley gasped in mock offense.

They heard a motor rev from around the bend behind them and turned to see a car speeding toward them. Mia had no time to think. She glanced back, noticing it was a classic gold Camaro. It was gaining on them.

"Oh my God!" she yelled as she peddled harder. Presley pushed her and Mia lost control of her bike. It careened to the left of the car while Presley controlled her bike straight. The car roared through the middle.

Mia's bike hit a rut. All at once, she stopped and flew off.

The Camaro caught up with Cole, who turned and rode faster. He looked back again, then steered his bike into some bushes. The car disappeared in the distance. He circled back to find Mia. She was sitting near her bike, her hands and knees muddy and bloody. She was trying to catch her breath.

"Are you okay?" Cole jumped off his bike to help her.

"What just happened?" Mia stared at the empty road ahead.

They turned to look across the road. Presley composed herself, smoothing her shirt. "Well, Mia. You can thank me later."

FORTY-NINE

In the darkness, Mia ran down the shore. The sand felt gritty and wet beneath her bare feet. The salt water that splashed up burned the cuts on her legs. She passed the red-and-white-striped umbrellas in front of the Wear National estate. They fluttered in the moonlight, waving at her to remind her of the first time she saw Ruby with Otto, when Presley and Cole tried to pull her away. A plastic toy shovel sticking from the sand jabbed her insole. She kept running.

She reached Brant Point and the lighthouse hugged by rocks. It was late, so no one was around. She climbed through the wood slats of the railing and up the rocks, maneuvering to the edge, where she had stood with Ruby. Her view was a black-blue canvas of melded sea into sky. Now all she wanted was to see the worn brick walls of the old buildings on her Southie street. She closed her eyes and wished she were back in the thrift shop, combing through gently loved clothing and imagining how she could make a piece her own.

She felt even more alone than when she had been out in that water searching for Ruby, her feet reaching for the sand she knew was beneath her but couldn't touch. She took a deep breath and instead of an exhale, pushed out sound from the depth of her soul. A long scream filled her entire body and echoed in her ears. Who would hear her? No one. *And if anyone could hear her on this fucking island, would they even care?*

She let the sea air cool her off. After some relief washed over her, she climbed down the rocks and started to walk back to the house, as much as she didn't want to. She stepped around the plastic shovel and let the gritty sand polish her soles, slipping away with the thin sheet of water that ran under them.

She reached the sprawling beach estates, set far back from the shore. In their lights, the shadow of a figure came over her. She could hear keys faintly jangling under the sound of the waves lapping.

She started to run.

The jangling didn't stop. The shadow and sound grew closer.

Mia sprinted down the beach at full speed. Her heart felt like it would burst from her chest. Her legs couldn't go any faster. She saw a sandy easement between two estates where kayaks and dinghies were stacked upside-down against each other. She scrambled in, crouching between outriggers.

"Mia!" She heard Cole's voice.

Mia tucked herself in tighter.

"Mia."

Mia scrunched her eyes closed. "Why are you following me, Cole?"

"You ran off."

"To be by myself," said Mia, suddenly overwhelmed by the fishy smell trapped in this small pocket of air.

"Come out, Mia," said Cole in a gentle voice. "Please, talk to me."

"Leave, Cole."

"I don't want to."

Mia rose, seeing Cole standing next to a paddleboard. "You need to get away from me," she said.

"It was just some crazy driver. We're all okay. No one is going to hurt you," replied Cole. He stepped toward her.

Mia picked up a wood oar and held it between them. "You're the one who's going to get hurt, Cole. Because that's what I do." In the moonlight, she could see Cole's confusion.

"What are you talking about?" he said.

"When people need me, I'm not there," Mia continued, shaking her head. "I let Grant go off the night he died because I was thinking about myself. I wasn't there for Ruby and look what happened. And I left my mom. I left her and she's sick."

"Stop. This is bullshit, Mia." Cole moved closer, but Mia lifted the oar.

"It's not bullshit. This is the real me. I never saw it before, but it's very clear. And now, I've pissed off Otto and he tried to kill us, because that was his car. I saw him driving it when I was with Vincent. It's my fault. I'm a terrible—"

Cole grabbed the arm holding the oar. "Mia, he wasn't after you."

Mia struggled away. "It wasn't an accident, Cole!"

Cole pointed to himself. "He was after me."

"What? Why?"

"I'm DEA," replied Cole.

Mia snickered. "If you're trying to be funny—"

"Believe me, there is nothing funny about this."

Mia smashed the oar down on a dinghy. "What is happening?" She chucked it and glared at Cole. "This whole time, you've been lying to us, to *me*?"

"That's kind of the job." Cole shrugged.

"We slept together!" Mia shoved him.

"That never should have happened."

"Did you even have a fiancée?" Mia glared at him.

"No. But I needed to give you a reason why I left the bar for so long that night. I had a lead."

Mia turned away from him. "Oh my God."

Cole nodded down the beach. "The Brant Point Lighthouse, where you just were—that's a drop point."

"For drugs?" scoffed Mia, whipping back at him. "I don't do drugs, Cole, and I sure as hell don't sell them."

"I believe you." Cole reached out to her, but she remained at arm's length. "Mia, you can't say anything to anyone. Lyndon knows I'm DEA, but Grace doesn't. Otto may be part of something bigger than this island," he said, motioning wide. "I had to get on the inside, but his seasonaires are longtime employees. The only way I could get close was to work for Lyndon Wyld. And we're not ready to move on him yet."

Mia stared out at the water. She thought about Ruby and the night at Brant Point. *That* was why Ruby went there. Maybe that was why she was so bold in taking Otto's ATV. He *wanted* her to take it to pick up drugs.

"Why would you do this to me, Cole?"

"You haven't exactly been honest with me either," continued Cole. He pulled his smartphone from his pocket. "I need to show you something I found today." He held out his phone for her. She took it and saw an Instagram repost of her, smiling in front of the fireworks. She *had* pressed the "+" button on her Insta Story. Someone had saved it and reposted.

She shrugged, handing the phone back to Cole. "I posted on the holiday, big deal. It's our job. Well, *my* job, not yours, apparently."

"My job now includes the murder investigation." Cole zoomed in on the photo. "There's a flag in the background. Do you see its colors?" He held out the phone. In the very corner of the photo was the tip of the red Wear National flag, lit by the fireworks.

Mia's relief over finding her mermaid teardrop necklace had been short-lived.

Mia sat on the curved bottom of a kayak and exhaled. "I was there that night." She looked down, digging a foot in the sand. "I found Grant and then I found Ruby. I panicked and left, but I called nine-one-one first."

"You did the right thing." Cole put his phone back in his pocket and sat next to her.

"No, I didn't." Mia hung her head.

"Neither did I—," said Cole, lifting her chin—"with you. I'm sorry, Mia."

Mia looked at him. "I'm ready to tell the truth if you are." She ran her index finger along the scar above his right brow. "Tell me how you got that."

"I was eleven, showing off to my buddies. I jumped over a fire hydrant." Cole tipped one hand over on the other. "Smack."

"You're badass DEA and *that's* the story you have for me?" scoffed Mia.

"That's my truth," Cole replied. "What's yours?"

Mia stared into his emerald green eyes, but didn't know if she could reveal it all.

FIFTY

In the morning, while Presley was still sleeping, Mia and Cole snuck out of the house. They rode cruisers through town. Mia's wounds were bandaged, but her knees stung as she peddled because scabs had started to form. The streets were quiet.

At the police station, Cole held the door open for her. He stepped in and she followed him to the bullpen. Mia recognized two of the officers from the scene at the Wear National fire and two others from the bust at The Rabbit Hole. As Cole's colleagues exchanged nods with him, Mia felt like an idiot. She reminded herself that he was doing a job.

Cole led her into the investigation room. Mia glanced around. The gray concrete walls felt suffocating and the fluorescent ceiling light was harsh against the metal table. Detective Miller rose from one of the chairs.

"Fitzpatrick," he said to Cole.

"Detective." Cole shook Miller's hand. Mia remembered their tussle after the Summer Solstice Soiree in front of the Seascape Restaurant. "Did Ruby Taylor get back to Stockton okay?" asked Cole.

Miller nodded. "She did." He turned to Mia. "You must be Mia Daniels. I hear you have some information for me."

"I'll be right back," said Cole. Mia shook her head slightly, but he gave her an assuring nod. Then he left, shutting the door. A two-way mirror reminded Mia that she was being watched, by whom she didn't know. Miller tapped the chair on one side of a metal table.

"Have a seat."

Mia sat opposite Miller. He slid over a small plastic bottle of water from the three clustered on the table.

"Thanks," said Mia, tucking a lock of hair behind her ear.

"It's been a dramatic year for fashion on the island." Miller shifted back and scratched his head. "So, what can you tell me about the drama on the Fourth?"

Mia took a deep breath and exhaled. "I ran into Ruby at The Rabbit Hole, where our company's party was happening. She was extremely intoxicated. After she left, Grant got a text message from her to come over. He was pretty wasted, too." Mia looked down at her hands. "I went to check on them both. When I got there, Grant was dead, in the pool. He'd been shot."

Mia tried to open the water, but her hands trembled. Miller opened it for her. Mia took a sip and put the bottle down.

"Then I saw Ruby. She was badly beaten. And I saw the gun."

"Do you think Grant beat her?" asked Miller.

"No." Mia stared at the water.

"Do you think he raped her?"

Mia looked up at Miller. "No. I don't think he raped her."

"Do you think he had sexual relations with her?"

"He may have," replied Mia. "But he could've just gone there to swim, too. He was like an overgrown kid. So was Ruby."

"She was an overgrown kid who did a hell of a lot of drugs," said Miller. "When we found her at the scene, she had Molly, heroin, weed, and traces of OxyContin in her system, not to mention alcohol, all of which are a problem on Nantucket."

Mia dropped her head and shook it.

"You and Ruby were close," said Miller. "Closer than any of the other—what do you call yourselves—seasonaires knew, so close you had friendship bracelets."

Mia crossed her bare wrists.

"I did a little digging myself in the wee hours this morning," continued Miller. "There are a host of posts with you wearing bracelets that matched one Ruby wore." Miller pulled his smartphone from his breast pocket. He placed it on the table and scrolled through Instagram posts tagged #TheMia showing Mia wearing the thin blue enamel bracelets. He stopped on the style tip video where Mia talked about taking off pieces of jewelry.

Mia's heart pounded. "I gave one to her."

"But there was a rivalry between the clothing line you work for and hers."

"Yes. It was silly." Mia gave a nervous snort.

"Would anyone on your side want to put her in a bad situation?" Miller rested his arm on the chair-back. "Or put Otto Hahn in a bad situation?"

Mia had to force herself to consciously breathe.

"How did this photo get on Ruby Taylor's phone?" Miller walked around the table to Mia, sliding over a file. He opened it to show Mia a smartphone photo printed out. It was taken from Ruby's point of view in the pool house: Mia's leg and a vague outline of her sunflower tattoo in the darkness. Miller's eyes went to Mia's ankle adorned with the ink.

"Where's Cole?" Mia's eyes darted around.

"Relax, Mia."

"Don't tell me to relax. I want a lawyer!"

Cole entered. Miller tapped the table in front of her. "Listen, I'm pretty sure, given that Ruby was too intoxicated to shoot a gun, she was also too intoxicated to snap this photo at the time it was taken."

The room was spinning. Mia thought about the blood pact with Presley, The Girl Vault, the proclamations of trust, how they would watch each other's backs. She stared at that photo and remembered @hounddogdayz. In her head, she saw Presley leaning on The Rabbit Hole jukebox when Mac and Eve were arrested. It had been playing "Hound Dog."

Cole bent down next to Mia. "Mia, we just want to know who was at the house with you. Grant's last post was around nine o'clock. You posted one in front of the Island Pie Shop forty-five minutes later, according to the shop's clock in the background. You're *not* a suspect, but who was there?"

Miller picked up his pen. "While you consider sharing, I'd like to see your driver's license. We need to include it in your statement."

Mia pulled her wallet from her purse and retrieved her license, avoiding Cole's gaze as she passed it to Miller.

Miller barely glanced at it. "Fake IDs were different back when I was young because we didn't have fancy computer programs," he said. "It was the job of an X-Acto knife and a laminator at Kinko's."

Mia looked at Cole. "When Mac and Eve were arrested, you knew?" she asked.

"Fitzpatrick here is a prince," remarked Miller, scribbling information on the report. "He gave you a pass on this one. He could have told your boss. He *still* could tell your boss."

"Presley Parker was there," blurted Mia. She looked at Cole. "And Ruby told me something at the house."

"What?" asked Cole.

"The last thing she saw was a blond woman," answered Mia, her body buzzing with certainty. "Presley tried to push me in front of a moving car. She would do anything to stay on top."

The washer sloshed. Presley was pulling clean whites out of the dryer when Mia entered the laundry room.

"I can't believe you," said Mia, her sharp inhale met with the fake flowery scent of fabric softener.

"Yes, it's true. I'm washing clothes," replied Presley, proudly shaking out a white nightgown and tossing it in the plastic basket on the folding counter. "Nadege has had as hard a time as anyone, so I decided to spare her our dirty laundry this week."

"You're hounddogdayz." Mia shoved her phone at Presley, pointing to the hounddogdayz Instagram account.

Presley ignored the phone, instead scooping a pair of Mia's white cotton underwear from the dryer. She held them up. "How do you wear these granny panties?"

Mia grabbed them out of Presley's hand and chucked them in the basket. "You posted the video of Grant and Axel's fight at The Rabbit Hole, and the one of me and Ruby at Nantucket Coffee Roasters."

Presley reclipped a still-damp white camisole to the clothesline. "Lyndon likes to have eyes on her seasonaires. I've been that for her." She straightened the camisole. "Vincent's probably been watching me. But what the fuck, Mia? We're all watching each other."

Mia stepped in closer to Presley. "Mac's arrest, that was because of you."

"Mac did that to himself," scoffed Presley, turning to lift the last item from the dryer, a lone sock.

"Did you take a photo of me with Ruby's phone the night of the murder?" demanded Mia.

"I might love you more than anyone else here, but I needed collateral," said Presley with a shrug. "In case you let it slip I was there."

"You don't love me." Mia slammed her hand on the dryer, her silver ring clanking against the metal. "You tried to kill me yesterday."

Presley glared at Mia, her mouth agape. "What? I tried to *save* you! That car would've hit you if I hadn't shoved you out of the way!"

Mia and Presley were inches apart. "You didn't want me here from day one," growled Mia.

Sirens could be heard coming up the driveway. Presley's eyes darted toward the sound.

—∞—

Mia watched the police arrest Presley. She stood with Cole and Vincent in the estate's driveway and she didn't look away as Presley stared at her with pleading eyes.

"Mia . . ."

Mia had never seen Presley so afraid. She had never seen Presley afraid at all.

FIFTY-ONE

Lyndon stood by the fireplace as Grace handed Mia and Cole each an envelope. "The remainder of your wages."

"Thank you," said Cole.

"No, thank *you*," replied Lyndon. "Both of you." Lyndon smiled at Mia.

Vincent entered, his camera bag over his shoulder.

Lyndon put her hand up. "You're off duty, Vincent. Although I'm grateful for these two gems"—she motioned to Mia and Cole—"I'm in no mood for photos."

"*Ça suffit.*" Vincent lifted both hands. "I'm ready to snap the French countryside anyway. I'm taking a vacation in Marseille before I have to return to more *chaos*, which is the same word in French as it is in English."

Lyndon shook her head. "I can't help feeling like Presley should be here." She turned to Mia. "I'm sorry, Mia. I know what she did

311

to you and I know what she's being accused of, but it's unbeliev-able to me."

"She wanted to trend on social and that's what's happening," said Grace, scrolling on her smartphone. "Everyone from her neighbors to her sorority sisters are posting. 'She had a smile that could light up the world,' 'A bright future snuffed out by injustice,' 'An angel,' and quite a few 'She's hot' comments with the fire emoji."

Lyndon touched Grace's arm. "That's enough, Grace."

"But *you* are not to talk to the press about the case." Grace wagged a finger at Mia and Cole.

"Anything you say could further damage the brand's reputa-tion," added Lyndon.

"I understand," said Mia. "Believe me, I don't want to talk about it."

Lyndon put her hands on Mia's shoulders. "We're chomping at the bit to move forward with the Mia Collection. We're going to show the world that we won't back down on any front."

Mia gave a small nod. Grace lifted a thick manila envelope from her work tote and handed it to her. "Here's the new contract. We think you'll like the terms, but it's time sensitive, so don't dillydally."

"I'll look at it before I leave tomorrow," said Mia.

"This will be brilliant for you, Mia. I promise." Lyndon embraced her.

"Smashing!" Grace grinned at Mia, rubbing her necklace's sapphire solitaire.

Lyndon caressed Cole's sleeve. "Don't be a stranger, Cole."

"I won't," replied Cole. Mia stared down at the hand-hooked rug. The sisters left. Vincent followed them out.

"You're good," Mia quietly said to Cole.

"Thank you for keeping what you know about me under wraps," replied Cole.

"I need a strong drink," said Mia. "But I'm not going to have one." She plucked a pen from the silver cup near the house phone and stepped outside onto the deck with the manila envelope. She settled into an Adirondack lounger and lifted out the contract. Staring at the stapled stack of pages, the words were a blur. She couldn't process any of it. She slid it back inside and put it on the side table, then stared out at the beach. The little boy who had given her the broken shell at the season's start ran past, giggling, his mom and dad traipsing behind.

"Lemonade," said Cole, joining her outside with two beverages.

"When life gives you lemons," remarked Mia as she took a glass.

"A lucrative contract doesn't seem like lemons." Cole sipped, nodding to the contract that stuck out of the top of the manila envelope.

Mia tapped the pen on it. "Then why doesn't this seem sweet to me?"

"Maybe you need time to think about it," replied Cole.

"I don't think I have any," said Mia, sipping. "Grace is strong-arming me."

"She's rougher around the edges than her older sister, but that's their story." Cole shrugged. "It's good cop, bad cop."

Mia stared out, then locked eyes with Cole. "Blond hair," she whispered.

———

Lyndon smoothed her golden bob and waved her tray of tea off with the humbled flight attendant. She lifted her smartphone to reveal Maz on FaceTime, his face filling the screen. "We have a call scheduled," she said to him. "Did you double book me, darling, just when we are having a *rapprochement*?"

Maz grinned. "I did, but I promise to make it up to you with some stellar news."

"I expect nothing less," replied Lyndon.

"Gotta jet." Maz hung up.

Lyndon clucked her tongue at the cutoff call. In the seat next to her, Grace scrolled through Twitter on her iPad, munching from a bone china bowl of nuts. "Where is he?"

"I have no clue, but he owes me another bonsai."

<hr />

Maz slipped his gold smartphone in his slacks pocket and turned to pluck one of his albums from the shelves in the loft office. Young, hot, and pin-thin male and female employees slunk around the glass-and-chrome industrial space marked by walls with floor-to-ceiling Wear National logos.

"Let's put on a little dance music to celebrate," said Maz.

Otto, propped against the edge of a desk custom-built from a DC-9 plane wing, gestured broadly. "*Mi casa es su casa*, especially since you bought my company. Lyndon is going to crap her fancy pants."

"You *did* sell it for a song." Maz handed the album to Skullcrusher, who placed it on a turntable and cranked up the volume. Maz paced in front of Otto. "You know I bought it with the full intention of firing your ass."

"You're not gonna do that, *boss*." Otto grinned and lifted a joint from a red ashtray.

"You're such a greedy bastard that you actually didn't consider why I would get into bed with you," replied Maz. "You've fucked every poor soul who worked for you. You tried to fuck my daughter—"

"Tried?" Otto laughed.

Wrecking Ball pistol-whipped Otto on the side of the head, knocking his white-rimmed sunglasses off. Otto laughed even harder.

"And now I'm fucking you." Maz pointed at him.

Wrecking Ball smacked Otto in the head once more. Otto dropped to his knees, the joint landing next to him. Blood dripped from above his temple.

"My friend here can aim a little lower," Maz said, pushed his forefinger into Otto's temple. "But someone else might like to do that."

Jade strutted in with J.P. on her heels. J.P. shut the door. Jade took the pistol from Wrecking Ball.

"Meet one of my newest business partners." Maz motioned to her.

Jade bent down to Otto. "I've done my due diligence on your management style, talked to some former employees, and watched a few videos. I had to wash my eyeballs," she said with disgust. "I should put you out of your misery."

"I'm not miserable." Otto jeered. "I'm happier than a pig in shit, baby."

"Don't call me 'baby.'" Jade pistol-whipped his cheek, breaking more skin.

Otto cackled, glaring at Maz. "Do you think I'll just slink away with my cock between my legs?"

Skullcrusher smacked Otto on the back of the head. "Hey! There are ladies present."

Maz stood over Otto. "I suggest you tap out gracefully, man."

"You love lobster," hissed Otto. "*I* love lobster. Bougie royalty *loves* lobster. Lobsters can lose their limbs, but they regenerate. I've gone bankrupt twice and came back bigger."

"But now you have Ruby Taylor's lawsuit," said Jade. "And mine, along with the other men and women you've treated like trash."

"I know a talented French fashion photographer who will also have a few choice words to say about you," added Maz.

"My pap pal, Vinnie," replied Otto. "Let him testify. Let all the whiny bitches testify."

"That shit's gonna stick. I'll make sure of it." Maz picked up the joint and exited.

"See you in court, motherfucker," said Jade with a sharp heel to Otto's kidney. She strode out in front of Wrecking Ball and Skullcrusher. J.P. brought up the rear, spitting on Otto before leaving.

Three pretty young women peered into the office at Otto, who was laughing and moaning. They walked away.

FIFTY-TWO

Lyndon crossed her sleek, professional-grade kitchen, holding a glass of Chardonnay as Grace cooked salmon with vegetables in a cast-iron pan on the eight-burner stove.

"You know I loathe fennel," said Lyndon. "Yet you still try to sneak it in." She slid onto the white leather bench in the breakfast nook and tucked her legs underneath her. She was barefoot and wearing a silk caftan.

"Fennel is fucking delicious," remarked Grace, wiping her hands on her apron.

"Let's hope your art of persuasion worked better on Mia," chuckled Lyndon as she thumbed through a file sitting on the nook's table.

"She won't be able to resist that contract." Grace sprinkled pepper into the pan. "And once you taste this, you won't be able to resist it either. It's a new recipe."

The doorbell rang. Lyndon glanced up. "If it's that sodding cow from below to harangue me about my renovations, cunt punch her, please."

"With pleasure." Grace turned the burner to low and walked out.

Lyndon heard an officious-sounding male voice. "I'd like to speak with you and your sister." She pursed her lips and made her way to the living room in the modern and monochrome penthouse overlooking Central Park. Detective Miller stood in the center with two NYPD police officers.

"What's going on?" Lyndon asked Grace.

"I'm Detective Miller." Miller held up his badge. "I'm with the Nantucket Police Department. I'm sure you've both seen me around that lovely little enclave."

"What can we do for you?" asked Grace, moving close to Lyndon, almost in front of her like a shield.

"I have some questions about your whereabouts on July Fourth. Can you tell me where you were that night?" asked Miller.

"In London," answered Lyndon.

"And you?" Miller nodded to Grace.

"I was here at our home," answered Grace.

Lyndon crossed her arms. "She was under the weather. We spoke on the phone throughout the day."

Miller eyed the Jasper Johns painting on the wall. "Mia Daniels, one of your seasonaires, told you about bruises on Ruby Taylor earlier in the summer. Did you share that information with your sister?"

"I may have," snapped Lyndon. "But that wouldn't be surprising to anyone, given Otto Hahn's history. He's the one you should be questioning."

"You both know what happened to Ruby the night of Grant's death," said Miller.

"Yes. She was raped." Lyndon shuddered.

"She was, but not necessarily by a man." Miller glanced at the vase of pink peonies on the credenza. "There was no evidence of that."

"Presley Parker is being investigated." Lyndon said, putting a hand on the top of the armchair next to her to steady herself. "I don't believe that she would do that."

"I don't believe she would either," remarked Miller.

"This is absurd." Lyndon squeezed the armchair.

"Here's what I believe." Miller walked closer to Lyndon. "Otto got a text from Ruby asking him to come to the Wear National estate. But the number was unknown, a burner phone."

Lyndon's brow knit.

Miller went on, "Ruby was beaten to make it look like Otto was her attacker. Her assailant held the gun for her, waiting for Otto to show up. But he didn't show up. Grant did—a surprise. Grant was shot accidentally, and the assailant fled, because it was so easy to leave Ruby holding the bag."

"I demand an attorney present for this type of ambush!" Lyndon stomped.

"Someone wanted Otto dead and I think you know who that was," said Miller.

The police officers made a beeline for her. Her eyes went wide, her mouth dropping open.

"No!" yelled Grace.

Miller held up his hand and the officers stopped.

Grace broke down, grabbing Lyndon's arm. "I did it for you."

"Grace?" gasped Lyndon, the blood draining from her face.

Grace looked at Miller. "My sister didn't know anything about it."

Miller nodded to the officers, who cuffed her.

"I'm sorry," whispered Grace as Lyndon wept. Miller and the police officers led Grace out as the kitchen's smoke detector went off. Lyndon stood there, stunned, smoke curling in.

FIFTY-THREE

Mia stood on the beach in front of the estate, staring out at the harbor. It would be the last time she looked at this view. Cole stepped up to her. "Presley was released," he said.

Mia exhaled. "Good."

"Are you sure you're okay dropping the charges?"

"Yes." Mia let the water wash over her bare feet. "I'm not sure she tried to kill me. I'm not sure of anything anymore." The tide slipped back out. "Actually, I'm sure of one thing. That I almost put away an innocent person because I couldn't see past myself."

Cole shook his head. "There you go again."

"We're all kind of assholes, Cole," chuckled Mia.

"Okay, I'll give you that." Cole kicked the water that came in. "I *am* sorry the summer turned out this way." He moved closer to Mia.

"It's not what I imagined, that's for sure," replied Mia.

"What are you going to do when you get back to Boston?"

"I'm going to reapply to MassArt, now that I have some tuition money. I think that's the right way to get what I want."

"Is there a 'right' way?" Cole squinted into the bright horizon.

Mia shrugged. "I think signing the Lyndon Wyld contract is the wrong way. I wanted to go to college from the start. And my brother is going to help out with my mom."

"Any chance you'll be out here in the next few months?" asked Cole. "I'm going to be hanging around for a while, tying up loose ends."

Mia brushed her hands together. "No chance."

"Did this experience spoil your picture of Nantucket?"

"How can you spoil a picture? It's not the real thing." Mia started to walk in the direction of Brant Point. Cole followed. "You remember when I told you that I don't like birds, on the way home from the bogs?" asked Mia.

Cole nodded.

Mia continued walking, the wet sand melting around her feet with each step. "Since my visit with the grief counselor, I've been thinking about my dreams. I had a recurring nightmare when I was a kid. A seagull sat on the foot of my bed."

"Seagulls are cool." Cole looked down the beach. There were no birds in sight.

"This seagull pecked out my eyes," said Mia.

"Oh." Cole grimaced.

Mia stopped walking. "Me, Presley, Grant, Jade, and J.P. . . . we wanted the world to look at us when we really need to look at the world. I lost sight of what I even came here for."

"Can I tell you something?" asked Cole. "That seagull image is not what I want to remember about you." He turned Mia's face to him.

Mia touched Cole's scar. "What image do you want to remember?"

"Your amazing smile."

Mia smiled at him, which made him smile. He lifted her chin and kissed her softly. The breeze felt good on her neck, but the soft graze of his fingers felt better. It was the most bittersweet kiss of her life.

———

That afternoon, Vincent drove Mia down Easy Street. He dropped her off at the harbor, where she had met Grant her first day.

"*Bonne chance*, Mia," he said.

They kissed each other on both cheeks.

"*Bonne chance*," replied Mia.

Mia climbed onto the ferry and never looked back. She knew what was behind her. It was a perfectly painted picture of beach paradise.

Sean picked her up at the Hyannis harbor terminal. They didn't say a word on the drive home—they didn't need to. Mia knew he loved her in a way that was real, and that sometimes he was pissed at her and thought she was doing the wrong thing. But he would *tell* her. He made it clear when he was angry or disappointed. Their family's love was based on truth, because Mia's mom was a terrible liar.

She thought about Cole and how different his life was from hers. She wondered if he'd actually liked one summer's life as a seasonaire or if it all seemed like bullshit to him. She felt they'd made a true connection, but would she ever trust that it was *real*? When they were together, she felt his longing to be with her. What would his life be like now? What would hers?

When she got home, she ran her hand along the brick wall of her dull, old Southie building. It was bumpy and sharp and inconsistent in color and feel, unlike the meticulous white wood shingle facades on Nantucket. They looked smooth and clean, but would surprise you with a splinter.

Her apartment smelled stale and musty, like the air at the hospital. She pulled a lavender candle from the Nantucket farmers market out of her Lyndon Wyld canvas tote.

"Think we'll ever be at a luxury resort again?" asked Kathryn. The lamp near her bed cast a dim light.

"If we want to be, we will," said Mia. "Besides, luxury is a state of mind. She fluffed Kathryn's pillows and wrapped Kathryn's Lyndon Wyld cashmere sweater more snuggly around her. She kissed her mom's forehead, her cheeks, and her nose, and they laughed.

She made dinner and Sean helped: spaghetti with magic marinara sauce. Her mom took an extra bite, especially for Mia.

After dinner, Mia sat at her grandma's sewing machine and worked on the lace inlay shirt she'd started before Nantucket. When her eyes got too tired to scrutinize the stitches, she turned in.

In bed, she opened her laptop and scrolled through Twitter. She clicked a news piece on Grace, who would stand trial for both Grant's death and Ruby's assault. It was possible she could be sentenced for life. Prison was a far cry from the rarified air Grace had been breathing most of her adult life. According to the story, Lyndon was inconsolable.

Mia's smartphone buzzed with a text. She picked it up from her nightstand and looked. It was from Presley:

You broke The Girl Vault.

Mia responded:

We both did.

Mia deleted Presley's texts and blocked her number. She closed her social media accounts.

Two weeks later, she went back to her job at the thrift shop. She enjoyed arranging the pre-loved clothing and realized why she appreciated it so much. Unlike the newest arrivals in the hottest clothing line, each piece told a story about life.

In October, she applied to MassArt and was excited to find out if she got in. February rolled around. She hustled through the snow into the thrift shop for her shift and saw a blond woman perusing the racks.

ACKNOWLEDGMENTS

I want to thank all those who helped make a dream my reality. To Jessica Case, my editor and fearless leader for her enthusiasm and thoughtful guidance. My deep appreciation goes out to the entire Pegasus team. To my literary agent, Adam Chromy, who prompted me to give it a go, and was there, tirelessly, all along the way. To Abrams Artists Agency, especially Manal Hammad, who has my back and keeps it real.

I would have been lost without Roz Weisberg, who is my creative guardian angel, as well as my wise friend. My thanks to Juliette Fassett for being the horse whisperer, and getting truly tickled about my endeavor. And to Aaron Berger, who is forever saying I can do it.

I must thank my mom, Joyce King Heyraud, who gave me my first journal and a pencil, and sent me to the park on my bike to write. I haven't stopped since. And to my siblings, Stephanie Estes and Danny King—we walk through the fire together. A double cheek kiss to my stepfather, Henri Heyraud, who is genuinely interested in all my work. A huge hug for my aunt, Margaret Debbané. She and her husband, Elie, created a warm temporary writing nest for me during a time I'll never forget. And I would thank my dad, Jeff King, if he were here. He was one-of-a-kind.

My thanks also extend to the other half of my immediate blended family—Kelly Kalichman and BG German. They help link together the important circle.

Gratitude from the bottom of my heart goes to my daughter, Izzy Kalichman, who reads what I write with a smart eye and an equally smart mouth. Her spirit inspires every ballsy female I invent. And to my son, Jake Kalichman, for doing the math and cheering me on with his wonderful kindness and humor.

Each step in this life adventure is made sweeter by my husband, David Samuels. His love, support and patience are a beautiful gift to me every single day. And for that, I give thanks.